Amy Cross is the author of more than 250 horror, paranormal, fantasy and thriller novels.

OTHER TITLES BY AMY CROSS INCLUDE

1689
American Coven
Angel
Anna's Sister
Annie's Room
Asylum
B&B
Bad News
The Curse of the Langfords
Daisy
The Devil, the Witch and the Whore
Devil's Briar
Eli's Town
Escape From Hotel Necro
The Farm
Grave Girl
The Haunting of Blackwych Grange
The Haunting of Nelson Street
The House Where She Died
I Married a Serial Killer
Little Miss Dead
Mary
One Star
Perfect Little Monsters & Other Stories
Stephen
The Soul Auction
Trill
Ward Z
Wax
You Should Have Seen Her

THE HAUNTING OF SAWARD ISLAND

AMY CROSS

This edition
first published by Blackwych Books Ltd
United Kingdom, 2024

Copyright © 2024 Blackwych Books Ltd

All rights reserved. This book is a work of fiction.
Names, characters, places, incidents and businesses are
the product of the author's imagination or are
used fictitiously. Any resemblance to actual persons,
living or dead, or to actual events or locations,
is entirely coincidental.

Also available in e-book format.

www.amycross.com
www.blackwychbooks.com

CONTENTS

CHAPTER ONE
page 15

CHAPTER TWO
page 23

CHAPTER THREE
page 33

CHAPTER FOUR
page 41

CHAPTER FIVE
page 49

CHAPTER SIX
page 57

CHAPTER SEVEN
page 65

CHAPTER EIGHT
page 73

CHAPTER NINE
page 81

CHAPTER TEN
page 89

CHAPTER ELEVEN
page 97

CHAPTER TWELVE
page 105

CHAPTER THIRTEEN
page 115

CHAPTER FOURTEEN
page 123

CHAPTER FIFTEEN
page 131

CHAPTER SIXTEEN
page 139

CHAPTER SEVENTEEN
page 147

CHAPTER EIGHTEEN
page 157

CHAPTER NINETEEN
page 165

CHAPTER TWENTY
page 175

CHAPTER TWENTY-ONE
page 185

CHAPTER TWENTY-TWO
page 193

CHAPTER TWENTY-THREE
page 203

CHAPTER TWENTY-FOUR
page 213

CHAPTER TWENTY-FIVE
page 223

CHAPTER TWENTY-SIX
page 231

CHAPTER TWENTY-SEVEN
page 241

CHAPTER TWENTY-EIGHT
page 249

CHAPTER TWENTY-NINE
page 256

CHAPTER THIRTY
page 265

CHAPTER THIRTY-ONE
page 275

CHAPTER THIRTY-TWO
page 283

CHAPTER THIRTY-THREE
page 291

CHAPTER THIRTY-FOUR
page 301

CHAPTER THIRTY-FIVE
page 311

CHAPTER THIRTY-SIX
page 323

CHAPTER THIRTY-SEVEN
page 331

CHAPTER THIRTY-EIGHT
page 343

CHAPTER THIRTY-NINE
page 351

CHAPTER FORTY
page 359

CHAPTER FORTY-ONE
page 371

THE BOOKSELLER'S CURSE
page 383

THE HAUNTING OF SAWARD ISLAND

CHAPTER ONE

EVIL ISN'T BORN. Evil grows like a cancer from the minds and bodies of the innocent.

Opening her eyes, Jacqui became aware of a gentle rhythm under her back as the boat bobbed up and down on the waves. Reflected sunlight danced on the cabin's roof, creating patterns that shimmied and changed constantly as water lapped at the boat's sides, and for a few seconds Jacqui felt absolute peace and tranquility – until a tray loaded with half-empty glasses slid off the table's edge and tumbled down, tipping over and spilling its contents all over her chest.

"What the -"

Sitting up, she inadvertently knocked the glasses aside onto the bench. The front of her shirt was already soaked and any sense of calm had been immediately dashed. She could hear voices talking up on the deck now, and she began to mutter a few choice curses under her breath as she turned and clambered off the bench, before heading through to the rear of the vessel and grabbing her backpack.

"Goddamn stupid -"

She pulled a fresh shirt from her bag with a theatrical flourish before taking a moment to change. After shoving the wet shirt into a plastic bag and stowing it in the backpack, she glanced at her own reflection in the scratched mirror above the shelving and immediately furrowed her brow. Leaning closer, she tilted her face to one side, chasing the shadows that seemed to be responsible for stubborn marks under her eyes.

"I'm not getting -"

In that moment the boat bobbed a little harder than before, and as she steadied herself she accidentally bumped her head against the shelf above the mirror. After letting out a gasp – more of frustration than of any actual pain – she took a few seconds to tie her hair back before turning and starting to make her way toward the rear of the boat. Holding her hands out to steady herself in preparation for any other unexpected lurching movements, she began to climb the small set of steps just as she heard a loud and depressingly familiar juddering sound coming from somewhere deep inside the boat's guts.

"There you are," her mother Vanessa said, smiling as she saw Jacqui emerging onto the stern. "I was just about to come and get you. How was your nap?"

"Eventful," Jacqui replied, before turning to see that her father was still at the boat's controls and still seemingly having all kinds of trouble. The juddering sound hadn't stopped yet and, if anything, seemed to be getting worse. "Has he fixed it?"

"I'm nearly there!" David called out defiantly, having heard the question. "Have faith in your old man!"

"He's not nearly there," Vanessa said, her voice betraying just a hint of the frustration that had been coursing through her body all morning. "He's not remotely nearly anywhere. And neither are we."

Holding up a hand to shield her eyes from the bright midday sun, Jacqui looked around and had to admit that her mother had a point. Whichever way she looked, she saw nothing but the vast sea stretching off to the horizon. She glanced up at the sky, remembering how her father had explained that birds usually indicated the presence of land nearby, but she saw absolutely no sign of life anywhere above. Turning to her mother again, she instantly spotted the long-suffering sustained smile that always came out whenever these little family jaunts turned to disaster. Which, with the best will in the world, was most of the time.

At that moment, the juddering sound shifted to become a kind of louder, higher pitched whistle.

"Are you sure you're not making it worse?" Vanessa asked patiently, raising her voice just a little. "David? You don't want to completely ruin the... gubbins, or whatever they're called."

"No, I've almost got it," he replied, causing his wife to roll her eyes. "It's just a matter of -"

Before he could finish, the sound changed yet again, this time returning to the calm and somewhat reassuring sound of the engine running in its usual mode.

"It's just a matter of patience," he continued, turning first to Jacqui and then to Vanessa. "See? I told you I could do it. We'll be back underway in no time."

"And then it'll conk out again, won't it?" Jacqui asked. "That's the problem, you fix it but it breaks again every half hour or so."

"Be more supportive," Vanessa whispered. "He's trying his best."

"Not this time," David said confidently,

closing the hatch and making his way over to the wheel. "This time I traced the root source of the problem. I told you I could do it, I've always had a very good engineering brain. I promise we won't have to stop again. The Sinclair family's tour of the islands is back on track and nothing can stop us now."

"Yay," Jacqui said flatly, with all the enthusiasm of someone who'd been dragged out on another long trip during the school holidays, and who could think of a hundred other things she'd rather be doing with her time. She turned to her mother, who was at least trying to pretend that she was having a good time. "Where's Bod?"

***

A short while later, having made her way around to the bow, Jacqui finally found her sister Marianne – or 'Bod' for short, thanks to some obscure and long-forgotten family joke – sitting idly with a notebook and some pens, drawing yet more pictures of monsters.

"Not bad," Jacqui said, taking care to hold onto the railing as she peered over Bod's shoulder. "For a ten-year-old, at least."

"You're only five years older than me," Bod

pointed out, glancing up at her with an unimpressed glare before breaking into a smile. "I'd like to see you do better."

"So out of the two of us," Jacqui continued, lowering herself down to sit cross-legged, "who do you think's the more bored right now? Because I totally think it's me."

"Daddy fixed the boat."

"He didn't fix anything. At best, he got lucky; at worst, it'll just break again long before we get back to Innisrach or whatever the place is called."

"No, it won't, because he knows what he's doing."

"You're an idiot."

"No, *you're* an idiot. I'm way smarter than you are, and you know it."

"Tell yourself that, Bod," Jacqui replied, looking around and spotting the faintest hint of a sliver of land in the distance. "If we're really lucky, do you think Dad'll let us get off and look around another completely featureless and depressing little island?"

"I like looking at islands," Bod told her, following her gaze, squinting for a moment to try to make out any details of the land in the distance. "Anyway, that one has a lighthouse. Don't you want to go to a lighthouse?"

"What are you talking about?" Jacqui asked, watching the land for a few more seconds but unable to spot anything even remotely resembling a lighthouse. "It's completely flat."

"I can see a lighthouse."

"You can't see a lighthouse. You're imagining things."

"How can you *not* see it?" Bod asked.

"You're driving me crazy," Jacqui replied, watching the distant island for a moment longer before turning to her sister again. "You know that, right? I must be the only girl in the whole world who actually wants to go to boarding school. At least then I'd be able to get some peace." She let out a loud sigh. "I thought I might get my chance when Dad made all that money selling his company, but no, instead he spent it on ridiculous things like paying off the mortgage and buying this ridiculous little excuse for a boat. Can you believe he actually tried to convince us that it counts as a yacht? Talk about a midlife crisis."

"I like the yacht."

"It's not a yacht," Jacqui countered. "It's a small, shitty little boat that Dad thinks will impress his friends. Now we're out here taking it for a test drive, looking at a bunch of stupid scattered little islands that nobody in the whole of Scotland cares about but Dad grew up near and -"

Before she could get another word out, the engine's hum once again shifted to become a series of loud juddering sounds, indicating that the problem – which had been plaguing them ever since they'd left Innisrach that morning – had returned.

"See?" Jacqui said, annoyed that her prophecy of doom and gloom had come true so quickly – but taking solace in the fact that at least she'd won the argument. "Dad didn't fix a damn thing. You realize what this means, don't you? We're gonna be stranded out here in the middle of nowhere and no-one'll ever find us and we'll starve to death. One of us might survive, I guess, but only by resorting to cannibalism. Which of us do you think would break first, Bod? Would it be Mum? Dad?" She leaned closer and bared her teeth. "Me?"

"You're disgusting," Bod replied, although she sounded a little concerned as she turned and looked toward the rear of the boat. "Dad'll fix it again. You'll see. Dad's really smart. He knows exactly what he's doing."

"*I* know what he's doing," Jacqui murmured. "He's ruining our entire summer. That's what he's doing."

CHAPTER TWO

"TOSS IT ROUND THE stump," David called out. "Turn it round first. You need to turn it round, that'll make it easier to throw. Jacqui, turn it round and then throw it gently and -"

"I know how to throw a rope, Dad!" Jacqui sighed, before tossing the looped section of rope and completely missing the wooden stump on the end of the little pier.

Annoyed by her own failure, and by her father's constant orders – and by everything, really – she pulled the rope up and grabbed the loop again, which was now soaking wet.

"You need to throw it slightly up," David continued. "I know you can do it, Jacqui. Just follow my -"

"Just give a moment!" she shouted, momentarily losing her cool. "I can do it, but only if you stop yelling at me constantly."

She took a deep breath, tried to match her movements to the bobbing of the boat, and then finally she threw the loop again. This time, to her immense relief, she managed to get it over the stump perfectly, and with a sense of satisfaction she quickly pulled it tight before checking that the other end was securely tied to the boat itself.

"There!" she continued, turning and looking over at the others. "I told you I could do it, I just need five seconds without people shouting in my ears."

She waited for someone to acknowledge her success, only to quickly realize that they were all completely ignoring her now as her father continued to work on fixing the engine problem. Making her way back around to the stern, she saw that he was on his knees in front of the same small panel that he'd been tinkering with each time, and in that moment she felt any lingering flakes of optimism falling away entirely from her body. The juddering sound was still running, although after a few more seconds that too ended, leaving the boat finally bobbing up and down in ominous silence.

"Is that it?" Jacqui asked finally. "Are we

marooned now?"

"Nobody's marooned," David replied. "I thought I'd figured out the root cause of the problem, but..."

His voice trailed off, and after a few more seconds Jacqui turned to see that her mother was examining Bod's latest drawings.

"Is nobody else concerned?" Jacqui asked, before pulling her phone from her pocket and unlocking the screen. "We don't even have signal out here. How are we gonna get rescued when Dad inevitably fries the electronics beyond all salvation?"

"I'm not going to fry anything," he insisted, but for the first time he sounded more than a little irritated. "You know, Jacqui, this would be a lot easier if I didn't have you constantly being negative in my ear. I need to concentrate. Can't you just let me work in peace?"

"Oh, now *I'm* the problem," Jacqui said, turning to her mother. "Did you hear that? It's not this rusty old boat that we could barely afford, and it's not Dad's lack of basic sailing knowledge. And it's definitely not the fact that we set out today with almost no preparation. It's me. And the things that I say."

"Why don't you two go and explore?"

Vanessa suggested diplomatically, setting Bod's drawings down. "Doesn't that sound exciting?"

Looking over her shoulder, Jacqui saw the rotting old wooden dock leading to what appeared to be a bunch of rocks at the island's edge.

"It doesn't exactly look very enticing," she admitted.

"Don't go too far," Vanessa continued, leading Bod over, clearly keen to get rid of them for a little while. "Not that you *can* go too far, I imagine. All the islands out here are pretty small, according to the map, and there shouldn't be anyone else around. Go and take a look. See what fun things you can find."

"Can we go to the lighthouse?" Bod asked excitedly.

"No," Jacqui replied, glaring down at her, "because there's no lighthouse to go to. You completely imagined that." She hesitated, before letting out a sigh. "Come on, I'll prove it to you."

***

"This is a deathtrap," she continued a few minutes later, as she climbed off the boat and set foot for the first time on the wooden dock. "How old is this thing?"

"Help me up," Bod said, reaching for her.

"Can't you make it yourself?"

"Help me, Jacqui."

"Help your sister!" Vanessa called out. "Jacqui, don't be mean."

"You have to help me," Bod insisted. "Mum said so."

"I wasn't being mean," Jacqui replied, reaching out and taking Bod's hand, then holding tight as the younger girl jumped up onto the dock. "I was trusting her abilities. There's a big difference. I would have thought that you might want me to encourage her independence."

"Don't go too far," Vanessa continued, just as the boat's engine began to let out a series of decidedly uninspiring clicking sounds. "Jacqui, you're in charge. I can trust you to be sensible, can't I? And Bod, I want you to listen to your sister all the time. She's the boss when Daddy and I aren't around, okay?"

"Yes, Mummy," Bod replied, already letting go of Jacqui's hand and starting to walk along the dock.

"Yes, Mummy," Jacqui said under her breath, mimicking her sister's tone of voice. "Whatever you say, Mummy. I'm a good girl, Mummy. Not like -"

Suddenly one of the wooden boards crunched away beneath her right foot. Startled, Jacqui dropped down as her foot burst straight through the wood, sending a shower of rotten splinters cascading down into the water; landing on her left knee, she felt a sharp pain in her other leg, and she immediately saw a few cuts as she began to extract herself from the gap.

"Is everything okay up there?" Vanessa called out.

"Absolutely," Jacqui replied, examining the wound but quickly determining that it was nothing more than a few cuts and scrapes on the surface. "I mean, this entire wooden dock is lethal, it's obviously been rotting away for hundreds of years and it just tried to kill me, but apart from that we're good to go."

She waited for her mother's inevitable overreaction.

"Okay, that's nice," Vanessa said finally, having clearly not really bothered to listen to the answer. "Remember, don't go too far. And Bod, always listen to your sister and do exactly what she tells you. Is that understood?"

"Yes, Mummy," Bod shouted, having already made her way to the rocks at the other end of the dock.

"Yeah, ignore me," Jacqui said, hauling herself up and taking a little more care now as she picked her way toward the rocks. "I'll probably die of tetanus anyway, but that's a small price to pay in the overall scheme of things. I probably won't be missed much. People will mention me now and again, maybe if Dad sells another company he'll set up a small memorial foundation in my name, but on a day to day basis I'll be pretty much forgotten by Christmas." Stopping, she looked down and saw that in fact the cuts were barely even bleeding. "That was a lucky escape, though," she added. "I could easily have -"

"Jacqui, hurry up!" Bod yelled, having already begun to clamber up the shallow pile of rocks. "I want to go and see the lighthouse!"

"There *is* no lighthouse," Jacqui said with a heavy sigh, setting off after her again, leaving the sound of the boat's spluttering engine behind. "Can't you get that through your thick head? The whole point of a lighthouse is that it can be seen by boats. I know it's the middle of the day, but still, if there was a lighthouse on this dumpy little island don't you think we'd have been able to see it earlier?"

"We did see it earlier!" Bod called out to her. "I saw it!"

"No, you imagined it," Jacqui said under her

breath, making her way up to the spot where her sister had stopped at the edge of the grass. "You're just a kid. An annoying, admittedly imaginative kid, but a kid nonetheless."

Once she was at the top of the rocks, she paused to get her breath back and looked out to see the island's rocky, slightly undulating terrain spreading out. And, to her surprise, she saw what appeared to be a cottage on the far side, sitting snugly near the base of a small but very much real lighthouse.

"See?" Bod said smugly. "I told you!"

"Alright, fine," Jacqui replied, slightly annoyed that had sister had turned out to be correct. "There's a lighthouse. Big deal. A lot of islands have lighthouses, they're there to stop boats and stuff hitting them."

"Come on, let's go!" Bod shouted, running across the rough grass. "I want to see!"

"Hey, stop!" Jacqui called after her, although she already knew that her sister wouldn't listen. "Bod, hold up! I'm in charge and I'm telling you to stop for a moment! Mum put me in charge!"

She waited, but Bod was getting further and further away. Fully aware that she'd only be wasting her breath if she shouted again, Jacqui briefly considered turning around and informing her mother that her little sister was being a pain. After a few seconds, however, she realized that she didn't want to turn into some kind of snitch; and besides, the prospect of exploring a little and checking out the lighthouse didn't seem that bad. Setting off, she began to make her way across the grass, trying her best to avoid the various rocks.

"Bod, wait for me!" she yelled. "Bod? We'll go and check out the lighthouse, but you have to wait for me!"

CHAPTER THREE

"IT'S NOT HERE," VANESSA said, furrowing her brow as she continued to peer at the map she'd laid out on the table in the boat's kitchenette. "David, I feel like I'm losing my mind but I swear... according to this map, there shouldn't be an island here."

"Have you got it the right way up?"

Turning to see him still tinkering with the electrics in the corner, she seemed distinctly unimpressed by that suggestion.

"Have I got it the right way up?" she asked, as if she couldn't quite believe that he'd even asked. "Yes, David, I've got it the right way up. That was one of the first things they taught us on the map-reading course I went to."

"You did a course in map-reading?"

"No, of course I didn't," she sighed, before looking at the map again. "It's not exactly complicated. But I've double-checked our route, I've used the compass, I've done everything right... and I keep coming to the same spot." She put a fingertip on the patch of blue on the map's surface, and then she looked out the window and saw long grass swaying in a gentle breeze at the top of the rocks. "The map definitely doesn't show there being any kind of island here."

"Check on your phone."

"I would, but I can't get any signal."

"Did you check you're not on airplane mode?"

"Yes," she replied carefully, annoyed that once again he was treating her like an imbecile, but fully aware that there was no point making a fuss. "I also checked that it's switched on."

"Then you must be reading the map wrong."

"Take a look for yourself," she replied, turning the map around in the hope that he might make his way over. "Come on, show me what I'm doing wrong."

"I'm only trying to help. There's no need to be snappy."

"I'm not being snappy," she told him, before taking a moment to pull herself together. "I'm not being snappy," she said again, this time a little more calmly, "I'm just wondering why this entire island has been left off the map. There are lots of other islands on here, and some of those seem to be much smaller than this one so -"

Before she could finish, the lights in the cabin fell dead.

"David?" she said cautiously. "You didn't break anything, did you?"

"No, I didn't break anything," he replied. "I'm just resetting the entire system. I think the problem with the engine is caused by some kind of safety device that keeps kicking in. Hopefully if I reset everything, the problem will just sort of... clear itself."

"So you're basically turning it off and on again?"

"That's a pretty major simplification, but I suppose I am. In a way."

"Is that likely to work?"

"I don't know for sure, but it's worth a try," he explained. "I just have to wait twenty seconds before restarting it, and that should sort it all out." He paused, counting silently to twenty, before flicking a switch and waiting again. "Any moment now."

Vanessa was also waiting, but she couldn't

help noticing that the lights remained off.

"Any second," David continued, as if he was trying to convince himself. "Just let it... think about things."

"I'm going to think about things outside," she sighed, trying not to worry that her husband might have made the situation even worse. Setting the map aside, she headed to the steps that led back up onto the deck. "Let me know when we're ready to get underway again. I want to see where the kids have got to. I really hope they haven't wandered off too far."

***

Reaching the top of the small rocky slope, Vanessa took a moment to steady herself before stopping to look all around. Long, unkempt grass was rustling in a gentle breeze, but – as she shielded her eyes with a hand to protect them from the sun – she saw absolutely no sign of her daughters.

"Jacqui?" she called out. "Bod? Where are you?"

She looked around again, and after a moment she spotted two tiny figures in the distance, making their way toward a lighthouse on the island's far side.

"Are you kidding me?" she sighed, amazed that they'd managed to cover so much ground in just a short amount of time – but also slightly impressed. Holding her hands up, she began to wave. "Jacqui! Bod! Get back here!"

She waved for a few more seconds, before sighing again as she lowered her arms.

"So much for not going too far," she said, although she knew deep down that she hadn't really expected them to pay too much attention to her instructions.

She stood in silence for a moment, wondering whether to simply set off after them. Even from a distance, she could tell that the lighthouse looked pretty rundown and derelict, and she wasn't too worried about anyone else being on the island. At the same time, part of her was slightly concerned about letting her two daughters loose on what appeared to be an uninhabited little patch of land in the middle of the North Sea; although she trusted Jacqui completely and knew she'd look after Bod, she was torn between wanting to let them have fun on one hand and wanting to coddle them on the other.

"You let them do *what*?" she imagined her own mother barking, horrified by the events that were now unfolding. "Are you out of your mind,

Vanessa?"

"They're smart kids," was her – again, imagined – response. "It's good for them to get out and about on their own. It's how they learn."

"This is gross irresponsibility of the highest order," her mother's voice continued in her head, "bordering on child neglect."

"You don't know half the stuff *I* got up to as a kid," she imagined herself replying, and she couldn't help but smile now as she saw the two distant dots getting closer and closer to the lighthouse. "They'll be fine."

For a moment, she thought back to the day when she and her brother had explored an old abandoned farmhouse near their childhood home. The pair of them had managed to get inside via a broken window, and they'd dared one another to explore the various rooms, constantly worrying that at any second they might be about to find the rotting corpse of the former owner. When no such corpse had appeared, they'd shifted to telling ghost stories, imagining that the dead farmer had returned and that he would surely gain vengeance over anyone who dared to enter his former home. In the end nothing much of note had happened, but that memory of hanging out with her brother was one of the happiest from her childhood.

And one of the last of her brother, too.

Not long after their day exploring the ruined farmhouse, he'd begun to get sick. Really sick. Even as a kid herself, she'd known immediately that something was really wrong with him. By the time he'd been hospitalized, she'd picked up on the cues from her parents and she'd understood that nothing was ever going to be the same again. Robert had spent almost exactly a year in the hospital, occasionally showing signs of improvement but mostly deteriorating – usually straight after brief moments of optimism. She'd gone to see him every single day, of course, and she'd worked really hard to hide any tears that threatened to reach her eyes. Finally she'd been there holding his hand when the end had come, and she remembered how reluctant she'd been to let go of that cold dead hand once he was gone.

That daring visit to the old farmhouse had ended up being their one and only true adventure together, and she couldn't help but wish dearly that they'd had a chance to explore more places together.

Now, with the first hint of tears in her eyes, she watched her own daughters running toward the lighthouse and she realized that she couldn't possibly be angry with them. In truth she was a little jealous, because deep down she wished with every fiber of her being that she and her brother could have had the same opportunities.

"Don't do anything stupid," she said under her breath, still slightly worried that she might be being a little too loose with the discipline. "And don't take too long. I want to get going as soon as your dad fixes the boat."

She thought for a moment.

"*If* he fixes the boat," she added with a resigned air, before turning to head back to the wooden dock. "No, when there's a -"

Suddenly she froze as she found herself face to face with a pale-skinned woman whose eyes and mouth appeared to have been sewn shut with thick black wire. Before she had a chance to react, the woman – whose eyes and mouth were straining as she desperately tried to force them open – reached out and placed a cold, clammy hand over Vanessa's face and squeezed tight.

CHAPTER FOUR

STOPPING SUDDENLY, JACQUI TURNED and looked over her shoulder. She saw the overgrown grass stretching back the way she'd just come, and she froze.

She'd heard nothing untoward, she was already sure of that fact, yet somehow the 'nothing' had briefly seemed louder somehow. Scanning the landscape, she watched out for something – anything – that didn't seem right; still she saw nothing, even though her heart was racing and she could feel a slow sense of panic stirring in her chest and threatening to grow.

"Jacqui!" Bod shouted somewhere in the other direction. "Look!"

Furrowing her brow, Jacqui still felt as if she was missing something. Finally, however, she turned to see that her sister had stopped on a slightly higher grassy mound. Still some way from the lighthouse, Bod was looking down at something that Jacqui couldn't quite see. Forcing herself to ignore the uncomfortable sensation in her heart, Jacqui climbed up the mound and stopped, and now she saw the simple wooden cross that had been left standing on an otherwise unremarkable patch of grass.

"What is it?" Bod asked.

"It's a cross," Jacqui observed, tucking a stray strand of hair behind her ear as the wind briefly picked up.

"I know that, but what's it here for?"

"How should I know?" Jacqui asked.

The cross, which appeared to be comprised of two rough lengths of wood bound together haphazardly by a length of rope, had been dug into the ground until its height was no more than perhaps four or five feet. Regardless of how it might have been set up originally, now the cross was leaning heavily to one side – to such an extent that one of its arms was almost touching the ground and indeed appeared to have been tilted slightly by the windswept grass. The wood itself, meanwhile, was dark and gnarly, as if it had been consistently battered by the elements. Whether that battering had taken place entirely after the cross was erected, or whether the pieces of wood had been in that condition to begin with, couldn't possibly have been discerned even by a seasoned carpenter, but the result was an overwhelming sense of amateurism suggesting that this particular cross had been put in place by someone unaccustomed to such operations.

Perhaps by someone who had never needed to build such a thing before.

After a moment of further contemplation, Jacqui began to make her way down the other side of the mound, approaching the cross.

"What are you doing?" Bod asked.

"What does it look like I'm doing?"

"Do you think it's safe to go near it?"

"I'll take my chances."

Once she reached the bottom, Jacqui began to approach the cross. In truth, she was starting to find the sight of the thing slightly unsettling, and she most likely would have halted the approach by now had it not been for her sister's presence. Not wanting to seem weak or fearful in front of Bod, Jacqui forced herself to keep going until finally she stopped directly in front of the object, and she could see now that while the rope was still holding the cross together, the fibers themselves were clearly tattered and in some places had broken entirely. The wood, meanwhile, only looked more damaged and fragile when viewed from up close. As the wind picked up once again, the cross shook slightly but somehow – seemingly against the odds – remained in place.

"What does it say on it?" Bod called out.

Jacqui turned and looked at her. Although she was only ten or so feet away, up on top of the mound, in some ways she seemed to be far more distant.

"What does it say on the cross?"

"Uh..."

Looking at the cross again, Jacqui tried to make out any words on the mottled wood, but she saw nothing. Stepping around to the other side, she once again drew a blank.

"Jacqui?"

"What?" she asked, a little less patiently than before.

"What does it say?"

"Nothing," Jacqui replied, before taking a step back. She wasn't sure why, but some part of her wanted to keep a little distance from the cross. "There's nothing on it."

"Why's it there?"

"I don't know," Jacqui said, looking at the ground and wondering for a moment whether there might be a dead body down there, rotting away in the soil or perhaps already turned to nothing more than bones. "I'm sure it's nothing. Hey, don't you want to get to that lighthouse?"

***

Although she'd very much hoped that resuming the journey to the lighthouse might make her feel better, Jacqui felt that the sense of unease – which she'd first developed right before finding the cross – was still clinging to her several minutes later.

Ahead, Bod had reached a small wooden gate set into a low fence running around the cottage next to the lighthouse. As she caught up, Jacqui saw that someone at some point had evidently seen fit to use the fence in order to mark out a small garden; this garden was similarly overgrown, yet there were various flowers mixed in with the piles of grass, suggesting that once somebody had at least made an effort to cultivate part of the land.

A tight creaking sound rang out as Bod pushed the gate open. She had to make several tries, since the gate's bottom continually bumped against – and tried to dig into – the ground.

"Do you think anyone lives here?" Bod asked.

"Not anymore," Jacqui replied, looking at the cottage itself and seeing that the place appeared to have been abandoned many years earlier. "It's kinda sad."

As the two sisters stepped into the garden, they both kept their eyes fixed on the cottage. A white front door showed clear signs that it had been open to the elements for a while, with a few dark marks left in the wood, while two windows – one on either side – featured cracked but not fully broken glass. These windows reflected the island's harsh landscape, and even as she picked her way closer through the overgrown garden Jacqui was unable to see anything inside the low, single level building.

One thing she noticed, however, as she approached one of the windows was a certain chill in the air. Sure enough, when she reached out and touched the pane of glass, she felt that its surface was decidedly cold; too cold, she felt, for the time of day. Keeping her palm against the glass for a moment, she began to wonder whether this low temperature was in some way reaching out from the room on the other side.

In the corner of the window, a fat orange-black spider sat on one side of a trembling web. The spider's legs moved slightly, as if the creature was deliberately trying to prove that it was still alive.

Hearing a bumping sound, Jacqui turned to see that Bod was trying the door handle.

"Hey!" she called out. "Don't do that!"

"Why not?" Bod asked.

"I don't know," Jacqui said, and that answer was true enough. "Just don't."

She looked at the window again, and she saw only her own face reflected in the split pane; the two pieces of glass were slightly at an angle, so the reflection wasn't entirely straight or true.

"I just don't know whether or not it's safe," she added finally, taking a step back. "Don't you want to check out the lighthouse? It's right next door and we might not have much more time before Dad thinks he's fixed the boat again."

"Yay!" Bod shouted, turning and running out of the little garden, hurrying toward the base of the lighthouse.

"Not that fast!" Jacqui called out, wondering how her sister could still have so much energy.

She turned to follow, but at the last second she glanced at the window again. Although she couldn't quite tell what had changed, she immediately realized that something seemed different. She saw her own face reflected in the glass, but somehow the split in that glass seemed more pronounced. Stepping closer again, she noticed a tiny gap between the two broken panes; she wasn't entirely sure, but she couldn't shake the feeling that the panes had tilted slightly, creating a slightly wider gap than before.

Leaning toward the gap, she tried to peer through. She saw only darkness, but she began to wonder whether she might see more if she gave her eyes time to adjust. Leaning closer still, she squinted in an attempt to see if there was anything on the other side, while her eyeball edged just a millimeter or so from a thin layer of glass dust that had been left on one of the sharp, broken panes.

"Jacqui!"

Startled, she pulled back and turned to see Bod waving at her from the open door at the base of the lighthouse. "We can get inside! Hurry!"

CHAPTER FIVE

"DID I *SAY* WE were going inside?" Jacqui asked as she reached the doorway and looked through into a surprisingly busy and over-filled room stuffed with equipment. "Bod? Seriously, do you recall me at any stage telling you that we were actually going to go inside?"

"I can't hear you!" Bod shouted mockingly as she climbed over some wooden panels that had been left propped against a set of shelves.

"Bod -"

"I still can't hear you!"

Sighing, Jacqui turned and looked back across the island. She could see no sign of the boat, of course, but she figured that her father was probably still hard at work on his latest attempt to fix the engine. There was something depressingly familiar about the way David tended to fumble his way through any kind of challenge; neither searingly brilliant or pathetically incompetent at anything, he could usually be relied upon to come up with some kind of solution eventually, even if the process took far longer than it should.

Hearing a clattering sound, she turned to see various pots and pans falling onto the rough and cracked concrete floor.

"Bod, seriously," she said, ducking under a set of cobwebs and stepping into the large circular room, immediately noticing the smell of what she could only assume must be damp bricks. "I don't want to sound like Mum here, but you can't just go diving in. We have no idea what might have been left in the place and it might not be safe."

"What about this?"

Having disappeared behind a large wooden wardrobe, Bod now emerged wearing an old flat cap.

"Take that off," Jacqui said.

"Why?"

"Because..."

For a few seconds, she tried to think of a reason.

"Just take it off," she continued. "It's not yours."

"I don't think it belongs to anyone now," Bod replied. "If it did, why would they leave it on the floor?"

"Fine, wear it if you want," Jacqui said, turning and looking around at the ramshackle room, seeing multiple machines and bits of machines and chunks of wood that had been distributed seemingly at random. "You look like an idiot, but I guess that's nothing new. Just make sure there aren't any spiders in it. You don't want them laying eggs in your hair and then crawling into your ears and taking over your brain."

At that moment, she spotted a familiar object leaning against the far wall. Climbing over the remains of an old bed, which had been left disassembled and scattered across the floor near the foot of the staircase, she made her way across the room to get a better look, and sure enough she soon found herself standing in front of another crudely-bound cross – just like the one she'd seen outside earlier. And then, to compound the strangeness of the scene, she looked to her left and saw two more crosses that had seemingly fallen over at some point.

"Someone was busy," she muttered under her breath, also noticing a large pile of rope that had been left on the floor.

Hearing footsteps, she turned just in time to see that Bod was starting to make her way up the staircase that ran up toward the wooden ceiling, following the curve of the wall.

"Hey, do you want to wait a moment?" she called after her little sister. "Bod, seriously, you're getting on my nerves now. Didn't you see how rotten that dock was? This whole place could fall apart at any moment!"

She waited, but already Bod had disappeared from view.

"It'd serve you right if you *did* fall through," Jacqui continued wearily as she began to follow, holding onto the wobbly metal railing as she climbed the stairs. "Then again, I'm the one who'd be left looking after you, aren't I? I guess it's in my best interests to keep you alive at least for a little while longer."

***

"We're already so high up," Bod said, standing on tip toes as she peered out through a small window in one of the upper rooms. "I can see all the way to the sea from here. I can see the boat!"

Stopping behind her, Jacqui looked out through the grimy window and spotted the boat far off on the other side of the island, still moored to the dock. She watched for a moment longer, hoping to spot some sign of her parents, but she figured that most likely they were working somewhere out of sight. She quickly looked at the rest of the island, still seeing no hint of movement, and then she turned to look around the room.

Slightly smaller than the one on the ground floor, this particular room was much more bare but also better organized, like an actual workspace. A desk had been pushed against one of the walls, and when she wandered over to take a closer look she saw assorted old notebooks that had been left scattered around. She picked a pen from its holder and saw that the nib was dry, and then she set it down before opening one of the notebooks at random and seeing that it contained carefully lined sections that someone had once drawn up as some kind of chart.

The handwriting, meanwhile, was neat but also very difficult to decipher.

"1872," she whispered, just about making out the date from one of the entries. "Hey, Bod, this book is from more than a hundred years ago. Isn't that cool?"

She ran a quick calculation in her head.

"One hundred and fifty-two years, to be precise," she continued, leafing through the notebook and finding page after page of seemingly identical entries. "It seems to be reports of boats that came here. Or that came past, at least."

Turning to another page, she couldn't help but notice that the handwriting was a little less neat now, almost as if written by the same person but in a more agitated state.

"Still 1872," she murmured. "I guess a lot used to happen around these parts, huh?"

She turned to yet another page, and she was shocked to see that the handwriting was now extremely messy, spilling out of some of the boxes and making only a rudimentary attempt to follow any of the lines. In a few spots, the person seemed not to have even noticed that his text had gone over the edge of the page, and the entries themselves had become simpler and simpler until – by the next page – most contained just one single word.

"Again," she read out loud, before spotting one with a little extra information. "Her. Again."

"Who?"

Turning suddenly, Jacqui found that Bod had crept up behind her and was trying to peer at the book.

"Who again?" the girl asked, grinning from ear to ear, clearly amused by the realization that she'd made her sister jump.

"How should I know?" Jacqui asked, not for the first time as she looked back at the notebook and leafed through a few more pages. "It just says the same thing over and over. And look at the dates."

"I can't read them," Bod admitted. "The writing's all funny."

"There are multiple entries per day," Jacqui pointed out. "It's like -"

Reaching another page, she was surprised to

see that the writing had ended abruptly, replaced by what appeared to be multiple sketches of the same dark crosses that she'd seen earlier. In each of these sketches, the rope had been tied in a different way, and attendant scribbles in the margins showed various attempts to design different types of knot.

"What do you think happened here?" Bod asked cautiously.

"Happened?" Jacqui set the notebook down and picked up another, only to find that this particular volume was from 1871 and featured much neater handwriting. "Who said that anything happened? This was probably just left behind by some total Victorian lunatic. They had idiots back then as well, you know." She looked Bod up and down for a moment. "People like you aren't a new phenomenon."

"I'm not an idiot *or* a lunatic," Bod replied, nudging Jacqui's arm hard with her shoulder. "You shouldn't say things like that to me, or I'll tell Mum and you'll get into lots of trouble."

"What kind of person would want to just sit around in a place like this?" Jacqui asked, flicking to the back of the notebook before picking up another. "Even if you had company, it'd be pretty boring. Even -"

And then, as soon as she opened the latest notebook, she found herself looking at a crude ink drawing of what appeared to be a woman glaring out from the page, while a note in the margin gave the date as some time in 1873.

"Who's that?" Bod asked, looking at the picture for a moment before taking a step back, as if disturbed by the image. "Jacqui? I don't like it. Who's that a drawing of?"

"I don't know," Jacqui replied, leafing through the notebook and finding scores and scores of similar sketches, with each drawing featuring slightly larger and angrier eyes. "But whoever lived here back in the day, I'm not sure that they handled the loneliness too well."

CHAPTER SIX

"VANESSA, CAN YOU PASS me a screwdriver?"

After waiting for a few seconds, David leaned out from the cabinet in the corner of the kitchenette and turned to see that he was alone.

"Vanessa?" he called out, looking at the steps leading up onto the deck. "Vanessa, are you there? What's going on?"

He waited again, before letting out a frustrated sigh as he got to his feet. He took a moment to wipe his slightly oily hands on a tea towel, and then he began to climb out into the midday sunlight.

"You know," he continued, "I think I'm really getting close to fixing it now. The basic problem is -"

Stopping, he looked around and saw that

there was still no sign of his wife. He turned and looked the other way, as if he genuinely couldn't believe that he was alone, and then he peered at the slightly rotten wooden dock leading to the rocks at the edge of the island.

"Vanessa?" he shouted, raising his voice a little higher this time. "I don't mean to be a pest, but do you think you could come and help me? I've fixed the engine and now I just need to test it out before putting the old panel back on. You don't mind helping a bit, do you?"

Again he waited, and again all he heard was silence. The boat's engine had been off for a while now, so that he could work on it, and the only sound came from water lapping gently at the vessel's sides. Looking toward the rocks, he could only suppose that his wife must have gone that way, but he felt quite sure that she would never have simply wandered off after the girls without telling him first.

"Vanessa?"

No reply.

"Vanessa?"

Again, he heard nothing.

"Vanessa?"

Stepping up to the controls, he fiddled with a few switches for a moment before starting the engine. Sure enough, the juddering sound was gone now and the engine began to run perfectly well. He gave it a few more seconds, just to be sure, and then he switched it off again.

"Vanessa? Kids? Who's laughing now, huh? Everything's fixed and I'm certain it won't break down again. We're ready to go!"

Feeling slightly frustrated now, he climbed onto the edge of the boat and then – with a little difficulty and awkwardness – he was able to clamber onto the side of the dock. Getting to his feet, he looked around once more, just in case his wife might miraculously appear from out of nowhere, and then he began to walk along the dock while taking care to avoid the small hole that (he didn't realize) had been left behind by Jacqui's right foot. He still noticed that several of the wooden boards were flexing slightly beneath his feet, and he felt slightly relieved that the dock held long enough for him to reach the rocks and start climbing up to the grass.

"Vanessa?" he called out. "Vanessa, where are you? Vanessa?"

***

"Vanessa?" he shouted, cupping his hands around his mouth as he stood on the grass and looked out across the island. "Vanessa, where are you?"

He waited, just as he'd waited every time he'd called her name, but he received the same answer: the wild grass rustled slightly in the wind, but otherwise he heard absolutely nothing and the island appeared to be completely still and calm.

"Great," he muttered under his breath, before spotting the lighthouse in the distance. "So that's it, huh? They've all gone off and left me to do the work. Muggins here has to stay on his knees the whole time, fiddling with the electronics, and then once he's done and it's time for the others to tell him he's a genius, there's no-one around."

Turning to go back to the boat, he stopped as he felt something hard under his left foot. He moved the foot aside and reached down, and a moment later he picked up Vanessa's necklace. To his surprise, he saw that the clasp was broken and twisted, as if it had been forced apart.

"Vanessa?" he called out, slightly troubled by the fact that his wife seemingly hadn't noticed the damage occurring. She was usually so careful when it came to her jewelry. "I've fixed the boat. We can leave now."

He looked all around, and then – as he glanced toward the lighthouse again – he spotted a solitary figure moving through the grass and disappearing behind what appeared to be some kind of small cottage.

"Great," he said, slipping the necklace away before pulling his phone out and trying one last time to connect. When that failed, he realized that he had few options left. "So they've gone sightseeing, have they? What's the point in me being smart and brilliant, and fixing everything, if they're not even around to congratulate me when I'm done?"

Setting off across the grass, he figured that he was simply going to have to go all the way to the lighthouse and find the others, and then drag them back. That process in itself would clearly take a couple of hours – perhaps even longer – so his plan to continue the day's tour of various local islands now lay in tatters. Instead, he reasoned that they were barely going to have time to get back to the harbor in Innisrach before sunset; although there was technically no reason to hurry, he'd never been out at night before and he wasn't entirely confident in his abilities just yet.

"This is typical," he said as he continued to make his way toward the lighthouse. "Why don't people ever listen to me? Everything would be so much easier if they all just accepted that I actually know what I'm doing."

As was his wont, he kept grumbling and complaining to himself for the next few minutes as he slowly but surely walked across the island. He glanced around every so often, watching in case his wife or daughters might appear, although deep down he'd resigned himself to the idea that they were probably having lots of fun without him at the lighthouse. He half expected to see them emerge onto the platform at the top and start waving at him, although so far even that prospect seemed unlikely.

His legs, meanwhile, were starting to ache a little. He was out of the habit of going to the gym, and the island's rough terrain made for tough going as he found himself going up and down a seemingly endless succession of little slopes and mounds.

And then, after he'd been walking for a while, he stopped as he saw a crude wooden cross leaning slightly as it stood on a patch of overgrown grass.

"Hello there," he mused, stepping around the cross a little before stopping to get a better look. "Looks like someone lashed you together in a hurry, doesn't it?"

Making his way closer, he reached out and gave the cross a push, immediately finding that it was only fairly loosely embedded in the ground.

"And a long time ago, too," he continued, running a hand across the warped wood. "A *very* long time ago. You must be at least a century old, if not more and -"

Stopping suddenly, he felt a flicker of doubt in the back of his mind. He told himself that he had to be wrong, that there was no way the island was anything more than some pointless little outcrop in the middle of nowhere, but for a few seconds he found himself thinking back to some old stories he'd heard during his childhood. The old men of Innisrach had loved recalling strange tales, usually embellishing them again and again with each telling. And then, figuring that there was no point getting paranoid, he managed to stuff those fears way back into the deepest recesses of his thoughts.

"No," he said out loud, trying to reassure himself. "No, it's just some dull little island."

He gave the cross another push, before adjusting his grip and taking hold of the two sides. He adjusted his position a little more, and then – with perhaps less effort than he'd expected – he was fairly easily able to lift the cross out. The lower part featured a fairly pronounced sharp tip, although this was mostly caked in damp soil now; a dark line indicated that only the bottom foot or so of the cross had actually been in the ground.

"Creepy," he said, turning the cross around so that he could inspect it a little better. "Almost -"

Before he could finish, the rope broke and one of the two wooden lengths fell down, hitting the ground with a dull thud.

"Damn it," he said, picking the piece up and trying to find some way to tie the cross back together. As he worked, however, he found that the rope was almost crumbling away in his hands, finally leaving him with just a few stray strands. "Well, that was unfortunate."

He picked up the second piece of wood, but he already knew that he had no way of tying them back together. Using his fingernails, he picked at one of the sections and found that the damp wood came away very easily, exposing a much lighter interior. After what he could only assume was at least a century left out in the elements, the cross had fallen apart almost instantly, and he told himself that it wasn't really his fault that the whole thing had broken.

Setting one of the pieces of wood down, he began to push the spiked end of the other length back into the ground. He had to really put his back into the work, twisting the wood several times, but finally he was able to drive the wood down far enough. Taking a step back, he hated to admit that he was a little out of breath, and he took a moment to brush his hands clean as he saw tiny flecks of rotten wood stuck to his palms.

"Sorry," he murmured, feeling slightly embarrassed that he'd disturbed the scene so badly. "I didn't mean to... cause a mess."

He gave the sole remaining part of the cross a gentle push and found that, if anything, it was now *more* sturdy than it had been when he'd arrived. With that, he turned and set off again, climbing up the narrow slope and resuming his slow march toward the lighthouse in the distance. As he left, he couldn't help glancing over his shoulder and looking one last time at the cross – but he quickly reminded himself that there was no reason to worry, and that he simply needed to find his family and head home.

CHAPTER SEVEN

"I WANT TO GO up," Bod said, standing at the foot of another staircase and trying to see where it led, but discouraged from going further by numerous cobwebs that were hanging down. "Jacqui, can we go up?"

"What?"

Having been looking through the notebooks for a few minutes now, Jacqui turned to see that her little sister had finally ventured onto the first step of the latest staircase.

"Just wait for me, okay?"

"But we might not have long left," Bod pointed out. "What if Mum and Dad suddenly tell us that it's time to go back?"

"Are you really scared of a few cobwebs?"

"I don't like spiders."

"There won't be any spiders living here," Jacqui suggested, not even trying to mask her irritation as she returned her attention to the latest notebook. "Just be careful, and whatever you do – don't go through any other doors. I'm serious, Bod, this place is rickety as hell. Call me before you go anywhere you shouldn't."

"But -"

"And you *know* exactly what I mean," she added firmly. "Don't act dumb with me, I know you too well. You know perfectly well what you should and shouldn't be doing. Just... use your head for once."

"Whatever," Bod replied. "You can be so boring sometimes."

Returning her attention to the notebook, Jacqui saw more drawings, this time with various scribbled lines of text interspersed between the images. Every page seemed crazy, like the ravings of a madman, yet she couldn't shake the feeling that there had to be some kind of logic enmeshed in such detailed and frenzied work. Frustrated by her ability to figure out exactly what was going on, she leafed from page to page and tried to decipher the handwriting, which seemed almost to be running out of control, until finally she reached a page where everything changed.

"It's gross up here!" Bod called out, having advanced a little higher up the staircase. "Jacqui, it's really disgusting!"

"Deal with it," Jacqui murmured as she saw that now the handwriting had become much clearer again.

Who are you?, the man had written.

Under that, an answer had been added by what appeared to be a completely different hand:

Her.

And under that, the original hand had written another question:

What do you want from me?

The rest of the page was mostly blank, until a little further down the other hand had answered:

Rest.

She turned to the next page and saw that the crazy to-and-fro continued. Although she considered the possibility that the same guy had lost his mind, and that he was faking a different style of writing, she couldn't shake the feeling that two separate people had been replying to one another via the pages of the notebook.

Why do you come here?
Patience.
Why do you torment me?
Shadows.

"That's not creepy," Jacqui whispered under her breath. "Not at all."

How can I get you to leave me alone?
Darkness.

Why won't you let us leave?
Misery.

Below that exchange, someone had once again drawn a picture of the dark figure, although the pen lines were so erratic that the human shape was almost lost.

"Losing your mind, huh?" Jacqui asked as she turned to the next page. "What -"

Suddenly let out a shocked gasp as she saw another image, this time showing a man clutching at his throat and screaming. Clearly drawn by someone else, this image filled almost the entire page and – in places – the nib of the pen had worn through the paper.

"Jacqui?"

Startled, she felt a bump on her elbow and turned to see that Bod had made her way back down.

"What's that?"

"Nothing," Jacqui replied quickly, snapping the book shut so that her sister wouldn't see the potentially disturbing images. The last thing she needed was for Bod's overactive imagination to run wild with an endless series of unanswerable questions. "What are you up to?"

"I went up those stairs," Bod explained, turning to look at the staircase, "but... there are way too many cobwebs up there so I need you to move them out of the way."

"I'm really not sure we should go creeping around in this place," Jacqui told her. "It's ancient and it might fall apart at any moment."

"I've never been in a lighthouse before," Bod said, grabbing her sleeve and trying to pull her once again toward the staircase. "Can we go up to the top, Jacqui? Please? Can we go up and take a look at the top?"

***

"It's stuck," Jacqui said a few minutes later, having reached the top of the staircase and found a wooden door. She tried the handle again, but with no better luck. "It's locked. We're not gonna be able to get through."

"Try again."

She turned the handle for the umpteenth time, still with no result.

"It's not happening, Bod. Sorry, but I think we've reached the -"

"We need a key!"

Filled with a sudden burst of energy, and apparently no longer troubled by the remaining cobwebs, Bod turned and raced back down the staircase.

"Wait!" Jacqui called after her.

"I'll find it!" Bod yelled, having already disappeared around the corner at the bottom. "Don't worry, I'm really smart! I bet I can find it faster than you can!"

"Come on," Jacqui sighed, trying to work out how she'd ended up in such a ridiculous situation, then turning and trying the handle yet again. She felt that the door wasn't locked, necessarily, but rather that something on the other side was holding it shut. "I've got to go back to school next week," she lamented. "Can't I just get one calm, relaxing week off before going back to all that crap?"

Hearing the sound of Bod rooting around downstairs, she had to admit that she slightly admired her sister's energy levels. She remembered when she'd been similar – not exactly the same, since Bod seemed to have some extra smidgen of sheer exuberance – but there had been a time when she'd felt less lethargic and more motivated. Could five years of extra existence really make such a huge difference? Not wanting to go down the steps in case she then had to turn around and make her way up again, she instead sat at the top and waited, while wondering whether the world would ever feel quite so exciting again.

"I still haven't found it!" Bod shouted from somewhere far below.

"No kidding," Jacqui said softly, making no real attempt to be heard.

"It has to be here somewhere!"

"Or nowhere."

"Where would you put it, Jacqui? If you were a lighthouse keeper in the old days and you had an important key, where would you put it when you weren't using it?"

"I don't know."

"You must know. If you were a lighthouse keeper -"

"I'm not a lighthouse keeper and I never will be," Jacqui said firmly, cutting her off. "Bod, seriously, I'm gonna tell Mum that she needs to change your diet, because you've got way too much energy. Whatever she's feeding you, she needs to stop because it's driving me crazy. You're like an insane puppy."

"Do you think it might be in a desk? Or a wardrobe? Or on a shelf? Or in a box? Or in a pocket?"

Rolling her eyes, Jacqui opened the notebook again. A small window nearby permitted just enough light, albeit through dirty and scratched glass, to allow her to once more see the lurid drawing of the man clutching his own throat. She couldn't help but wonder whether this was an answer to the earlier drawings, in the same way that someone appeared to have used the notebook to answer a bunch of other questions. She had to admit that the whole idea seemed pretty unlikely, but evidently *something* unusual must have happened.

Hearing a faint clicking sound, she looked up over her shoulder and saw that the wind seemed to be slightly shaking the door.

Once the wind had died down again, she turned back to the book and -

In that moment, she saw to her horror that the entire book was now caked in blood, much of which was soaking onto her hands and dripping down onto the steps. Shocked, she pulled back and let the book fall away, and then as she held her hands up she saw more and more blood sloughing down between her fingers and running as far down as her wrists. She could feel the blood's heat now, and after a few more seconds she realized that she could even smell the extra iron in the air, but a moment later she saw a bloody drip falling onto her left hand; looking up, she realized that blood was dribbling down from a crack in the ceiling.

"Jacqui?"

Looking down, she found herself staring into Bod's smiling face. A moment later she checked her own hands again and saw that the blood was gone. When she peered past her sister, she saw that the book was now similarly unstained, merely resting on the dusty steps.

"I found it!" Bod continued with glee, holding up a slightly rusty metal key. "I told you I'm a genius!"

CHAPTER EIGHT

THE DOOR CLICKED OPEN, its hinges groaning slightly as Jacqui pushed it all the way and blinked in the bright afternoon sunlight that was streaming down onto the lighthouse's top deck.

"Yay!" Bod gasped, slipping past – only for Jacqui to grab her by the back of the collar.

"Listen to me *very* carefully," she told her sister. "Do you see that railing?"

"Yes."

"You are not to go anywhere near it," Jacqui continued, before stepping past her. "In fact, you're not going anywhere at all without me. This is serious, Bod, we're really high up and I'm not taking any prisoners right now."

Reaching down, she took hold of her sister's slightly clammy hand.

"If you let go of me for even one second," she added, "we're going back down. Do you understand?"

Smiling, Bod nodded.

"Don't smile when you agree."

After taking a moment to banish the smile, Bod nodded again, before smiling once more as if pleased with her self-control and attempt at seriousness.

Still holding the girl's hand, Jacqui stepped out onto the upper deck, which turned out to be a fairly narrow pathway running around the top of the lighthouse. A double-barred metal railing had been fixed to the outer edge, but this railing had plenty of gaps that could easily allow a human figure to slip through and plummet over the side, in which case any unfortunate individual would fall the full hundred and fifty or so meters all the way down to the ground far below. As a cold wind blew across the island, Jacqui led Bod forward for a few steps before stopping again and looking over the edge.

"Oh, I do *not* like heights, Bod," she murmured, slightly surprised to feel a cold sweat breaking out across her face. "That's new information. I mean, I never particularly enjoyed them, but this is something different."

"This is amazing!" Bod gasped, before pointing to the far side of the island. "Look! There's the boat!"

"Yep," Jacqui replied, struggling to summon any real enthusiasm as she spotted the boat still tied to the wooden dock. In that moment she saw the island spread out before her, and she couldn't help but notice that most of the land looked so wild and untamed.

"I want to be a lighthouse keeper when I'm older," Bod told her.

"No, you really don't."

"Yes, I do!"

"You don't, Bod. You'd be lonely as hell."

"I'd get my friends to come over for parties."

"What friends?"

"I'm gonna have lots of friends when I get older," Bod explained. "I won't be sad and lonely like you."

"Do you want me to let us stay up here or not?"

Realizing that there was no immediate danger, and slightly liking the idea that she'd later be able to freak their mother out, Jacqui began to edge along the platform while taking care to stay well away from the edge. She found that it helped if she didn't look down, although in truth there weren't many other places she *could* look, but after a moment she turned and saw a huge lamp on the other side of a large pane of glass.

"It looks like a giant kaleidoscope," she

suggested, trying in vain to focus on something – anything – other than the sheer drop. "It's beautiful, in a way."

"Was it really used to warn ships?"

"See those rocks down there?" Jacqui replied, nodding toward a set of particularly nasty-looking rocks far below, against which waves were already crashing as the sea became a little rougher. "In bad weather, and at night, those things could rip a boat apart in minutes. So it was the lighthouse keeper's job to come up here and make sure that the lamp was burning all the time. They probably didn't have electricity back then, so I guess they used some kind of oil."

"What type of oil?"

"I don't know."

"The type Dad puts in the car?"

"I really don't know, Bod," she continued, still leading her slowly along the platform that ran around the top of the lighthouse. "The point is, the lives of all the people out there on the sea depended on the lighthouse keeper doing his job properly. Can you imagine that? Can you imagine what it must have been like, knowing that if you got it wrong and if you let the light go out..."

She turned to see that, for once, she had her younger sister's undivided attention.

"Lots and lots of people," she added for effect, "would die. They'd get dashed against the rocks, or they'd sink into the depths of the freezing cold sea and drown.

"That's horrible," Bod admitted.

"Yeah, it is," Jacqui told her, "and don't forget that the weather out here probably gets completely insane. It's one thing for us to be up here right now, on a fairly boring day, but imagine being here when there's wind and rain howling all around, and it's the middle of the night and you're trying not to slip. And you know there's a boat out there, and you know it could hit the rocks at any moment, and you have to somehow force your way through the storm. Do you *still* want to be a lighthouse keeper?"

"I... don't know," Bod said cautiously.

"Well, it doesn't matter either way," Jacqui added, "because most of them are probably automated these days, so they don't even need anyone to live in them. In fact, I wonder why this one doesn't seem to have been spruced up. The rocks are still there, but I guess modern technology means most boats aren't in so much danger."

Feeling something bumping against her back, she turned to see that they'd found another door. She tried the handle, and to her relief it turned easily, allowing her to open the door and peer inside.

"What is it?" Bod asked.

"Mirrors," she explained, still holding the girl's hand and leading her into the cramped room.

"This is the heart of it all, Bod. This is what kept all those sailors safe."

In the center of the room, a large brass lamp stood on a pedestal, festooned with assorted outlets and compartments that Jacqui couldn't even begin to understand. She assumed that somehow this was the part of the structure that actually burned, no doubt fed by some kind of oil that had to be topped up regularly, while various large mirrors all around would be used to reflect the light and spread it far and wide. Reaching out, she touched the base of the lamp and felt the cold metal, and she couldn't shake the feeling that in some way she was touching the past. Having never seen anything quite so grand, she momentarily fell silent as she tried to imagine how bright the lamp would be when it was being used.

"What's this?" Bod asked.

Looking down, Jacqui spotted a metal plate screwed to the side of the base. She crouched to get a better look, but she had to wipe some grime away before she could make out any of the words.

"A. Dilnot & Sons," she read out loud, "manufacturers. 1850."

"What does it mean?"

"It must be the company that made this thing," she replied, looking up at the huge lamp that even now towered above her. After a moment she got to her feet. "Can you imagine all the work that would be required? They couldn't have made it here, they'd have made it somewhere on the mainland and then it would have been brought here by boat. And then it had to be carried all the way up here so it could be installed."

"They must have been strong," Bod suggested.

"Yeah, they must have been," she agreed, before turning to see her own face reflected scores of times in differently-tilted mirrors all around. "You know, I've never been very much into history, but even *I* have to respect something like this. It's insane to realize what people can do when they're really motivated. And then for someone to live out here, year after year, must have taken real guts. I don't want to sound like Dad right now, but you've got to admit... people back then were made of sterner stuff."

"What does that mean?"

"It means they could put up with more shit without complaining."

"You shouldn't swear in front of me," Bod replied. "Mum says I might start copying you."

"I wouldn't bother doing that if I were you," Jacqui said, before looking once again at her own reflection. Stepping closer to the glass, she saw her reflected face breaking apart into all sorts of different fragments, some of them warped by curves in the surface. For a moment, she felt as if she was seeing her own features all shaken up and jumbled and then reassembled in various crazy arrangements. "Trust me, if you're the kind of person who copies people, there are way better options out there than me."

CHAPTER NINE

FINALLY REACHING THE PATCH of land directly in front of the lighthouse, David stopped for a moment to get his breath back. He'd found the hike across the island way more physically demanding than he'd expected, to the extent that for much of the time he'd begun to wonder about hiring a personal trainer when he got home.

After all, he figured that now he had a little more money, he might as well try to get fit.

He took a moment to lean against the low wooden fence running around the cottage. Glancing in both directions, he looked out for any sign that his wife and daughters had passed this way, but so far he appeared to be entirely alone. He knew that wasn't possible, of course, but he was also surprised that so far he'd spotted no sign of them at all. He looked up and saw the very top of the lighthouse, although he quickly reminded himself that there was no way Vanessa would let the kids go all the way up there.

The door at the lighthouse's base was wide open, however, and he figured there was no way they could have resisted going in there.

And then, just as he was about to follow them, he heard a creaking sound. He turned and looked toward the cottage, and to his surprise he saw the front door slowly swinging open to reveal the dark interior beyond. He waited, wondering whether Vanessa or the kids were about to come out into the light, but with each passing second he felt more and more alone.

"Hello?" he said cautiously.

Silence.

"Vanessa, are you there?"

No reply.

"Jacqui? Bod?"

Still nothing.

"Hey, I fixed the boat," he continued. "I know I've said that before, and I know you won't believe me, but this time I really *have* fixed it. We're all good to go."

This time, as he watched the open doorway, he couldn't help but notice that the grass was rustling a little louder and that a slightly colder wind had begun to pick up. He glanced over his shoulder and saw that the clouds looked just that tiny bit darker, and he began to wonder whether a front of bad weather might be getting closer. A moment later he turned to look at the lighthouse again, before suddenly hearing a brief but very distinct bumping sound coming from inside the cottage.

"What are you doing in there?" he muttered, opening the gate and making his way along the path, before stopping at the open doorway and peering inside. "Can we please get going? I'm not sure the weather's going to be on our side for much longer, and I know none of you like it when it's rough out there so..."

Again he waited, and now his eyes were starting to adjust to the gloom. He could see a dark, dull little entrance hallway with a few doors leading off in different directions, but the most striking aspect of the cottage was the musty smell that even now seemed to be drifting out of the place. The more he peered into the cottage, the more he felt as if the place appeared to have been shuttered and sealed for quite some time, as if this was the first moment in many years that the accumulation of dust and staleness had been able to escape.

"Vanessa?"

"Jacqui?"

"Bod?"

Once he'd called all three of their names and

heard nothing in response, he once again turned to go to the lighthouse. Before he could take so much as another step, however, he heard a brief crashing sound coming from inside the cottage, as if something had fallen over.

"Okay, now this is getting silly," he sighed, stepping into the hallway. "Are you playing silly games here? I'm serious, we need to get out of here before the weather turns on us."

He waited yet again, but now he was starting to think that the others were messing with him. He knew Bod loved playing games, and that Jacqui might be persuaded to join in, but he was honestly surprised by the idea that his wife would even consider engaging in such lunacy.

"Alright," he said, emphasizing his sense of weary irritation as he walked a little further into the hallway. "I'm here now. Is that the end of the joke?"

Glancing into a small room to his right, he saw a couple of very old-looking armchairs positioned at the far end in front of a cold hearth. He stepped into that room and spotted a bare table, and he couldn't help feeling that this particular space seemed very dull and uninviting. Sure, the years clearly hadn't been kind to the place and he figured that the original inhabitants would have made things a little homelier, yet the graying walls and the low cracked ceiling seemed like imposing markers of some kind of very strict austerity.

Curtains hung in front of the window, but they were dark and very thick-looking curtains that kept out most of the light, while the dusty floorboards had been warped by the passage of time.

Two framed photographs hung on a nearby wall.

Making his way over, David took out his phone and switched on the flashlight app. Holding the phone up, he was able to see that the photographs showed two very glum-looking people – a man and a woman – posing for their portraits. The images were slightly faded and the overriding color was a kind of dull gray-green mix, and a thick layer of dust covered both panes.

Reaching out, he wiped away the dust from one photograph and saw an older man with a heavily-lined face and a large, dark mustache. He wiped the other pane and saw a plump and slightly younger woman who somehow had an even starker expression than the man; this woman looked permanently unimpressed, and David could only assume that the man – if he was her husband – must have lived a rather meek and controlled existence.

"Nice couple," he said under his breath, before turning and shining the flashlight's meager beam around the room once more.

Looking at the chairs, he tried to imagine the dour couple sitting there back in the day, no doubt engaged in polite and very respectable conversations about their life at the lighthouse. In truth he pitied them a little, and he wondered how anyone could live in such a remote location. He knew that he and Vanessa, for example, would be at one another's throats constantly if they were ever forced to live in such confinement, but he figured that people back in the old days were cut from a very different cloth.

"Each to their own," he said, before turning and making his way back out into the hall, where he stopped again and tried to work out not only *where* his family might be hiding, but also why.

With the flashlight app still running, he looked through into another room and saw a sparse white table with two chairs.

"I guess you didn't get many visitors," he muttered, and once again he felt sorry for the couple.

Stepping back, he turned and saw the third and final door. Having checked the first two rooms of the compact little cottage, he figured that Vanessa and the girls had to be in the room directly ahead. There was clearly no bathroom in the place, and he could only assume that any relevant activities were carried out somewhere beyond the cottage. As he made his way to the next door, he saw a fairly small metal-framed double bed with a pile of dirty old sheets that had been left in the middle. This, he realized as he stopped in the doorway, was undoubtedly the source of the fusty smell that had been released when the door was opened.

"Okay, game's over," he called out, although he was puzzled by the fact that he still hadn't managed to locate any members of his family. "Do you really have nothing better to do than hide from me? Seriously? Vanessa, can you get the kids gathered up so we can leave?"

As if to reinforce his point, the panes in the bedroom window rattled gently in their frames. Even in the space of just a few minutes, David could tell that the light was a little duller outside, suggesting that the clouds were gathering.

"I really don't want to waste more time in here," he muttered, stepping into the room and pushing the door shut a little, to make sure that nobody was hiding there. "This place really isn't that interesting."

He turned to look toward the bed.

"It's just -"

In that moment, he froze as he realized that there was some kind of shape under the bed, with what appeared to be a pair of boots and a pair of dark shoes poking out. He felt a niggling sense of fear in his chest, and he knew already that nobody in his family possessed such footwear, and as he tilted the phone a little he realized that these particular shoes very much appeared to be attached to something more substantial.

"Everything okay here?" he asked, even though he knew he was unlikely to receive an affirmative answer.

He waited, wondering whether he should just turn around and leave, but deep down he already knew that he had to at least take a look. As the wind blew against the window once more, he stepped around the bed, making sure to stay as far back as possible, and then he very slowly got down onto his knees. His heart was racing now and part of him still wanted to simply leave, but he figured that he might yet be able to prove that there was nothing to worry about.

Slowly leaning down, and very much aware that the air in this room smelled a little worse than anywhere else in the cottage, he tilted the phone again, until finally he froze as he spotted the two human corpses tucked away beneath the bed, seemingly locked in an embrace as their withered and dried faces stared back out.

CHAPTER TEN

"THIS PLACE IS TRIPPING me out," Jacqui said, still in the lamp room at the top of the lighthouse as she looked down at the notebook in her hands. "It's getting into my head somehow."

She couldn't help thinking back to the moment – just a few minutes earlier – when the notebook had suddenly seemed to be covered in blood, much of which had been leaking down from the ceiling. The whole awful vision had felt way too macabre to be real, and she was absolutely certain that she'd imagined it all, but she still wasn't quite sure why her mind had suddenly started to burp up such vivid fantasies. Even now, as she turned the book around in her hands, she wondered what might have triggered such a thing – and whether it might happen again.

"Can I have your phone?" Bod asked.

Jacqui turned to her.

"Your phone," Bod continued. "I left mine on the boat."

"It doesn't work," Jacqui reminded her. "There's no signal here."

"I know *that*," Bod replied impatiently, holding her hand out, "but I want to take photos. I want to show people when we get back home."

Not really knowing how to counter that request, Jacqui slipped her phone out and handed it to her sister, who snatched it away and immediately unlocked the screen.

"Bod, how do you know that pattern?" she asked.

"I know everyone's patterns," Bod told her with a sly smile. "I sneak and I spy."

Holding up the phone, she began to take photos of the lamp. Slightly impressed but also a little worried, Jacqui watched her for a moment before looking at the notebook again. She wanted to dismiss everything, to tell herself that there was absolutely no reason to be concerned, yet she couldn't shake the feeling that the various notebooks represented fragments of something pretty bad that must have once happened at the lighthouse. At the very least, the person who'd written all those entries seemed to have been pretty confused, perhaps even out of his mind. Then again, she figured that anyone would go crazy if they were stuck living on a remote rock in the North Sea for so long.

Nearby, Bod was still taking photos, this time of the mirrors.

"How many do you need?" Jacqui asked impatiently.

"Just a few more."

"You've already taken way too many."

"Why does it matter?"

"It's my phone."

"Yeah, but you let me borrow it."

"Give it back."

She reached out to take the phone, but Bod – having seemingly anticipated the attempt – darted back and made her way to the door before turning and stating to take more photos of the island.

"You're so immature," Jacqui told her.

"I'm documenting our time here!" Bod protested, stepping out onto the platform but staying back from the railing. "Don't you want to have some proof of our adventure?"

"It's not an adventure," Jacqui replied, feeling increasingly annoyed now by her sister's constant attempts to wind her up. "Bod, this isn't the right moment for you to try to annoy me, okay? We've been up here long enough, we need to go back down and then head to the boat. Dad's probably bodged the engine back up enough for us to leave by now."

"You go," Bod replied, before walking out of sight. "I want to take more photos."

"Not with my phone, you won't," Jacqui sighed, before storming after her. "I'm serious, you little rat, give it back! If you want to take so many photos everywhere we go, you should remember to bring your own damn phone, shouldn't you?"

"Can't hear you!"

Storming out onto the platform, Jacqui felt her blood starting to boil as soon as she spotted her sister taking yet more photos of the admittedly spectacular view. Although she wanted to race over and grab the phone out of her hands, she told herself that she had to be the calm and mature one, so she forced herself to instead grip the railing and start making her way along the platform in a far more measured manner.

"Bod," she said firmly, "I appreciate that you're a budding photographer, but -"

"You'll thank me later," Bod replied with a grin, turning to her. "You can upload these for all your friends to see." She took a step back. "Oh, wait, I forgot – you don't have any friends, do you? You're just -"

In that moment she bumped against the railing, which suddenly snapped away. Falling back, Bod tried to reach out and grab something – anything – for support, but she could only flail helplessly as she tipped over the edge. At the very last second, however, Jacqui managed to rush forward and grab her left hand, hauling her back until the pair of them crashed down hard and landed on the platform's metal floor.

"Are you okay?" Jacqui gasped, and now her heart was racing as she looked past Bod and saw the gap where the railing had given way.

"I was only playing!" Bod sobbed with tears in her eyes.

"Where's my phone?" Jacqui continued, pulling out from under her and then looking over the edge. Although she couldn't see anything as tiny as a cellphone down on the ground, she felt sure that she'd seen the damn thing slip from her sister's hand.

"I'm sorry!" Bod whimpered. "It wasn't my fault!"

Jacqui turned to her.

"I didn't know that was going to break," the younger girl continued, crawling back until she was pressing against the side of the lamp house. "It's not my fault it was old and damaged! I didn't know!"

"I told you to behave," Jacqui replied, and now her initial fear was starting to give way to a rush of anger. "What the hell's wrong with you, Bod? I told you to stay close to me!"

"It's not my fault!"

"Of course it's your fault!" Jacqui snapped. "Are you out of your mind? Do you have any idea how close you just came to falling?"

"I -"

"You'd be dead by now if I hadn't caught you," she added, determined to push her point home this time. "Do you get that? You'd have fallen a hundred meters, and do you know what would have happened when you hit the bottom?" She could see more tears running down her sister's face now and she knew she should stop, but she just couldn't hold back. "You'd probably have exploded. That's what happens to bodies when they fall that far. They burst open when they hit the ground, and there's no surviving that! There's zero chance, Bod! You've had had two or three seconds of falling, watching the ground coming toward you, and then you'd have been splattered everywhere!"

Shaking her head as if she couldn't quite comprehend how close she'd come to death, Bod seemed to be in a state of shock.

"You're such a dumb little child sometimes," Jacqui continued through gritted teeth. "You act all smart and adult, and you wind me up about things, but at the end of the day you're just a stupid little girl!"

"I'm sorry!" Bod shouted, turning and racing along the platform, quickly disappearing through the doorway that led back down into the lighthouse. "You don't have to hate me for it!"

"I don't hate you!" Jacqui called after her,

before sighing as she realized that she'd gone a little too far. Still, as she looked over the edge once more, she felt slightly dizzy as she spotted the rough grass far below.

Pulling back, she leaned against the side of the lamp room and tried to regather her composure. She knew she was going to have to find Bod in a moment and apologize, but she could still feel the anger and fear coursing through her veins and she couldn't help but imagine what would have happened if she hadn't managed to grab her sister's hand in time. Everything had happened so fast, and deep down she blamed herself for letting the situation get that far.

After glancing around to check that there was definitely no sign of her phone, she hauled herself up. She looked at the broken section of railing and once again imagined Bod vanishing over the edge, and then she very carefully began to pick her way to the door so that she could go downstairs and make things up to her sister. The last thing she wanted was to have another long argument, so she figured she was just going to have to accept that her phone was gone and hit her father up for a new one as soon as they got home.

Behind her, as she disappeared down into the lighthouse, a broken section of the railing was hanging loose, swaying a little harder now as the wind continued to pick up strength.

AMY CROSS

CHAPTER ELEVEN

AS SOON AS SHE reached the old office on the lighthouse's first floor, Jacqui realized she could hear a sobbing sound.

"Great," she whispered under her breath. "Best sister ever."

She stopped to look around, and after just a few seconds she was able to work out that the sound seemed to be coming from underneath the desk. She knew that Bod had a tendency to lurch from one extreme to the next, and it wasn't particularly unusual for her to be laughing one moment and then crying the next. Still, she never liked being the one responsible for her sister's mood swings and she couldn't help but wish that she'd reacted differently.

She also knew that a simple apology would never be enough.

"Well," she said out loud, as she slowly made her way across the room, "I guess I really screwed up, huh?"

She stopped at a set of shelves and pretended to be interested in the ancient-looking leather-bound books. To add to the effect, she put her hands on her hips.

"Yeah, I really blew a gasket. And now I have no idea where to find Bod, she's run off and I might never find her. What if she's fallen down a hole?"

She waited, but the sobbing continued and – if anything – seemed to be getting a little more intense.

"Or she'll probably run off and become a lonely old women living here on the island," she continued, hoping that her usual tactic – making Bod laugh – would work as well as ever. "That'd be ironic, wouldn't it? She's totally the more popular out of us, but she'd be the one who'd end up as a hermit. I mean, that's some kind of crazy irony."

Setting the notebook on the shelf, she pulled out a larger tome and opened it up, quickly finding that it contained various diagrams and schematics showing the lighthouse itself.

"Saward Island," she whispered as she read the text beneath what appeared to be a map of the place. "Huh. So that's what it's called."

She began to flick through the yellowing

pages and discovered that they contained a bunch of very dull charts and tables, most of which made no real sense to her whatsoever.

"Yeah, I really screwed up today," she continued, raising her voice just a little more in the hope that Bod would finally respond. "Why am I such an idiot? Why have I got this short temper and this angry side? I mean, it's just a phone. An expensive phone that I only got a few months ago for my birthday, the kind of phone that people actually notice but..."

She let out a loud, expansive sigh.

"It's just a phone," she said again. "I shouldn't get so touchy about it and -"

"Who are you talking to?"

To her surprise, she saw Bod appearing at the top of the staircase leading to the ground floor. She stared at her for a moment – blinking, trying to work out what was happening – before turning to look at the desk just as she realized that the sobbing sound had stopped.

"Where did you just come from?" she asked cautiously.

"Downstairs," Bod replied, sniffing back more tears. "I heard you talking and I wondered who you were talking to."

Furrowing her brow, Jacqui made her way across the room and crouched down. When she looked under the desk, she saw that there was no sign of anyone; she wasn't certain that the sobbing sound had come from this exact spot, but it had certainly been in the room – yet now it was gone.

"I'm sorry I didn't listen to you," Bod said, "and I'm sorry I dropped your phone."

Holding her hand up, she revealed the broken phone that had fallen off the top of the lighthouse.

"I went out to find it," she explained as Jacqui walked over and took it from her hand. "I hoped that maybe it didn't get broken in the fall, but it did. The screen's all smashed."

Pushing a button on the phone's side, Jacqui found to her surprise that the phone actually worked, even if the screen was so badly damaged that any images were badly distorted. Figuring that it must have hit some bushes or something else slightly soft on its way down, she picked at the cracked sections for a moment before looking at her sister and seeing that fresh tears were dancing in her eyes.

"You know what, Bod?" she said after a moment. "Screw the phone. It can be replaced, unlike you. If you'd fallen -"

She caught herself just in time, and she quickly reminded herself that there was really no need to upset her sister again.

"Well, let's just be glad that everything's okay," she added, "and if you don't mind, can we *please* not tell Mum and Dad about what happened? They'll only get mad at me for letting us go up there in the first place, and it'll be me who gets into a whole load of trouble. You wouldn't want that, would you?"

Bod stared up at her for a moment, still sniffing back tears, before finally her mischievous grin returned.

"Bod!" Jacqui said firmly, holding up a little finger. "Pinkie promise."

"Fine," Bod replied, briefly offering her own little finger for the requisite shake. "I won't tell Mum and Dad, but how are you going to explain how your phone got broken?"

"I'll just tell them that I dropped it or something like that," she suggested, before glancing at the window as she heard the first drops of rain starting to fall. "Great, it's not looking too brilliant out there. I don't suppose you've seen an umbrella on your travels, have you?"

***

By the time they got downstairs and reached the lighthouse's main door, the initial drops of rain had transformed to become an absolute deluge, cascading down from an ever-darkening sky high above. Already, the rain was so bad that a loud hissing sound was filling the air as the bad weather hammered every surface around.

"We... don't have to go out in that, do we?" Bod asked cautiously, feeling a fine spray against her face even though she was still in the doorway. "*Do* we?"

"I think we'd be drowned before we made it ten feet," Jacqui replied, shivering slightly as a cold wind blew against them both. "We'd better -"

Before she could finish, thunder rumbled ominously above the island, and the sound continued for several more seconds until finally it petered away to nothing.

"We'd better stay here," she continued, "until it eases up a bit. I'm pretty sure that Dad won't be wanting to set sail while there's a storm brewing."

"Does that mean we're stuck here?"

"No, of course not," Jacqui replied, although she immediately realized that her sister might have a valid point. Somehow, impossibly, the rain seemed to be getting even more intense now. "We're just... temporarily delayed, that's all. The sensible thing is just to hunker down and hope that the worst of it passes soon. Which it will."

She swallowed hard.

"I'm sure."

Above, another rumble of thunder seemed a little louder than the first and lasted longer too.

"I don't like storms," Bod said, reaching out

and gently taking hold of Jacqui's hand for comfort. "I know it's stupid, but they scare me."

"Relax," Jacqui replied, "at least there's no lightning." She looked out across the rain-lashed island for a moment, worried that those last words might have tempted fate. "It's weird, though. I'm sure the forecast for today was supposed to be really good. I looked at the weather radar and I didn't see anything that could possibly cause this. It must have just rolled in really fast."

"Will Mum and Dad be okay on the boat?"

"They'll be fine, although they might get a little seasick if the water's too choppy. Can you imagine that? They'll both be puking their guts up."

Bod began to giggle.

"Dad'll go nuts," Jacqui continued, glad that she was finally managing to cheer her sister up again. "Even more nuts than usual. He'll be spitting feathers."

Bod's giggle grew a little, and she seemed genuinely amused even as the rain continued to fall and another peal of thunder rumbled across the sky.

"It's so desolate," Jacqui said under her breath, struck by how much the island had changed in just the short time since she and her family had arrived. "Look at it. I always heard that things could get pretty choppy out here in the more remote islands, but it's still kinda crazy to witness it firsthand. People always say that nature can be so powerful, but this is the first time I've ever seen it really unleashed."

"But we're safe in here, right?" Bod asked nervously.

"We're safe in here," Jacqui told her, trying as hard as possible to sound like she felt confident about that fact. "I bet this lighthouse has withstood more than its fair share of storms over the years. All we've got to do now is try to ride it out."

CHAPTER TWELVE

AS RAIN BATTERED THE window, David remained on his hands and knees in the cottage's bedroom, unable to stop staring at the horrific sight of the dead couple beneath the bed.

He blinked, but even this couldn't disturb his gaze. One moment he found himself studying the face of the dead woman, with its mouth wide open in an apparent final scream, and then the next he instead focused on the relatively calm and somehow stoic expression of the dead man. Both had died in an embrace, with the man's arms wrapped around the woman from behind as if he was trying to hold her in place, and now their bodies remained locked in the moment of their death. Evidently the unusual atmosphere of the cottage, perhaps of the entire island, had caused them to become more mummified than rotten, with pale flesh mostly clinging to the bones beneath as strands of white hair remained attached to their scalps.

Suddenly, as thunder rumbled again, David pulled back and bumped hard against the wall.

"No," he whispered, as if disturbed from some kind of reverie as he got to his feet and began to back out of the room. "Hell, no. Absolutely not. Definitely not."

He stumbled and almost fell back, but at the last moment he managed to reach out and steady himself against the sides of the doorway. By the time he reached the hall, he'd already begun – in his mind's eye – to connect the two corpses to the photographs in the other room, and when he turned to look over his shoulder he saw the pair of empty chairs seemingly still waiting for their dead occupants.

Thunder rumbled once more, and the entire cottage seemed to shake slightly as David shuffled to the door and stepped outside. As soon as he was beyond the door, he found himself standing in the strongest downpour he'd ever experienced in his life, yet he could only remain completely still as his clothes became drenched in a matter of just a few seconds.

Barely even aware of the elements, he began to slowly turn and look back into the cottage. He saw the empty hallway, but somehow – above the crashing sound of more and more rain falling – he felt that he could also hear the faintest cracking sound. He told himself that he had to be imagining things, but as he peered into the gloom he saw the door leading into the bathroom and he realized that somehow the shadows on the far wall, just beyond the edge of the bed, appeared to be shifting slightly, almost as if -

In that instant a bright flash of lightning filled the air, followed a fraction of a second later by yet another crack of thunder.

Turning away from the cottage, David looked around but still saw no sign of anyone. He quickly spotted the open door at the base of the lighthouse, however, and now he was becoming more aware of the fact that his soaked and cold clothes were starting to cling to his body. He stared in open-mouthed horror at the door for a moment longer, before hearing the cracking sound once again coming from inside the cottage.

Not daring to turn and look, he began to hurry toward the lighthouse.

***

Once he was inside, he pushed the door shut and stepped back, using his body weight to keep it closed. He was soaking wet and dripping all over the floor, and more than a little short of breath, but so far he couldn't quite convince himself that everything was alright.

A moment later, to his surprise, he heard a familiar giggle coming from somewhere above.

Stepping across the cramped room, and struggling a little to pick his way past and over and around various items that had been left haphazardly all over the place, he finally reached the foot of a staircase and looked up. He listened carefully, and after just a couple more seconds he heard the giggle again. Still not quite believing his deepest suspicions, he began to make his way carefully up the staircase, brushing repeatedly against the wall as he struggled to remain on his feet.

As he finally reached the top, the giggle rang out again, and to his surprise and bemusement David saw his two daughters sitting cross-legged on the floor with a chessboard between them.

"What... what are you doing here?" he asked.

"Hey Dad," Jacqui replied, turning to him and immediately bursting out with a brief laugh. "What happened to you? You're completely soaked!"

"You're so wet!" Bod added unhelpfully.

"It's raining," he stammered.

"We know," Jacqui said matter-of-factly. "That's why we took an executive decision to stay here until the worst of it passes. We found an old chessboard and figured we could see who's better. To be honest, we thought you and Mum would be waiting for us on the boat."

She waited for a reply, but after just a few seconds her smile began to fade as she saw the shocked expression on his face.

"Dad?" she said cautiously, getting to her feet as lightning flashed outside the window again. "What's wrong? You look kind of... freaked out."

"Did you go into that cottage?" he asked.

"No," she replied cautiously. "Why?"

He opened his mouth to reply, but at the last second he held back. Looking around, he saw the desk with its pile of notebooks and the various sets of shelves, and then he turned to see another staircase leading up higher into the lighthouse.

"What the hell is this place?" he continued.

"Just your average everyday spooky abandoned lighthouse," Jacqui explained with a smile.

"It's your turn," Bod said after moving a piece on the chessboard.

"I..."

For a few seconds, David simply seemed lost for words. He looked around once again, as if trying to make sense of the bizarre scene, but his mouth was hanging slightly open even as rainwater ran down his features. After a few seconds he turned suddenly and looked over his shoulder, as if something had caught his attention, but he saw nothing. He swallowed hard, but in truth he seemed almost to have stalled, no longer able to make any sense of his surroundings.

"Jacqui?" Bod said again. "It's your turn."

"Dad, everything's cool," Jacqui continued, ignoring her sister. "Just chill out and we'll wait for the storm to pass. If you think about it, this is actually kinda funny."

He turned to her. "Funny?"

"In a way. How many people do *you* know who can honestly say that they got stranded in a lighthouse on some random remote Scottish island in the middle of a storm? And that's before you factor in the spooky notebooks and all that stuff."

"Did you go into the cottage?" he asked again.

"No, but -"

"Do *not* go into the cottage," he continued, interrupting her. "Do you hear me, Jacqui? Whatever else happens, you and your sister are under express orders to stay out of there. This isn't a joke, it isn't one of those situations where it's fun for you to break my rules. This is extremely important and I need to know that I can rely on you. Do not go in there."

"Alright," she replied, clearly wondering exactly why he was being so insistent. "We won't go in the stinky little cottage, but... why not?"

"Where's your mother?"

"Isn't she with you?"

"She left," he explained. "One minute she was on the boat with me, the next minute she was gone. I assumed she'd followed you guys."

"We haven't seen Mum since we set off," Jacqui said cautiously, before looking toward the window and seeing that – somehow, impossibly – the weather now seemed even worse. "She'll be okay, won't she?"

"Of course she will," he replied, before shaking his head for a moment. "She might be soaking wet, in which case she'll be pissed off, but she'll be fine. I just don't quite get where she could've gone, that's all. It's not like there are any other places nearby."

He turned and looked the other way.

"It's almost like..."

His voice trailed off for a few seconds, and then he shook his head.

"No," he added, clearly talking to himself now. "Don't even go there, David. Don't even think about it. It's not possible."

"Trust Mum to get lost on a small island in a storm," Jacqui said, rolling her eyes as she sat back down and looked once more at the chessboard. "She'll show up eventually. It's not like she can go far wrong on this Saward Island place."

She studied the board for a moment, before

moving one of her bishops.

"What did you just say?" David asked, and now the color appeared to have drained from his face in a matter of seconds.

"Just that Mum can't really get too lost. Like you said, there aren't many other places for her to be."

"No, after that," he replied, staring at her with a growing sense of fear in his eyes. "What... what did you call this place?"

"Saward Island?" She shrugged as she watched Bod moving one of the black knights.

"Why did you call it that?" David asked.

"Because that's its name?" she suggested, before pointing vaguely in the direction of some of the books. "According to one of those things over there, anyway. Why, does it matter?"

"Why would you say something like that?" he continued. "Were you listening to stupid stories when we stayed in Innisrach? Do you think you're being funny?"

She moved her other bishop, and then she turned to see that he looked white as a sheet.

"If you don't believe me," she said, "then see for yourself. But why does it matter, anyway? Have you heard of this place?"

"Saward Island doesn't exist," he told her. "It can't. It's a stupid myth people used to tell each other years ago, but it's not based on a true story.

You have to be wrong, Jacqui. A place like Saward Island just can't be real."

CHAPTER THIRTEEN

AS SOON AS HE opened the book, David saw the name Saward Island and froze. At that moment, as if to underline the intensity of the moment, thunder rumbled again and wind – blowing through a tiny gap in the window – carried a whistling sound into the room.

"See?" Jacqui said, with an air of satisfaction in her tone. "It says it right there. Saward Island. *Now* do you believe me?"

She waited for him to admit that she was right and that he was wrong, and that she was incredibly smart and he should never ever doubt her again, but instead he simply stared at the book before slowly starting to turn its pages. He seemed shocked to his core and unable to quite get any words out, even as his mouth continued to hang slightly open.

"Dad, chill," she continued, nudging his arm. "What are you getting so worked up about? So we're on an island that you thought didn't exist. Does it matter?"

"This must be some kind of joke," he muttered, as if he hadn't even heard her question. He continued to look through the book, before coming to a page showing a map of the entire area. "But why would someone do that? Why would anyone go to such lengths to..."

He hesitated, before carrying the book over to a table in front of the window. Setting the book down so that he could see a little better, he muttered under his breath as he pointed at various spots on the map. As she made her way over to join him, Jacqui was starting to worry that her father might be losing his mind.

"It's your turn!" Bod called out brightly, still sitting patiently at the chessboard.

"Dad, what's going on?" Jacqui asked. "Don't get me wrong, I'm all for a little mystery now and again but you're starting to freak me out."

"We came this way," he whispered, and it still wasn't entirely clear whether or not he'd heard her as he indicated an open patch of sea on the map. "I know I was right about that, so we should have come over here." He moved his finger slightly. "But the engine trouble put us off the original course, so we *would* have pitched up here..."

He moved his finger again.

"This isn't on any of the usual lanes, so no-one really comes here much," he continued, "but if my navigation was correct, then..."

He hesitated again, before lifting his finger to reveal that it had been covering the exact spot showing the location of Saward Island.

"Your mother said the maps showed nothing here," he added. "I didn't pay much attention at the time, I was just annoyed by the engine, but she insisted that there shouldn't be an island. And she was right. According to all the maps, there should be nothing here but -"

"But there *is* something here," Jacqui pointed out. "There has to be, because... we're standing on it."

"That doesn't mean it has to be Saward Island, though," he replied, turning to her with an increasingly worried expression in his eyes. "Not definitively. There are lots of other possibilities."

"What's so wrong if it's this Saward Island place?" she asked.

"Jacqui, it's your turn!" Bod said again, this time sounding a little more whiny.

"I grew up round here," David reminded Jacqui. "On the mainland, sure, but lots of people in the village were fishermen."

"I know," she replied. "You tell us about

your childhood whenever you get a chance. You grew up in a tiny fishing village, blah blah blah, and you worked really hard and made something of yourself, blah blah blah, and you left the village when you were eighteen with nothing but the clothes you were wearing, blah blah blah, and then twenty years later you came back as a self-made man with loads of money. Blah blah and indeed blah. But you've never forgotten your roots because you're a true Scotsman at heart, even though you worked hard to get rid of your accent and until this week you hadn't been here for years and years. Have I more or less summed it up correctly?"

She waited for a reply, but slowly she began to realize that this perhaps hadn't been the right moment for her to try to be smart.

"I remember the stories," he told her. "They stick with you, even when nothing else does. They become part of how you see the world."

"Okay, now you're starting to freak me out a little bit," she replied. "Dad, what's actually going on here? Why are you acting so weird?"

"It's your turn!" Bod said firmly, clearly frustrated now that she was being ignored.

"I remember people talking about Saward Island," David murmured, looking paler than ever. "I remember the story about the Millers, but... I was so sure it was all made up. I thought it was one of those stupid tales that old fishermen tell each other in the pub." As the wind picked up outside and the entire lighthouse creaked and groaned slightly, he looked once more at the rain-lashed window. "To be honest, I never even though that the Millers were real."

***

January 10th, 1872...

"This'll be your new home, then," Martin Bellwether said, pulling the rope tight and then wrapping it around the post on the end of the wooden dock. "Can't say that I envy you, but for the right people... I suppose a place like this might be idyllic."

He reached down to help William Miller up off the boat, but the older men steadfastly – and clearly very deliberately – refused the offer. Instead, despite his advancing age and obvious stiffness, William took hold of the post and hauled himself up. His gangly figure allowed him to climb up the ladder two rungs at a time, and once he was on the dock he stopped and took a moment to straighten his black shirt.

"Wouldn't do much for me, though," Martin added with a smile, still trying to make pleasant conversation even though the journey from the mainland had been entirely silent. "I need a little more... rambunctiousness from life, if you catch my drift."

"Rambunctiousness?"

"Yes. You know... energy... vim and vigor... action..."

William turned to him, glaring with humorless intent, before turning the other way and looking down to see his wife Margaret preparing to climb the ladder.

"Mind you hold on tight," he said, his voice sounding scratched and croaky, almost as if he was having trouble getting any words out at all. "Be careful, Margaret. The sea's at its coldest at this time of year. The shock of falling in wouldn't be good for anyone's heart."

"Goodness, yes," Martin replied, refusing to bow down to the grim atmosphere of the situation. "Only a complete madman would dip so much as a toe in there. Oh, but Mrs. Miller, where are my manners? Let me help you up."

He stepped toward the ladder, but William immediately held out a long, thin arm to keep him back.

"It's better for a person to do it alone," the older man intoned. "While it might make you feel better to help her, and you might think it part of your chivalrous duty, if you think about it you'd only be increasing the likelihood of an accident. The ladder's sturdy enough and my wife is a strong woman. Best to avoid interfering and, instead, let her climb up under her own steam."

"Well, I suppose that's one way of looking at it," Martin muttered, watching as Margaret slowly but surely made her way up the ladder and joined them on the dock.

"You'll be turning around and heading back now, I assume," William continued. "There's no need for you to stay here."

"I thought I might show you the -"

"We can find our way perfectly well," William added, stopping him before he could say more. "This is where I'll be meeting the boat with supplies once every month, is it not?"

"It is."

"Then I know everything I need to know. My wife and I did not choose to come out here lightly. We seek a life far away from the excesses of modern life. People talk too much these days. They rabbit on and on, speaking even when they have nothing to say. I despise that, as I despise most aspects of our present society, and I understand that things are even worse in the cities. Out here, meanwhile, Margaret and I shall surely be able to live better, more devout lives. We are looking for simplicity."

"You'll undoubtedly find it here," Martin told him, as he felt just the slightest drizzle of rain against his face. After a moment he turned to

Margaret. "And you, Mrs. Miller, will -"

"My wife feels the same way," William said firmly. "Mr. Bellwether, I must thank you for bringing us out here, even though I know the company has remunerated you for the effort. I shall pray for you to return safely."

"That would be nice," Martin told him, looking down at the small collection of cases he'd already transferred from the boat and realizing that there was little for him to do now. "All that's left, I suppose, is for me to wish you a pleasant time here on Saward Island." He glanced toward the top of the rocks and felt a shiver run through his bones. "I'm sure you'll be absolutely fine. You'll be quite alone here. Completely alone, in fact. Just the two of you, just the way you seem to want it."

CHAPTER FOURTEEN

A SHORT WHILE LATER, as he carried the cases across the island, William stopped and felt a sharp pain in the small of his back. Although he hated to show any form of weakness, he had no choice: he set the cases down against the rough grass and took a moment to stretch, trying to rid himself of the annoying crick.

"Are you sure you don't want me to carry something?" Margaret asked, turning to him.

"It's not a woman's place to convey luggage," he told her.

"Yes, but -"

Stopping for a moment, she wondered whether there might be any way she could persuade him. Almost ten years her husband's junior, Margaret Miller – nee Clarendon – had only just passed her thirtieth birthday, although a harsh life in the village first as a washerwoman and then as a cook had left her with plenty of niggling injuries of her own. She knew that her new husband didn't like much fussing, however, so she held her tongue and waited as he continued to stretch, and after a few seconds she bowed her head and looked down as she reminded herself that he probably did not want to be observed.

Slowly she turned and looked across the island, and she felt a flicker of dread as she spotted the lighthouse in the distance. William had given her no say in their move; he'd merely returned home a few weeks earlier and informed he that he'd taken a position as master of the lighthouse on Saward Island, and that the pair of them would be moving shortly. In truth she'd been aghast at the idea, not only because it meant leaving her childhood home but also because she'd heard the rumors about this particular island. Even on the journey from the mainland, she'd been secretly hoping that some barrier to their move might emerge at the last moment.

Yet no such barrier had made itself known.

"I am ready to continue," William said, and she turned to see that he was already picking up the cases again. "We should hurry. There'll be rain soon, I think."

"William -"

"We don't want to get caught out in that," he continued, carrying the cases past her, clearly struggling a great deal. "There's plenty to be doing, though, and I want to get started before sundown. You'll be busy too, you'll need to start making the cottage ready and sorting through the supplies. We shall both be ready for a good meal later."

She opened her mouth to once again offer some help, but she already knew that William had very strict rules on such things. He wasn't old-fashioned, exactly, but he had explained many times that some jobs fell to men and some fell to women, and that there was nothing to be gained from mixing the two up. Finally, resolving to try to support him a little better, she set off again on the journey to the lighthouse, and she told herself that things could only get better.

***

"It's a fine little place," William said, standing in the cottage's hallway and looking around at the three doors that led into different rooms. "Strong and sturdy. It'll protect us from the elements, which is the main thing. How do you find the kitchen?"

"Slightly dirty," Margaret replied, still sorting through the cupboards, "but nothing a good clean won't fix up. Did you say that the previous tenants here left in something of a hurry?"

"That they did."

"And..."

She set a couple of pots down and saw a thin-legged spider stirring in one, and then she turned to look out at her husband in the hallway.

"And *why* did they leave, again?"

"That is none of our concern."

"I heard that nobody has stayed here for very long," she told him, desperate to learn a little more about her new predicament – but aware that she had to be diplomatic. "Mother Corstairs claims that even the men who built this lighthouse insisted on rowing out each morning and rowing away at night, on account of them not liking to stay here during the hours of darkness."

She waited, but now William was glaring at her with an expression that almost burned into her soul.

"But Mother Corstairs loves to gossip," she added, forcing a smile in an attempt to lighten the atmosphere, "and I shouldn't set any store by her words, should I?" Taking the pot, she carried it across the room and opened the window, and then she carefully removed the spider and threw it out onto a bush. "As you always tell me, gossip is for idle minds. We should be grateful for what we have here."

She waited for her husband to respond, but a moment later she heard footsteps. Looking outside, she saw him already leaving the cottage and making his way toward the lighthouse, and she reminded herself that she was so lucky to be married to such a strong man. After all, William had long been known in their little village as a bastion of decency and proper conduct, whereas she had begun to gain a reputation for wildness; in marrying him, she had sought to tame her worst impulses in an attempt to better become a proper wife.

So far, that plan was working. And if William was a little... difficult to engage in conversation, then she could only assume that all husbands were the same.

"Lord," she whispered, looking up at the sky and seeing vast roiling clouds that clearly threatened rain, "I ask that you watch over us in this place, and that you keep us safe so that we – in turn – can strive to keep others from harm."

She took a deep breath as she listened to the stillness of the cottage, which was in marked contrast to the life she was used to back on the mainland.

"And if you wouldn't mind helping me to appreciate this place more," she continued, "I would be very grateful. Help me to forget all the foolish tales I used to hear. Silly old Mother Corstairs can be especially free with her tongue, I'm quite sure she could conjure up a chilling tale about even the sunniest and happiest of places so -"

Before she could finish, she spotted a figure in the distance. She felt her heart skip a beat as she looked out across the island and saw that someone appeared to be standing way off on the very far side, seemingly completely still and unafraid of being noticed.

Telling herself that she had to be wrong, that nobody else was supposed to be on Saward Island, Margaret kept her eyes fixed on the figure and waited for it to resolve into something else. She blinked a couple of times but the figure remained and – although she was determined to remain calm and rational – Margaret couldn't help but wonder whether some other soul might have ended up on this small patch of land far out in the wilds of the North Sea.

And then, feeling something brushing her hand, she looked down and saw another spider. Wincing, she tipped this spider out onto the bush to follow its companion, and then she looked across the island again.

This time, to her immense relief, there was no sign of anyone, and she began to notice that there were several dark shadows on the grass that could – to an impressionable mind – seem like human figures. She looked once more toward the spot where the supposed interloper had been standing and she satisfied herself that there was nobody there now, and she began to focus on the idea that she had merely seen another of those shadows. At the same time, a growing sense of worry was starting to uncurl itself at the back of her mind.

"Only a fool would set foot on Saward Island," she remembered Mother Corstairs saying a week or so earlier. "You and that Miller gentleman won't last long out there, not if you know what's good for you."

Those words echoed in her thoughts now, and she had to force herself to stop thinking about any of the other comments she'd heard about the island. Some of those comments had been aimed at her directly, by people who wanted her to reconsider traveling to the island at all, while some had been overheard while she was going about her duties. And while the details differed from one telling to the next, the various voices had all been agreed on one important point.

"They shouldn't go out to that island."

"I pray every morning and every night that Margaret will change her mind."

"Why would she follow that dour man out to such an awful place?"

"No living soul should set foot on Saward Island ever again. That place should be forgotten."

"Pray for them."

"I shall pray for their souls."

"I shall include Margaret and William in my

prayers from now on."

So many concerns. So many promises of prayer.

Finally, with more than a little effort, Margaret managed to stop dwelling on such memories. She knew that there was a danger she might trick her mind into inventing all sorts of impressions, and she recalled her husband's warning that the female brain was especially prone to hysterics. After looking across the island one more time and satisfying herself that there had never been anyone else out there, then, she closed the window and carried the pot back over to the table, where she set it down so that she could continue with her work.

William would expect a meal at the end of the afternoon, and it was her job to prepare that meal. Nothing else, she reminded herself, should occupy her thoughts at all.

"And look after Mr. Bellwether," she whispered, finishing her earlier prayer as she pulled some cans from another of the cupboards. "Please, Lord, see to it that he makes it safely back to the mainland. Also, please keep William and I in your thoughts. We can be happy here, I know it. I feel such hope in my heart."

CHAPTER FIFTEEN

ONE YEAR LATER, REACHING the top of the staircase in the lighthouse with a plate of food in her hands, Margaret saw that once again her husband was sitting hunched at his desk on the far side of the room.

She waited, hoping that he would already have noticed her arrival, but she quickly realized that as usual he was scribbling in one of the journals.

"William?" she said cautiously, watching as candlelight caught the side of his face and accentuated the already strong lines that ran down his cheek. "I brought you something to eat. I hoped that you might come down to the cottage and join me for supper, but..."

As her voice trailed off, she realized that

such a hope had been foolish all along. Within days of their arrival on the island, William had stopped joining her for any meals at all, and instead she always had to bring something up to him. He rarely liked to leave the lighthouse at all, insisting that he had to remain constantly alert in case any passing vessels required assistance; and while she admired her husband's dedication to his job, she couldn't help but wish that he might just occasionally take a few hours off to spend time with her.

"William?" she said again. "It's only some dried bread and half an apple, and a glass of water, but you should eat something to keep your strength up."

When he still failed to respond, she began to make her way across the room. Night had fallen outside and a fair wind had picked up, although the winter weather had so far not been quite as harsh as it might. As she reached the desk and set the plate down, Margaret hoped very much that her husband might finally at least acknowledge her presence, yet he remained utterly devoted to the journal. Looking down, she saw that he was making notes about a vessel that had passed close to the island, although a moment later she saw that he'd also added a crude drawing of what appeared to be a woman.

"Who's that?" she asked.

All she heard in return was the sound of his pen's nib scratching against the page. He appeared to be paying particular attention to the woman's mouth, running the pen over that area in different directions.

"Is it me?" she continued, still desperately trying to engage him in conversation. "It doesn't quite look like me, but... who else could it be?"

She swallowed hard, but in truth she was growing more and more accustomed to her husband's inward nature. After a moment she left the desk and walked over to the window, although when she peered outside she was able to see little more than darkness.

"I believe," she said, having saved this information for a few hours, "that today marks one year since we arrived on this island. Can you believe that? So many people whispered that we'd barely last one day, yet here we are. I must say that, although times have been difficult occasionally and we certainly struggled to begin with, I have come to enjoy our time here."

She waited again, still hearing only the scratching of the pen against paper.

"I do find myself wondering, however," she added cautiously, "whether it might be possible to pay a brief visit to the village. When the supplies next arrive, I should like to return with them just for a day or two, just to see how everyone is. Then I can arrange to come back out with someone. You could even come with me. Would you like to do that, William? Do you think that we might -"

"No," he said gruffly.

She turned and saw that he was still writing in the journal.

"It would be for but a day or -"

"No," he said again.

"I understand that you have much to do here," she told him, "but I -"

"No," he said for a third time, still not looking up at her.

"I understand," she replied, trying to hide her disappointment. "Perhaps next year, then."

She hesitated, wondering whether there might be anything else she could say to elicit more of a response, but she quickly admonished herself in silence for demanding too much of her husband. Instead of disturbing him further, she turned and began to make her way back over toward the staircase.

"She would not let us leave, anyhow," William added.

Stopping, she took a moment to try to make sense of those words before slowly looking back at him.

"I beg your pardon?" she replied.

"She would not let us leave," he repeated, turning to another page in the journal. "We're safe for now, since we aren't part of the cursed bloodline, but her patience surely has limits."

Although she opened her mouth to ask her husband what he meant, Margaret held back at the last moment. He had been prone, since their arrival on the island, to issue occasional pronouncements that made little sense, and she could only assume that this was the latest example. She certainly knew that there was nobody else anywhere on Saward Island, and the figure she'd spotted on her first day had by now entirely slipped her mind. She also knew that it was not her place to question anything her husband said, or indeed to disturb him more than she already had.

"I shall retire to the cottage to read," she told him, "and then I shall retire to bed. I hope you shall join me shortly."

She waited for a reply, and then – when nothing was forthcoming and she heard only the scratching of the pen – she made her way alone back down the staircase.

***

Flat on her back in bed, staring up at the dark ceiling, Margaret wondered why she couldn't sleep. Several hours had passed since she'd returned to the cottage; she'd read for a little while before her eyes had become tired, and finally she'd given up waiting for William to join her. She'd settled in the bed and had hoped to fall swiftly asleep, yet on this particular night something was keeping her wide awake.

She had no idea of the time, but she felt sure that midnight must soon be rolling around.

And then, after a little while longer, she heard the sound of footsteps emerging from the lighthouse. Her first reaction was relief, for she always slept so much better once William was beside her in the bed, but slowly she began to realize that these footsteps were not approaching the cottage at all and instead already seemed to be getting further and further away. Not wanting to question her husband's actions, but also wondering what he might be doing, she rose from the bed and headed to the door, and then she walked through to the small sitting room and made her way to the window next to the two empty chairs.

Outside, a cold moon cast just enough light for her to spot William walking away past the little fence surrounding the cottage, seemingly intent on marching out across the island.

"What are you doing?" she whispered, puzzled by this latest instance of unusual behavior.

She told herself that William of course would have a perfectly good reason to venture out, but a moment later she realized that the lighthouse stood bathed in darkness. This in itself was highly unusual, since the weather had become a little worse and she'd assumed that the lamp must remain burning, but again she told herself that William must know what he was doing. Nevertheless, after a moment she walked through into the hall and opened the front door, and she felt cold night air blowing against her as she looked out across the moonlit island and saw that William was already much further away by now.

Worried that he might be walking in his sleep, she considered the various possibilities for a moment longer before deciding that for once she was going to take action.

After pulling the door shut, she began to make her way after her husband, determined to see where he was going. She'd already suspected that he occasionally ventured out across the island at night, yet this was the first time that she'd been awake enough to catch him leaving. She could just about see him in the distance, and she told herself that while she would prefer to go unnoticed, she also wasn't actually doing anything wrong. Should not a wife go after her husband, she wondered to herself, if she worried that something might be amiss?

Finally, after walking for quite some time, she saw that William had stopped on what appeared to be a perfectly nondescript patch of land at the bottom of a shallow slope, and that he was seemingly just staring now at the ground. She waited, wondering what he might do next, yet he was clearly focused very much on the grass and after a few more seconds she realized that her earlier assumption must be correct.

She felt a rush of relief as she understood that William was merely walking in his sleep, and she told herself that she would simply stay close and make sure that he remained safe until he returned to the cottage.

CHAPTER SIXTEEN

THE FOLLOWING MORNING, FEELING rather tired after spending a couple of hours keeping track of her husband during the night, Margaret stood at the kitchen window and continued to wash the pots.

Hearing footsteps outside, she looked up just in time to see William walking past with a fairly large dark cross. After watching him for a moment, she quickly dried her hands before hurrying outside and heading to the fence just as he began to head out across the island.

"Where are you going?" she called out.

He stopped and turned to her.

"William, where are you going," she asked again, "and what is that you're carrying?"

"Isn't it obvious?" he asked.

"It looks like a cross."

"Then that is your answer," he told her, although his voice betrayed a little less certainty than usual. "You have no need to concern yourself over this matter. I shall be back presently."

"What is it intended to mark?"

"Woman, you are full of questions this morning," he muttered, before turning and setting off again, evidently believing that he had no need to explain further.

As she watched him go, Margaret wondered whether she ought to go after him, but she supposed that he was clearly awake now and that there was no point risking his anger. Instead she waited until he was far enough away, before glancing over at the lighthouse and thinking about the desk where he spent so much of his time. Truthfully, she had begun to notice that he often slipped his most important duties and that the lighthouse's lamp was seldom burning, and she wondered just why he tended to spend so much time scribbling in his journals.

She knew that she had no right to interfere, and that he would be furious if he discovered her snooping, yet she couldn't quite escape a rippling sense of concern in her belly. She looked out across the island again and saw that he was getting further and further away, and then – slightly against her better judgment – she began to hurry toward the door at the lighthouse's base.

***

As she reached the top of the staircase, Margaret felt the wooden board shift slightly under her left foot, letting out a faint creaking sound that seemed almost to serve as a warning.

She stopped, waiting for silence to settle again, and then she walked over to the window and looked outside. She could just about see William in the distance and – although she couldn't be sure – she felt that she could just about spy him having stopped on the same patch of ground that had occupied his attention during the night; he had set the cross down and looked to be getting down onto his knees, for reasons that Margaret felt she couldn't possibly fathom.

Then again, she had long since come to the conclusion that she couldn't hope to understand her husband's every action. After all, he was an intelligent man and she was just an uneducated woman from the village.

Deciding to ignore such concerns for now, she instead turned and walked over to the desk. William had filled copious journals in the year since the pair of them had arrived on the island, and she knew that he often stayed up long into the night working on logs and notes and all manner of other entries. He'd always been careful to hide them from her, although she'd occasionally spotted some of the passages and even the odd drawing.

Now, feeling a tightening sense of fear in her chest, she picked one of the journals at random and opened it out, and to her surprise she found that it contained not only her husband's handwriting but also several lines that appeared to have been written by somebody else entirely.

I do not know where, William had scribbled at the top of one page. *You must show me.*

A little further down, in a script that she felt sure could never have come from William's hand, she saw what appeared to be a reply.

I shall lead you.

Puzzled, she looked to the next page and saw that, although the questions and answers were fairly spaced out, they seemed to continue in some kind of order.

I shall do as you ask, William had written.

"You... have no... choice," she whispered, struggling a little to read the response.

Below that line, one or other of the hands had drawn a simple cross, with a few added details seemingly included to show how the two sections might be joined together.

Like this? William had asked.

Like this, the other hand had replied.

Staring at the page, Margaret told herself that one thing was very clear. Nobody else lived on the island, and certainly nobody was visiting the lighthouse, which meant that all the entries in the book had to have been made by her husband. She couldn't even begin to understand why or how William would do such a thing, yet she supposed that he must have a good reason – and that she herself was simply not of sufficient intelligence to understand. Why, for all she knew, was it not possible that all men wrote in such a manner, perhaps in an attempt to give better order to their thoughts?

The alternative, that William was in some way strange or unusual, was almost too horrible to contemplate.

"My husband is a completely normal man," she said, hoping that – by saying the words out loud – she might be more likely to believe them, "and he is merely acting as any other man would. Indeed, he is in many ways superior to other men, so it stands to reason that he needs to write out his thoughts in this seemingly slightly unusual... manner..."

Even as that last word left her lips, she felt on a deeper level that she didn't really believe this theory, yet she quickly forced herself to get over any doubts. William Miller might have a few minor faults, she was perfectly aware of that fact, yet on the whole he was strong and decent and reliable, and she quietly admonished herself for even daring to try to question his habits. If he found that there was something to be gained from writing to himself in this manner, then how could she ever dare to question him?

She turned to another page and saw a scratchy drawing of a rather terrifying-looking woman, and then she demurely closed the journal and took a very deep and deliberate breath.

Resolving to not tell William that she had looked in his journals, while feeling bad for keeping things from him, she hurried to the window again. This time, when she looked out, she saw no sign of her husband but instead she immediately spotted the cross that he had now erected far away toward the center of the island. This cross stood stark and alone, looking utterly desolate, and she still couldn't work out why William would have built such a thing. Certainly, the cross had all the characteristics of something that one might find on a grave, but Margaret felt certain that there would be no need for a grave on Saward Island, not unless...

No.

No, she knew she could not allow herself to think such superstitious thoughts.

And then, just as she was about to turn away, she spotted William walking back to the lighthouse – and she realized that he was much closer than she could have expected. Suddenly filled with panic at the very idea that she might be chanced upon, she hurried to the staircase and made her way down, but she already knew that she couldn't possibly leave without being spotted. Rather than trying to come up on the spot with some explanation for her intrusion, she instead opted to hide behind one of the many items of furniture that had been stored in the lighthouse's lower room. As she did so, she saw several more of the crosses leaning against a nearby wall, as if William had constructed a number of specimens before picking the one that he liked best.

A moment later she heard him entering the lighthouse, and she listened as his weary footsteps crossed the room and began to head up the staircase.

"I have done what is right," he called out, seemingly to nobody at all. "I am a good man and I have my faith. I did what I know is right, and that should be the end of the matter. I can only pray that you will leave us well alone now."

Looking up at the ceiling, Margaret heard him crossing the room above, followed by the sound of the chair's legs scraping against the floor. She knew that William had returned to his usual spot in front of the desk, and after a few more seconds she even fancied that she could hear the sound of his pen's nib once again scratching against paper. She so desperately wanted to hurry up and ask him about the journals, and about the cross, and about his new habit of speaking out loud as if to some invisible person, but she quickly told herself that under no circumstances should she do any such thing.

    Instead she stepped out from behind the wardrobe and quickly made her way out of the lighthouse, while telling herself that she was worrying for no reason. As far as she knew, *all* husbands acted the way William had been acting recently, and she was simply worrying over nothing.

CHAPTER SEVENTEEN

ONCE AGAIN, THAT NIGHT Margaret went to bed alone. She had stayed up in the sitting room, reading in one of the two chairs for a while, clinging to the hope that William might join her. Eventually she had given up and had decided to retire, although she had briefly stopped to straighten the two photographs – one of herself and one of William, taken separately but on their wedding day – that hung on the wall.

Anything to delay the moment of climbing into that empty bed all alone.

Now, staring up at the ceiling, she found herself replaying the day's events, wondering over and over whether she could truly describe her husband's actions as entirely normal. She had no doubt that her understanding of the male mind was sorely lacking, yet as the day had worn on she had begun to doubt her earlier conclusions. Could it really be true that all – or at least most – men jotted down their thoughts on paper and then answered those thoughts in another hand? Did even a majority of men draw strange, wild women in those journals and then go out to construct crosses on seemingly random stretches of land? Did so much as one third of men talk out loud to themselves in a seemingly agitated tone?

Despite her lack of experience, she felt that the answer to all these questions must be in the negative. With that being the case, however, she was left wondering what compelled her William to act in such a manner.

A short while later, as she continued to contemplate this concern, she heard the cottage's front door swinging open and then bumping gently shut. To her surprise and delight, she realized that her husband was making his way early to the bed, and she couldn't help but smile gently as she allowed herself to hope that – for the first time in many months – she might actually be able to gently fall asleep with her husband by her side.

For the next few minutes William pottered about in the kitchen, but finally he made his way into the bedroom and began to undress. Not wanting to alert him to her wakefulness, Margaret simply stared at the ceiling and waited for the beautiful sensation of his body settling next to hers; she had to wait quite some time, however, as he took longer than usual to get out of his clothes, until eventually he pulled the sheet aside and climbed into the bed. As he did so, however, Margaret couldn't help noticing that something seemed different. It was not until he settled alongside her, though, that she understood what was wrong.

He was shivering.

"William?" she said cautiously, supposing that there was no harm now in letting him know that she was awake. "What -"

"Hush!" he gasped, reaching over and putting a firm hand on the side of her arm.

"William -"

"Hush!" he said again, still shaking and now unable to stop his teeth chattering.

She waited for a few seconds, but now she simply couldn't keep her concerns to herself.

"Are you ill?" she asked, worried that he might have a fever. "Are you coming down with something?"

"Woman," he replied, squeezing her arm tighter still, "you must be quiet, else she will hear."

"She?"

Furrowing her brow, she felt sure now that this behavior was most unusual.

"Who are you talking about?" she continued, and now she too sounded most unsettled.

"William, I confess that I am struggling to understand. I know I am only a woman, but I have these fears and I must beg you to explain in a way that even I can take in. What exactly is making you shiver like -"

"Quiet!" he hissed, and somehow he squeezed her arm even tighter – until she felt a mild pain.

Before she had a chance to ask him to stop, she heard the front door slowly starting to ease open again.

"It is the wind," she whispered, trying to convince herself of that fact. "It... it is just the wind."

"You wretched woman," he replied, "why couldn't you just be quiet? Oh, but in truth I don't suppose that it would have made any difference. I have done what I have done and I hoped she would now leave us alone, but I fear that I have merely angered her. I tried to follow the teachings of the Lord. I tried to do what is right."

"Who?" she begged. "Who are you talking about?"

"Yet there might be one last chance," he continued, suddenly climbing out of the bed. "Get up! We must hide!"

"Where?"

He looked around, and then he dropped to his knees.

"Under the bed," he explained, leaning down and clambering into the space between the bed and the floor. "Hurry, lest she might come in here and spy you!"

Margaret wanted to ask again what he meant, but for a moment she felt utterly flustered. At the same time, she knew that she had promised on her wedding day to always obey her husband, so she quickly got out of bed and dropped to the floor, and then she crawled into the gap and found that William was still shivering in the darkness.

Once they were both in position, she waited for him to explain further, but in truth she felt rather foolish and she couldn't help wondering whether William might in fact be behaving a little strangely. As hard as she tried to focus on the fact that her husband knew better, a niggling doubt at the back of her mind told her that there was perhaps no harm in asking a few mild and discreet questions.

"What are we doing here?" she whispered. "I... I cannot help but wonder..."

Hearing no reply other than his chattering teeth, she began to feel as if she might never make any progress. She tried to think of some other way to get her husband to explain things, even though she felt that she was on a hiding to nothing. After a few more seconds she resolved to ask a little more gently in a bid to nudge at the truth; before she could do so, however, she heard the unmistakable sound of the bedroom door very slowly starting to ease open.

Looking down past the bottom of the bed, she saw the door bumping against the wall. And then, impossibly, a pair of bare and slightly bloodied feet stepped silently into the room.

"Who is that?" Margaret gasped. "What kind of -"

In that instant, William turned and clamped a hand over her mouth. She turned too, until her back was to him, and she could feel him shaking more wildly than ever. Finally she understood that sheer terror itself was making him act this way, and she felt the same terror entering her own body now as she looked down and saw the bare feet shuffling past the bottom of the bed.

Now that they were closer, she could see that the feet had several broken, twisted toes.

"Dear Lord," William whispered, his lips just half an inch or so from Margaret's right ear, "deliver us from this evil. We are your humble servants and we have tried to do nothing but good deeds. If we have failed in that, it is only because we are mere foolish mortals who cannot always divine your grand plans, but we still have only love for you in our hearts."

She felt his hand tightening a little over her mouth.

At the bottom of the bed, meanwhile, the

feet had stopped for a moment.

"We have never turned away from you," William continued, "nor shall we ever. Even in the face of this presence, I have tried to do what is right. We ask only that you keep us safe and that you give us further chances to serve you, and that -"

He stopped suddenly.

Margaret waited, but now his trembling had abated. She began to hope that something had changed, but after a few seconds she heard a series of pained groans coming from his throat and his hand fell away from her mouth. She had no idea what might be happening to him now, but slowly the groans became a kind of wheezing sound that lasted for a couple more minutes before he fell entirely still and silent.

Not daring to move, Margaret remained frozen in place with her husband's arms still around her. She wanted to ask him what was wrong, but this time she resolved once again to simply wait. Convinced that her husband knew best, and that he would keep them both safe, she looked down toward the bottom of the bed and saw that the bare feet were still in the same spot, with the cuts and scratches picked out by moonlight. And as she waited patiently for William to tell her what to do next, Margaret could only keep her eyes fixed on those feet.

Several hours passed and nothing changed.

Margaret had barely dared to move at all, while William still had his arms around her. The bare feet, meanwhile, remained at the bottom of the bed. Finally, realizing that morning must come soon, Margaret tried to turn and look at her husband, only to find that his arms – which remained wrapped around her body – were now stiff and difficult to move.

"William?" she whispered, touching his hand and finding that it was unusually cold. Tears were in her eyes now but she still told herself that this was all part of her husband's plan. "William, can we go? William, I must admit this to you... I am scared."

On some very deep level, she had a stirring sense that something far more serious was wrong with him than a mere fever. Slowly she turned her head as much as she could manage, until finally she was able to look at his face; in that moment she saw that his eyes were wide open and unmoving, and that he seemed locked in an entirely still rictus that she had only seen once before. Many years earlier, her own grandmother had died in bed, and Margaret had discovered the corpse. Now her own husband had the same countenance about him, and when she tried again to move, she felt that his arms remained stiff and unyielding.

"William?" she whimpered, hoping against hope that he might suddenly answer. "William, please..."

Again she waited, but his cold dead stare was the only answer and after a few more seconds she was just about able to see that his lips looked to be abnormally discolored, tainted almost blue.

Hearing a shuffling sound, she turned and saw to her horror that the bare feet were now right next to her. She could see the rough, slightly torn nails and the various scratches and crosses marking the flesh, particularly around the ankles. And although she felt utter terror filling her chest, she knew that she couldn't simply remain under the bed forever, even if that had seemed to be her husband's initial plan. Telling herself that things couldn't be as bad as they seemed, she began to lean out from under the bed, trying to force herself to look up – only to pull back at the last second, unable to summon the last scrap of strength that she needed.

"It's alright," she whispered, even as her voice trembled with fear. "William knows what to do. Don't you, William? I'll just... I shall wait here until you tell me the plan. I trust in you, William, and I know you won't let me down."

She squeezed her eyes tight shut, hoping against hope that the feet would be gone when next she looked.

"Dear Lord," she continued under her breath, "we are your loyal servants and we pray that you will see us to safety. Lord... William... please, somebody... anybody... help us..."

CHAPTER EIGHTEEN

AS LATE-NIGHT RAIN BATTERED the windows, Martin Bellwether sat at his usual table in the corner of the *Three Compasses* public house in the small Scottish fishing village of Innisrach.

Finally, after an interminable wait, the door opened and a tall man entered wearing a rainproof jacket. He struggled for a moment to push the door shut, and then he pulled his hood down to reveal a weathered and lined face; he nodded at Martin, and then he made his way over to the bar – dribbling water in his wake – to order himself a drink.

Martin, meanwhile, sat with a worried expression on his face. He'd been in the same spot for a while now, patiently waiting with a growing sense of doom for word from the crew. Now that Albert Foster had arrived, however, Martin was suddenly gripped by the sense that perhaps he didn't want to know the truth, that maybe it was better to simply forget all about Saward Island and its poor, miserable inhabitants.

After exchanging a few pleasantries with the barman, however, Albert finally carried his drink over and took a seat opposite Martin.

"Well?" Martin asked. "What's the news?"

"Are you sure you want to hear?"

"No," Martin admitted, "I'm not sure at all."

They sat in silence for a moment, each of them daring the other to speak next.

"But I must," Martin continued. "I don't know that you're aware, but it was I who transported those two unfortunate souls to Saward Island last year. That means I am possibly the last person to have seen them in -"

He stopped himself just in time.

"I mean, if they are..."

"Dead?" Albert replied, raising a skeptical eyebrow. He hesitated, and then he nodded. "Aye, they're dead alright. Found underneath the bed in the little cottage."

"*Under* the bed?"

Albert nodded.

"What would they be doing there?"

"I wouldn't have the first clue," Albert admitted. "You probably know why we ended up going to check on them. The supply ship turned up with a delivery and found that the previous crates were still on the dock. The men didn't want to go ashore for obvious reasons, so they came back and asked around. Yannick and I were the only two fools in the whole village who were willing to do the job."

"The Millers should never have been there in the first place," Martin said with a sigh.

"They lasted longer than most out there."

"That doesn't change anything," Martin continued. "It's wrong to let people even *try* to live on that island. It's tantamount to murder and I... I played as great a part as any in seeing that they were led to their fate."

"A lighthouse was deemed necessary many years ago," Albert reminded him. "Have you not heard of all the boats that were wrecked on the rocks of Saward Island?"

"There must be another way."

"Aye, perhaps there is. We can only hope so."

"That island must be left completely untouched," Martin said firmly.

"I agree with you now," Albert explained, "although I can't say that I would have done last year. There have been stories about that island for years, but every so often someone decides to try putting a keeper back in the lighthouse. Usually the poor bastards leave within a day or two, but something about William Miller and his wife meant that they stuck it out for much longer. Who can tell why, eh? But they're dead now and I think something's going to have to change."

"Nobody must be sent there again," Martin said firmly. "If they are, I certainly won't be responsible for transporting them."

"I believe the alternative plan is to scrub the island from all maps," Albert said, taking a long swig of beer before letting out a burp and wiping his lips. "It's not on any essential routes, not these days. With a little work, things can be set up so that nobody ever goes there again. The lighthouse can be left dark and we can all just try to forget that Saward Island ever existed." He hesitated again. "You know what they say happened there many years ago, don't you? Do you know the story of Jane Moore and -"

"Let us not speak of that," Martin replied, cutting him off. "Nobody should."

"I should get going," Albert muttered, finishing his beer and getting to his feet. "I must be out early with the fishing boat. Are you going to stay?"

"For a little while longer," Martin admitted, glancing at his own beer and already fancying another. "I think I need to... dull my senses so that I might try to sleep tonight. Otherwise I shall surely be plagued by thoughts of William and his wife."

"Mind that you don't drink too much," Albert said, turning and heading to the door. "That's how bad habits area formed."

"Did you bury them?"

Stopping, Albert glanced back at him.

"The Millers," Martin continued. "Did you at least take them out from under the bed and bury them?"

"We did not," Albert told him. "Truth be told, we didn't want to interfere, and besides... it was getting late." He paused again. "There was one odd thing, though. We found a strange cross that someone had erected out there in the middle of nowhere. We didn't know what it was about, so we just left it. If you want the Millers buried, you'll have to find someone else to go out there, but I don't think you'll have much luck. The best thing is just to forget that the entire island exists, and to hope that no other poor souls ever end up there."

"If there's any mercy in the world, they will not," Martin replied darkly. "Enough people have suffered now because of that place."

***

Several hours later, having finished off another five pints of ale, Martin stumbled slightly unsteadily out of the public house. He stopped for a moment and looked out across the dark harbor of Innisrach, and then he turned as he heard the landlord sliding the bolt across on the other side of the door.

"Go straight home, Martin," a voice called out from inside the building. "I've not seen you this drunk before. Don't get into any mischief now, or Maureen'll be here tomorrow claiming it's my fault."

"I'll be fine," Martin muttered, setting off along the quayside, determined to walk in a straight line but not quite managing. "Don't you worry about me," he continued, slurring his words a little. "This is one of those rare nights when being drunk is better than being sober, but... ah, you wouldn't understand. Nobody would."

Reaching the far end of the quayside, he stopped and looked at the fishing boats moored nearby. The harbor was usually a hive of activity, but late at night there was no sign of anyone else at all. Even the gulls were gone, no doubt sleeping so that they could be ready to follow the fishing boats at first light. The entire village was based solely around the boats and the catches they landed; as many men had observed over the years, without the boats Innisrach would more than likely empty out fast and cease to exist. After all, there was precious little available work for able-bodied men in the area.

Now, as he looked out toward the sea and saw moonlight dancing on the gentle waves, Martin couldn't help but think of the Millers again. Indeed, he soon realized that he'd been standing in almost this exact spot more than a year earlier when he'd first been introduced to William Miller and had been asked to convey him and his wife to Saward Island. Even though he'd harbored certain doubts at the time, Martin had been glad of the money and had convinced himself that there was no need to be too superstitious. He wasn't the first for whom the stories of Saward Island had lost their sting over time, but he resolved now that he would never again make the same mistake.

Sure, the island was still out there in the North Sea, alone and cold, but that didn't mean that any man ever had to set foot on the place again. He wasn't quite sure of the practicalities, but he felt sure that with some hard work he and the other men of the village would be able to scrub that wretched place from the minds of all those nearby; the harder job, he supposed, would be to erase it from maps and ensure that future generations didn't discover it again, but he knew that a solution could be found.

Certainly he would be praying for help every day from now on.

"I'm profoundly sorry for you both," he whispered, removing and lowering his hat as he thought one last time of the Millers. "I hope that your deaths were at least -"

Stopping himself just in time, he realized

that there was no point trying to deceive himself. The Millers would undoubtedly have died in abject terror, and there was no way he could ignore that fact. All he could do, as he turned and continued his unsteady walk home, was work with others to make sure that nobody else would ever fall victim to the horror of Saward Island.

And pray. Always pray.

CHAPTER NINETEEN

Today...

"THAT'S IT?" JACQUI SAID after a moment, once her father had finally finished talking. "*That's* the story about this place?"

"That's the most common version," David replied, ashen-faced and clearly shocked by the tale he'd just told. "There are others with slight variations, but that's the gist of it."

"So this Margaret woman... how's she supposed to have died, exactly?"

"After her husband's heart attack, she was too scared to come out from under the bed," he told her. "She stayed under there, watching the feet, for days and days until she died. Dehydration probably got her in the end."

"It's your turn!" Bod said again, sounding more annoyed than ever as she remained in front of the chessboard.

"That's ridiculous," Jacqui told her father. "I don't care how terrified she was, no-one would ever just... allow themselves to waste away under a bed."

"You're a young girl in the twenty-first century," he pointed out. "Margaret Miller was a terrified woman living two hundred years earlier and she obeyed her husband almost without question. Plus, if the story's to be believed, those feet would have been horrifying and her death..."

He hesitated, before looking over at his younger daughter.

"Well," he added, "maybe there's no need to talk about that right now."

"Okay," Jacqui replied, "but you're forgetting another thing, and this pops the entire balloon of your insane story."

"What's that?"

"If it happened exactly as you just told me," she continued, folding her arms across her chest as she adopted an I've-got-it-all-figured-out kind of pose, "and the Millers were alone at the lighthouse, then how exactly does anyone else know the details? *How* do people know that she saw him putting that cross up? How do they know that she waited up for him but he rarely joined her in the bed until the morning? How do they know all those tiny little details that – let me remind you again – would have only been known to the two people who lived and died here?"

She waited for her father to admit that she was right, but instead she saw a slow hint of dread crossing his face.

"Because you can't," she added. "No-one can."

"Ordinarily you'd be right," he admitted.

"I'm totally right. I'm as right as anyone can ever be. There's no way around that problem."

David glanced at Bod again, before taking hold of Jacqui by the arm and leading her over to the farthest side of the room.

"I'm only telling you this because it's really important," he said, lowering his voice, "but while the people of Innisrach worked hard to erase all memories of Saward Island, a few local residents were determined to figure out the truth. They weren't willing to actually go out to the island, but eventually they came up with one way to find out what had really happened."

"And what was that?" she asked. "There literally *isn't* a way. All the witnesses were dead."

"Exactly," he said cautiously. "So they had to do something pretty extreme."

***

March 17th, 1901...

"We are joined here tonight," Astrid West said softly, once the others gathered holding hands around the table had fallen silent, "to seek communion with the spirits of the dead. In particular, we want to speak to the soul of someone who once lived in this very house here in Innisrach before she was taken away to her death."

Everyone had their eyes closed as they waited for a response; everyone, that is, except Leonora Slumkey, who couldn't resist keeping one eye slightly open so that she could watch the other five members of the little group.

"Margaret Miller," Astrid continued, "you were born Margaret Clarendon in this very room, I believe. Eventually you married William Miller shortly after he arrived in the village and you moved with him to Saward Island, where you ultimately met your doom in the year 1873. We are but a small and humble gathering of local women who have sought to uncover the truth about your final moments, and now we are trying our most direct appeal yet."

She waited.

Silence.

"Margaret Miller, is your soul here? Do you hear us?"

Leonora looked at each of the other faces in

turn, and she couldn't help but smile a little as she saw that everyone seemed so very serious. For Leonora, the entire séance was rather a joke, for she had no inkling whatsoever that ghosts and spirits were real. As far as she was concerned, when someone was dead they were simply gone, and there was no further use for them except as food for worms. They certainly couldn't be called back to the land of the living for brief chats, or to give accounts of their own demises.

"Is it getting cold in here?" Martha Coates whispered. "Is it just me or -"

"No, it's not just you," Alexandra Mafferty added eagerly, with her eyes still shut. "I feel it too. There's a chill in this room, the likes of which I haven't felt in the house before."

"Everybody stay focused," Astrid said firmly. "I sense something approaching, some kind of... spirit from the afterlife. My dear ladies, we are not alone."

Leonora bit her bottom lip as she waited for something – anything – to happen. She had no real expectation of encountering an actual ghost, since she felt sure that such things didn't exist, but she loved seeing the anticipation and excitement of her mother's friends – who were usually so demure and reserved. Ever since Astrid had arrived earlier, Martha and the others had begun to work themselves up into an utter frenzy, and now they all seem convinced that they were about to make contact with the famous Margaret Miller.

Deep down, Leonora was hoping for something really spectacular. She had once heard an account of a similar event in London, which had ended with copious amounts of strange so-called ectoplasm getting scattered across the room. She felt sure that this unusual ectoplasm couldn't possibly be real, yet she was keen to witness a proper show.

"She is here," Astrid whispered.

"Can we open our eyes?" Alexandra asked.

Hearing no answer, the rest of the women began to open their eyes and look around. Astrid, meanwhile, remained at the head of the table with her eyes very much closed, yet something about the older woman's face had changed, as if the very muscles themselves had become rearranged. As the silence continued, Leonora couldn't help but note that Astrid was certainly a very fine performer, and that the whole séance was being presented as a marvelous piece of theater.

The other women whispered to one another for a few more seconds before falling silent, each of them now waiting for Astrid's cue and -

Suddenly Astrid leaned back in her chair and gasped, opening her eyes wide and looking up toward the ceiling. Her expression had changed again and now her features appeared gripped by some new kind of tension, and she slowly opened her mouth as if she was on the verge of speaking.

"Could you let go of my hand?" Caroline Lemone asked, wincing slightly. "Ms. West, you're... hurting me and -"

"She's coming for us!" Astrid gasped, as if each word had to be forced from her mouth with great effort. "Why has my darling William done this? Why has he left us at her mercy?"

"Who's she talking about?" Alexandra asked.

"William was Margaret's husband," Martha reminded the others. "They were together on the island and -"

"Her touch is death!" Astrid whimpered, and now tears – genuine tears, from the looks of things – were streaming down her face. "How much longer must I hide here under the bed, locked in the arms of my poor dear William as I wait for salvation?"

Leonora looked around at the other women; she had to admit that Astrid's commitment to the theatrics of the séance was remarkable, and that her performance was exemplary. So far she had seen no sign of ectoplasm, nor any hint of where the sticky substance might come from, but she lived in hope.

"I cannot leave," Astrid sobbed, sniffing back more tears. "My belly burns, but I can never leave! Will nobody come and save me? Why do these feet remain before me? I just want to go home. I want to go back to Innisrach and never think of this place again! William, why did you bring me here in the first place? We all heard the warnings, but you told me to pay them no mind! Why -"

In that instant her body tilted forward and her head dropped. Leonora, who was enjoying the evening far more than she'd ever expected, felt a flutter of disappointment as she realized that perhaps the show was coming to an end. Was there, after all, to be no ectoplasm?

"Ms. West," Alexandra said cautiously, "are you -"

"We were doomed," Astrid said softly, her voice now sounding much quieter and more melancholy than before. "I see it now. From the moment we first set foot on that island, our souls were condemned and we..."

Her voice trailed off, and once again silence fell. A solitary candle, flickering on the center of the table, seemed now to be on the verge of being extinguished, yet somehow its plucky light managed to keep burning.

"You," Astrid growled finally, "who dare disturb me shall find that I am not easy to overcome. Nor do I forgive those who made me like this. You want to come and disturb my resting place? Then you may try, but be warned that I do not forget the crimes that were committed against me, or against -"

She became silent again, and her head nodded slightly as if she was struggling to stay awake. For Leonora, who had entered into the venture in a spirit of much mirth, the proceedings had now become so terribly exciting – and she even caught herself wondering whether there might be some element of truth in everything she was witnessing. She glanced around the table and saw the terribly serious expressions on the faces of all the other women, and then she turned to see – to her shock – that now Astrid was glaring at her and her alone.

"There will come others," Astrid snarled angrily, "and they too shall pay. For I am not done yet with my vengeance, nor shall I ever be."

Feeling distinctly uncomfortable now, Leonora could only stare back at her while inwardly praying that the older woman's attention might soon turn to one of the other guests at the séance.

"You do not believe what you are witnessing," Astrid continued after a moment. "Well, then... perhaps I shall have to prove myself to you."

"You're really hurting my hand," Caroline complained. "If -"

Suddenly Astrid lunged forward, emitting an anguished scream as she lunged at Leonora, crossing the table and throwing herself against the other woman with such force that the chair tipped back. Screaming, Leonora fell to the floor with Astrid landing on top of her, and the other women could only pull away in horror as the family manservant rushed into the room and tried to intervene.

CHAPTER TWENTY

"YOU'LL FEEL A LOT better in the morning," Martha was saying to Leonora as they left the house, heading along a dark and winding lane that led away from the row of homes next to Innisrach's harbor. "I'm sure of it. You've just had a shock, that's all."

"Well," Caroline murmured, having followed Alexandra out of the house, "that was certainly rather eventful, wasn't it? I must say, I wasn't expecting things to go quite that way."

"I don't think anyone was," Alexandra replied, stopping and watching as Martha and Leonora disappeared around a far corner. "I'm all for a little light fun in the evenings, but I'm not sure I want women screaming and ranting in the house. I think -"

Before she could finish, she heard footsteps approaching and she turned to see that Astrid West was being helped across the hallway by the gentleman who appeared to function as her assistant. Clearly in some distress, Astrid was muttering to the man and dabbing at her face with a handkerchief, and as she reached the doorway she stopped and looked back into the house as if she had forgotten something.

"It's alright," the servant, who had been introduced earlier in the evening as a fellow by the name of Charles, explained calmly. "Everything is done here now. It is time for us to leave."

"Yes, I know that," Astrid told him. "You... you are quite right."

She stepped forward, only to stop again as she found herself directly in front of Caroline and Alexandra.

"I do hope," Alexandra said politely, "that your journey home will be comfortable."

"The young lady who fell from her chair," Astrid replied, "is she... has she left?"

"Ms. Slumkey will be quite alright, I'm sure," Alexandra told her with a smile. "She's a tough young thing."

"I do so hope that she is not injured," Astrid replied. "The truth is, in all my years conducting seances of this nature, I have never once had my body become so... animated."

"You certainly gave it your all," Caroline suggested. "It was really something to behold."

"I felt such pain," Astrid told her, "and such fear. And a complete loss of hope. I felt the harrowing terror of that poor woman. She is locked in the most indescribable torment, with no end in sight. But toward the end, there was another presence in the room. I am not sure how, but another damned soul reached out to me, I think she reached out to me from the island itself." She stopped and looked out toward the harbor, thinking for a moment of the island waiting out there in the darkness. "I do not believe," she added, "that anyone should ever go to that place again."

"After what you told us tonight," Caroline said brightly, "I doubt that anyone would want to."

"There is something evil there," Astrid continued. "Whatever killed William and Margaret Miller... it is not done yet. I believe it reached out to me tonight, perhaps after sensing my connection to poor Margaret. That suggests a level of power that I have never experienced before. Please, promise me that you shall do everything within your capabilities to make sure that the island is never disturbed again."

"Nobody ever goes to Saward Island these days," Alexandra told her. "Certain... efforts have been undertaken to ensure that the place remains abandoned."

"We were just curious, that's all," Caroline added. "That's why we wrote to you and invited you to come to our little village tonight. We wanted to find out what happened to poor Margaret. Some of us remember her, you see, and... well, I suppose we hoped for happier news."

"There is no happy news," Astrid replied, turning to her with a shocked expression on her face. "Margaret Miller died in terror, and while I cannot tell you what she was fearful *of*, I can assure you that tonight's proceedings were by far the most shocking I have ever conducted. Never before have I come close to anything so terrible. Whatever waits out there on that island, it seeks fresh victims. I beg of you... leave it well alone. Promise me that nobody else will ever set foot on that place."

***

Today...

"Years later, Astrid West wrote a memoir of her exploits in the spiritualist world," David explained. "I didn't read it, but apparently she described her visit to Innisrach as the most profoundly disturbing of her long career. She claimed that it was the only séance she ever terminated early, since she simply couldn't handle the connection she had made to Margaret Miller and..."

His voice trailed off for a few seconds.

"And whatever else she contacted on that night. But she set down everything she had sensed, including all the details of the Millers and how they died."

"I'm still not buying it," Jacqui replied, although her smile seemed a little more uneasy now as wind and rain continued to batter the lighthouse. "Cool story, but are you seriously trying to tell me that we've accidentally stumbled upon this island, after it was left alone and untouched for all these years? I mean... even if the story was true, the odds would be insane. Not to mention the sheer amount of bad luck we'd have needed."

"After I moved away to London," her father replied, "I tried very hard to forget all the stupid stuff I heard about when I lived in this part of the world. I don't know why, but the story of Saward Island always stuck with me, even though I assumed it couldn't have been real."

"Okay, so the island's real," Jacqui said. "I'm willing to consider that possibility. But that doesn't mean the rest of the story is."

She waited for her father to reply, but for the first time in her life she felt as if he was truly lost for words. She wanted him to suddenly burst out laughing, for him to admit that he was just trying to wind her up, but after a moment longer he took a step back.

"We should go," he stammered. "Right now. We need to leave."

"In the middle of a storm?"

"Yes, in the middle of a storm!" he snapped, turning and heading to the top of the staircase. "Girls, come on, we're getting out of here."

"Bod, let's go," Jacqui muttered, heading over to her sister and holding out a hand. "Time to get soaked out there."

She waited for an answer, but Bod was merely staring at the board. Looking at the pieces, Jacqui took a moment to remind herself how the game was developing, before realizing that several more moves had been played since she'd stepped away.

"Have you been playing both sides?" she asked. "That's impressive."

Bod continued to stare at the board for a few more seconds, before looking up at her sister with a fearful expression on her face.

"I didn't move the other pieces," she whispered. "They moved themselves."

"Not you too," Jacqui sighed, grabbing the girl's hand and forcing her up. "I admire the effort, and it's kinda cool that you're trying to join in with the whole spooky atmosphere, but we -"

"Girls, hurry up!" David shouted from halfway down the stairs. "I'm not joking!"

"Let's just get out of here," Jacqui said,

leading Bod to the stairs as thunder rumbled louder than ever high above the lighthouse. "I've got to admit, there's a kind of freaky atmosphere here, thanks to Dad and his sudden determination to tell all these spooky stories." They began to head down to the lighthouse's ground floor. "It's not really his usual style, is it?" she continued. "I think his inner Scottishness is really starting to come out. Next he'll be going on about haggis and telling us we all have to wear kilts. As long as he never gets his hands on a set of bagpipes, I guess we'll survive."

Reaching the bottom of the staircase, she saw that her father was peering out through one of the windows, seemingly engrossed in the sight of the storm.

"Dad, are you ready?" she asked, still holding Bod's hand.

She waited.

"Dad?"

"I thought I saw something out there," he replied, still looking out the window. "I don't know, I might have been wrong, but just for a second I thought I saw someone."

"I'm pretty sure you've just worked yourself up into a tizzy over nothing," she told him. "Seriously, Dad, I'm all for you reconnecting with your roots and all that stuff, but you need to know when to -"

Before she could finish, they all heard

something bumping against the lighthouse's wooden door. Jacqui opened her mouth to insist that there was absolutely no reasons to be scared, but already she was starting to notice a faint scratching sound coming from the door's other side, and this particular sound seemed somehow to exist separately from the various swirling noises of the continuing storm.

"Is somebody out there?" Bod whispered, still holding her sister's hand but pulling back slightly and hiding behind her.

"No," Jacqui replied cautiously, although she was unable to entirely banish the fear from her voice. "Dad, tell her. Tell us both. Ghost stories are all fine and good, but there come a point when you just have to... stop."

Hoping that he was going to agree with her, she waited for him to say something but instead he was simply watching the door. The scratching sound came and went, occasionally fading for a few seconds but always returning, and the storm seemed somehow to be getting stronger and more violent by the second. Although she was still waiting for her father to take charge, Jacqui couldn't help but worry that he now seemed to be almost frozen, and finally she realized that someone was going to have to show a little initiative.

"It's just the wind," she pointed out, slipping her hand free from Bod and walking to the door, reaching out for the handle so she could pull it open. "Dad, you've really worked us all up."

She turned the handle and opened the door.

"There's no -"

In that instant, a soaked figure fell through and crashed down against the floor, before rolling onto its back and staring up at Jacqui while letting out an anguished gasp.

"Mum?" Bod shouted, stepping back against the wall. "Daddy? What's wrong with Mum?"

CHAPTER TWENTY-ONE

"VANESSA?" DAVID SAID CAUTIOUSLY, hurrying over and looking down at his wife as she remained flat on her back on the floor. "Vanessa, what the hell are you doing? Have you been out there in that storm?"

Although she tried to say something, all that emerged from Vanessa's mouth was a series of frantic, pained groans.

"I thought you were back on the boat," David continued, "or that you'd come here or... I don't know, but I assumed you were hiding out from the storm. Where have you been?"

"Mum, are you hurt?" Jacqui asked, dropping to her knees and looking for any sign of an injury. "Mum, can you even hear me? Talk to me."

Vanessa turned and stared at her, but she

seemed almost too horrified to respond. Her eyes were wide open and she was still trying but failing to speak, yet something was clearly holding her back. After a moment she reached up and grabbed her throat, clawing at the skin as if some hidden force was pushing down on her, and a few seconds later she rolled onto her side and began to shake violently.

"Dad, is she having a fit?" Jacqui stammered, struggling to hold back a sense of sheer panic. "Dad, do something!"

"I've never seen her like this before," he replied as he knelt to take a closer look. "She doesn't have a history of fitting."

"Why's she doing this?" Bod cried, still watching from a distance. "Daddy, make her stop."

"I don't know how," David said helplessly, "it's almost as if she -"

Suddenly Vanessa rolled onto her back again and let out a long, anguished gasp, before closing her eyes and falling still. Jacqui immediately put two fingers against the side of her mother's neck, checking for a pulse.

"Her heart's racing," she said, before waiting a moment longer. "I think it's calming down a little bit now, though. Whatever's happening to her, it might be passing."

"Vanessa, can you hear me?" David asked, reaching out and touching the side of her face.

"She's so cold," he continued. "Her clothes are soaked. She must have been caught out there in the storm and she just couldn't get to shelter."

"Could she have pneumonia?" Jacqui suggested.

"Vanessa, can you say something?" David continued, forcing one of her eyes open, only for it to quickly close again. "I think she's passed out now. You're right, whatever was going on... hopefully it's starting to calm down." He took a moment to wipe some of the wet, matted hair from across his wife's forehead. "She seems much better. If that was some kind of fit, it's obviously fading. I think now we just have to wait for her to wake up."

"She's so cold," Jacqui pointed out. "Should we get her out of these clothes? Should we try to start a fire and warm her up?"

She waited for her father to come up with a plan, for him to show at least some semblance of leadership, but instead he was simply staring down at Vanessa as if he was in a state of shock.

And then, very slowly, Vanessa's eyes began to open.

"Where... where are am I?" she whispered, barely managing to get any words out at all. "What happened?"

***

Lightning flickered in the darkening clouds as thunder rumbled across the island. Standing at the window of what seemed to be the lighthouse's office, Jacqui stared out at the storm for a moment as drops of rain were blown almost horizontally across the outside of the glass pane.

"Is Mum going to be okay?"

Looking down, she saw that Bod had made her way over. After a moment they both looked toward the far side of the room and saw that their mother was now sitting on one of the chairs, still wearing her soaking wet clothes.

"Yeah, she's gonna be okay," she said, although she felt that she didn't sound particularly convincing. "She's just getting over whatever happened to her out there."

"I didn't like when she was shaking," Bod continued, before furrowing her brow for a moment. "Jacqui, how much longer are we going to have to stay here? I know I wanted to come and see the lighthouse, but I think I've seen it as much as I need to now, so... can't we go back to the boat?"

"The boat's gonna be pretty choppy right now," Jacqui pointed out. "I don't think it'd be very nice to be on it in this storm. Do you remember that time you got seasick? It'd be like that but ten times worse."

"I thought the lighthouse was going to be fun," Bod said softly, before looking up at the ceiling as a stronger gust of wind caused the entire building to creak and groan slightly. "Now I'm not so sure."

"We're gonna look back on this and laugh one day," Jacqui replied. "You realize that, don't you? We're gonna tell people all about the time we got stranded on some wacky weird island in the middle of a massive storm, and about how Dad freaked us out with some kind of spooky story, and about how Mum was being weird and..."

Her voice trailed off, and after a moment she reached out and tousled the hair on top of her sister's head.

"It's gonna be hilarious," she added before glancing out the window again. "We'll be -"

In that moment she froze, as she spotted what appeared to be a figure standing down on the grass near the corner of the cottage. She leaned closer to the window, trying to see past the constantly moving raindrops, convinced that she had to be wrong; already, however, she could tell that there was definitely a woman standing out there, wearing some kind of pale dress and with dark lines criss-crossing and mostly covering her eyes and mouth.

"What the..."

"Who's that?" Bod whispered, having stood on tiptoes so that she too could see out.

"I have no idea," Jacqui replied, and now

she couldn't help but notice that the woman seemed to be staring straight back up at her with a penetrating gaze.

"I don't like her," Bod said, stepping back from the window. "I thought there wasn't supposed to be anyone else on the island."

"There isn't," Jacqui murmured, before turning to look over at her parents. "Dad?"

"Just a minute," David replied, still sitting with Vanessa as if he was worried that she might experience another fit at any moment.

"This is kind of important," Jacqui said, glancing out the window again and seeing that the woman was still there, before turning back to him. "Dad, I know how this is going to sound and I really don't want to add to the weirdness, but... there's someone outside."

"What are you talking about?" he asked.

"I'm saying that there's a woman outside and she's looking up at the window and... I'm really not sure what it means."

Stepping away from Vanessa, who seemed exhausted and quiet but was otherwise mostly back to her usual self, David headed to the window and looked out. He immediately saw the woman, and for a few seconds both he and Jacqui could only stare back at the woman until suddenly – with no warning – David pulled his daughter back so that she wouldn't be seen.

"Who is she?" Jacqui asked. "It looks like she's got some kind of... stuff over her mouth. And maybe her eyes too."

"Someone's playing a joke on us," he replied, shaking his head slowly. "That must be what's going on here. Someone's... playing some kind of elaborate prank, they're probably filming us and laughing and planning to put it online somewhere and make us look like complete idiots."

Although she wanted to ask her father exactly what he meant, Jacqui instead headed back to the window. She was desperately hoping that the woman might have vanished, and that she might be able to come up with some kind of explanation for what was happening, but instead she saw that the woman hadn't moved at all and was still staring up at the window. A moment later, just to banish any lingering doubt, another flash of lightning briefly lit the scene and confirmed the woman's presence.

"She's just... standing there," she murmured. "She -"

"Get back!" David hissed, grabbing her arm and pulling her away again. "Don't let her see you!"

"I'm pretty sure she's already seen us," Jacqui replied, shocked by her father's reaction. "Dad, what's going on here? Who's that woman and why's she just standing out there in the rain?"

Again she waited for him to say something reassuring, but she could already tell from the fearful expression on his face that something was very wrong. She thought back to the story he'd told her earlier, to the whole tale of the Millers and their time on the island, and finally she remembered the part about the woman with bare feet. She hesitated a moment longer, and then she cautiously approached the window and looked out; sure enough, the woman down on the grass appeared to be wearing nothing on her feet at all. Once she'd ascertained that fact, Jacqui pulled back out of sight and turned to her father again.

"Dad, now would be a really good time to tell us how this is all going to be okay," she said, and now her voice was tense with fear. "Dad? Can you please tell us what the hell is going on?"

CHAPTER TWENTY-TWO

"LOOK AT THIS ONE," Jacqui said a few minutes later, having searched through the notebooks to find the drawings she'd seen earlier. "I didn't notice before because the pen lines are so crazy, but look..."

She turned the notebook around so that her father could see.

"There are lines all over the eyes and mouth," she continued. "Just like the woman who's out there now. It's the same person."

Although he looked at the picture, David said nothing and after a moment he instead turned and looked toward the window. Vanessa, meanwhile, had been mostly silent ever since she'd woken up on the floor and now she was simply watching the wall as if in some kind of trance.

"Dad, say something," Jacqui added, struggling to contain a sense of frustration. "Dad? Do you think we should just... go out there and *ask* who she is?"

Again, David said nothing.

"What if she's some kind of serial killer?" she asked. "Is that what you're worried about? Damn it, Dad, have you stranded us here with an escaped murderer? Is -"

"Can you just let me think?" he replied suddenly, cutting her off. "I'm trying to think."

"It's going to get dark soon," she reminded him. "It's already looking murky out there and there's no sign that the storm's going to go anywhere. We're not... we're not going to be stuck here overnight, are we? Dad, please tell me that we're not going to be stuck here overnight."

"We..."

For a moment, David seemed completely frozen, as if he couldn't even begin to come up with a plan. He looked around, clearly searching for something he might be able to use, and then finally he shook his head as if trying to clear his thoughts.

"Just give me a minute or two," he muttered.

"Dad, this is serious," Jacqui continued. "I don't want to stay here overnight!"

"Just let me think."

"Dad -"

"Let me think!" he snapped angrily. "Will you just shut up for one second, Jacqui? How am I supposed to think when you're constantly badgering me like this?" He sighed. "I'm sorry, I shouldn't have been short with you but I really just need a moment to think. Can you give me that?"

"Sure," she murmured, turning and walking away toward the far side of the room, then stopping near the top of the staircase.

She could hear her parents talking, but she couldn't quite make out what they were saying; in truth, she didn't much care, since she felt as if they weren't quite grasping the severity of the situation. Light was fading outside and while a few candles had been left dotted around in the lighthouse, she really didn't like the idea of spending an entire night on the island. Turning, she looked toward the window and thought of the woman standing out there, and then she thought of the quasi-ghost story her father had regaled them all with earlier.

"Jacqui?" Bod whispered, having made her way over. "Can we go now?"

"I think Dad's losing his mind," she replied, keeping her voice low before thinking for a moment. "He's getting paranoid and superstitious. It's time someone took charge and tried to figure out what's really going on."

***

A couple of minutes later, having made her way down to the ground floor without attracting her parents' attention, Jacqui looked at the door and thought once more about the woman.

"Jacqui?" Bod said, just a few paces behind. "What are you going to do?"

"I'm going to do what any normal, sane person would," she replied, trying to dismiss the sense of fear that even now was threatening to spread further and further throughout her chest. "I'm going to see what's going on with that woman out there."

"She looks scary."

"You've been listening to Dad too much," she replied, before swallowing hard. "We both have. What we need right now is a cold dose of reality and common sense."

"But -"

"Trust me on this, Bod," she continued, turning to her sister. She knew she was intentionally delaying the next step, but she figured she had a couple more seconds to play with at least. "Dad gets these weird ideas sometimes, and it's natural that we're kind of... influenced by the dumb stuff that comes out of his mouth. At least, that's what I'm hoping has been going on here. Meanwhile, that woman out there is probably just some local who can actually help us."

"Do you really think so?"

"Yes," Jacqui lied, before taking a moment to convince herself a little more.

"Yes," she said again, and this time she was just about able to believe that she was telling the truth.

"Just stay here," she added, nodding at the staircase. "I mean it, Bod. I know you love messing around, but I need you to promise me that you won't do anything stupid right now."

"I promise," Bod replied, with a tinge of fear in her voice.

"Pinkie promise?" Jacqui continued. "Cross your heart and swear to die? On Granny's life? All that stuff?"

Bod thought, and then she nodded.

Realizing that the moment had come, Jacqui turned and made her way toward the door. She could hear the wind and rain still howling outside, but she knew she couldn't keep delaying. Part of her was hoping that the woman would be gone, and that she could then try to convince herself that the whole thing had been some kind of mirage. As she reached the door, however, she knew that was unlikely.

Lifting the latch, she pulled the door open and saw that the woman was still out there, watching from near the corner of the cottage.

"Oh, you're creepy, aren't you?" she whispered under her breath. "I bet you know exactly what you're doing."

"What does she look like now?" Bod called out to her.

Jacqui turned and raised a hand to quieten her, and then she looked at the woman again. Her plan had been to go out there and try to talk to the new arrival, although now the driving rain made her reconsider that option. Instead she wondered whether she could just stay in the doorway and perhaps shout a few questions, even if that meant attracting her father's ire.

"Hey!" she called out finally, smiling in an attempt to seem as friendly as possible. She even held up a hand and offered a wave. "Hello? Can I talk to you?"

She waited, but the woman merely continued to stare at her, although from this distance her eyes and mouth still appeared to be covered in a series of black lines – almost like wire, sealing them shut.

"Hello?" Jacqui shouted again, a little louder this time. "Do you live here? Sorry if we're intruding, we thought this island was deserted. We ended up here by accident and we're kind of stranded by the storm, and I'm sorry again if we went into your place without asking but..."

As her voice trailed off, she realized that the woman still hadn't reacted. Instead, simply remaining by the cottage in the pouring rain, the strange woman seemed to be strangely impassive.

"Jacqui?" Bod whispered.

Startled, she turned to see her little sister standing right next to her.

"I told you to stay on the stairs!"

"I wanted to see," Bod replied, looking out at the woman. "Why are her eyes and mouth shut?"

"They're not," Jacqui said, although she was already starting to think that Bod might be right. "I mean... are they?"

She squinted slightly, trying to make the woman out a little better, but she had to admit that there certainly appeared to be some kind of string or wire keeping her eyes and mouth sealed. And although she told herself that the idea was crazy, Jacqui couldn't help but feel a shiver run through her bones as she began to wonder just what kind of person would stand out there in the rain with no apparent care about getting wet. With each passing second, the strange woman seemed more and more unusual.

"Hey," she called out again, even though she hadn't quite figured out what she was going to say next. "If you don't mind, can we just stay here for a bit? If -"

Suddenly the woman stepped forward, and Jacqui fell silent as she saw that she was now very slowly but surely walking through the rain and making her way toward the lighthouse.

"I don't like this," Bod said, tugging at Jacqui's sleeve. "Jacqui? I don't like her."

"Yeah, I'm not loving this situation either," she replied, although so far she was just about resisting the urge to panic as the woman made her way closer and closer. "Just... chill, okay? I'm sure there's a perfectly reasonable explanation for all of this and we'll laugh about it later."

The woman was now halfway between the cottage and the lighthouse, and as she edged closer the glistening black wires sealing her eyes and mouth were becoming much more visible.

"*Much* later," Jacqui added, hoping against hope that suddenly everything might start to make sense.

Bod squeezed her hand tighter.

"Just don't freak out, Bod. This is probably just some kind of weird way they welcome people up here. Remember, we're way up in the north of the country. People here are probably just... cut from a different cloth."

The woman was still heading straight toward the lighthouse and now she was only ten or twelve paces away. Jacqui had held her ground so far, refusing to let fear take control, but now she could be in no doubt at all: the woman's eyes and mouth were sealed shut by black wire that had been sewn through her flesh, and similar wire appeared to have been used on her ears as well. And while she still clung to the hope that this was all some kind of cheap carnival trick, Jacqui was finding it harder and harder to just wait for the woman to arrive.

"Jacqui," Bod whimpered, "I don't like -"

In that moment Jacqui stepped back and slammed the door shut, and then she pushed her weight against the wood in an attempt to keep it from opening.

"We can talk to her through the door," she told her sister, before waiting to hear something – anything – from the other side. "Hello?" she continued, raising her voice slightly again. "I'm sorry if you're pissed off, that really wasn't our intention. We're just out here on a day trip from Innisrach and we're kind of stuck, so if we can just hang out until the storm clears, we'll be really grateful. We won't take anything, I promise."

Again she waited, but all she heard was the sound of the storm.

"I don't believe in ghosts," she added under her breath, trying to remind herself of that fact over and over again. "I just don't. They're not real and they're made up."

As those last words left her lips, she told herself that she was actually starting to believe them, but a moment later she heard Bod letting out a faint gasp.

"Be cool," she said, looking down at her

sister. "Let's not freak out over nothing."

"Don't you hear it?" Bod whispered.

"Hear what?"

"The footsteps," Bod continued. "On the stairs."

Although she opened her mouth to tell Bod to shut up, after a moment Jacqui realized that perhaps her sister had a point. She turned slowly and looked toward the staircase that led up to the office space, and now she could be in no doubt. The sound was faint, barely audible over the sound of the ongoing storm, but she could just about make out a set of footsteps – as if some invisible figure had walked straight through the door and was now making its way upstairs.

"Who's that?" Bod asked, still clinging to Jacqui's hand. "Who is it, Jacqui? Did someone else just come inside?"

CHAPTER TWENTY-THREE

REACHING THE TOP OF the staircase, keeping hold of Bod's hand, Jacqui looked across the room and saw that her parents were still sitting by the desk and talking.

The footsteps, meanwhile, had now faded away to nothing.

"We can't sail in this weather," David was saying in hushed tones. "It's just not possible."

"So we're stuck here," Vanessa replied. "Great, we -"

Suddenly spotting her daughters, she hesitated before offering a smile.

"Girls, hey," she said, clearly trying to put a positive spin on the situation, "we were just talking about what we want to do tonight, and we were thinking that you might enjoy a good old-fashioned night camping. Doesn't that sound like fun?"

Jacqui looked around the room, but so far she saw nothing that might explain the footsteps.

"We can make the best of it," David suggested, and he too was trying way too hard to make things seem alright as he stepped away from the chair where Vanessa was sitting and began to approach the girls. "We're mostly kinda dry, which is good, and there are a few candles. Granted, it's a little chilly here, but I'm sure we can make do and... and I'm not quite sure what we'll do about food, but we'll figure something out."

He began to reach into the pockets of his coat, pulling out a spare flare gun and some packs of chewing gum.

"Um, we might have to be a little hungry," he added. "I don't think going back to the boat right now is a good idea, not while the storm's still raging."

A flash of lightning filled the window, followed by more thunder.

"See?" he continued, obviously trying to hide his nerves. "But that only makes it more fun, in a way," he added. "If you think about it, we're going to be experiencing what it was like for people hundreds of years ago, and that's an experience that money just can't buy. Even those supposedly authentic historical reenactment groups always cater to modern needs and sensibilities, whereas this..."

He paused, trying to think of some better way to sell the situation.

"Think of it as an escape room," he added finally. "You like escape rooms, don't you?"

Spotting a faint shadow that appeared to be moving across the wall and heading toward her mother, Jacqui hesitated for a few seconds. She told herself that the shadow had to be an illusion, but she couldn't quite stop watching as it continued to slip across the room.

"No, Dad," she whispered, seeing that her mother was still a little slumped in the chair, as if she was unable to summon the strength to stand, "actually I *hate* escape rooms and -"

She fell silent as the shadow reached Vanessa and vanished. Telling herself that she'd simply imagined the whole thing, she continued to watch her mother for a few more seconds before turning to her father again.

"Those old people who died here," she continued, "the lighthouse keeper and his wife..."

"Let's not talk about that right now," David replied.

"The Millers, right?" she added. "You told us about them, but do you know anything else about the history of the island? You said old fishermen used to tell stories, but did any of those stories go back further? If something was here when the Millers arrived, do you know what it might have been?"

"Nope," he replied, shaking his head. "And can you please stop with all these questions?"

"You're lying," she told him.

"Jacqui, this isn't the right time for silly stories."

"It's the *perfect* time for stories," she said firmly, annoyed by his unconvincing attempt to act as if everything was perfectly alright. "It's the best damn time for stories ever. You know something else and you're not letting on what it is."

"Jacqui -"

"I'm not an idiot, Dad," she added. "What do you know about the bare-footed women the Millers saw?"

He opened his mouth to reply, no doubt to tell her to stop worrying.

"What do you know about a woman with her eyes and mouth and maybe even her ears all sewn shut?" she continued, and she immediately saw a flicker of recognition and fear in his eyes. "And if you try to tell me there's nothing to worry about, or that you don't have a clue, then I think I might just scream."

"Jacqui?" Bod whispered, tugging on her sleeve again. "What's wrong with Mum?"

"Just a second," Jacqui replied, watching her father's expression. "I need -"

Suddenly realizing what her sister had said,

she turned and looked over her shoulder, and she immediately saw that something had changed. Whereas a moment earlier Vanessa had been sitting slightly slumped in the chair, now she was bolt upright and staring back at the rest of the family; a candle on the nearby table was flickering fast, casting multiple versions of her shadow on the wall.

"Honey, just relax," David said. "You don't need to stress about any of this. We're just having a little discussion about the practicalities, that's all."

"She doesn't look right," Jacqui whispered.

"Nonsense," David replied. "Jacqui, I really wish you'd stop trying to get us all riled up. How about this for a suggestion? Let's get ourselves all set up for the night, and *then* we can each take turns to tell campfire ghost stories. I'll even offer a little prize for whoever does best. But... let's avoid any set on little islands, okay? Or in lighthouses. Or about witches with their eyes and mouths and ears sewn shut."

Jacqui continued to watch her mother for a moment, still unable to ignore a growing sense of unease, but then she suddenly turned to her father as she finally processed everything he'd just said.

"Witches?" she stammered. "Dad, who said anything about a -"

In that moment, Vanessa let out a loud, pained gasp as if inhaling a huge amount of air; gripping the sides of the chair, she leaned back and pushed her chest out, and she opened her mouth wide as she looked up toward the ceiling.

"Make her stop!" Bod sobbed.

"Is she having another fit?" Jacqui asked, watching as her mother's body began to tremble violently.

"I'm sure that's all it is," David said. "I'm sure it's just... it's another fit."

"Don't just stand here!" Jacqui hissed, before slipping free from Bod's gasp and rushing over to her mother. "She might swallow her tongue! We have to help her!"

"Jacqui, you maybe shouldn't get too close," David said, pulling Bod nearer and holding her tight. "Jacqui? Sweetheart? Don't you think you should come over here with us?"

"She needs help!" Looking down at her mother, she saw that Vanessa's entire body was shaking – but she wasn't sure where to even begin trying to help her out. "Dad, do something!" she shouted as tears began to fill her eyes. "Dad, I'm serious, it's like she -"

Suddenly Vanessa leaned forward and stared straight at her, and Jacqui instinctively took a step back. Although she was no longer trembling, Vanessa appeared to be tensing every muscle in her body and after a couple more seconds a bead of blood began to slowly dribble down from her left nostril.

"Mum?" Jacqui said cautiously, almost too scared to speak. "Mum, are you okay? Can you hear me? Mum, if you can... please, say something."

She waited, but Vanessa was merely glaring at her as the bead of blood ran down over her lips and onto her chin. At the same time, a second bead had begun to emerge from her right tear duct, pooling in her eye for a few seconds before starting to trickle down her cheek.

"Dad, I think something's really wrong," Jacqui said, torn between the desire to help and the need to run away. "Dad, she's bleeding," she added, and now tears were running down her own face. "Dad, I think Mum's really sick and we need to get her to a hospital."

She waited a few more seconds, and then she turned to see that he was still standing with Bod over on the other side of the room.

"Dad, do something!" she screamed. "She needs -"

In that moment Vanessa lunged forward, tumbling from the chair and dropping to her knees but reaching out and grabbing the sides of Jacqui's arms so that she could hold herself up. Letting out a harsh retching sound, almost as if she was gasping for air, Vanessa stared up at her daughter with an expression of open-mouthed horror as more blood began to trickle from her eyes and nostrils.

"Jacqui, I think you should get away from

her right now," David said firmly, holding a hand out toward his daughter. "Jacqui, this isn't advice, this is an order. You need to get over here."

"What's wrong with her?" Jacqui replied, before realizing that her mother seemed now to be trying to say something, even if she could only manage a repetitive clicking sound that was coming from the back of her throat. "Dad, I don't think she can even breathe! She's having some kind of fit but it's worse than the one earlier."

As those words left her mouth, she saw that blood vessels were bursting in her mother's eyes – and that one of the irises was becoming detached as more blood seeped out from deeper inside the eyeball.

"What the hell?" Jacqui whispered, feeling her mother's hands gripping her arms more tightly than ever. "Dad, I think she's -"

Dying.

That was the word she'd been about to say, but she'd managed to hold it back partly to protect Bod, and partly because she didn't want to admit the truth. She could tell that her mother was trying to say something, yet the words just wouldn't quite leave her mouth.

"Mum?" she whimpered, desperately wanting to help but not sure where to start. "Mum, please, I don't know what to do. I want to help you but -"

"Gray," Vanessa gasped, finally managing to spit out the word that had seemingly been trapped in her mouth for so long.

"Gray?"

Jacqui stared at her, trying to understand, before looking over at her father.

"Dad, what does she mean?" she asked. "I don't get it. Dad, she's being really weird and I think -"

"The gray!" Vanessa screamed, reaching up and grabbing Jacqui's shoulders, trying to drag her down onto the floor even as more blood erupted from her eyes and mouth. "Help me!"

And then, as suddenly as she'd lurched into action, she sighed and slumped down, landing in a heap on the floor.

AMY CROSS

CHAPTER TWENTY-FOUR

"SHE'S BREATHING," DAVID SAID, having checked the side of his wife's neck with two fingers, "and she has a pulse. It's racing, but... she's definitely unconscious."

"What was she trying to tell us?" Jacqui asked, sniffing back more tears as she looked at her mother still resting on the floor. "Why did she mention the color gray?"

She looked around.

"What's gray in here? That doesn't really narrow things down very much."

"I don't know," David replied, sounding exhausted as he sat back a little. "I just... I don't have a clue."

"It was like she really had to force it out," Jacqui continued. "She was trying for a couple of minutes, but something was stopping her. And her eyes... one of them looked like it was breaking apart, like the pressure from inside was -"

"Maybe not now," he said firmly, before nodding toward the far side of the room.

Looking over toward the desk, Jacqui realized what he meant; Bod was sitting on one of the chairs, sobbing gently as the storm continued to gather strength outside. Although she knew that her little sister was pretty tough, Jacqui figured that she still needed to protect her as much as possible.

"The woman came in through the door," Jacqui whispered. "She walked right up to it, and then she made her way to the stairs. I didn't see her once she came inside, but that's what happened." She looked at her father again. "I didn't believe it at first, but I now I can't see any other explanation. She's a -"

"Don't say the word," David said, cutting her off.

"But you know I'm right," she insisted. "She walked inside and she came up here, and then..."

She looked at her mother again, and now she was starting to wonder whether in some way the strange woman from outside had entered the lighthouse and had then possessed – or tried to possess, at least – her mother's body. She knew that idea sounded completely insane, and ten minutes earlier she would have laughed at the proposition, but now she was starting to realize that all bets were off.

"Dad, what happened here?" she asked, turning to him again. "I mean, what *really* happened here? Before the Millers came... there was obviously something here already. And I think you know more than you've admitted so far."

"We'll talk about it later," he replied. "Right now, our priority has to be getting out of here."

"Which will be easier if we all know the truth," she pointed out. "Dad, I'm going to be completely honest with you. I'm terrified. I'm more terrified than I've ever been in my life, and I'm pretty sure you are too. But this isn't the right time to start protecting us, like we can't handle it."

"If I'd believed for one second that Saward Island was real," he said cautiously, "I never would have brought us within a hundred miles of this spot."

"I know that," she told him, "but we're here now, so we need to understand what we're dealing with. No-one blames you. What kind of -"

Before she could finish, she heard a faint scratching sound. She looked around, wondering where the sound could possibly be coming from. After a few more seconds the scratching came to an end, just as Jacqui found herself looking over at the desk. She couldn't be certain, but although now she could see that one of the notebooks was open on the desk, she felt fairly sure that they'd all been left closed just a moment earlier.

Realizing that nobody else seemed to have noticed the change, she hesitated before making her way over. Darkness had fallen entirely outside now, and the light of a solitary candle was the only illumination as she reached the desk and looked down to see that a single word had been scratched onto the page. The pen lay nearby, but the ink had long since run dry so the nib had been used to cut the word into the paper.

"What is it?" David asked. "What do you see?"

"Grave," she whispered, before turning to him again. "What if we misunderstood what Mum was trying to say just now? What if she just couldn't finish the word properly?"

"It was probably there before," David suggested, looking at the notebook with an expression of concern, although his tone of voice suggested that he didn't believe his own theory. "It was probably there and your mum read it and... and then she..."

Jacqui looked around the room, but she saw no hint of the strange woman.

"What grave?" she said cautiously, wondering whether the woman could hear her. "What are you talking about? I don't understand what you want."

She glanced down at the notebook again, but there was no sign of a reply.

"What grave?" she asked again, raising her voice a little more this time. "Can you tell us exactly what you mean?"

She waited again, and then she turned and walked back over to join her father and sister.

"This is going to sound pretty crazy," she continued, "but can we all look away?"

"Look away from what?" David asked.

"From the desk. From the notebook. I don't know why, but I think the answer will only come when nobody's looking at it."

Although he clearly didn't quite understand what she meant, after a moment David rolled his eyes and did as she'd requested, while also forcing Bod to turn too. Jacqui did the same, and they stood in silence as they listened to the sound of the storm still battering the outside of the lighthouse.

And then, very slowly, the scratching sound returned.

"Don't look," Jacqui said, having spotted that her father was on the verge of turning around. "I can't explain it, but she won't write if we're looking."

"Who are you talking about?" Bod asked quietly, as if she was scared of the possible answer. "There's no-one else here."

The scratching sound had already stopped,

and after a few seconds Jacqui allowed herself to turn and look back toward the desk. She could already see that the pen had been laid down in a different position, and she felt a tightening sense of dread in her chest as she began to make her way over.

"Be careful," David said suddenly.

"Sure, Dad," she murmured as she reached the desk. "*Now* you're worried about keeping us all safe."

As soon as she looked down at the page, she felt her heart skip a beat.

"Well?" David called out, as lightning briefly lit the window and thunder shook the glass pane. "What does it say?"

"Trapped," she read out loud, before turning to him. "One word. Trapped."

"What do you think it means?" he asked.

"There was a cross on the island when we came to the lighthouse," she told him. "It was right out there in the middle of nowhere."

"I saw it," he replied. "I didn't think anything much of it at the time. I certainly didn't connect it to the story of the Millers. Actually, I..."

He thought for a moment.

"Actually," he continued, "I might have... slightly... damaged it."

"Come again?" Jacqui replied, raising both eyebrows at once.

"It was so delicate and so frail," he protested. "I barely touched the damn thing and the crossbeam bit – or whatever you call it – fell away. I can't believe it hadn't disintegrated already, the wind would've blown it away soon if I hadn't been there." He pointed toward the window. "There's no way it would've survived this storm, not for a second. It was totally rickety, Jacqui."

He waited for her to answer.

"It's not my fault," he added with a hint of desperation.

"No-one's saying that it's anyone's fault," she replied, "but I think maybe we ought to... put it right. There are some other crosses downstairs, they're probably in much better condition. If we take one and replace the cross you damaged, then whatever's going on... it might just stop, right? That's what happens in films. Don't you think there's a chance that this ghost -"

"Please don't use that word," David said firmly, putting his hands over Bod's ears. "Let's keep things rational."

"Don't you think there's a chance that this... thing," she continued, choosing her words with a little more care, "might stop being so angry if we put everything right?"

Although he was clearly uncomfortable with the direction the conversation was taking, David seemed unable to actually disagree with his daughter.

"I've seen horror movies," she added. "That's what happens in them, the ghost is annoyed at something and then the people try to fix it, and sometimes that's enough to make the ghost stop bothering them. I know it sounds kind of simple, but it makes sense if the ghost is angry and wants it all fixed. It's got to be worth a try, right? Those crosses are right there downstairs, it shouldn't even be that hard. One of us just has to go out there into the rain and -"

"I'll do it," David said.

"It might be better if -"

"I started this," he continued, interrupting her, "so it's only right if I fix it. Besides, there's no way I'm letting you go out there alone and someone has to stay here with Bod. If you're right, it shouldn't even take me very long." He still seemed uncertain, as if he was struggling slightly to find the necessary courage. "You'll just have to wait here."

"Here?" Jacqui said, shocked by the suggestion. "In the lighthouse?"

"Can you think of a better place?"

"We'll come with you," she said firmly. "Dad, if you think about it, it makes total sense. It's on the way back to the boat, anyway."

"Your mum's in no fit state to make the walk," he reminded her. "Jacqui, just let me do this. If it's what the ghost wants, it won't even try to stop me." He turned and headed toward the top of the staircase. "I'll be quick," he added, "and -"

Suddenly a loud thud rang out from somewhere on the ground floor. David froze, listening as something hit the door from the other side, and a moment later he heard the sound of wood splitting. At that moment the candle blew out, plunging them all into darkness, but something could be heard breaking through the door below, followed by the sound of footsteps slowly approaching the bottom of the stairs.

"Dad, what's happening?" Jacqui asked, leading Bod over to join him, holding a hand out in an attempt to keep herself from slamming into anything. "Dad, you heard that, right?"

"I heard it," he replied, staring down into the darkness as thunder continued to rumble outside, "but I don't know what -"

In that instant a flash of lightning briefly lit the scene, revealing – for a split second – the sight of a tall, thin man looking up at them all from the foot of the staircase.

"What was that?" Jacqui asked, having spotted the figure without managing to make out many of its features. "Dad? What was that thing down at the bottom of the stairs?"

"I think it was William Miller," he replied, already thinking back to the two bodies he'd found hidden away under a bed in the cottage. A moment later he heard a foot pressing on one of the bottom steps. "And I think he's coming up to join us."

CHAPTER TWENTY-FIVE

LIGHTNING FLASHED AGAIN AS Jacqui, Bod and David slowly backed away from the top of the staircase. They were too far back to see William now, but lightning flashed again and they briefly spotted his shadow cast against the wall as he made his way up.

"What does he want?" Jacqui asked. "How can you even be sure that it's him?"

"I'm sure," David said, fumbling for his cellphone before activating the flashlight app. He stepped forward and aimed the beam down the stairs, and he shuddered as soon as he saw the dead, withered figure of William Miller still slowly and stiffly walking up. "Don't ask me how right now, but I'm very sure."

A moment later, he saw a second figure following William – he realized in an instant that Margaret Miller was also on her way up.

He turned and looked around.

"Is there another way out of here?" he asked.

"There are rungs on the outside," she told him. "I noticed them earlier, but in this rain they'd be lethal."

"Your mother would never be able to climb down," he replied as he heard another footstep pressing on the stairs. "Jacqui, I don't know what William Miller wants with us right now, but I'm pretty sure it's not going to be anything good. Do you understand what I'm saying to you? I need you to take your sister and get up as high as possible, and I'll bring Mum. Once we're up there, we'll block the door and figure something else out."

"But -"

"Do you have a better idea?" he spluttered.

"Bod, come on," she replied, grabbing her sister's hand and heading her toward the stairs that led higher up toward the top of the lighthouse.

"What about Mum?" Bod sobbed.

"Dad's going to bring here," she said, leading her up the first few steps before turning to see that her father was already scooping Vanessa's unconscious body up into his arms.

A moment later she spotted William Miller reaching the top of the stairs.

"Dad, hurry!" she screamed. "He's here!"

Once he had hold of Vanessa, David carried her across the room, easily bypassing William's animated corpse and quickly managing to start following Jacqui and Bod.

"Move!" he barked, as they set off ahead of him. "Hurry! There's a door at the top, right?"

"Yes, but -"

"Then we'll find a way to block it somehow," he said, already sounding breathless as he struggled to carry Vanessa up the stairs. "Get moving and we'll come up with the next part of our plan later!"

***

Spilling out through the door at the top, Jacqui led Bod out into the rain and then stopped to look back. She saw her father carrying her mother up, and once they were clear she slammed the door shut.

"How do we keep it sealed?" she shouted, struggling to be heard over the sound of crashing rain. Already drenched, she looked over and saw that Bod was pressing herself back against the side of the lamp house, having evidently realized that she mustn't go anywhere near the edge this time. "Bod, be careful! It's slippery up here!"

"We need to try to jam the door shut," David gasped.

"There's another door round the other side," she told him. "It leads into the lamp room. It's the only place up here where we can shelter from the rain."

Heading past her, David carried Vanessa along the curving walkway. Jacqui, not daring to move too far from the door, watched and waited for even the slightest hint that the dead figure of William Miller might try to get through. A moment later, spotting some rusty old tools that had been left on a shelf, she grabbed a spanner and tried to lodge it through the lower half of the handle, trying desperately to hold the door shut. Almost immediately, however, the spanner fell to the floor.

"Here," David said, having returned already.

He grabbed the spanner and positioned it at a different angle, wedging it into the small hook near the door. Pulling on the handle, he satisfied himself that the door was sealed for now and then he turned to his daughter.

"Where's the ladder?"

"Dad -"

"I know what I have to do, Jacqui," he said firmly. "You need to stay here and look after your mum. Where's the ladder?"

"It's not really a ladder," she replied, holding Bod's hand tight and leading them to the railing. "It's a set of rungs that starts here and leads down to the ground."

"That'll have to do."

"But it's going to be so slippery," she continued as rain continued to crash down. "Dad, it's not safe."

"It's the only option," he told her. "Don't worry, I'll be fine. All of this started after I damaged that cross. Fixing it seems like the only idea right now."

He looked down toward the ground but saw only darkness. A moment later he turned first to Bod and then to Jacqui.

"I get it," he said. "It's scary. There's no way around that, but you're just going to have to tough it out up here. I won't be long, I swear, and hopefully once they see that I'm trying to do the right thing..."

His voice trailed off for a few seconds, before he kissed Bod and Jacqui on their foreheads and began to maneuver himself onto the top of the ladder that led down to the rungs.

"I'll be quick!" he continued over the sound

of the rain. "Keep an eye on your mum. And stick together!"

Feeling completely helpless, Jacqui watched as he began to climb down. A thousand thoughts were rushing through her mind and she desperately wanted to stop him, but she knew she had no better plan. As her father disappeared from view, she felt as if she'd been left in charge, although when she looked down at Bod she realized that she really had no idea what to do next. She glanced back at the door, which so far seemed to be holding, and then she began to lead Bod through into the lamp room.

"Hey," she said as soon as she saw that her mother was beginning to stir. "How are you feeling?"

"Like my head almost exploded," Vanessa murmured, sitting up and leaning against the wall. Looking around, she quickly spotted the huge lamp. "Are we at the top of the lighthouse?"

"It's complicated," Jacqui explained as Bod sat on the floor nearby.

"What did I do?" Vanessa asked, touching the side of her head but immediately flinching. She touched her nose and felt the dried blood. "It hurt so much. Something else was in my head, it was pushing so hard, I thought my skull was going to crack."

"You're okay now," Jacqui replied, looking into her mother's eyes and still seeing patches of blood. "I think. Mum, can you see properly?"

"It's a little blurry," she murmured. "Where's your dad?"

Not quite knowing how to explain, Jacqui hesitated.

"Where is he?" Vanessa asked again, sounding a little more concerned this time. "Jacqui, where's your father?"

"He went to fix things," she said cautiously. "He thinks this has to do with a cross he damaged, he's not sure and to be honest I'm worried he might be making a mistake, but I couldn't stop him."

"Is he alone?"

She nodded.

"No-one should be alone on this island, Jacqui," she continued. "I saw something out there, just after I got off the boat. It was a woman, but... it was like her eyes and mouth had been sewn shut. She put a hand on my face, and the next thing I remember is arriving here. I think she somehow got into my thoughts and tried to control me. I felt so much chaos in my mind, and I saw..."

Again she fell silent for a few seconds.

"It's okay, Mum," Jacqui said, trying to sound optimistic. "I'm sure Dad's right and he'll get everything sorted."

"She was in my mind," she replied, "but at the same time, I was in *her* mind. I saw and felt everything. Her name was Jane Moore and she's been dead for a long time. Hundreds of years. She died here on this island and she's been trapped ever since. She can only walk on the island, but she yearns to leave and get revenge on the people who did this to her."

"What did they do?" Jacqui asked. "Did they strand her here and leave her to die? Why would anyone do that?"

"I only saw scraps of it at first, but I think I started to make sense of it by the end. She was feeling my pain and I was feeling hers, and I got glimpses of her memories." She hesitated, staring at the open doorway and seeing a flash of lightning, before turning to Jacqui again. "They thought she was a witch," she added finally. "They were terrified of her and they thought there was only one way to stop her."

CHAPTER TWENTY-SIX

September 7th, 1752...

"CONFESS!"

As soon as the burning hot metal pressed against her back, Jane screamed again. Held in place by two men, one holding each arm, she tried desperately to get to her feet, only for the shackles around her ankles to pull tight. The flesh on her back was burning, and a moment later – when the metal rod was pulled away – blood began to run down from the thick, heavy wound just below her shoulder blades.

Nearby, several onlookers were watching from the safety of the observation area beyond the cell's bars. A number of men and women from the local village had arrived to witness the confession, although so far this latest witch was refusing to buckle nearly as easily as all the rest.

"The time has come," Alistair Hopgood said, stepping around Jane as she remained kneeling on the floor. Torches burned nearby, casting a flickering glow across the cell. "Why put yourself through more of this pain? Your powers can't help you now."

He stopped in front of her and looked down at her bowed, trembling figure.

"You are a wretched and cursed thing," he continued, "but that does not mean that you were not a good woman once. I do not like to inflict this pain on anyone, even one such as yourself. Confess to your crimes, Jane Moore, and your suffering can be brought to a satisfying and swift end for all concerned. We have brought you all the way up here from your home in Kent, and now you are to be dispatched."

He waited, but Jane merely took a series of heavy breaths as she fought against the agony.

"I have the list of charges here," Hopgood said, stepping back as the two guards continued to hold his prisoner's arms. He took a scrap of paper from his pocket and took a moment to remind himself of the text. "Three counts of murder, all relating to the deaths of your husband Thomas Moore, his mother Elizabeth Moore and his sister Cordelia Moore. Two counts of causing grievous harm to the men who were sent to find you. One count of using your powers against a bookseller of some renown, who was indeed the one who first alerted me to your evil. And finally, we have twenty-seven counts of witchcraft and sorcery, witnessed by other women who lived near your husband's land. Thirty-two charges in total, yet still you have the temerity to claim that all of this is somehow wrong, that this veritable mountain of proof is a mistake or, worse... a lie."

He folded the paper carefully and slipped it away with a sense of great ceremony, and then – fully aware that the observers were watching him closely – he took his time as he waited for Jane to speak.

"Your silence condemns you as much as your lies might," he continued. "The only thing that can help your soul now, Jane Moore, is the truth. Can you bring yourself to confess?"

Stepping forward, he reached down and took hold of her dark, matted hair. He forced her to look up at him; she resisted at first, but finally he won out and her terrified eyes stared up at him.

"You *are* a witch," he said firmly.

She tried to shake her head as tears streamed down her face.

"You are a witch," he said again, "and judgment must be passed. The only question is the ultimate fate you shall suffer. We cannot allow a witch to prosper, but there are still... different ways that we might dispatch you from this world. If you will just confess, matters can be dealt with in a way that will cause you far less suffering. Do you not see that we are trying to help you? The Lord pays particular attention to these affairs, and He sees all that transpires here today. If you confess and beg the Lord for absolution, you shall die quickly. If you do not confess, however, you shall be taken from this place and you shall face a far harsher fate."

He paused, watching the fear in her eyes but noticing also a hint of defiance. In truth, he already suspected that he knew how she was going to respond.

"What will it be?" he asked finally. "Will you confess, or must we punish you fully?"

"I am not a witch," she stammered, barely able to get the words out. "In your heart, you know that I speak the truth."

"And still you lie," Alistair murmured, determined to make sure that the observers recognized his sadness at this latest turn of events.

"Remember Margaret Lockheart!" one of the women called out from the other side of the bars, her voice filled with panic. "Remember how she -"

"Silence!" Alistair roarer, holding up a hand to warn her that she must fall silent, while keeping his eyes fixed on Jane. "I remember Margaret

Lockheart and *all* the other witches we have dealt with over these past six years. I know the mistakes that were made, and I also know how to avoid those mistakes this time. That is why I have prepared a slightly different method of dealing with this latest infestation of evil."

He snapped his fingers and a man stepped through into the cell carrying a velvet cushion.

"What is that?" Jane asked, watching with a growing sense of horror as the cushion was set down on a nearby chair. She saw a large needle and what appeared to be several lengths of black wire. "What are those for? What are you going to do to me?"

"We have dealt with other witches," Alistair explained as he walked over to the chair and picked up the needle. He began to attach one of the pieces of wire. "We have heard how they try to trick us, even after their final judgment. They have silver tongues that they can use to confuse even the most devout of men. Even if they cannot use their tongues, their eyes can tempt and terrify. And even if they lack that chance, they can hear what is said around them – and they are able to conspire with Satan to come up with fresh evil."

He walked back over to her and held up the needle, letting its sharp tip glint in the torchlight.

"And all the while," he purred, "Satan looks out through the witch's eyes, and listens through her ears, and speaks with her tongue."

"No," she stammered, trying again to pull away even as the men maintained their grip on her arms. "If Satan is in this room, it is not *me* he uses as his vessel in this world."

She turned and looked over at the observers.

"Do you not see?" she shouted frantically. "How can you stand there and condone this, and still call yourself good people? You are supporting a follower of Satan!"

"Listen to her," Alistair called out confidently, allowing himself a faint smile as he saw Jane still trying to break free. "She proves me correct with her every attempt to wriggle free. If anyone still has any doubts, listen to her final words and know that she is the worst of all the witches we have dealt with in this court."

"He's a liar!" she screamed. "I'm not a witch!"

"Your words might have worked on lesser men," Alistair sneered, "but fortunately I am here to save these good people from your evil." He looked at the guards. "You know what to do. Hold her in place so that I can administer the only course of justice that will end her lies for good."

"What -"

Before she could get another word out, Jane felt one of the guards letting go of her left arm. She immediately tried to pull away but the guard quickly put an arm around her throat, holding her more firmly in place; the second guard, meanwhile, ducked down and grabbed her jaw, clamping her head and stopping her moving as Alistair began to pull at her lips. She'd been struggling already – indeed, she'd been struggling for hours, ever since some men from the village had found her hiding in the forest – but now she found a whole new surge of energy.

Launching herself up, she almost managed to break free, only for the guards to quickly subdue her again. She tried to stay on her feet, and as the guards pushed her back down several of her toes broke.

"See how she struggles," Alistair said, waiting as the guards adjusted their grip and then pulling on her lips again. "When a child of Satan is cornered, she fights with all she has left. Fortunately there are too many of us here now and she cannot overcome us."

"Praise the Lord," one of the men observing the trial whispered, making the sign of the cross against his chest.

As several others said their own prayers, Alistair put the needle against Jane's bottom lip and looked into her terrified eyes, and then he dug the metal tip deep into her flesh.

"I shall not merely connect her lips," he sneered as blood began to dribble from the wound.

"She might break that. It shall be far harder for her to escape, however, if her entire mouth is sealed shut."

With that, he began to push the needle into her gums, forcing the tip through until it broke out on the other side; and then, for good measure, he pushed it through her tongue as well, before forcing it back out through her upper gums and then out from beneath her top lip as well. Jane was sobbing now, fighting frantically as frothing blood bubbled and burst from her mouth, but Alistair continued to work, sewing her lips and gums and tongue shut with slow, methodical patience – and pulling the black wire tighter and tighter each time.

"It is done," he said finally, clipping the wire and taking a moment to tie it in place. "Now for the eyes."

Trying desperately to scream, Jane turned her head away, but he quickly forced her to look at him again. She was murmuring, unable to get any words out, and this inability brought a fresh smile to Alistair's lips.

"You thought we could not stop you," he sneered. "You were wrong. You are not the first witch to be dragged before me, and I fear you shall not be the last. But I have learned some tricks of my own over the years, and these shall be put to good use now."

"I can't look," one of the women said,

turning and walking away from the cell. "Forgive me, but I just can't."

Alistair ignored the woman's weakness as he slowly reached down and pulled out the lower eyelid of Jane's right eye. He touched the needle to her skin, just below her eyelashes, and then he began to force the tip through.

"As with the mouth," he said softly, "here too extra measures shall have to be taken to make sure that she does not tear them open."

With that, he pushed the needle out through the other side of the eyelid and then he started to slowly sink the sharpened end into the white of the eyeball itself.

CHAPTER TWENTY-SEVEN

A BELL RANG OUT in the cold morning air as Jane stumbled and dropped to her knees. Bound by ropes, one of which tied her wrists together so that she could be pulled along by the guards ahead, she managed a faint murmur – but nothing more.

Her eyes and mouth had been sewn tightly shut, and now – after several days – the thick black wire still glistened as a few drops of fresh blood dried on its length. Her ears had also been sealed, albeit a little less successfully, and although she occasionally tried to force herself to break the wire, in truth she found the effort far too painful. She could just about hear a hint of the crowd that had gathered to line the streets of Innisrach, but otherwise her only impression of the outside world came from the cold and damp cobbles that even now scratched her knees.

One of the guards tugged on the rope, another stepped behind her and pulled on her arm, and slowly Jane got to her feet and began to walk again. Several of her toes remained broken, but this pain was nothing compared to the agony of her eyes and mouth and ears.

"Good people of Innisrach," Alistair said, waiting up ahead next to a simple wooden boat that bobbed gently up and down on the peaceful water of the harbor. "Be not afraid, for the witch is entirely bound and can cause you no harm."

A murmur of concern spread quickly through the crowd.

"Would I have brought her north to your fair village," Alistair continued, "if she posed even the slightest threat? Of course not. I know of this village from times past, and I know that you are all good people. I hear that your church is full each and every Sunday. This witch, who even now possesses no ability to harm anyone, is merely passing through on her way to her final destination. After today, you shall have no need to think of her at all."

He turned to see a man making his way from the nearby public house. With rounded shoulders and a slovenly, shuffling gait, the man clearly had no great enthusiasm for his task, although he managed to straighten himself up a little once he realized that he was being watched.

By the time he reached Alistair and looked down at the boat, he'd even wiped a few stray specks of beer from the side of his mustache.

"Mr. Anderson," Alistair said firmly, with an air of great importance, "are you sure that you're the right man for this task?"

"There's no righter man in the whole of Innisrach," Jonathan replied. "There's also no other man in the village who'll do what you're asking. Unless you want to row the boat yourself."

"I was charged by the Lord with rooting out evil," Alistair told him, "not simple manual labor."

"You've told me what you want done, and I'll do it," Jonathan insisted. "Provided you have the payment, that is."

Reaching into his pocket, Alistair took out a small velvet purse. He loosened the strings and tipped a few coins into the palm of his other hand, and Jonathan quickly took those coins with perhaps a little too much haste.

"And half upon your return," Alistair reminded him. "As we arranged."

Having so far managed to avoid looking directly at his passenger, Jonathan now knew that he had no choice. He turned and saw Jane on her knees, and a shiver ran through his body as soon as his gaze settled upon her bloodied and wired face.

"Saints preserve us," he whispered under his breath.

"This is the witch Jane Moore," Alistair announced loudly, so that the entire crowd would be able to hear, "and she is to be transported away from this place to another place where her life will be ended. If this seems like an unusual method of dispatching any mortal soul, then let me remind you that pure evil courses through her veins."

"And I'm to be on a boat with her alone?" Jonathan asked.

"That evil has been contained," Alistair added. "She cannot speak to cast a spell, nor can she use her eyes to enchant any man or woman."

"Then why not kill her here and now?" a voice called out from the crowd.

"And risk having her ghostly presence walk through these pleasant streets?" Alistair asked. "I would not have thought anybody wants that. Instead she is to be taken to one of the many barren islands far away from these shores, where her blood shall be spilled upon the ground and any lingering presence shall have no power. And this brave fellow, Mr. Jonathan Anderson of the parish, has volunteered to do the deed."

"I have," Jonathan murmured, "although now I wonder -"

"Put her onboard!" Alistair shouted to the guards, who immediately began to haul Jane toward the boat. "Tie her down! She must not be allowed to end her own life here, lest she might return to plague these good people!"

He turned to Jonathan.

"Do you have a location in mind?" he asked.

"I do, as it happens."

"And when the time comes..." Reaching under his coat, he pulled out a dagger and handed it over. "Will you be able to do the deed?"

"I've killed before," Jonathan told him, with a flicker of dread in his voice. "Men, women and even children. You don't have to worry about me, Mr. Hopgood. Your witch'll be dead by sundown."

***

The oars dipped once again into clear blue water as Jonathan continued to row the boat away from shore. Innisrach was barely visible now, just a faint smudge on the horizon, and when he glanced over his shoulder he was just about able to make out a speck on the horizon.

"Nearly there," he muttered under his breath, before looking over at his passenger. "And then..."

Since leaving Innisrach, Jane had sat completely still and silent. Thick ropes were holding her in place, yet in truth she hadn't pulled on those ropes at all; instead she had finally accepted her fate, and she knew that soon she would set foot on land for the last time. The wire sealing her ears shut had only partly done its job, and she had been able to hear everything that had been said about her in the village; she had heard Alistair Hopgood's instructions as well as the sound of the baying crowd.

Her eyes, meanwhile, remained sealed shut – save for the tiniest speck of light that was just about able to break through the smallest of gaps. Blood had pooled in her eyes and she could barely see a thing, but she knew when the sun rose and set. As for her mouth, which remained sewn shut, she had occasionally tried to move her tongue, only to find that it would not budge at all. She was able to breathe only through her nostrils, although these two small holes did not permit enough air whenever she became agitated, so instead she was trying to remain as calm as possible.

Her hands were resting on her knees, bound at the wrists.

"Can you hear me?" Jonathan asked finally. "Do you even know where you are?"

He waited, still rowing the boat gently forward, but Jane offered no reply.

"It'll all be over soon," he continued as he felt a growing sense of fear rising through his chest. "I won't drag it out any longer than I have to."

In truth, he had no idea whether or not his passenger was truly a witch. He paid little attention to such matters in his daily life, and although he reasoned that a man like Alistair Hopgood would have no obvious cause to lie, he was also well aware that there were men in the world who twisted and abused the name of the Lord in attempts to justify their villainy. At the same time, he believed that witches were most certainly real, so he couldn't shake the fear that he was traveling with such a creature now, in which case he could only hope that she had been properly bound. Had he not been in such dire need of the money, he would have erred on the side of caution and would never have undertaken the journey out to Saward Island.

Nor would he have lied about his experience.

"I've killed before," he'd told Alistair earlier. "Men, women and even children. You don't have to worry about me, Mr. Hopgood."

He'd never actually killed anyone before, even though he'd been given plenty of opportunities, although he told himself that the task should prove to be easy enough. All he had to do, he told himself, was quickly cut the woman's throat or perhaps just stab her in the heart, and then she'd be dead.

"Not long now," he said, even though he wasn't sure that she could hear him at all. "Then this will all be over."

CHAPTER TWENTY-EIGHT

IN THE YEAR 1752, around a century before anybody thought to construct a lighthouse there, Saward Island was nothing more than a rough scrap of flat land rising just a short way above the surface of the North Sea.

"Come on," Jonathan said, holding the rope that had been attached to Jane's wrists as he led her up from the rocks and onto the long grass. "Be careful. You don't want to slip."

As those words left his lips, he rolled his eyes. Why should the woman bother to be careful when she was about to be dispatched from the world? Still, he'd been raised to treat everyone – especially women – with kindness and respect, and he was determined to do so even in the most trying of circumstances. Part of him even wanted to offer

Jane a final meal, or at least a drink, but as he looked out across the island he supposed that he was only putting off the inevitable.

Watching as the grass swayed in the wind, he tried to work out where best to do the deed, but again he understood deep down that there was no reason for such caution.

The time had come.

"It's a peaceful enough place," he said, turning to see that Jane was standing patiently and obediently nearby. "I've passed this way a few times but never came ashore before."

He wanted to think of something that might make her feel better, a few words that might bring a sense of calm to her heart. Even a witch, he supposed, might feel fear – and he wondered, too, whether in her final moments she might be feeling a pang of regret.

"I -"

Suddenly Jane dropped down onto her knees, as if attempting to hasten the moment of her death.

"I was going to ask whether you have any final words," Jonathan said, "but I suppose... in the circumstances, that's not going to be possible, is it?"

He hesitated, before taking the knife from the loop on his belt and starting to make his way around until he was standing behind her. Although he'd considered plenty of different methods by which he might end Jane's life, he'd come to the conclusion that the best approach might be to simply slit her throat from ear to ear. Death would surely take just a few seconds, perhaps a minute or two at most, and he supposed that he didn't even have to watch. He could look away and wait for a few minutes before quickly checking that the whole thing was over, and then he would be able to leave the island forever.

Reaching around, Jane felt for his arm. Quickly finding his wrist, she moved it up toward her throat as if encouraging him to get on with the task. All the fight had left her body and she and Jonathan were united in a common cause: to end the misery.

"Are you ready?" he asked, unable to rid his voice of a sense of true fear.

Silence.

"Are you sure?"

He waited, even though he knew the answer. As the seconds passed, he looked out across the island and told himself that he simply needed to end the woman's life. He glanced toward the heavens and offered a brief, silent prayer – for what, he wasn't quite sure, but he thought it was the right thing to do – and then finally he slashed the knife across the witch's throat.

***

"Is it done?"

As he stepped off the boat, Jonathan saw Andrew MacDonald from the public house standing a little way back from the harbor. The rest of the crowd had long since dispersed, although voices could be heard shouting and cheering in the distance as night began to fall.

Jonathan paused, before nodding and leaning down to double-check that the ropes were secure.

"Was it quick?" Andrew asked.

"Quick as anyone could have made it."

"Did she fight it?"

"She did not," Jonathan replied, not particularly keen to talk about the matter. "What's important is that it's done."

He turned and looked around.

"Where did Mr. Hopgood go?"

"He left right after you rowed away," Andrew told him. "I suppose he has other witches to root out. He asked that word be sent to his office in Aberdeen, so that he might know that Jane Moore met her fate. I suppose he had faith in you to get the job done."

"Have word sent," Jonathan murmured, wiping his hands clean. "And then I should very much like to forget that any of this happened."

"He left this for you," Andrew said, holding

out some coins. "The rest of your payment."

Jonathan hesitated, as if he couldn't quite stomach the sight of the money, but after a moment he took the coins and – without counting them – slipped them into his pocket.

"You look like a man who's in need of a drink," Andrew told him. "There's one waiting for you inside, and it's on the house. I hate to see someone in such a state. What you did today was for the good of the whole nation, but I know it can't have been enjoyable. I hope you know that we all prayed for you."

"That's fine," Jonathan replied, adjusting his coat, "but -"

Before he could finish, the dagger fell out and landed on the cobbles. Looking down, both men saw blood glinting on the blade, and after a few seconds Jonathan picked it up and quickly washed it in a barrel of water that had been left next to the old flagpole.

"You did the right thing," Andrew told him.

"So I hear."

"Hopgood never gets it wrong," Andrew continued. "You're aware of his reputation, aren't you? They say he's brought scores of witches to justice, and never once has he ever been shown to have made a mistake."

"I never claimed to doubt him."

"I know, but in the circumstances... no man

would blame you if you'd had a few questions."

"Why? Because I had to murder her in cold blood?"

"It's not murder when it's in such circumstances," Andrew said as Jonathan stepped past him and headed toward a nearby street. "Are you not coming for a drink?"

"I think I'd rather be alone," Jonathan called back to him. "I'm feeling a little unusual, to be honest. I'm sure some sleep will do me good."

"That drink'll be waiting for you whenever you're ready to come and get it," Andrew said, before turning and heading to the *Three Compasses* public house, where some men had emerged to get some air.

"Did he do it?" Ralph Irman asked cautiously.

"Aye, he did it," Andrew replied.

"I knew he would," Ralph continued. "A few of the others wondered whether he might be too soft, but I told them that Jonathan wouldn't shirk from his responsibilities."

He watched as Jonathan disappeared around the corner, and then he turned to Andrew again.

"And now what?" he asked. "That island's out there now with a dead witch on it, and with the witch's blood no doubt soaked into the soil. If you want my opinion, nobody should ever set foot on it again."

"We'll see to it that everybody knows to stay away," Andrew told him. "No-one has cause to visit the place anyway, so that shouldn't be too difficult. So long as the tale of Jane Moore is remembered around these parts, what fool would ever want to venture out to Saward Island? There's nothing there but grass and rocks, and we've got plenty of both those things in abundance right here on the mainland. So long as the fishermen understand to stay away, I don't see how there can be any further problems."

"I hope you're right," Ralph said darkly, looking out past the harbor as the sky continued to darken. "Something about this still doesn't quite sit right with me. It'll be a while, I'm sure, before I manage to forget what happened today. I don't doubt for one second that Mr. Hopgood was right about that woman being a witch, but I still didn't like the sight of her being paraded through the streets with her mouth and eyes all -"

"Then stop talking about it," Andrew said firmly. "We can keep the story alive without dwelling too much on the details, can't we? Nobody *liked* what happened today, it just... it had to happen, that's all. And so long as people stay away from that island, it can all be put in the past."

As Andrew made his way back inside, Ralph and the other men were left in the cold and the wind to contemplate those words. Nobody spoke, but they were each watching the sea and wondering about the woman's corpse out on Saward Island. And even though they didn't give voice to their fears, they were each privately wondering whether the right thing had been done that day, and whether the evil of Jane Moore had truly been contained and destroyed forever.

CHAPTER TWENTY-NINE

May 5th, 1840...

"BRING THEM ALL ONSHORE!" a voice shouted above the sound of the storm, as men with lanterns hurried through the rainy night and made their way to the harbor. "Alive and dead, how many have you got?"

"No survivors," another voice called out. "Three bodies recovered and three lost to the sea."

A small crowd had gathered now, taking shelter in various nearby doorways to watch as the fishing crew hauled three sodden corpses onto the cobbles.

"Where did you find them?" a voice asked.

"Where do you think?" one of the other men replied. "As soon as we heard another boat was missing, we knew where to look. There was debris all around the north shore of the island and we found these three corpses floating with the wood. We called out for any sign of survivors having made it to land, but there were none."

"How can you be sure?"

"Nobody answered."

"And you didn't go ashore yourselves to check?"

"Are you out of your mind? Of course we didn't. We shone our torches onto the same rocks that had dashed the boat apart, but there was nobody to be seen. If anyone had survived, they would have been there waiting for us."

"This can't go on," the first voice said bitterly as the three corpses were laid near his feet. "That's the fifth boat we've lost to those rocks in the past five years alone. Eighteen good men have drowned, by my count. It's time we finally did something to stop more of these tragedies happening."

***

"Then we're agreed?" Marshall Irman called out, struggling to be heard over the din of voices in the *Three Compasses*. "Listen to me! Are we agreed on what's to be done?"

"We don't have a choice," Ezekiel Withers

replied, having listened to the entire hurried debate from his usual chair in the corner. "Too many lives have been lost on the rocks of Saward Island. We simply *have* to raise the funds to build a lighthouse there, or any one of us in this room might be next."

A murmur of agreement spread through the crowd.

"But will we be able to raise the money?" a voice asked.

"We'll have to," Marshall replied. "I'll go to Marsham Hall in the morning and see if the family can be counted on for a contribution. That ought to get us started nicely. Then we'll have to source the remaining funds ourselves. It'll be cheaper if we can find some laborers from nearby who'll do the work." He paused for a moment as the storm continued to rage in the darkness outside. "And that brings our business to a conclusion," he added, "at least for tonight. I'm sure that, like me, you all want to get this terrible evening over with. There are four families grieving the losses of their loved ones tonight. Let us keep them in our prayers."

As the meeting began to disband, Marshall made his way to the bar, where Tom Lester had already poured him a pint of ale.

"Do you really think it can be done?" Tom asked.

"I think is *must* be done," Marshall told him before taking a sip. "I'm sick of us having to send search parties out there when we all know the most likely outcome. Those rocks on the northern tip of Saward Island are lethal, and boats coming back to shore are prone to getting blown off course in that very direction. If we don't find a way to get a lighthouse built out there, we shall have the deaths of more souls on our consciences."

He took another sip as Leonard Pottinger wandered over to join him.

"So it's to be a lighthouse, is it?" Leonard murmured darkly. "Are we sure that's a good idea?"

"How could it not be?" Marshall asked.

"I just mean..."

Leonard looked at Tom, who rolled his eyes and turned away to dry some glasses.

"I just mean," Leonard continued cautiously, "that we all know the stories about that place."

"You mean the ones about the witch?" Marshall asked, raising a skeptical eyebrow. "How does it go again? Oh, that's right... so a hundred years ago, or roughly that, a witch was dragged out there and killed, so that she could never again trouble the good people of our nation. And now nobody's supposed to go to Saward Island, because her ghostly figure haunts the place. Is that about the gist of it?"

"Yes, and -"

"It's pure bunkum," Marshall replied before the other man could get another word out. "I'm surprised, Leonard, that you'd even entertain such nonsense. I remember my old grandfather telling me spooky tales about that island, but I never took them to be anything more than foolish attempts to scare young children."

"You don't think the witch existed?"

"Perhaps she did and perhaps she didn't. And perhaps she was taken out and killed there, or perhaps she wasn't. And perhaps her ghost might even haunt the place, or perhaps it doesn't. But do you know what *is* certain? Those rocks are real and we're losing too many good men to them. Saward Island is the perfect place for a lighthouse that'll keep our fishermen safe. Do you really want to let more people die, just because of some old superstitions?"

"Sometimes superstitions should be respected," Leonard suggested. "Sometimes they're based on a whole lot of truth."

"William Archer died tonight," Marshall replied. "William Merriman, Thomas Caggard, Thomas Peterson, Thomas Low and Cameron Riley too. Six good men, six sons of Innisrach, each with family in this very village and roots that go back for generations. Do you really want to go to their parents, their wives, their children... and tell them that you're willing to let more people die just because of some ghost stories you were told when you were a lad? Can you look them in the eye and tell them that?"

"I just think we need to consider the matter better," Leonard said, although he was clearly struggling to come up with a more convincing argument. "That island... it's not a good place."

"I shall go to Marsham Hall at first light," Marshall said, downing the last of his ale before heading to the door. "That lighthouse is going to be built whether you like it or not, Leonard. We can't remain beholden to childish tales. We have to look after our fishermen. Without the fishermen, soon there'd be nothing left of this village at all. You'd do well to remember that fact."

Once Marshall was gone, Leonard looked down at his own pint of ale.

"He's right, you know," Tom said finally, having listened to the entire conversation.

"He hasn't been out there," Leonard replied. "He wasn't out there tonight, trying to save some of the men who drowned. I was, just as I've been out there every time a boat hits those rocks."

"So you know better than anyone why we need the lighthouse," Tom suggested. "Do you really want to have to keep going out there and hauling dead men from the water?"

"Of course I don't," Leonard spat back at him, clearly insulted by the mere suggestion.

"Then -"

"But I've seen her," he added. "Don't think I

haven't, because I have. The others have too, even if they won't admit as much." He hesitated, as if he was scared to reveal the truth. "Sometimes, when I raise my lantern up to cast its light across those rocks on Saward Island, the glow catches part of the grass higher up. That's when I spot her. She's standing there staring out at us, almost like she's wanting us to go ashore so that she can claim more victims. I try to keep the lantern low so that I won't spot her, but occasionally I can't help it. She's just like my grandfather told me she'd be, with her mouth and lips sewn shut. She's out there on that island still, a century or more after she died there, and nobody who goes to build that lighthouse will be safe."

"You don't really believe in such things, do you?" Tom asked, clearly struck by the tale.

"It's not a matter of believing," Leonard replied. "It's a matter of having seen it. "I can tell that I won't be able to stop anything happening. I can tell that the lighthouse most likely will get built, but let me promise you that I shall never go out there, and I shall never set foot on that island. And I shall pray every morning and every night for any poor soul that doesn't heed my warning."

He took another sip of beer, and then he turned and looked toward the window, thinking now of the island waiting out there in the darkness.

"I understand the arguments in favor of the

lighthouse, but nothing good will come of this scheme. Only pain and misery and more death."

CHAPTER THIRTY

Today...

"THAT'S... HORRIBLE," JACQUI SAID once her mother had finished telling her about Jane Moore. With tears in her eyes, she tried to imagine the pain the woman must have felt. "How could they do something so awful to another human being? What the hell was wrong with them all?"

"They were driven by fear, I suppose," Vanessa said softly, still wincing occasionally as she felt ripples of pain running through her skull. "Fear and superstition."

"But how could they be *so* ignorant?" Jacqui continued. "It's one thing to be scared of something, but how did they convince themselves that witches are real? And even if they did that, why did they have to kill her in such a horrible way? Why did they have to march her through the streets like that?"

"You're judging those people by modern standards," Vanessa warned her.

"And? Why shouldn't I do that?"

"Just remember that times change. You look back at those people and think they were -"

"Savages," Jacqui said through gritted teeth. "They were savages."

"You look back at them and think that," Vanessa continued, "but two hundred years from now, people might look back on us and think the same thing."

"There's one big difference," Jacqui told her. "We're not murderers!"

"I'm not defending them," Vanessa replied wearily. "Far from it. I just think we need to try to be more understanding, that's all." Now it was her turn to pause for a moment. "I felt every flicker and heartbeat of Jane Moore's pain," she added. "I felt what it was like for her to have her eyes and mouth sewn shut. I felt what it was like for her to kneel on the grass and await death. Parts of it are a little murky in my mind, but I also felt the sheer fear that was pounding in her chest. Believe me, I know that it was wrong."

Jacqui looked over at Bod, who was examining the huge glass lamp, and then she turned to her mother again.

"If you got into her mind while she was trying to possess you," she continued cautiously, "then... do you know the truth? Was she a witch or not?"

"That part I'm not sure about," Vanessa admitted. "Like I said, I wasn't able to experience all of it. Instead I got these... flashes of what happened to her, and of what she sensed. There's so much pain and confusion and anger in her soul, it's honestly terrifying to even think about her. And I think -"

Before she could finish, they heard a single loud thud coming from somewhere outside on the walkway.

"It's her," Jacqui stammered, getting to her feet. "Isn't it? Or it's that dead lighthouse keeper."

Rushing over to the door, she pushed her weight against the wood in an attempt to keep it shut.

"Mum, help me!" she called out. "We can't let them get inside! We have to keep them out until Dad somehow puts things right."

"I'm scared," Bod whimpered, pulling back around behind the lamp. "I don't want to be here."

"No-one wants to be here!" Jacqui yelled, still pushing against the door. "We just need to give Dad time to sort it all out. I've seen loads of horror films, I bet he just needs to fix the cross and then she can rest in peace again."

"But you don't *know* that'll work," Bod pointed out as tears began to run down her cheek.

"Have you got a better idea?" Jacqui snapped, before turning to her mother. "Mum, can you tell her to stop asking stupid questions? And can you guys both help me here? I don't know that I'll be able to keep this shut when they start trying to force their way through."

She waited, but Vanessa – who had fallen silent now – slowly began to lean forward before letting out a series of faint gasps.

"Mum?" Jacqui continued. "Are you okay?"

"What's happening to her?" Bod asked, stepping back the other way around the lamp room now.

"She's trying again," Vanessa said, putting a hand on the side of her head as she looked up at Jacqui. "I can feel her in my mind. She's trying to get into my thoughts again and push them aside."

"So push her out!" Jacqui hissed.

"I don't know if I can," Vanessa replied, leaning back against the wall as a fresh bead of blood began to dribble from one nostril. "She feels... stronger this time, as if she's getting better at it. She's weaving herself into my mind... into all of me. We're starting to feel each other's thoughts and pain and... I don't know if I can hold her back forever."

"Mum, you have to try!" Jacqui replied.

"I *am* trying!" Vanessa gasped, slowly getting to her feet on unsteady legs that seemed ready to buckle at any moment. "Believe me, I'm trying harder than ever, but it's like she's swamping my mind." As if to emphasize that point, she leaned back against the wall and let out another pained gasp. "She's too much for me, Jacqui," she continued. "She keeps pushing and pushing. Occasionally I manage to push back, but she only comes back stronger than ever. Eventually she's going to take over completely and then... I'm not sure what she'll do once she has full control."

"Can we help you?" Jacqui asked, reaching out and taking hold of Bod's hand. "Mum, tell us what to do."

Vanessa shook her head slowly.

"Mum, tell us what to do!" Jacqui sobbed, no longer able to stay strong. "Mum, you have to tell us what to do because right now I don't have a clue."

"I think... you need to go and find your father," Vanessa replied cautiously. "It's not safe for you to be around me."

"Bod can't climb down!"

"You don't need to climb," Vanessa told her, before pointing toward the door. "It's safe. You can go that way now."

"Those things are out there."

"No, they're not," Vanessa continued, struggling for breath now. "I think they've gone to find your father, but they're slow. If you hurry, you can reach him first and then... I'll be right behind you, I promise."

"You have to come with us," Jacqui said firmly.

"No, I want you to go first," Vanessa replied, before stumbling toward the door and pulling it open, letting wind and rain blow into the lamp room. "Hurry, Jacqui! You and your sister have to get out of here!"

"Not without you," Jacqui insisted.

"Jacqui, please!" Vanessa hissed. "This isn't up for debate! I need you to get your sister out of here and I... I'll come a little later."

Jacqui opened her mouth to reply, but at the last second she realized that her mother perhaps had a point. Figuring that she needed to be strong and brave for Bod, she kept hold of the girl's hand and squeezed tight as she led her over to the door.

"Don't look back," Vanessa said through gritted teeth. "I mean it, Jacqui. Whatever else you do, don't look back."

"Why can't -"

"Just promise me!" Vanessa snarled.

"I promise," Jacqui said, although her mother's insistence was scaring her now. "But you're coming soon, right?"

"I just need to hold her back for a little while longer," Vanessa said, pushing her out through the open doorway. "I can only do that if I know that you're both safe. Find your dad and tell him that you all need to get to the boat. Tell him that I'll try to keep this bitch out of my mind for as long as possible!"

"And then you'll meet us at the boat?"

"Yes," Vanessa replied, "but only if you leave right now!"

"Mum, promise me," Jacqui said, struggling to contain her fear as she and Bod stepped onto the gangway and turned to look at her again. *"Really* promise me."

"Of course," Vanessa said, clinging to the side of the door in an effort to stay on her feet. " I promise. Just go right now, okay? And whatever you do, remember that I love you. You're the two most adored girls in the whole world and you mustn't ever forget that. But you have to go now and I have to stay here, but we'll see each other again soon. I swear."

Reaching into her pocket, she pulled out her phone and handed it over.

"Take this," she continued. "There's still a little battery left. You can use it to light your way."

Jacqui hesitated, still worried that her mother was acting strangely. After a moment she saw a hint of steely determination in Vanessa's eyes, but she told herself that there was no reason to worry and that her mother simply had a plan that she couldn't fully explain.

"We'll see you at the boat, Mum," she said finally. "Won't we?"

Unable to get any words out, Vanessa nodded.

"Mum -"

"Go! Go now!"

Turning and hurrying along the gangway, Jacqui led Bod to the door. She stopped and listened, but she heard no sign of William and Margaret Miller on the other side. Although her hand was trembling, she managed to move the spanner her father had earlier used to block the door; a moment later she pulled the door open and she braced herself for the sight of the Millers, but to her immense relief she saw nothing but the dark staircase leading down into the lighthouse.

"Do we really have to go down there again?" Bod asked, barely managing to raise her voice over the sound of the storm.

"We do," Jacqui told her, "but... we'll be fine. Mum said the Millers were gone and it looks like she was right. Now we just have to make our way to the ground floor and go to find Dad."

"Are you sure Mum'll come after us?"

"I'm sure," Jacqui replied, forcing herself to ignore the sense of doubt in the pit of her belly as she activated the flashlight on her mother's phone and began to lead her sister down into the darkness. "Watch your step, Bod," she added. "Don't worry, I think I can figure out the way."

AMY CROSS

CHAPTER THIRTY-ONE

"I'M SURE," JACQUI SAID, her voice drifting back along the gangway so that it could just be heard over the raging storm. "Watch your step, Bod. Don't worry, I think..."

Now the voice became too murky, lost in the sound of howling wind and pouring rain as Vanessa stood in the doorway and waited for the presence to return. For several minutes now she'd been feeling a series of surges in her mind, and she had no doubt that the ghost of Jane Moore was trying over and over again to take control; each of those surges felt just a little stronger than the last, pushing a harder and further and requiring more effort to repel. There was a relentlessness about Jane's efforts that showed no sign of letting up, and Vanessa had already accepted that eventually she was going to lose the battle.

At least, however, she'd managed to get her children away.

"And then you'll meet us at the boat?" she remembered Jacqui asking desperately.

"Yes," she'd replied, "but only if you leave right now!"

"Mum, promise me," Jacqui had insisted, as if she'd sensed that something wasn't quite right. "*Really* promise me."

"Of course," she'd lied. " I promise."

Now, leaning against the side of the door in an attempt to remain on her feet, Vanessa looked out at the storm and felt a pang of regret for lying to her daughter.

"I'm sorry, Jacqui," she whispered. "Bod. I just had to get you away from here before -"

In that instant she felt something bursting through her mind. Stumbling forward, she bumped against the railing and dropped to her knees. Jane Moore's soul was forcing its way deeper and deeper into her thoughts, and Vanessa could feel herself starting to absorb the dead woman's experiences and pain. Still clinging to the railing, she felt the rain blowing against her face and she told herself that she just needed to be strong; in truth, however, she had no idea what Jane really wanted with her body and she was determined to stop her.

She had a plan, one that she'd hidden from

her daughters, and as she looked down past the railing and saw the darkness below she realized that the time had come.

"I don't think you were a bad person," she said through gritted teeth, hauling herself to her feet and shuffling toward a gap in the railing. "Not at the start. You've been driven insane by everything that happened to you, but I can't let you hurt my daughters. You need to understand that."

Stopping, she looked down at the gap and thought of the ground far below.

"I can feel everything you feel as you scratch and claw your way into my mind," she sneered, "but I'm pretty sure that goes both ways. You feel everything *I* feel as well, so hopefully you'll feel this and it'll distract you so that the rest of my family can get away." She flinched, preparing herself for the final moment even as she felt Jane blossoming in her thoughts. "They say that all parents eventually have to sacrifice themselves for their children. I guess this is just more literal than usual."

With that, she tried to let go of the railing and tumble forward, but already she could feel Jane fighting to hold on.

"I won't let you hurt them," she snarled as she tried to loosen her fingers one by one. "I won't let you get anywhere near them."

***

"Jacqui, I'm scared," Bod whispered as they finally reached the bottom step and saw the door ahead. "Where's Mum?"

"She'll be right behind us," Jacqui replied, stopping and shining the flashlight all around, seeing nothing but the various items of furniture and a few old crosses. After a moment she turned and shone the light back up the stairs, but she still saw no sign of her mother. "She promised."

"Where did those scary people go?"

"I think Mum was right, they went after Dad."

"Will he be okay?"

"You're asking a lot of questions that I don't have answers for," Jacqui admitted, before reminding herself that she needed to sound a little more confident – for her sister's sake, at least. "You know what? It's all going to be fine. Dad's plan actually makes a lot of sense, at least according to the rules of every horror movie I've ever seen. He's going to put things right and then the ghost... I mean, she should start pulling her shit together."

"You're not supposed to swear."

"I know, but I think in the circumstances..."

As her voice trailed off, Jacqui realized that she could hear the storm still battering the lighthouse but that – crucially – there was no sign of her mother following them down the stairs. She knew she should just keep going and lead Bod away, yet at the back of her mind she couldn't help thinking that something about her mother's promises had seemed a little wrong earlier, as if something had been slightly off.

"Bod," she said finally, "I need you to do something."

Bod squeezed her hand tighter.

"Okay," Jacqui continued, slipping her hand free – only for Bod to grab it again. This time Jacqui pulled away more firmly. "Bod, listen, you need to be brave for just a few minutes. I'm going to go back up and check that Mum's okay."

"She said not to."

"I know, but I'm going to do it anyway."

She led her sister across the room until she found a spot behind an old cabinet, next to the crosses.

"This looks like a good hiding place," she added, forcing Bod into the gap. "You'll be completely safe here, I promise. I'm going to run up and check that Mum's still coming, and then we'll all go and find Dad. Do you understand?"

"I don't want to be by myself."

"It's just for a few minutes," Jacqui told her, before handing her the phone. "Take this. I can find my way without it."

"I'm really scared."

"I know, but you're also really brave." She hesitated, before leaning over and kissing the top of her sister's head and then stepping back. "Two minutes. Three at most. Just... let me do this, Bod."

Bod hesitated, before finally nodding – even if her reluctance was palpable.

After a moment, Jacqui turned and began to pick her way back over toward the stairs. She knew that getting back up to the top of the building would be difficult without the phone, but she couldn't leave her sister in the dark so she fumbled with her hands along the wall until she found the right spot, and then she slowly began to make her way up the staircase.

"Hurry!" Bod called out, and already her voice sounded so small and far off.

"I promise!" Jacqui shouted back to her, before quickening her pace until she reached the next level.

Now she really struggled, and she had to keep her hands on the wall as she slowly made her way around the room. Her heart was racing and with each step she worried that she was making a terrible mistake, but she couldn't ignore the sense of dread in her chest; there had been something strangely final in her mother's voice just a few minutes earlier, something that made her worry that she hadn't been planning to keep her promises at all. And as she found the next set of steps and began to make her way up, Jacqui was unable to shake the fear that somehow things were much more dangerous than her mother had been letting on.

Finally she reached the top and managed to get the door open. Stepping out onto the platform, she immediately felt the storm blowing against her, almost pushing her back down. Forcing herself forward, she managed a couple of steps before coming to a halt as she saw her mother standing at the gap in the railing.

"Mum?" she called out.

Vanessa stared out at the storm for a moment, before turning to look at her. In that moment Jacqui saw two faces; her mother's features were mixed with those of the dead woman, allowing hints of the sewn eyes and mouth to show through. Somehow two people were occupying the exact same space, and while she could see her mother trying to cry out she also saw the dead face of Jane Moore becoming stronger and stronger.

And then, with no warning, Vanessa toppled forward and fell off the top of the lighthouse.

"Mum!" Jacqui screamed, rushing forward and slamming against the railing, then looking down into the void. "No!"

She waited, but a moment later she heard a very distant and muffled bumping sound. Telling herself that everything was going to be alright, she stared down and a moment later another flash of lightning briefly lit the scene, revealing Vanessa's crumpled body at the foot of the lighthouse with blood splattered across the grass.

Pulling back, Jacqui fell down against the side of the lamp room and clamped her hands over her mouth, desperately trying to stop herself screaming. Staring at the gap in the railing with wide-eyed horror, she replayed the moment of her mother's fall again and again as tears began to run from her eyes. A moment later she leaned forward, and now – even with her hands over her mouth – she managed a slow, rattling sobbing sound as she realized that her mother was truly gone.

CHAPTER THIRTY-TWO

LETTING OUT A LOUD grunt, David finally pulled hard enough to rip the post out of the ground. Falling back, he landed hard in the mud with the wooden beam in his hands, and a moment later he grabbed his phone and tilted the flashlight to see that the cross was now entirely gone.

"Nearly there," he whispered, stumbling to his feet and picking up the second cross, which he'd grabbed from the lighthouse before making his way across the island.

Every muscle in his body was aching, but he knew he couldn't afford to slow down, not even for a second. The rainwater had turned the ground into a muddy bog, and he had to force his feet up with each step as he carried the new cross over to the right position. He hesitated for a moment, wondering whether he simply had to force the bottom section down into the ground, and a few seconds later a flash of lightning briefly lit the entire island.

He saw the lighthouse over on the far side, and he thought of his wife and daughters hiding out at the top.

"This is for you," he said, before holding the cross up high and then driving it down into the ground with all the strength he could muster.

Stepping back, his feet once again sank a short distance into the mud.

"I did it!" he shouted at the top of his voice, desperately hoping that the ghostly figure would now see that everything had been put right. "I'm sorry I damaged it in the first place, but it's fixed now! Do you see?"

He pointed at the cross while looking all around, convinced that at any moment the woman might appear. He wasn't quite sure how he expected her to let him know, but he felt sure that he'd done what she'd wanted.

"So now you can leave us alone!" he yelled. "That's how it works, right? Now you're going to leave us alone, and then we'll leave this island and you can get back to whatever the hell you were doing before we ever set foot on the place! Or you can... be at peace, or something like that."

He waited.

The storm continued to rage all around him.

"Right?" he continued, although now he was starting to feel just a little more worried that for some reason nothing was happening. He still wasn't sure *what* he'd been expecting, but he figured that somehow there should be some kind of recognition of his actions.

He looked the other way.

"Right?" he said again, before taking another step back. "Come on, where -"

Before he could finish, he lost his footing and fell back, landing hard in the mud. Reaching out, he tried to steady himself, only for his hands to sink deep beneath the surface. He immediately began to pull them out, only to stop as he realized that his right hand was brushing against something hard that had been buried in the ground. Pushing his hand a little deeper, he felt some kind of cold, partially rotten fabric, and then he slipped his fingertips through a gap and felt something harder and colder.

The mud squelched as he pushed his hand deeper still, and finally he let out a gasp as he realized that his fingers were brushing against a collection of bones.

***

Still hiding behind the cabinet on the lighthouse's

ground floor, Bod couldn't help but shiver slightly in the cold air as she waited for her sister to return.

Several minutes had passed since Jacqui had gone back upstairs, and while she hadn't exactly been counting, Bod felt sure that she was already taking way longer than she'd promised. She wanted to call out, but she knew that nobody would be able to hear her from the top of the lighthouse, and she also wanted to prove that she could be brave. Still, a moment later she began to tilt the phone, casting its electric glow across the assorted items of furniture until she spotted the crosses that had been left leaning against the wall.

Something about those crosses left her feeling decidedly uneasy.

"Jacqui, can you come back soon?" she whispered. "I -"

Suddenly she turned and looked the other way. She held the phone up again, but all she saw in its glow were more items of furniture.

"Jacqui?" she said cautiously. "Are you there?"

She waited, telling herself that all she'd really heard had been a very faint and very brief clicking sound. A moment later, however, she heard the sound again, this time coming from the other side of the room. She turned to look, but now all she saw was the door.

"Jacqui, is that you?" she called out, barely

daring to raise her voice above a whisper.

Again she waited, and after a few more seconds the lighthouse's door began to slowly creak open, revealing the pouring rain outside.

Swallowing hard, she told herself not to panic. Part of her wanted to run to the stairs and go up to find her sister, but she knew that was exactly what a scared little kid would do; instead, she was determined to prove for the first time that she could be brave and strong, and that she wasn't going to let a stupid door scare her to death.

Still, she kept her eyes fixed on the open door now, determined to prove to herself that it had only opened because of the wind.

And then a figure walked past, disappearing from view just as quickly as it had appeared.

Letting out a gasp, Bod pulled back, but a moment later a second figure walked past and then a third. They were all going in the same direction, all walking through the storm as if they had some kind of singular purpose, and a few seconds later she spotted a couple more following, this time a little further from the door and slightly harder to make out.

Looking up, she saw that she was almost directly underneath one of the windows. Although she wanted to simply curl herself into a ball and hide away, she tried instead to work out what her sister would do in the same situation, and she quickly came to the conclusion that Jacqui would *definitely* try to figure out what was going on. She stared up at the window for a moment longer, and then she forced herself to stand.

Glancing at the door, she saw another figure stumbling past, and she told herself to focus on the fact that so far none of the strange people had shown any interest in actually entering the lighthouse.

"Be brave," she whispered, still trying to act like her sister. "Make Jacqui proud of you."

She had to stand on tip toes to have any chance of seeing outside at all, but finally she managed to look out the window, only to find that the view was completely dark. She could hear thunder still rumbling high above, and she figured that she needed to wait for another flash of lightning, but so far all she saw was more rain hitting the window's other side. She held up the phone and tried to illuminate the scene using the flashlight, but this only caused a bright reflected glare. Lowing the phone again, she told herself that Jacqui would totally keep looking and waiting for more lightning, so she resolved to do the same thing even though her heart was racing and -

In that moment another flash of lightning arced across the sky, and Bod gasped as she briefly spotted a dozen or more people walking away across the island.

Pulling back from the window, she turned to run, only to bump into the side of the cabinet and trip over the trailing leg of a chair. Letting out a startled cry, she slammed down against the floor and the phone fell from her hand, quickly sliding away until it bumped against the wall.

Stumbling to her feet, she grabbed the phone and raced through the darkness, and then she pushed the door shut before dropping down onto the floor. Using her back to try to keep the door shut, she struggled to get her breath back as she felt panic spreading throughout her body.

"Jacqui!" she screamed, no longer able to stay calm. "Jacqui, there are more ghosts! Help me!"

She waited, and now she couldn't help but wonder why her sister wasn't coming to find out what was wrong.

"Jacqui!" she sobbed, trying in vain to hold back more tears. "There are lots and lots of ghosts! Jacqui, where are you?"

Hearing a bumping sound, she looked toward the stairs and finally saw her sister making her way down. Stumbling to her feet, she raced over and put her arms around Jacqui, before looking up to see her shocked face.

"There are lots of ghosts outside," she spluttered, "and they're walking away and they're really scary and I saw them but I don't think they saw me but there are so many of them and Jacqui I'm really scared!"

Staring back down at her with tear-filled eyes, Jacqui tried to work out exactly what her sister was talking about.

"There are so many of them," Bod whimpered. "Jacqui, why are there so many ghosts on this island?"

CHAPTER THIRTY-THREE

"WHERE'S MUM?" Bod asked as Jacqui held her hand tight and led her out of the lighthouse, out into the raging storm. "Jacqui, where -"

"I just told you, she's -"

Turning to her sister, Jacqui couldn't help but relive that moment over and over again. She saw the sight of her mother falling from the platform, and then she saw the brief burst of lightning that had revealed her broken corpse far below on the ground. Looking around, she tried to calculate exactly where the body would have landed. Holding up her mother's phone, she tilted the beam around until she spotted the crumpled and bloody figure just a few feet away.

Immediately turning Bod away, she put a hand over the girl's eyes.

"What is it?" Bod asked, and now her voice was filled with terror. "Jacqui, you're acting really weirdly. Where's Mum?"

"Don't worry about Mum right now," Jacqui said as more tears ran down her face. "Mum's... going to look after herself. We're going to stick to the plan she gave us and... we're going to go and find Dad, okay?"

"But -"

"And that's the end of the story," she added, telling herself that she couldn't possibly reveal the truth right now, and that she had to make sure that Bod didn't see the body. "Just do what I tell you to do, Bod, and everything will be alright." She looked out across the island for a moment. "I don't see any other ghosts. You must have imagined them."

"I didn't imagine them," Bod complained. "They were real, Jacqui! Why don't you believe me?"

"Where would they have come from?" Jacqui replied. "Bod, you need to calm down and stop imagining things, okay? We've got enough problems on our hands without pretending that there are more."

"I want Mum and Dad," Bod whimpered. "Jacqui, can we find them and go home now?"

"We're going to go and find Dad," she said, looking over her shoulder and imagining her mother's body on the ground somewhere nearby in the darkness. "That's all we *can* do right now. And we both need to be strong, Bod. Really strong. If we start panicking, we might never manage to get away from this island."

***

"There!" Bod gasped a short while later, stopping as they made their way through the rain, looking back over her shoulder. "You must have heard it this time!"

"I didn't hear anything," Jacqui replied, pulling on her hand, trying to get her to start walking again. "Seriously, Bod, we can't stop every ten seconds just because you think you heard a spooky noise."

"But I *did* hear something," Bod insisted, before turning to look in the other direction. "There are other ghosts out here, Jacqui! I think they're all around us."

"Can we just walk?" Jacqui asked with a sigh, still struggling to keep from replaying the moment of their mother's death over and over again. "I just want to get the hell out of here and never come back again."

Bod hesitated, still looking into the darkness, before reluctantly allowing her sister to pull her along again. Still alert to the possibility that the other ghosts might appear at any moment, she continually looked first one way and then another, but for now all she could hear – apart from the sound of crashing rain and howling wind – was her own footsteps squelching in the mud plus occasional rumbles of thunder in the sky. The storm seemed relentless and endless, and if anything was becoming worse.

"Is Mum coming?" she asked finally.

"Don't worry about Mum right now."

"But -"

"I said, don't worry about Mum!" Jacqui snapped angrily, before sighing again. "I'm sorry, Bod, just... stop asking questions all the time. We have to find Dad."

"Is Mum standing guard at the lighthouse?"

"Not quite."

"Is she going to meet us at the boat?"

"Yes, Bod," she said finally, figuring that she could stall for time and then her father would have to break the news, "that's probably it. Let's just get to the boat and find out."

"When we find her, will she be -"

"Just shut up!" Jacqui screamed, suddenly losing control as she turned to her sister. "Bod, seriously, stop asking me about Mum!"

"Why?"

"Because I can't... because I don't know, okay? Because we're stuck on this stupid island and everything's going wrong and I don't know if we're ever going to get off! And because I keep telling myself that everything's going to be okay, but now I really don't know whether that's true and I'm scared we might all -"

Stopping herself in the nick of time, she felt utterly hopeless for a moment before pulling her sister closer for a hug.

"I'm sorry," she continued as tears streamed from her eyes, flowing down her face with the rain. "I didn't mean to yell at you, just... *please* stop asking me about Mum right now, okay?"

"Okay," Bod said weakly.

A few seconds later Jacqui spotted a faint glow ahead, and she set off again – pulling Bod along – as she realized that they'd finally located their father. Sure enough, as they made their way down a narrow slope they spotted David kneeling in the mud in front of the new cross, although as she reached him Jacqui noticed that he didn't seem to be celebrating.

"Dad," she said slightly breathlessly, "how did it go?"

The light from his phone allowed her to see the cross, which was shaking slightly in the wind but otherwise seemed to be fairly sturdy.

"You did it," she continued. "So... that's it all sorted, right?"

"Is it?" he asked.

"You tell me," she replied, before waiting

for him to say something. "Dad, what's going on? Can we just leave now?"

"Where's your mother?"

"She's... at the lighthouse," she explained, not wanting to tell the truth right now, not in front of her sister. "Dad, I think it's really important that we go to the boat. I know the weather's really bad, but we have to get off this island as quickly as possible."

"She's buried here."

"The witch? I guess so."

"I can feel her body."

"What -"

"Her bones," he added, looking down at his right hand, which remained embedded in the mud. "She's not that far beneath the surface."

"Okay, that's creepy," she replied, wondering why he was still on his knees. "Dad, I really don't think that we need to go around trying to solve every mystery here. We just have to get out of here."

"Something's wrong with the bones."

"What are you talking about?"

"I can feel it," he continued, still slipping his fingertips between the bones in the buried fabric. "I haven't dared to pull them out but -"

"I think pulling them out might be a very bad idea," she told him. "Dad, don't you think you've already done enough to piss this ghost off?"

"I don't think she's buried here."

"*Now* what are you talking about?" She gave him a chance to answer, but so far his comments were making no sense at all. "Dad, something really bad happened back at the lighthouse, something that I... I need to tell you." She looked down at Bod, who was staring at the cross, and then she turned to her father again. "It's about Mum."

"This isn't her," he said, pushing his hand a little deeper into the mud.

"What do you mean?"

"It's not her buried here," he continued. "It's not Jane Moore, or whatever her name was."

"How can you tell that?"

She waited for him to answer, and then – to her horror – he reached his other hand into the mud and began to pull the bundle up.

"Dad, I think this is a really bad idea," she said firmly. "Are you out of your friggin' mind right now? Did you learn absolutely nothing after you damaged that cross? What -"

Before she could finish, she saw that he'd pulled up a small object wrapped in some kind of decaying white fabric. Already the rain was washing away much of the mud, and she could only watch as her father gently set the pile down.

He hesitated, as if he was nervous about what he might find, and then he pulled the fabric aside to reveal a small collection of surprisingly tiny bones.

"Where's the rest?" she stammered.

"This is all of her," he replied.

"That's not possible," she said. "Dad, why are we even doing this? We need to be getting off this island right now, and there's something I have to tell you about Mum. Dad, she -"

"There's something I have to tell *you*," he replied, interrupting her as he began to sort through the bones. "All those years ago, Jane Moore was brought to this island by a man named Jonathan Anderson. There's a reason why I always found that particular story so fascinating, Jacqui. It's because there's something you don't know about our family history." He picked up one particular bone in particular. "Jonathan Anderson was my direct ancestor. Our direct ancestor. He was something like my great-great-grandfather. Maybe there's another great or two in there. The point is, the man who did this to Jane Moore was part of our family."

"Okay," Jacqui replied, trying to make sense of everything he'd just told her, "that's clearly far from ideal, but it doesn't change the fact that we need to get out of here."

She waited for him to agree with her, but after a moment she saw the piece of bone he was holding. Although she wanted to tell him to ignore the skeleton, she was starting to realize that she could just about make out the bone's shape, and sure enough he then turned it around until she found herself looking at a small human skull.

"There were always rumors in the family about Jonathan Anderson," David said, looking up at her with fear in his eyes. "About what *really* happened on that day when he brought Jane Moore out to Saward Island. And I think..."

He looked down at the skull again, which had now been washed entirely clean by the rain.

"And I think," he added with a sense of dread in his voice, "that some of those rumors might have been true after all."

CHAPTER THIRTY-FOUR

1752...

JONATHAN ANDERSON HESITATED, BEFORE taking the knife from the loop on his belt and starting to make his way around until he was standing behind her. Although he'd considered plenty of different methods by which he might end Jane's life, he'd come to the conclusion that the best approach might be to simply slit her throat from ear to ear. Death would surely take just a few seconds, perhaps a minute or two at most, and he supposed that he didn't even have to watch. He could look away and wait for a few minutes before quickly checking that the whole thing was over, and then he would be able to leave the island forever.

Reaching around, Jane felt for his arm.

Quickly finding his wrist, she moved it up toward her throat as if encouraging him to get on with the task. All the fight had left her body and she and Jonathan were united in a common cause: to end the misery.

"Are you ready?" he asked, unable to rid his voice of a sense of true fear.

Silence.

"Are you sure?"

He waited, even though he knew the answer. As the seconds passed, he looked out across the island and told himself that he simply needed to end the woman's life. He glanced toward the heavens and offered a brief, silent prayer – for what, he wasn't quite sure, but he thought it was the right thing to do – and then finally he slashed the knife across the witch's throat.

As soon as he was finished, however, he realized that the job wasn't done. Looking down, he saw that he'd barely scratched the surface of her flesh, so he quickly reset, trying again with a little more force. Once more, however, he looked down and saw that he'd left little more than a faint red line, so he resolved to be far more powerful for what he hoped would be his third and final attempt.

Cutting a woman's throat, he was starting to learn, could be a difficult task. It was as if, on some deeper level than his conscious mind, part of him hesitated to apply the necessary pressure.

After taking a moment to pull himself together, he tried again to slice her open. This time he managed to cut her deeper on one side, yet somehow he still wasn't quite able to force the blade deep enough; he knew that he needed to feel the metal ripping through her flesh, perhaps catching on some ragged strands, and that the sensation would not be clean. He told himself to try yet again, but he could feel a growing sense of anger in his chest and finally he threw the knife aside before stepping back and letting out a grunt of rage.

"What the hell is wrong with me?" he snarled as he saw Jane still kneeling with her back to him, patiently waiting for her fate. "It's a simple enough task, to be sure. Other men kill all the time. Why can't I manage it?"

Jane remained in place, with her head bowed as wind blew across the island and rustled the long grass. A moment later a small rodent emerged from the its burrow, before turning and disappearing from view. Above, gulls called out as they circled the island.

Meanwhile the back of Jane's head seemed almost to be taunting Jonathan, and inquiring why he wasn't man enough to kill a poor defenseless woman.

"Are you protecting yourself?" he sneered, feeling as if the eyes of everyone back in Innisrach were somehow watching him and waiting for him to step up. "Is that it, huh? Are you somehow using your witchcraft to keep your throat uncut? Is that it?"

Realizing that his right hand was trembling, he tried to work out how else he might be able to dispatch the witch from the world. Although he'd never killed before, he'd never imagined that he would ever find the task difficult and he worried that everyone back on the mainland would laugh at him when they discovered that he was such a failure.

A moment later, as if wondering what was causing the delay, Jane turned her head slightly.

"It's you," Jonathan said after a moment. "That's the only possible explanation. You're using your powers to stop me. How am I, a simple and honest man, supposed to fight against such evil powers? Hopgood might know what to do, but I..."

Looking around, he spotted a rock on the ground. He stepped over and picked it up, and then he slowly turned to Jane and imagined himself bashing her head in and spilling her brain across the ground. Although he didn't like the idea of dealing her such a violent end, he knew that he at least had to find *some* way to kill her.

"What a task I have been given," he murmured. "And I, a good man..."

Stepping up behind her once more, he looked at her scalp and tried to pick the best spot for the first strike. He knew that he was unlikely to be able to finish her off with one blow, but he felt sure that no witch could ever save herself from brute force. He had to prove that his was a good and righteous soul.

Yet as the seconds passed, he began to realize that he could never possibly do such a thing. A moment later, clearly sensing that something was wrong, Jane turned to face him; reaching up, she felt his arm and moved her hand to his wrist, and then she felt the rock. At the same time, a very faint murmur came from behind her sealed lips, as if she had resorted to begging; her breath, forced through her nostrils, was ragged and harsh now.

"I can't do it," he complained. "I just -"

Before he could finish, she tried to pull his hand down – as if she hoped to use the rock to crack her own skull open. He instinctively resisted, even as she tried again and again, and after a moment he found himself having to pull back.

"This won't work," he told her. "Stop it! Let go of me!"

He threw the rock aside, and then he watched as Jane dropped down onto her hands and knees and began to crawl across the ground. She was reaching out, clearly trying to find the rock again, so Jonathan stepped past her and kicked several possible specimens aside. And then, as he watched her scrambling about in the dirt, he realized that he was actually starting to feel profoundly sorry for her.

For a few seconds, alone on that infernal little island, the two of them merely waited for some kind of divine intervention, for something – anything – that might end their shared misery.

"Stop that," he murmured, even though he doubted she could hear him. "Listen to me, this will do you no good."

Ignoring him, she began again to reach around in a desperate search for a rock. Finally locating one, she picked it up and began to bash it against the side of her head, although she was unable to muster sufficient strength.

"Stop it," Jonathan said again, unable to hide a sense of frustration. "Do you really believe that you can end your life in this manner?"

He waited for her to cast the rock aside; when she tried again to crack her own head open, he pulled the rock from her hand and threw it into the long grass, and then he grabbed Jane by the arms and pushed her down against the ground. To his surprise, he found that she was able to almost push him aside, so he used a knee to press down onto her chest and hold her in position.

"Why do you struggle so?" he sneered, just about managing to hold her in place. "What power compels you to act in this manner? Is Satan in your heart? That's what they said back in Innisrach, yet I see no sign of such evil myself. I'm not even sure that you're a witch after all, I fear you are perhaps merely a woman instead!"

For a moment he had to adjust his grip on her, trying in vain to make her settle – yet still she fought back with a ferocity that he had scarcely ever imagined could be possible. After a few more seconds, however, he felt her strength starting to fade and he realized that she was finally becoming subdued. She let out a few more angry kicks, although these seemed to be more out of frustration than any real attempt to get free, and then she fell still.

"Are you done now?" he asked, still slightly breathless as he waited in case she might try to surprise him with another effort. "You can kick like the best of them, can't you? That's a fine skill that -"

Before he could finish, she reached up and touched the side of his face, running her fingertips against his cheek as if feeling his stubble.

"What are you doing?" he continued cautiously, having never been touched by a woman in this manner before. The tenderness was new. "Is this some kind of trick or spell? Woman, are you trying to enchant me?"

He wanted to pull away, but something about her touch made him instead fall still and silent. As much as he knew that he had to finish the job that he'd tried to start, he also felt as if this poor wretched woman might have been misunderstood. He had heard Alistair Hopgood's pronouncements, and he'd heard the jeering of the crowd in Innisrach too, yet he had seen no evidence of Jane Moore's witchery with his own two eyes. And as she moved her fingertips to the edge of his mouth, he was shocked by her tenderness.

Staring at her face, he saw the thick black wires cutting through her flesh and he tried to imagine what she might have looked like before she had been bound in such a manner. Had she been beautiful?

And then, with no warning, he felt a surge of anger in his chest as he realized that she was attempting to get the better of him. He thought of the embarrassment he would surely feel if he returned to Innisrach and confessed that he'd been unable to complete the job, and he told himself that he had to find some way to kill her. First, though, he was going to teach her a lesson that would last for the rest of her miserable life.

***

The boat bobbed on the water as, around one hour later, Jonathan rowed away from the island. His face was stiff with anger, and a bloodied knife was near his foot; he'd cut his own palm, so that he could show the knife to any man who asked – and so that he could pretend that the deed had been done.

Looking back at Saward Island one last time, he saw Jane Moore standing at the edge of the rocks, seemingly listening to the sound of his oars as he departed.

"Rot and die there," he sneered, having convinced himself that nobody would ever learn her true fate. "It's better than you deserve. Murder would have been too quick for you anyway, and too merciful. This way, you shall know the misery of wasting away to nothing."

AMY CROSS

CHAPTER THIRTY-FIVE

NINE MONTHS LATER, A small brown rodent slowly began to emerge from a burrow on the south side of Saward Island. The creature hesitated, twitching its nose as it waited to make sure that there were no threats nearby, before scurrying over to the bones of a dead gull and started to search for scraps of meat.

Suddenly Jane Moore's hands reached down – with the swiftness she had learned during her time on the island – and she pulled the panicking animal up from the ground. Feeling it shaking as it tried to break free, she held the rodent up and quickly broke its neck, ending its suffering as quickly as she could manage. She had waited almost a whole hour for something to emerge from the burrow, and she had forced herself to remain entirely still and quiet for the whole time.

Although her eyes and mouth remained sewn tightly shut, the wire in her ears had been less successful and she had learned to use her hearing to hunt creatures on the island.

She was painfully thin now, yet she was still clinging to life and after a moment she began to tear the rodent apart, saving as much of its warm blood as possible and pouring the precious liquid through a small gap on one side of her mouth, where she had been able to tease the wire open. When she was done with that, she began to rip away some of the meat; whereas at first she had struggled with this task, after almost a year on the island she had become something of an expert.

She made sure to rip the shreds into smaller pieces that she was then just about able to poke through the solitary gap at the very edge of her mouth. Chewing was impossible, but by tilting her head in different directions she could eventually get the meat to the back of her throat so that it might finally be swallowed. That was another trick she'd learned during her time alone on the island.

As she ate, a few specks of blood dripped down onto her large, swollen and very pregnant belly.

***

Leaning back and letting out an agonized scream that filled the island's cold night air, Jane tried yet again to push. She had been in labor for several hours now, struggling to give birth alone, yet she felt as if the child was now somehow trapped in her body.

    Gripping the ground for purchase, she tried to adjust her position a little, only to find that nothing seemed to help. The child was almost out, yet something was keeping it trapped and she worried that she had made no progress for quite some time. Her strength was poor and she knew that her dwindling diet of rodents and gulls had left her woefully unprepared for this moment, but she also knew that she had to try.

    Many months earlier, when she'd first realized that Jonathan Anderson had left her with a child in her belly, she had tried – for that child's sake – to end her pregnancy and her life. She had never quite managed, however, and now as she leaned back against the cold grass she couldn't help but wonder whether she had merely condemned both herself and her child to a slow and agonizing death.

"You shouldn't have made me do that," she remembered Jonathan saying once he'd been finished with her. "It's your fault, you know. I wouldn't be surprised if you used a spell on me."

"What spell?" she'd wanted to reply – and she would have uttered exactly those words if only she had been able to open her mouth. "I have said it so many times before, and I shall repeat it until the end of my days. I am not a witch."

"I should kill you now," he'd told her. "You know that, don't you? I should cut your throat, and I wager that this time I'd get the job done properly."

He'd hesitated for a moment and she'd begun to hope that he might finally gained the courage required to finish her off. In those precious seconds, she had been ready to embrace death.

"Or I could just leave you here," he'd suggested. "Wouldn't that be better? The people of Innisrach are superstitious enough, it won't take much to scare them into leaving this place well alone, at least for as long as it takes you to die. And once the gulls and other animals have picked your bones clean, nobody will know what I did or did not do to you."

Just about able to hear him, she'd begun to crawl forward, hoping to beg for her death. Instead she'd heard him walking away, crossing the grass and making his way down the rocks, and in that moment she'd understood that he truly intended to abandon her on the island. Sheer terror had filled her heart as she'd stumbled to her feet, and now she recalled the awful sound of him rowing slowly away.

Each splash of the oars had sounded like another nail in her vast, invisible coffin.

Suddenly another burst of pain ripped through her body, pulling her away from those memories as she tried again to squeeze. This time she felt some movement, then a little more, and in an instant she felt the weight shift. After taking a moment to get her breath back, she sat up and reached down, and to her astonishment she felt a child on the grass between her legs, attached to her still by a thick cord. She felt a rush of hope, mixed with a desperate need to help this precious new life, as if in an instant she knew how it felt to be a mother.

And yet...

And yet she knew instantly that her worst fears had come true.

She thought back to the roughness of Jonathan Anderson's touch, and to the way he'd imposed his will upon her. She hadn't fought back, she hadn't even objected, yet now she realized that he must have always been planning to abandon her to such a lonely fate. He probably assumed that she was dead by now and he certainly would have no idea that she had become pregnant, yet she felt the rage and bitterness starting to slowly rise up through her body as she told herself that he was still entirely responsible for what had happened.

At least Alistair Hopgood had believed that he was doing the Lord's work. She hated him for his hypocrisy and lies, but she understood him.

Jonathan, meanwhile, had seemed so ordinary and unpretentious, like just another normal man, yet he'd shown himself to be capable of such cruelty.

She sat for a long time as wind, sweeping across the island and disturbing the long grass, seemed almost to mock the lack of a child's cry.

Finally Jane realized that she was going to have her revenge. She had no idea how or when, but she told herself that in this life or the next she was going to find both Jonathan and Mr. Hopgood and she was going to make them pay – not for her own suffering, which she could handle, but for everything they had done to her unborn child. And if they died before she was able to get to them, she was going to find their children or their children's children or anyone carrying their blood and she was going to rain her vengeance down upon them instead.

Reaching up, she tried to pull the wire from her eyes, but the pain was too much; she tried to do the same to the wire sealing her mouth shut, but here again she was unable to make any progress.

As her anger grew, so too did the darkness of the clouds above the island, as if the weather itself was starting to pick up on the rage and fury of this one desperate woman. She knew that her own death would not be a long time coming, not now that she had no reason to keep living; but she swore to herself that rather than seeing death as a hindrance, she was going to find some way to make it work to her advantage. Eventually someone would arrive on Saward Island, and she knew that she needed to be ready for that day, even if she had to wait long beyond her own mortal years.

Even if she had to wait until the end of time.

***

Twenty years later, Thomas Beaumont and Wilf Leland sat in their usual seats at the *Three Compasses* in Innisrach and looked down at the plans they'd sketched out on a piece of paper.

"That's where we'll do the best fishing,"

Wilf said, jabbing at one spot on the paper. "Right there. There's no doubt about it whatsoever. Haddock, cod, pollock... we'll have more than enough to sell."

"What about that island?" Thomas asked. "What's it called again? I'm talking about the one that most people pretend isn't even there."

"Saward Island," Wilf muttered, his voice already betraying a hint of concern. "I've heard plenty about the place. There's not a fisherman around here who'll go within sight of that island, they're far too scared of all the foolish stories that get told about it. But that's precisely the point, because it means that we have a crucial advantage. Because we're *not* superstitious idiots, we can make hay while the sun's shining and we'll be able to catch the fish that take refuge in those waters."

"I'm not sure that's such a good idea," Thomas replied, glancing around and seeing that one of the drunks in the corner appeared to be eavesdropping on their conversation. After a moment he turned to his friend again. "What if they're right? What if it's too dangerous to go anywhere near that island?"

"Not you too," Wilf said with a sigh. "If you don't want to be part of this venture, then nobody's forcing you. Just don't get angry with me when I'm rich and you're still scrabbling about in the dirt."

He hesitated, before holding out a hand.

"What's it to be?" he asked with a faint smile. "Are you in or are you out? Because if you're out, I need to know immediately so that I can find someone less superstitious to take your place."

Thomas hesitated, worrying that he might be about to make a dreadful mistake, before finally relenting and shaking Wilf's hand.

"Saward Island is going to make us very rich," Wilf said with a leering grin. "Richer than we can possibly imagine. Now, why don't we get another drink and celebrate our business plan?"

Hearing footsteps, they both turned to see that the drunk from the corner was slowly but surely stumbling toward them.

"Did I hear you right?" the man asked gruffly, slurring his words slightly. "I can't believe I did, but I'm sure I heard one of you mention Saward Island and something about a business proposal."

"It's none of your business," Wilf replied, looking the stranger up and down for a moment. "Go back to your corner. You're an old man, and we have no use for anyone who can't pull their weight."

"But is it true?" the stranger continued. "Are you really foolish enough to go anywhere near that place? Nobody has dared for two decades or more, everyone round these parts knows that the stories are true. I should have known that eventually some fools would decide to take matters into their own hands."

"Leave them be," the barman said firmly. "Jonathan, they haven't done anything wrong. Instead of harassing my new customers, why don't you go home and sober up? It's not good for you to be drinking every night. Eliza and the children will be waiting for you."

"You should listen to the fellow," Wilf chuckled, turning back to his beer. "No-one asked for your opinion. We're new to this area and perhaps it's time for someone to introduce a few fresh ideas. You'll all be thanking us when we bring fresh money to -"

Suddenly he let out a gasp and leaned forward, revealing the large knife that had been plunged into his back. Before anyone had a chance to react, Jonathan pulled the knife out and turned, swiftly slashing the throat of the other man with such force that blood immediately began to spray across the window. And then, before he could strike again, Jonathan was tackled from behind and dragged to the floor; holding him tight, the barman knocked the knife from his hand and kicked it away, and then he turned to look at the kitchen boy who'd run through to check on the commotion.

"Fetch Mr. Warner and Mr. Abbott!" he snarled. "Tell them that Jonathan Anderson has finally lost his mind, and that we've got two dead men here! Tell him to prepare the gallows!"

***

Many miles away, Jane Moore's bones lay partially hidden beneath the rocks, in the small space she'd found while searching for somewhere to die.

Nearby, her ghostly figure stood at the edge of the grass, looking out to sea and thinking of Innisrach. Over time, she had trained herself to reach out with her mind, to tease the edges of the village; she couldn't influence anything there, not from such a great distance, but she was just about able to sense certain changes. In that moment, she could tell that Jonathan Anderson was filled with greater madness and chaos than ever, but a few seconds later that sensation ended abruptly and she understood that he had finally died.

In which case, he had slipped away before she could get to him.

Tilting her head slightly, she told herself that she would simply have to go after his descendants, and their descendants too, and that her revenge would never be complete until the entire wretched bloodline had been wiped away for good. And as these latest plans began to form in her mind, she was almost able to ignore the sound of wind still rustling the long grass that grew all over the island.

Sometimes, just for a second or a two at a time, that rustling sound seemed to also contain the cry of a dead child.

CHAPTER THIRTY-SIX

Today...

THUNDER RUMBLED ABOVE AS Jacqui pulled Bod a little closer. The storm was still raging, but for a moment she was barely aware of the rain that had already drenched her clothes; instead she was staring down at the meager collection of bones as she tried to come to terms with the horror of Jane Moore's story.

"I don't blame her," she said finally.

"Jacqui," her father replied, "I -"

"I don't blame her for being angry," she continued. "Why did no-one come and check on her? Why did no-one care that she might have been left stranded out here? Why did they all just believe the word of that bastard who brought her to the island?"

"It was a long time ago," he pointed out. "Our generation can't be blamed for something that someone from our family did two hundred years ago."

"I know that," she told him, "but still, I get why she -"

Stopping herself at the last moment, she thought back yet again to the sight of her own mother falling from the top of the lighthouse.

"Someone should have fixed this a long time ago," she continued as fresh tears began to fill her eyes. "It shouldn't have been left this long. Someone should have found a way to put it all right before anyone else had to get hurt."

"Jacqui -"

"Before Mum had to get hurt," she sobbed, no longer able to hide her sorrow. After a moment she pulled Bod even closer, holding her tight. "She got Mum. I'm sorry, Dad, there was nothing we could do to stop it and now she's not coming home with us. The ghost got Mum, and I think maybe by doing that Mum was able to distract her for a while, but that won't last forever. We have to get off this island before -"

"Look!" Bod shouted, pointing past David.

At first Jacqui saw nothing, but after a few seconds she realized that the dead lighthouse keeper and his wife were slowly emerging from the darkness and approaching the grave.

"That's William Miller and his wife," her father said, taking a step back. "It has to be."

"I guessed," Jacqui replied, before turning to see several more ghostly figured stepping into view, "but who are *they*?"

All around them, ghosts were starting to gather. Most were men, and they were wearing clothing in a variety of styles. Turning to look in every direction, Jacqui couldn't help but feel that these ghosts appeared to be from different eras, yet they all seemed drawn to the grave.

"It's the ghosts of all the people who died because of this island," David said, trying to make sense of the chaos. "It must be. So many boats hit the rocks here before the lighthouse was built, and I'm pretty sure that these are all the souls that were lost over the years. Eventually the lighthouse wasn't needed, they could rely on modern navigation tools, but before that boats were lost here all the time. All these people died because Jane Moore was left to die here. Isn't that amazing? The ripple effect from the decision to persecute Jane caused all this horror."

"They don't look too impressed," Jacqui pointed out as Bod clung to her. "Dad, what do they want?"

"I don't know," he replied, before hesitating for a moment. Suddenly he dropped to his knees and began to rebury the child's remains. "We need to put things back how we found them, and then we need to get to the boat. There'll be time to figure this out later, but right now I want to get far away from Saward Island and never set foot on the place again."

He took a moment to cover the bones with mud, before getting to his feet and grabbing Jacqui's hand, forcing her and Bod to follow him up the narrow slope.

"This way!" he hissed. "Hurry!"

"What about Mum?" Bod cried.

"Mum's going to be fine," Jacqui told her, figuring that she could explain later. "Mum's going to... catch up to us on the mainland."

"But -"

"Move!" she added, slipping past the gathered ghosts, relieved that so far they appeared to pose no threat. "We'll talk about it later, Bod. Right now we just have to get away from here as fast as possible."

***

"It's just down here," David said a short while later as they reached the top of the rocks that led down to the wooden dock. "We just need to -"

Stopping suddenly, he stared at the stormy sea. After a few seconds Jacqui and Bod joined him, and together the three of them look at the boat – or, rather, at what remained of the boat, which was now little more than a collection of debris.

"What happened?" Jacqui stammered. "Dad... that's not *our* boat, is it?"

"It must have been smashed to pieces on the rocks," he replied, "or against the dock or..."

His voice trailed off as he contemplated the possibility that the ghostly figure of Jane Moore might have something to do with the destruction. He knew that the storm was bad, and in the back of his mind he'd worried about potential damage to the boat, but he'd never even considered the possibility that the entire vessel might have been destroyed. Now, as he saw part of the hull resting on the rocks, he felt for a few seconds as if he was truly all out of ideas.

"Dad?" Jacqui said cautiously. "What are we going to do now?"

Turning to her, he realized that he needed to come up with an answer.

"Dad?" she said again. "What are we going to do? How are we going to get off the island?"

In that moment he saw the terrified faces of his daughters and he understood that they were utterly relying on him to keep them safe. Rain was still pouring down and wind was howling across the island, and when he looked out across the darkness he thought of all the ghosts waiting in the darkness;

sure, Jane Moore hadn't appeared for a while, but he knew with absolute certainty that she was still around somewhere.

He also knew that he had to find his wife, even if the only task left was to collect her body and take it home.

A crack of lightning briefly flashed across the sky, illuminating the island and revealing the scores of ghostly figures still dotted all around.

"Dad?" Jacqui continued, sounding just that little bit more desperate now. "What are we going to do?"

"Are we stuck, Dad?" Bod added. "Are we going to die here?"

"No," he replied, looking down at her. "No, we're not going to die here. Are you crazy? Haven't I taught you that no matter how bad things look, there's always a way forward?"

"What's the way forward now, Dad?" Jacqui asked. "Without a boat, there's no way we can get off the island. You're not going to suggest that we try to swim to safety, are you?"

"Of course I'm not," he told her, and now he was starting to form the bare bones of a plan in his mind. "That'd be suicide, but we're three intelligent, resourceful human beings and we're not done yet."

"Then what -"

"We have to go back to the lighthouse."

"*Back* to the lighthouse?" Jacqui replied.

"We can't go back to the lighthouse, that's... that's insane."

"No, it's not insane," he replied as the plan became more solid with each passing second. "It's not insane at all, because there's stuff at the lighthouse that we can use."

"Use? What are you planning to do, MacGyver our way out of this?"

"There's wood in there," he continued, "and rope, and that should be enough for us to build a simple raft. The storm can't last forever, by the time I've finished working hopefully the sea will be a little calmer. I don't know what your mum did, but it's clear that she's managed to keep Jane Moore distracted for a while."

"Mum's gone," Jacqui said, and now her voice was trembling with fear as she thought back yet again to the sight of her mother falling from the top of the lighthouse. "She's not coming back."

"She wouldn't want us to give up," he said firmly. "If we roll over and accept our fates, everything she did was for nothing. She bought us time to find another way off this island, and we're going to use that time."

"What about all those other ghosts?"

"I don't think they're on her side," he replied, grabbing Jacqui and Bod by the hands and starting to lead them back across the island. "The Millers aren't, either. They never have been.

William Miller was trying to get Jane to leave him alone, but she just killed him and his wife anyway. The ghosts aren't helping her, they're trapped here just like we are. The only difference is that at least we've still got a chance to escape."

CHAPTER THIRTY-SEVEN

STANDING IN THE LIGHTHOUSE'S doorway, Jacqui looked out through the rain and saw the darkness around the side of the building. Although she couldn't see anything in that moment, she knew that her mother's corpse was somewhere in that darkness, and that a flash of lightning would allow her to see the crumpled mess.

"Jacqui?"

Turning, she saw that Bod had walked over to join her. A little way back, their father was still furiously joining the spare crosses together with rope, and slowly the raft was taking shape.

"Let's look that way," Jacqui replied, shifting Bod around so that she wouldn't accidentally see their mother if the lightning returned.

"Where's Mum?" Bod asked cautiously, as if she was scared of the answer she might receive.

"We'll talk about it later."

"She's not coming with us, is she?"

"We'll talk about it later."

"Did she know she wasn't going to be able to come with us?"

Lightning flashed high above the lighthouse, and Jacqui instinctively turned to look over at the spot where her mother's body had landed; to her relief, the lightning had already faded before she had any chance to witness the grisly sight.

"I think so," she whispered, staring once more into the darkness. "I think she knew exactly what she was doing."

"Does that mean she was brave?"

"She was the bravest person in the whole world," Jacqui continued, blinking and seeing her mother fall again. In truth, every time she blinked now, the effect was like a bolt of pitch black lightning in her mind, bringing that awful vision back to haunt her again. "She did what she did because... she figured it was the only way the rest of us had any chance to get away."

Inside the lighthouse, her father was still working on the raft.

"Wasn't there another way?" Bod asked.

Looking down at her, Jacqui realized that while she hadn't told her sister exactly what had happened, somehow Bod had put all the pieces together. In that moment she understood that perhaps Bod was a little smarter and a little more mature than she'd recognized before; she was capable of linking different clues together and coming up with the right answer, no matter how awful that answer might be.

"I guess not," she said softly. "She -"

Another flash of lightning filled the scene, and she just had time to spot the crumpled shape on the ground; while the shape wasn't recognizably human from a distance, she knew that her mother's mangled body was out there, and she quickly thought back to the warning she'd given Bod just a few hours earlier.

"You'd be dead by now if I hadn't caught you," she remembered saying angrily. "You'd have fallen a hundred meters, and do you know what would have happened when you hit the bottom? You'd probably have exploded. That's what happens to bodies when they fall that far. They burst open when they hit the ground, and there's no surviving that! There's zero chance, Bod! You've had had two or three seconds of falling, watching the ground coming toward you, and then you'd have been splattered everywhere!"

A shudder ran though her bones, and she wondered why she couldn't stop imagining her mother's final moments over and over again. She thought back to the sight of her up at the top of the lighthouse, with the ghostly face of Jane Moore somehow twisting its way out of Vanessa's features, and she wondered how much her mother had even known of that fatal plunge.

"Nearly done!" David called out breathlessly from inside. "Just give me a couple more minutes!"

Pulling Bod closer, Jacqui felt a sudden need to hold her tight – and protect her.

"You don't have to cuddle me," Bod said, looking up at her. "I'm not that scared."

"Yes you are," Jacqui replied, "and so am -"

Before she could finish, another flash of lightning split across the sky, accompanied by a rush of thunder, and Jacqui once again saw her mother's body on the ground. This time, however, something was different; darkness had already returned but in that fraction of a second she'd seen something moving, almost as if her mother's corpse had been somehow rearranging itself.

"Hey Bod," she said cautiously, "do you still have Mum's phone?"

"Yes, but -"

"Give it to me."

Bod hesitated, before passing the phone into her hand.

"Now turn around," Jacqui said, grabbing her sister's shoulders and forcing her to look back into the lighthouse. "Whatever you do," she continued, as another flash briefly illuminated the scene, "don't turn back around until I tell you to, okay?"

"Why not?"

"Bod, I swear, just do what you're told for once."

She hesitated, and then she looked back out into the darkness. Her heart was racing now and she told herself that she had to be wrong, but at the same time she knew she needed to be sure. What if, by some miracle, her mother was somehow still alive? Stepping out into the rain, she fumbled to active the flashlight app on the phone, while keeping the device mostly sheltered from the rain by holding one hand over its screen; she edged closer and closer to the spot where she knew her mother had landed, and she told herself that any sane person would turn around already, but she felt herself drawn forward until finally her right foot nudged against something on the ground.

As soon as she felt the object budge slightly, she somehow knew that it was a human body.

"I'm sorry, Mum," she whispered in the rain, "I don't want to look at you right now, but I saw something move and... I have to know. You can't..."

She waited for a few seconds.

"You're not alive, are you?" she continued, feeling a flicker of hope in her chest – but also a hint of dread. "Are you in pain? Did you somehow survive the fall?"

She took a deep breath, desperately trying to think of some excuse to just go back and *not* look, but slowly she turned the phone around until its cold electric glow bathed the body in a buzzing light. In that moment she saw that her words of warning to Bod had been partially correct; Vanessa's corpse had landed with its limbs broken and part of the shoulder torn away, although persistent rain appeared to have washed off most of the blood.

Tilting her head slightly, Jacqui struggled for a few seconds to spot a face, until suddenly the mash of conflicting flesh suddenly resolved in her eyes and she saw her mother's features. One of Vanessa's eyes was open and one was closed, and her mouth was partly agape as if the impact of the landing had forced one last burst of air from her lungs and one last scream from her lips.

Her left hand, meanwhile, was sticking up slightly with the fingers curled, and rainwater was gathering in the palm and swilling off either side.

As she leaned down and tilted the phone again, Jacqui saw that the other side of her mother's face had been crushed, with the cheek having been completely shattered. She told herself that she'd seen enough now, that she could turn away, but she felt compelled to keep looking – and now she began to worry that there was something very wrong with her, that only a complete freak would actually stand in the rain inspecting the broken corpse of her own mother, except...

Except in that last flash of lightning she'd spotted something moving, something stirring, and she worried that even in death her mother wasn't being left in peace.

"Jacqui!" David shouted suddenly from the lighthouse. "It's ready! Let's go!"

"Just a moment," she replied, still watching her mother's dead face. "I think -"

Letting out a sudden gasp, Vanessa turned and looked straight up. Jacqui instinctively pulled back, almost dropping the phone in the process, and she could only watch in horror as her mother's smashed and broken body tried slowly to get to its feet. The arms reached out in opposite directions, attempting to grip the grass, but already – even over the sound of so much rain – the shattered bones could be heard grinding and cutting against other. No longer fit to stand, the body was still trying to force itself up, and a moment later the face turned slightly and began to bulge, finally allowing the sewn features of Jane Moore to start breaking through as the ghostly figure tried over and over again to take possession of the destroyed body.

"Leave her alone!" Jacqui screamed. "Get out of her!"

The body twisted first one way and then the

other, before finally crumpling back down again. Jane Moore's features were still just about visible, but now she was slowly starting to pull herself clear of the bloodied wreckage, as if she'd understood that Vanessa's body was no longer going to be of any use to her.

"Jacqui!" David yelled. "Run!"

"I hate you," Jacqui sneered at the ghost. "I don't know how, but once we get out of here, I'm gonna find a way to come back and make you pay! If you think we're just going to run away and hide and try to forget you, you're wrong. I'm going to -"

In that moment the ghostly face tried to scream, succeeding only in ripping the wire partly out of its lips. Horrified, Jacqui took another step back and then – realizing that she could hear both her father and her sister calling her name – she turned and scrambled away through the mud.

***

"It's still choppy but I think the storm's calming down a little," David said as he finally finished lugging the raft down to the edge of the rocks. "You're going to have to hold on tight, and you're going to have to row as soon as you get a chance."

"Won't we just get washed back onto the island?" Jacqui asked.

"I think this should work," he replied,

handing her the oars he'd hastily tied together. "It's the only chance we've got."

Looking down at the raft, Jacqui saw that it was little more than a set of crosses bound tightly together, with a few other pieces of wood added in an attempt to provide some more structure. The whole thing seemed incredibly flimsy, yet as she turned to look out to sea she realized that her father was right; the storm certainly appeared to be calming down a little, and there had been no more thunder or lightning for a few minutes now.

"We don't have any time to waste," David continued, placing the raft in the water. "Get on."

"I need to tell you about Mum," she replied, turning to him as Bod clambered onto the raft and grabbed the post in the middle. "She -"

"I know," he said firmly.

"No, Dad, you don't know everything," she replied. "Mum died to save us. She threw herself off the lighthouse while that ghost was in her, and that's how she gave us a chance to escape. I think it's taken Jane Moore a while to break back out of her body."

"I figured that part out," he insisted.

"But it's dragging itself out of her bones now," she continued as tears filled her eyes. "It's relentless and -"

Before she could finish, she heard the sound of a baby crying in the distance. Turning, she looked out into the darkness, but the sound was faint and seemed almost to be drifting in and out of earshot.

"Do you hear that?" she whispered. "Is it real?"

"Take this," he replied, thrusting the flare gun into her hands. "As soon as you're far enough from the shore, wait for any sign that someone might be near enough to see you and then fire this thing into the air. Do you understand?"

"Of course," she said, climbing onto the raft and joining her sister in the middle, then turning to him. "But you're coming with us, right?"

"The raft won't hold three people," he told her. "I'm sorry, Jacqui, but it just won't. Not reliably, at least. You'll have a much better chance of success if it's just the two of you."

"We're not leaving you behind!" she snapped angrily. "Dad -"

"I'm sorry," he replied, pushing the raft away from the rocks and then climbing a little way back up. "Now row!" he yelled. "Jacqui, you have to get away from here! I'll be fine, I can look after myself, and when you get to the mainland send someone to pick me up!"

"Dad, you have to come with us!" she shouted, struggling to be heard now over the crashing rain as the raft lurched and almost tipped in the rough sea. "We can't leave you here!"

"Remember to use the flare gun when you get a chance!" he shouted. "But don't waste it too soon. Jacqui, I'm relying on you to keep your head! Remember -"

"She's behind you!" she screamed, suddenly filled with fear as she saw the spectral figure of Jane Moore in the darkness directly behind her father. "Dad! She's right there!"

The raft tipped again, turning on the rough waves. Momentarily losing sight of the mainland, Jacqui turned to try to spot her father again. She held up the phone, hoping against hope that its light might help, but instead she saw only darkness. After a few seconds she was just about able to make out the shore again, but there was no sign of her father on the rocks now.

"Where is he?" Bod whimpered. "Jacqui? Where did he go?"

"He'll be fine," she replied, pulling her sister closer as they both continued to hug the central post tightly. Beneath them the raft lurched again, carried further and further away from the island by the fierce waves. "Hold on tight, Bod," she continued as the island faded into the distant darkness and the storm continued to fade. "It's going to be okay. Don't be scared. Everything's going to be fine."

CHAPTER THIRTY-EIGHT

A COUPLE OF HOURS later, with the storm having passed remarkably quickly and the first rays of morning sun starting to spread across the sky, Jacqui continued to look all around in the hope that she might spot the mainland.

"I don't see anything," she whispered, trying to keep from panicking. "The sun's over there, which means that way must be east, but..."

She turned and looked in the other direction, but saw saw only water spreading to the horizon.

"Does that mean we got blown the wrong way?" she asked, thinking out loud as she desperately tried to find some cause for optimism. "I can't quite work it out. I guess... it's a miracle we got this far. It'd be another miracle if we just happened to be blown in the right direction."

Hearing a gasping sound, she turned to see that Bod was shivering wildly.

"Hey, it's going to be okay," she continued, inching her way around the post and reaching out to put a hand on her sister's shoulder. "I promise. Someone's going to find us. There'll be... fishing boats and stuff like that, there'll be loads of them out here. Just wait and see."

"Is Dad going to be okay?"

"Yes," she lied, thinking back to the sight of him on the shore with Jane Moore's ghost, and then to the sight of the empty shore with no sign of either of them. "Dad knows what he's doing. He's really smart and... I bet there was a part two to his plan. I bet there was a part about saving himself too. It was probably some totally convoluted plan that only Dad could pull off."

She waited for another question, but Bod was shivering too much to speak and now her teeth were starting to chatter. Reaching down, Jacqui moved some hair from across the girl's face, and in that moment she realized that her sister was starting to look strangely pale.

"Hey, stay awake," she added. "Do you hear me, Bod?"

"I'm so sleepy," Bod replied, already starting to close her eyes.

"No!" she said firmly, shaking her gently and managing to force her eyes open again. "This is really important, Bod. I need you to -"

Suddenly a slightly larger wave caught the raft, causing the entire structure to lurch and creak. Hearing a bumping sound, Jacqui turned just in time to see the flare gun sliding toward the edge. She reached out and grabbed it at the last second, saving it from the water, and then she stared at the trigger for a moment.

"Should I fire it now?" she asked. "I don't know how far away it can be seen. I don't know if it just fires once, or if I can fire it several times. I don't know how it works at all. Why didn't Dad tell me? Why didn't he teach me to use this thing properly?"

Feeling the anger rising through her chest, she tried to stay calm. Instead, however, she felt fury starting to fill her mind, and finally she slammed the flare gun down with such force that she immediately worried she might have broken it.

"Why didn't he just come with us?" she snapped. "Hell, why did he take us out on that stupid boat in the first place? This is all his fault! Do you realize that, Bod? If he hadn't been so determined to show off and take us all on some dumb boat trip, we'd be on dry land right now and we'd never even have heard of Saward Island or that stupid lighthouse, and Mum would still be alive and Dad would be here and I'd still be angry with him but at least it'd be for something else and I wouldn't be scared that he's -"

Stopping herself just in time, she turned to see that Bod's eyes were closed again.

"No no no!" she gasped, shaking her harder this time and just about managing to wake her up. "Bod, this is the most important thing I've ever told you. You really have to stay awake for me. Do you promise you can do that?"

"I don't know," Bod whispered, barely managing to keep her eyes open. "I'm *so* tired, Jacqui. Why can't I just sleep for a few minutes?"

"Because you'll..."

Holding back, Jacqui realized that she had to be smarter.

"Because I'll be lonely," she added cautiously. "You don't want me to be lonely, do you? You don't want me to be all alone and... the only one of us left. Do you?"

"No," Bod murmured.

"So don't go anywhere," Jacqui continued, sniffing back tears. "Please, Bod. If you can't do it for yourself, then do it for me. I'm begging you, okay? There, I admitted it. I need you."

"I'll try," Bod said, before furrowing her brow. "Did you see that?"

"What?"

Turning, Jacqui instantly felt a burst of hope in her heart, although she saw absolutely no sign of any land on the horizon.

"I thought I saw something moving," Bod said softly.

"Where?" She continued to watch the horizon for a few more seconds. "I don't see anything out there, Bod."

"Not out there," Bod replied. "Here. On the raft."

"What the hell are you talking about now?"

"There's someone else on the raft."

"Huh?"

Turning to her sister, Jacqui tried to make sense of this latest wild claim, but after a moment she realized that she too was somehow sensing a presence nearby. The sun was edging a little higher now, almost clearing the horizon as she slowly turned and looked around the raft. For a few seconds everything seemed strangely calm, almost peaceful, yet Jacqui was already starting to feel as if someone else was staring back at her.

"The storm passed really quickly, didn't it?" she whispered, once again thinking out loud as she tried to make sense of the situation. "Almost too quickly. Almost too conveniently."

"She died here on this island," she remembered her mother telling her, "and she's been trapped ever since. She can only walk on the island, but she yearns to leave and get revenge on the people who did this to her."

The raft bobbed a little more for a moment,

causing the wooden crosses to strain against the ropes.

"She can only walk on the island," Jacqui said, once again repeating the words her mother had used.

The crosses creaked and strained again.

"But where did these come from?" she continued, reaching down and touching the crosses. "If that Miller guy made them, where did he get the wood? If the wood came from the island, then doesn't that mean that the crosses are *part* of it all? And then if the crosses were used to make the raft, then doesn't that mean that the raft is also part of the island?"

"What do you mean?" Bod asked wearily, sitting up a little.

"I mean that she might have been able to reach the raft," she explained, "and then the storm passed, and the storm started pretty suddenly too, so maybe she had something to do with that to begin with."

"How could someone make a storm happen?" Bod replied.

"She's a dead witch, she can probably do a lot of crazy shit!" Jacqui pointed out. "That's what they accused her of being, at least. They said she was a witch, so what if... what if they were right? We just assumed she wasn't, because we assumed all those people back then were a bunch of reactionary misogynistic assholes, but what if they were right about one thing? What if Jane Moore really was..."

As her voice trailed off, she tried to think of some other explanation. Watching the other side of the raft, however, she began to wonder whether she could just about make out a figure in the morning light. She instinctively began to hold the flare gun up, while wondering exactly what a ghost would look like in the glow of morning. She swallowed hard and told herself that most likely she was wrong, that she was just imagining things, but very slowly she began to make out a figure – and she saw that this figure's eyes and mouth had been sewn shut.

"Jacqui, she's here!" Bod shouted.

Before she had a chance to stop herself, Jacqui pulled back and aimed the flare gun. She wanted to believe that she was wrong, that there was no way Jane Moore's ghost could possibly have joined them on the raft, but as the seconds passed the image only became stronger. Finally, as Bod yelled again and again for her to do something – and as she realized that she had no idea what else she *could* do – Jacqui instinctively pulled the trigger and fired a flare straight at the center of the raft.

A huge blast of light hit the post, knocking the raft heavily to one side and almost throwing both girls into the sea. They managed to hold on, but now the ropes were burning and already the raft had begun to fall apart. Clinging to one of the crosses as it separated from the rest, Jacqui showed Bod how to do the same, and they both began to paddle furiously away from the rest of the disintegrating raft as the flare gun's canister continued to burn brightly. For a fraction of a second the ghostly figure could be seen sinking beneath the waves.

"Is she gone?" Bod gasped as the raft broke up. "She's gone, isn't it?"

"I see a boat," Jacqui replied, spotting the tiniest dot on the horizon and immediately waving. "They might spot the flare. Bod, wave at them! They might be our only chance!"

CHAPTER THIRTY-NINE

"I'VE SPOKEN TO THE grandparents," Detective Scott said a few hours later, as he stood in the bar at the *Three Compasses* in Innisrach, "and they're going to get the first plane they can back to the country. They're in Canada right now on a holiday, so it's going to take them a day or two."

"What are you going to do with them in the meantime?" Shirley asked, looking past him and spotting Jacqui and Bod sitting shivering in blankets in the far corner.

"Ordinarily I'd take them to one of the temporary homes down south," Scott explained, "but that's not going to be possible right now. The storm did some real damage to the bridges round here and it's going to be a while before anyone can get out of Innisrach. That's why I was going to ask you... I spoke to my bosses back in Aberdeen and they told me the best option is to try to find rooms here for the night."

"For you *and* the girls?"

He nodded.

"We can put you up," she told him, "and we can feed you too, but... don't they need medical attention?"

"They don't have any obvious injuries, and I don't think they're going to get hypothermia." He looked over his shoulder and watched them for a moment. "If it's just one night, they should be okay, but obviously tomorrow I'll hopefully be able to get them to a hospital. I'm also going to have to arrange to get out to that island at some point and see what really happened."

"I heard they were talking about ghosts," Shirley told him. "One of the boys from the fishing boat that picked them up... he said the older girl in particular couldn't stop yelling about a ghost on Saward Island. Just when I thought people had finally stopped going on about that place, it has to rear its ugly head again."

"I'm not from round these parts," Scott replied, "so I don't know anything about any local superstitions. All I can tell you is that in my line of work we don't give much credence to talk of ghosts or haunted islands. I don't know what happened out on that island, but I'm going to get to the bottom of it and when I do, I'm fairly certain that there's going to be a perfectly rational explanation." He watched the girls for a few seconds. "I've got to admit, though, I'm a little out of my comfort zone in one department. These kids need to see a shrink, and someone who's generally more... sensitive than I am."

"I'm sure you'll do fine," she replied.

"It's just bad luck for all concerned that I was in the area this morning," he said with a sigh, turning to her again. "Now I'm trapped here working the type of case I usually run a mile from. I guess I just really don't know how to talk to children."

"Talk to them like they're ordinary people," she advised him. "Talk to them like they're two young women who just lost their parents. Kids are smarter than most adults realize. Take it from me, they already know how bad things are. Don't try to convince them that they aren't living through a tragedy."

***

"So this is the room that the nice lady downstairs picked for you guys," Scott said a few minutes later, opening the door and stepping inside. "It's much nicer than the one I'm in."

Turning, he saw Jacqui and Bod following

close behind, still holding hands. Although he felt extremely sorry for them, he also knew that he was absolutely the last person in the entire department who would ordinarily be chosen to deal with this type of case. *Cyberdan* was the nickname some of his colleagues often used for him, due to his general inability to deal with any kind of display of emotions, and over the years he'd given up trying to fight back against that notion. If anything, he'd leaned into the stereotype a little too heavily.

"You've got a single bed each," he added, "so that's pretty cool."

He watched as they made their way together across the room.

"I'll level with you," he continued. "Normally a specialist or two would have arrived to talk to you both. He or she would be someone who knows all the right things to say. As you might have noticed, my skills are more to do with solving cases rather than dealing with victims. Just as soon as the roads and bridges are clear, some people'll show up who'll make you feel a lot better."

"Are all the roads and bridges really out of action?" Jacqui asked, turning to him. "Is there no way in or out of the village?"

"Not unless you want to take another boat," he replied, before wincing. "Sorry, I didn't mean that to sound quite so bad. But the point is, I'm sure everything'll be better tonight, or by tomorrow at the latest, and your grandparents are on their way back to the country as we speak."

He paused, wondering what to say next – and even whether he needed to say anything at all.

"Would you like me to leave you alone for a few minutes?" he asked, praying that they'd like that idea as he stepped back out of the room. "I'll be downstairs when you're ready, and we can see what kind of food this place serves. It's been here for hundreds of years so you'd think that they should know how to rustle up a decent burger, right? I don't now about you, but when I'm in a pub, I get these cravings for a good juicy burger. And since when did any pub *not* do burgers? Am I right?"

He waited for one of them to respond, but he quickly realized that they seemed to be in a state of shock. Although he'd so far avoided grilling them too much about their experience, he was now starting to think that he should just leave them alone entirely and wait for them to ask him for help. Deep down, he felt fairly sure that he was getting the whole situation extremely wrong, but he also knew that he – a man in his early thirties – really needed to be careful when dealing with two extremely traumatized young girls.

For now, he was simply going to try to keep them safe until someone more appropriate arrived to deal with them.

"Door open or shut?" he asked.

He waited for a reply before realizing that shut would probably be better.

"I'll see you downstairs, then," he added. "Whenever you're ready."

Once he'd pulled the door shut and left, Jacqui and Bod stood alone in silence for a moment. Finally Jacqui made her way to the window and peered out at the harbor area, and for a few seconds she watched some fishermen unloading their catch. Several boats were bobbing up and down in the water, attached by ropes to the harbors long wall. There was something strangely serene about the world of Innisrach, but she couldn't help thinking back just a couple of days to the afternoon she and her sister had spent in the village with their parents.

"That cop's so awkward," she said finally, turning to Bod. "I actually feel bad for him."

Bod simply continued to stare at one of the beds, almost as if she hadn't heard her sister's words at all.

"I think he just doesn't know how to talk to us at all," Jacqui continued. "For his sake, I hope someone else turns up soon. I hate seeing someone so uncomfortable."

Again she waited for an answer, but her sister had barely said a word ever since they'd been rescued by the fishing boat.

"It's going to be okay, Bod," she added. "I mean, not okay exactly... Mum and Dad are still..."

Her voice trailed off. Deep down, she knew her father had stood no chance alone on the island with Jane Moore's ghost.

"We've got each other," she explained, "and we'll be fine just so long as we stick together. You understand that, Bod, don't you? We'll be fine as long as we work as a team. Granny and Gramps'll be here tomorrow. Did you hear him say that? It's just bad luck that the storm cut this stupid little village off from the rest of the world, otherwise I'm sure we'd be out of here by now."

Realizing that her sister seemed almost catatonic, she walked over and put a hand on the side of her arm.

"Bod, are you even hearing a word I've been saying to you?" she asked. "I know it's hard, but please try not to replay everything that happened in your mind. That's never going to help, it'll only make you feel worse. Mum and Dad would want us to just stay strong and tell everyone exactly what happened, so that maybe we can at least stop it happening to anyone else. Doesn't that sound like a good idea?"

"I don't know," Bod said softly, not even managing to look up at her.

"Let's take it one day at a time," Jacqui continued, giving her arm a gentle squeeze that she hoped might make her feel better. "And one night at a time too. We just have to get through tonight and then tomorrow we'll be able to leave Innisrach. I don't know about you, but I'm pretty sure that I'll feel better once we're out of here. Don't you agree?"

"Maybe," Bod whispered.

"You'll see," Jacqui said firmly, hoping against hope that soon they'd both be able to start dealing with the horror they'd experienced – and determined to stay strong, if only for her sister's sake. "Tomorrow everything's going to start feeling better."

CHAPTER FORTY

"MUM, NO!" SHE SCREAMED, lunging forward just as her mother disappeared from the top of the lighthouse.

Stumbling, she bumped against the railing and then stopped to look down. As rain fell all around her in the darkness, she could only watch as Vanessa's body fell into the void, followed a moment later by the sound of a crunching thud far below.

"Mum!" she sobbed, realizing that she'd been just a fraction of a second too late.

And then, hearing a clicking sound, she turned to see the ghostly figure of Jane Moore standing right behind her. In that instant she saw the thick black wires that had been sewn into the woman's eyeballs, and more wires holding her mouth shut; every last inch of the dead woman's mottled and pale flesh seemed to be so much clearer, and for a few seconds Jacqui could only stare at the horrific sight until – finally – Jane stepped forward and pushed her in the chest.

Before she could save herself, Jacqui tumbled back into the void, falling just like her mother had fallen, twisting in the air and looking down to see the ground racing up toward her. She blinked, preparing herself for the impact, and then she closed her eyes as -

***

"No!"

Sitting up suddenly, drenched in sweat, Jacqui stared across the pitch black bedroom and tried to remember where she was and how she'd ended up there. She could see a pair of curtains swaying in a gentle breeze, but several more seconds passed before she heard the sound of water lapping against the harbor wall and she realized that she was in Innisrach, and that all the awful events on Saward Island had really taken place.

Wiping sweat from her brow, she thought back to the nightmare in which she'd seen her mother falling yet again – and then she'd fallen too. The dream had seemed so real, and she felt sure that she'd almost smashed straight into the ground before waking up. She'd heard so many times that if someone died in their dreams, they died in real life, and as she climbed out of bed and headed to the bathroom she wondered whether she'd just had a close call.

At least, she figured, she'd managed to fall asleep at last. She glanced over at the other bed as she reached the bathroom door, and then she froze as she saw that the covers had been pulled aside and there was no sign of her sister.

"Bod?" she said cautiously, before checking the bathroom and then turning to see that the door to the room had been left slightly ajar. "Bod, where are you?"

***

As soon as she stepped out from the back door of the *Three Compasses*, she saw her. Bod was standing in the middle of the narrow cobbled street, caught in a patch of moonlight and seemingly staring out toward the harbor.

"Bod?" Jacqui said again. "Hey, it's cold out here. Come back inside."

She waited, but Bod showed no sign of a response. Looking over her shoulder, Jacqui saw that the streets of the little fishing village were deserted. When she turned to her sister again, however, she couldn't help wondering whether something was really wrong. Bod had never shown a tendency to sleepwalk before, but she'd been quiet all day – ever since they'd been picked up from the raft, in fact – and deep down Jacqui had begun to worry that the girl was in some kind of state of denial.

"I'm sure a proper psychologist will arrive tomorrow," the hopelessly-out-of-his-depth and clearly-extremely-uncomfortable-around-young-girls cop had said during the previous evening. "Someone who knows how to... handle this sort of thing."

She'd hoped at the time that the guy was right, and now she realized more than ever that she and her sister both needed to talk to a professional about what they'd experienced on the island. Either that, or they needed to hurry up and develop serious psychiatric problems, although she still had some vague hope of emerging from the situation with at least a few shreds of her sanity.

"Bod, I'm sorry I fell asleep," she continued. "I didn't think I would, I thought I'd be up all night reliving everything that happened but -"

Before she could finish, Bod set off again, walking away along the street.

"Bod, where are you going?" Jacqui called out, hurrying after her and putting a hand on her shoulder, then stepping around so that she could look into her eyes. "Bod, you're being creepy and -"

In that moment she gasped and pulled back as she saw Bod's calm eyes staring back up at her. Something about those eyes, however, struck her as being distinctly un-Bodlike, and she felt a shiver run through her bones as she remembered the sight of Jane Moore's ghostly figure on the raft. She'd assumed that they'd left the ghost far behind, but now – as she continued to look down at her sister's strangely blank face – she began to worry that things weren't quite that simple.

"Bod," she said cautiously, "are you okay in there? Can you hear me, Bod?"

She waited, but after a moment her sister simply stepped around her and began to once again walk away. Jacqui turned and watched her for a few seconds, but already her fears were starting to crystallize and she knew she had to be sure.

"Jane Moore, is that you?" she called out.

Bod stopped again, still looking toward the harbor.

"*Is* it you?" Jacqui continued. "Did you follow us here?"

Again she waited, and she could feel a sense of genuine dread slowly creeping through her body.

"You can't have her," she said firmly, through gritted teeth. "You took my parents, but you're not taking my sister. I won't let you."

She watched the back of Bod's head. After a moment the girl slowly turned to look at her, and this time Jacqui saw just the slightest hint of a smile on her lips.

Suddenly she heard a bumping sound, and she turned to see that Detective Scott had emerged from the back of the hotel.

"What's going on?" he asked, clearly a little befuddled and sleepy, and with the worst case of bed hair that Jacqui had ever seen. "Girls, what are you doing out here? I went to the bathroom and looked out the window and..."

He hesitated for a moment before making his way over.

"Couldn't sleep, huh?" he said as he reached Jacqui. "Okay, I get that, but you really shouldn't be out here in the middle of the night. If you come inside, we can... talk or something. If you really need to."

He looked over at Bod, and then he stepped closer to her.

"I'm sorry I'm not much good at talking to you about this stuff," he continued, with a hint of resignation in his voice. Reaching out, he began to put a hand on her shoulder – only to immediately pull back. "Sorry," he added, "I didn't mean to..."

He sighed.

"Listen," he added, taking a moment to squeeze the bridge of his nose – as if he was trying to somehow reset his thoughts. "We definitely need to go back inside. That much is pretty clear. Do you want me to wake up the woman who runs the place? She might be better if you want to talk about... feelings and stuff."

He looked at Bod for a moment longer before turning back to Jacqui.

"Would that work?" he asked plaintively, with a little desperation creeping into his tone.

"I don't think you should stand too close to her," Jacqui replied as she saw the smile on Bod's face growing slightly.

"What do you mean?" he asked. "How -"

In that moment his body was flung back, smashing against the side of the pub with bone-cracking force before he slumped down with a heavy thud against the cobbles. Jacqui pulled back in horror, while Bod looked down at Scott for a few seconds before turning and starting once again to walk away.

"Stop!" Jacqui shouted, hurrying after her and grabbing her by the arm, holding her back. "I told you, you can't have her! You've taken everything else from me. I won't let you take her as well."

Holding her arm firmly, she waited for a response. After a few seconds, Bod merely turned and looked up at her once again.

"I know it's you," Jacqui continued, trying to banish the fear from her own voice. "I don't know how you made it here, I thought you were confined to the island but I guess once you got closer to the mainland... What's your big plan? Are you going to take revenge against the entire village for what happened to you? My dad was descended from one of them, but I bet half the people in this village have got some sort of connection to everyone who lived here back then. Are you going to kill all of them? Are -"

As that last word left her lips, she saw her sister's face shimmering slightly. A moment later, thick black wires began to emerge from her eyes and mouth as the face of Jane Moore began to appear.

"I'm sorry for what they did to you," Jacqui added, "but no-one can change it now. Your child's still out there on the island, I heard him crying. Or her. You've left your child alone now, all alone on that island with just a load of ghosts for company. Is that what you want? What's more important to you? Revenge... or being there for her?"

She knew she risked the ghost's anger now, but she couldn't help herself. She had no idea whether Bod was aware of what had begun to happen, but she desperately wanted to find some way to get rid of Jane's ghost forever – and she had no other ideas.

"That lighthouse keeper guy was trying to give your child a proper burial," she continued as she tried to figure out everything that had happened.

"But that meant he or she was buried without you. Is that what this is all about? You've been separated from your child for hundreds of years and you just want to be reunited, but you can't because your bones aren't together and your face... are you worried that she'll be scared of you? Are -"

Suddenly Bod grabbed her by the throat, and then – with more strength than a young girl should ever possess – she swung her around and slammed her against the wall as Jane Moore's features emerged more strongly than ever.

"This isn't the way!" Jacqui gasped, struggling to break free. "Even if you kill every last person in this village, then what? You'll still be stuck here all alone, haunting the place forever! Is that what you want? Do you just want to be some pathetic ghost who can never move on?" Slowly Jane's ghostly form was rising up from Bod's body. "I'm so sorry for everything they ever did to you, and I don't even care whether or not you were really a witch. But I'm not going to let you take my sister."

As she tried to work out how to escape, she realized that she could once again hear the child crying in the distance, as if the voice was echoing from the island. She looked toward the harbor and wondered whether the cries might be coming from one of the houses, but a moment later she saw that Jane had also turned – as if she too was trying to track the source of the sound.

"And you'll be trapped here," Jacqui continued, struggling for air now as Bod's hand squeezed her throat tighter and tighter, "but you'll still be able to hear those cries. You'll be able to hear them forever but this time you'll never have a hope of getting back to her. Is that what you really want?"

She waited, but Jane's ghostly face was becoming clearer with each passing second as the cries continued to drift through the village's dark streets.

Finally, figuring that she had no better ideas, Jacqui reached up and put her hand on the dead woman's features, and to her shock she found that she could actually feel the cold wire poking out from the cold flesh. She hesitated, worried that she might be about to make a terrible mistake, and then she began to pull on the wires, slipping her fingers through the rough loops and tugging as hard as she could manage, slowly ripping them free to reveal two tattered eyes and – a few seconds later – the ragged remains of lips.

Parts of the wire snagged in the flesh, as if doomed to remain forever, but Jacqui twisted them and turned them around until she was able to pull more and more sections free. Pieces of wire were embedded in Jane's ears too, but these came out a little more easily. She had to dig into the flesh at some points, almost gouging the wire out, but after a few more seconds she was able to pull most of the wire away, with just one last section catching on Jane's left eye. She pulled harder, ripping part of the eyelid away, and then she let go, allowing the wire to drop down against the cobbled ground.

For a moment she stared at the ghost's ravaged face, seeing bloodied eyeballs that were barely able to move in their sockets. When the dead woman opened her mouth, she revealed gums that had been cracked apart and a tongue with a deep split down the middle. And then, in an instant, Jane Moore screamed and pulled back, vanishing into the night air and finally allowing Bod's unconscious body to slump into a heap.

"Bod!" Jacqui gasped, dropping to her knees and shaking her sister, frantically checking to see whether she was alright. "Can you hear me? Bod, are you okay?"

AMY CROSS

CHAPTER FORTY-ONE

A GENTLE BREEZE BLEW across the island, rustling the long grass as footsteps traipsed toward the rocks beyond the lighthouse.

"Stop!"

Sighing as she climbed up the rocks that led away from the wooden dock, Jacqui realized that she could no longer ignore him. He'd been calling out to her from his boat for a while, rowing frantically despite their head start; once they'd reached the island, she'd hoped to outrun him. Now she turned and saw that Detective Scott had finally managed to catch up.

"Seriously?" he continued, clearly exasperated. "You decided to steal a boat and row back out here to the island?"

"You didn't have to chase after us," she

replied.

"I have to keep you safe," he pointed out, "and technically this is a crime scene."

"Do you remember what happened last night?" she asked, before nodding at Bod. "Do you remember what she did to you?"

"Maybe," he said cautiously, before furrowing his brow. "How *did* she knock me out, anyway? She's just a..."

His voice trailed off.

"We came out here this morning to finish this once and for all," Jacqui told him. "Ignoring the problem of Jane Moore won't make her go away. Eventually more innocent people are always going to end up on the island. It can't just be sealed off and forgotten about."

"Are you sure this is a good idea?" he asked, rubbing the back of his head, wincing slightly as he once again felt the bump. "The roads are supposed to be clear soon and -"

"If we leave it, someone'll just persuade us not to come," Jacqui replied, holding Bod's hand as they made their way past the top of the rocks. "Trust me, we have to do this quickly. After what happened last night, we have a chance to put this right for good, but if we wait then it might drag on forever."

"I'm really not sure I should let you stay here," Scott murmured, tilting his head first one way and then the other, trying to get rid of the crick in his neck. He turned and looked back across Saward Island, and he quickly spotted the patch of grass where a simple tarpaulin covered Vanessa Sinclair's body. "How am I going to explain it all in my report? How am I even going to start when -"

"I found her!"

Turning again, he saw that Jacqui and Bod were at the far end of the rocks, and a moment later Jacqui got down onto her knees.

Making his way over to join the girls, Scott looked down and saw nothing but more and more rocks. Jacqui was pulling some aside, however, and finally she uncovered a set of human bones, including a skull with pieces of thick black wire hanging from the jaw and empty eye sockets.

"This must be the spot where she finally died all those years ago," Jacqui explained. "I don't know how long she survived after she gave birth to her child and buried it, but I guess she probably just starved to death. Or bled out. Maybe she tried to crawl in here when she knew the end was coming, and she's been here ever since. It's weird, as soon as we arrived this morning I had a sense of where to find her. It's almost as she was trying to guide me."

"This is definitely a crime scene," Scott said. "I don't know how old those bones are, but we absolutely can't touch them or -"

"Take this," Jacqui said, lifting the skull up

and handing it to Bod, then grabbing more of the bones and holding them up for Scott. "I know what to do," she continued, "but if these get taken away and loads of police start interfering, Jane's ghost won't ever be able to rest. I think last night she agreed to give us a chance to fix things, but we don't have long."

Scott opened his mouth to reply, before hesitating at the last moment and finally taking the bones.

"I'm going to regret this," he muttered under his breath. "This is breaking so much protocol."

"I think that's all of them," Jacqui said, gathering the last of the bones into her arms and getting to her feet. "Well, there are a few left, but hopefully we've got enough. We've got the main ones, at least." She turned and began to head back across the island. "Come on, you saw the cross just now. That's where we're going."

"Is this a good idea?" Scott called after her, before looking down at Bod.

"She's usually right about most things," Bod suggested, before setting off after her sister.

"I really -"

Before he could finish, Scott thought back once again to the way the little girl had slammed him against a wall and knocked him unconscious. No matter how hard he tried to convince himself otherwise, deep down he knew that she should never have been able to do that, so he began to hurry after the girls even as he contorted his thoughts and tried to come up with some kind of explanation.

"When we're done here, we're going to have to work out exactly how to phrase it for the report," he said. "There are certain things that -"

"You'll find a way!" Jacqui called back to him. "Plus we're kids, so they'll be really sensitive around us. People have been covering up the truth about this island for centuries. I've got a feeling one more set of lies won't be too hard to arrange. Just tell them that someone attacked you, and when you woke up you saw us rowing away from the harbor and you gave chase. That's not even a lie!"

"Sometimes lying is good," Bod explained. "That's what *I've* learned, anyway."

"I'm not sure that's a good moral to take away from all of this," Scott told her.

Once they reached the cross, they began to dig and eventually they located the bones of the child, which David had hurriedly tried to bury during the previous night. They dug a little deeper and set Jane's bones down next to those of her dead baby, and then they worked to cover the grave properly. Jacqui pushed the cross down a little harder, just to make sure that it had a good chance of staying in place, and finally the three of them stood back and looked at their handiwork. A breeze was still blowing across the island, but in that moment the scene seemed strangely peaceful.

"What now?" Scott asked.

"You're not going to like it," Jacqui told him.

"What am I not going to like?"

"I didn't mention this part until now, because I figured you'd be totally against it," she continued, "but if you think about it, there's really only one way to make sure that this is over."

"And what's that?" he asked.

She hesitated, before pulling Bod closer.

"We have to spend one more night here," she explained.

"Absolutely not," he said firmly. "Help's on the way, they should reach the village by this evening and then a proper investigation is going to take place."

"We're staying for one more night," Jacqui told him, "and you can either stay with us or you can go back and then pick us up in the morning. I'm pretty sure you can use the radio in the boat to let everyone on the mainland know that we're okay, and you'll be able to come up with some kind of excuse. We've come this far and we really just need to be absolutely certain that it's all over for good."

She waited for an answer, but she could tell that he was struggling.

"Detective Scott, please let us do this," she

added finally. "When it's over, I'm pretty sure that Bod and I are going to freak out about everything that happened. Hell, I for one might even end up having some kind of complete breakdown, but if that's the case... I need to at least know that Jane Moore's at peace now and that nobody ever has to fear this island again. And nobody has to lost their parents."

"I -"

"We saw Dad's body," she told him. "From a distance."

"I'm sorry," he replied. "You need to tell me exactly where to find him."

"This island has been haunted for centuries," Jacqui said firmly. "There's been so much pain and fear and death here, but we have a chance to end all of that forever. It won't bring our parents back, but at least we'll know that they didn't die completely in vain. I'm not sure, but I feel like that's something I want to be able to say to the inevitable succession of doctors I'm going to have to see over the next few years. I know we probably seem flippant, but that's just a defense mechanism. I'm delaying so much trauma right now, I'm almost shaking."

"Me too," Bod said. "I'm probably going to go totally mad."

"I'll see what I can do," Scott replied reluctantly, rubbing the back of his head again.

"You really should have told me what you were planning, though. You'll be lucky if the owner of that boat doesn't press charges."

He watched Jacqui for a moment, as if trying to understand her a little better.

"I'm starting to think," he added, "that you're both having some kind of manic episode."

"Think about it this way," she told him, "you'll be the hero who finally solves the mystery of the island for good. If someone had just faced the ghost instead of running away from her, this could have been over so much sooner. There are loads of bodies here, but maybe now people won't have to be so scared of Saward Island. Not anymore. Isn't that worth breaking the rules for one more night? I mean, you've already broken them a few times."

***

Once Scott had made the necessary arrangements with his colleagues on the mainland, and had fudged a few of the details, the three of them began to figure out how they were going to spend one last night on the island. Although he tried to talk them out of it a few more times, Scott had to admit that the girls seemed absolutely determined, and by the time darkness fell he figured that he'd committed to the plan. And as the night progressed and he forced himself to stay awake, he listened out to the sound of grass blowing in the seemingly constant wind and he had to admit that there was something strangely peaceful about Saward Island.

"She's gone now," Jacqui said around three in the morning, pulling Bod tight so that they could share their warmth. "I can feel it. The island's completely empty. There's nothing to be scared of here anymore."

"I wish Mum and Dad were with us," Bod replied, sniffing back tears.

"Me too," Jacqui replied, and she too felt as if the full enormity of the night's events was finally settling on her shoulders.

Tears filled her eyes; she couldn't wondering whether the frantic return to the island had – in part, at least – been inspired by a desperate attempt to stop thinking about the awful things that had happened. Now the mania was fading away, replaced by nothing but grief.

"They're gone, though," she sobbed, struggling to see now as she started crying and pulled Bod closer. "*All* the ghosts are gone."

A few hours later, with morning light breaking above the horizon and reaching out across the North Sea, the three of them began the long row back to Innisrach.

AMY CROSS

AUTHOR'S NOTE

Originally, this is where *The Haunting of Saward Island* was going to end. Shortly before publication, however, a short story was discovered that might cast fresh light on the awful events that took place.

Written at some point in the nineteenth century and lost for many years, *The Bookseller's Curse* was recently uncovered in a chest in Gravesend, Kent. This short tale – written by an unknown author – claims to tell the true story of a young couple named David and Jane Moore, and their encounter with an infamous bookseller named Horatio Bentwhistle.

Historical records prove that Mr. Bentwhistle and his shop really existed, and that a married couple named David and Jane Moore lived in the area too.

While we can't be certain that the Jane Moore in this story is the same Jane Moore from *The Bookseller's Curse*, all the details match up. Although written in a different style, the short story is therefore included over the following pages, so that the reader can determine in his or her own mind whether the Jane Moore who encountered Horatio Bentwhistle is the same Jane Moore who later ended up haunting Saward Island.

This author's opinion is that the similarities are too striking to be ignored.

THE BOOKSELLER'S CURSE

Prologue

Although – for the most part – the reader must trust that this story is true, there is one tiny morsel of proof that can be offered before we begin our tale.

If one were to visit a certain small town in Kent, and if one were to amble approximately two thirds of the way along the High Street from the station, one might stop and observe a small, dark building leaning haphazardly between two much taller structures on either side. This particular building stands out very much from its neighbors, and it is here that a certain Mr. Horatio Bentwhistle esq. spent a lifetime running a bookshop. I cannot in good faith give the exact location of this domicile, for it is now a private dwelling and I should hate to cause embarrassment for the current owners, but if one were to examine the exposed wood above the door one would still make out the particulars of the shop and its owner:

H. Bentwhistle esq., bookseller and antiquarian, established 1701

Knowing then that this proof is out there somewhere, and that certain readers might well chance upon it one day while out exploring England's most beautiful county, we can get to our real business. For while in 1701 Mr. Bentwhistle had indeed established his shop in a fit of hope and optimism, fifty years later he was filled with entirely opposite qualities, namely bitterness and disappointment. The bitterness came from a belief that his career should have been more successful and more respected, and the disappointment arose from a singular hatred of those moneyed London enthusiasts who had never bothered to make the journey down to see the marvelous old titles – some of them exceedingly rare, if a little overly specific – that sat dotted around the shop's gloomy interior.

And while Mr. Bentwhistle might soon come across as an almost comically inept and arrogant man, it is important at this point to clarify that his instincts as a bookseller were second to none; he possessed copies of some of the rarest and most valuable books in all of England, yet from his little shop in Kent he was never able to sell more than a handful. Even when some passing customer happened to step through the front door, and even if that customer had both the interest and the wherewithal to make a purchase, Horatio Bentwhistle was possessed off a uniquely abrasive personality that often proved most offensive. Sometimes the keenest purchaser might leave empty-handed, even if he had previously resolved to buy a book or two.

So it was, then, that Mr. Bentwhistle became more and more angry at the world, believing that all other men had conspired to rob him of the success he (believed) he so richly deserved. As he sat and brooded and stewed in his shop, he thought of the great sums of money that should have been paid for his books, and he often cursed – under his breath, of course, and with no actual supernatural powers – all those whose shadows moved past the dusty windows of his little home. The years passed, and the years became decades, and eventually this wretched man became too destitute and wrecked to maintain his business. He had nobody to hand it all over to, however, so he persisted long past the point at which anyone else would have given up, until eventually in the year 1752 and at the grand age of more than ninety he had to be carried out insane from the front door by neighbors who had grown tired of his loud late-night cackling.

A place was found for Mr. Bentwhistle at the local lunatic asylum, where he was confined to a small stone-walled room barely half the size of his shop floor. Magistrates ruled on the ruined and burned shop and saw to it that the building was disposed of, with the few remaining books donated to a library where nobody knew their value, although in truth by this point there were precious few books in the shop at all. Meanwhile the building was sold to a man who wished to restore its burned timbers and turn it into a home, and the money was given over to the fine ladies of a nearby church who wished to do up the rafters and perhaps improve the state of the cemetery. All the while, Horatio Bentwhistle remained in his cell, laughing manically and appearing for all the world to be as mad as any other resident of the asylum.

Sometimes the nurses and guards would stop outside his cell and listen, trying to make sense of his impenetrable cries. They would speculate as to the reason for the man's insanity, yet although they knew of his general history, none of them could possibly have understood exactly what had tipped Mr. Bentwhistle over the edge. The true facts of that case, indeed, must instead be relayed in these pages, told to the world for the first time as a warning and cautionary tale, and titled – for reasons that shall soon become clear – rather ominously as *The Bookseller's Curse*.

I

Some two years before he was dragged away to the asylum, on a bright July morning, Horatio Bentwhistle was – as usual – sitting all alone in his shop and contemplating the utter failure that had come to mark his existence. Surrounded by his precious books, he sank ever deeper into his large armchair, ruining his posture as he watched galaxies of dust drifting through the air. For this man, as has been made clear already, life's despair was complete and his only advantage was a complete lack of hope.

Until, finally, the door shuddered a little, as it was wont to do when somebody was trying to push it open; and then, once it *had* opened, the little bell above rang briefly to announce two things: first that, after such a long time of torpor, it still functioned; and secondly that a visitor was actually making his way into the shop.

"If you're looking for the lady who does the embroidery," Mr. Bentwhistle murmured, not even bothering to look up, "then you shall find her two doors down. Really, I don't know why she doesn't have a clearer sign in her window. People are always mistaking my house for hers, and I'm damn sick of it."

"I am sure that the lady in question is a fine embroiderer," a man's voice replied, "but it is not her services that I seek today. This is your bookshop, is it not?"

At this curious turn of phrase and even more curious question, Mr. Bentwhistle finally roused himself. Sitting up, he turned and saw a slim, fairly well-dressed man standing just inside the doorway, although he quickly realized that this man was in fact exceedingly uncomfortable in such elegant clothing. In other words, this was undoubtedly a man with little money who was trying to pass for someone with a great deal, or perhaps someone new to minor wealth, and as he hauled himself to his feet the old shopkeeper felt sure that the fellow needed to be sent packing as swiftly as possible.

"What do you want?" he barked.

"I am in a bookshop," the man replied, "which is lucky for me, since it is a book that I require."

"Well, I've got plenty," Mr. Bentwhistle said, unable to summon much enthusiasm at all. "Not that most people care. The vast majority have neither the intelligence nor the wit to read."

"I wouldn't know about that," the man said, "but I myself am an extremely keen reader and I have come quite some way. I heard about your little shop and I perceive that this might be the perfect place in which to make a modest purchase."

"You *perceive*, do you?" Mr. Bentwhistle replied, more convinced than ever now that this man was merely acting the role of a wealthy gentleman, rather than truly being such a thing. "And you wish to make a modest purchase? How modest are we talking?"

"That... depends," the man said cautiously, before stepping closer and removing his gloves, then holding out a hand. "My name is David Moore, I live in the village of Wollophampton which is about -"

"I know where Wallophampton is," Mr. Bentwhistle replied quickly, giving the man's hand only the most cursory of shakes, as if he had no time for such a thing at all. "And what kind of book do you wish to purchase?"

"That is the slightly embarrassing part," the guest explained. "You see, I am neither an educated nor a rich man. I have made a small amount of money as the proprietor of a mill and the adjoining farm, and I wish now to raise my mind a little by reading nourishing and important books. I must admit that, when it comes to selecting such things, I rather must set myself at your mercy. I merely wish to start building a small library of my own, merely for my own delectation at home."

"You want a recommendation?"

"I suppose that is what I am trying to get at, yes."

"Well..."

For a few seconds, Mr. Bentwhistle could

only think that this was an extremely unusual predicament, but also that it was one he might be able to exploit. This David Moore gentleman was clearly an idiot in possession of a sum of money he knew not how to spend, in essence a complete fool, and the shopkeeper was starting to believe that for once he might actually be in luck. He looked Mr. Moore up and down, tried his best to estimate the full extent of the man's gullibility, and finally he walked calmly to a set of shelves over near the window.

"You have come," he purred, "to the right place."

"I certainly hope so," Mr. Moore replied.

"Oh, but you have; you have."

Reaching out, Mr. Bentwhistle tried to decide which of these lowly and rather unimportant titles he could possibly fob off onto his foolish guest. He had a plethora from which to choose, but finally he slid out a rather old and dusty – not to mention practically worthless in financial terms – tract on the history of England's place in the world. The book was of no real value, nor did it contain any interesting information, and in truth the old man barely remembered how or why it had become part of his inventory. Nevertheless, he held the book for several seconds, caressing its rather worn spine, before turning to Mr. Moore and trying to work out how much he could squeeze out of the gentleman.

"I cannot help but notice," Mr. Moore remarked, "that you are now holding a title in your hands."

"Oh, that I am," Mr. Bentwhistle said, carrying the book over to him and then setting it down onto the table. "Might I ask... how much are you looking to spend?"

"I am not rich," Mr. Moore explained, "even if I have made a lot more of myself than many others of my station. I wish to learn about the world, and I know that I cannot afford to travel extensively. I have a young son and I want to eventually ignite in him a passion for learning."

"Then I have just the book for you," Mr. Bentwhistle murmured, sliding the book toward him. "You cannot go too far wrong by learning the history of our great nation."

"Oh, but I -"

"Pick it up," the bookseller added, before the other man had a chance to finish his sentence. "Peruse it. Feel its weight and the touch of its pages. One must get to know a book as one gets to know a man, which is to say that you must be sure it is the right one for you."

He stepped around behind Mr. Moore and headed to the cabinet in the corner. After hesitating for a few seconds, wondering whether his little plan might work, he saw reflected in the glass the sight of Mr. Moore slowly leafing through the book. A smile reached the antiquarian's lips as he opened the cabinet and took out two glasses.

"This seems fascinating," Mr. Moore exclaimed. "It's exactly what I'm looking for, at least to start with. I can learn a great deal from this book. Tell me, how much do you want for it?"

"Oh, only what it's worth," Mr. Bentwhistle said, taking a bottle of wine and quickly uncorking it – for he did not want to waste time or effort opening a new one entirely – and then modestly filling the two glasses up to about their halfway points. "I'm not a greedy man, it is just that I tend to deal in rarer books, in the type of books that cannot be acquired elsewhere. Why, I'd be surprised if there's another copy of that particular book in all of England."

"I shall take your word for that, but again I must ask – how much would it cost me?"

"One mustn't fuss over petty things such as prices," the older man said, carrying the glasses over and holding one out for him. "A book's value cannot be measured in pounds or shillings or pence."

"Of course not," Mr. Moore replied, before looking at the glass. "Thank you, but I do not imbibe."

"But you must."

"I -"

"Evidently those do-gooding priests have

got to you," Mr. Bentwhistle sighed, taking Mr. Moore's right hand and forcing the glass of wine into his grip. "'Tis truly a sad state of affairs, the way they get their thoughts into the minds of other people, but you're not the first and unfortunately I very much doubt that you'll be the last. That's good wine, Mr. Moore, and it might hit you even better if you're not used to such things. Go on, have a drop."

"I must decline," Mr. Moore said, reaching over to set the glass on the table. "Instead -"

"At least hold it," Mr. Bentwhistle stammered, taking hold of his arm and preventing him from putting the glass down. "Humor me. When one is holding a glass of fine wine, one can appreciate a book so much better."

"One can?"

"I think it's the fumes."

"I had no idea."

"You clearly have a great deal to learn," Mr. Bentwhistle suggested, "so it's fortunate that you have come to the right place."

"I -"

"This is a fine book indeed," the learned gentleman continued, almost purring as the words slithered from his lips. "You made a very wise choice."

"I don't think that it was I who -"

"All the knowledge of the world is in your hands right now, Mr. Moore. All the wonders, too.

Why, I have had many well-dressed men through my doors, always searching for the latest fashionable titles, but not one of them ever had the wisdom to pick this particular volume. That is why my heart is filled now with such astonishment, for it is rare in the life of a humble bookseller to come across someone such as yourself."

"It is?"

"You and this book were made for one another, and it would be a crime upon humanity for you not to take this tome away with you and read it a thousand times over! Why, if I did not sell it to you, I am quite sure that I would end up in the Tower of London itself, charged with the most dreadful crimes against reason!" He reached over and tugged slightly on Mr. Moore's coat. "Sir, you have afforded me this most wonderful honor, or at least a glimpse of it. Now, please... you will not snatch such perfection away, will you?"

Momentarily lost for words, Mr. Moore looked down at the book in his hands. He wasn't quite sure what he'd expected when he'd entered the bookshop, but it had certainly been nothing like this; he hadn't even been certain that he intended to make a purchase, at least not immediately, yet something about Horatio Bentwhistle's entreaty had stirred a sense of joy in his own soul. Indeed, the more he looked at this particular book, and the more he held it too, the more he felt certain that fate had somehow guided him into this shop and that all the answers to all the questions in his mind could be found between the slightly shabby red covers in his hands. This book, and this book alone, could come to function as the veritable foundation stone of his humble library.

"I... well, I..."

"Yes?" Mr. Bentwhistle wheezed.

"I suppose..."

Swallowing hard, Mr. Moore realized that the emotional side of the decision was already over; all that remained now were the financial details.

"How much is it?" he asked.

"It is a life," Mr. Bentwhistle beamed, "and a soul, and a journey that will surely take you to fresh heights of imagination."

"That's all well and good," Mr. Moore continued cautiously, "but I mean... I don't want to sound petty or foolish, but I must ask about the price of the book. Sir, will you tell me how much I must pay, in order that you might hand it over to me?"

"Oh, it is so hard to put a monetary value on such a thing."

"Indeed, but I must persist in asking."

"I would give it away if I could."

"I am sure, but that would hardly seem fair on you."

"No, no, I suppose not," the older man

lamented, before hesitating again as he looked at the book and tried to work out exactly how to proceed. "I suppose," he continued, "that given the circumstances, I could sell it to you for the grand sum of..."

He took a moment to wipe a fleck of spittle from one corner of his mouth.

"A thousand pounds."

"A thousand pounds?" Mr. Moore replied, and now his eyes grew almost as large as a pair of dinner plates.

"It's a small sum for such a valuable -"

"I can only apologize," Mr. Moore gasped, holding the book out toward him with trembling hands. "Evidently I much mistook the nature of this shop, and perhaps I also misrepresented the scope of my ambition. I was after something at a much more ordinary level, for I am but a humble man with a small business of my own. Please, take the book back."

"Allow yourself to consider the matter first."

"There's really nothing to consider," Mr. Moore continued, desperately waiting for the other man to take the book back. "I fear to even touch so valuable a thing."

"You merely need to get used to it."

Turning, Mr. Moore was about to set the book down on a nearby table when – with a sudden burst of hitherto hidden energy – Mr. Bentwhistle rushed over and held his arm back.

"Not there, Sir," he said breathlessly. "The wood of the table is varnished, and that varnish would certainly damage the book."

"Over here, then?" Mr. Moore asked, hurrying to another table.

"No!" Mr. Bentwhistle shrieked, his voice filled with alarm. "Not there either, Sir, for the varnish on that table is worse still! How do you not know these things?"

"Where, then?" Mr. Moore replied, clearly now in the grip of some sort of panic as he held the book in his increasingly tremulous hands. Sweat was running down his face. "Sir, you must aid me at once. I do not trust myself to hold such a valuable item!"

"Let me think for a moment," Mr. Bentwhistle replied, reaching up and scratching his chin.

"Please hurry!" the other man begged. "What about the shelf? Can it not simply be placed back on its shelf?"

"Well, I suppose that's one possibility," the proprietor admitted, although he was still carefully giving the impression that he was lost in a great deal of thought, "but one cannot simply slide such a book into position."

"One cannot?"

"No, not at all," the old man continued sagely, rubbing his chin now before picking up one of the wine glasses and holding it out to him. "Here, hold this."

"Why?"

"Just hold it for one moment, so that I might better think on the matter."

Not understanding what was happening at all, but equally not wanting to disturb the great bookseller in his contemplation, Mr. Moore did as he was told. Now holding the book in one hand and the glass of red wine in the other, he waited with baited breath for his next instruction, and he didn't dare to take his eyes off the esteemed Mr. Bentwhistle for so much as a single second.

"Yes," the elderly gentleman mused, "this is a most perplexing situation."

"What shall we do?" Mr. Moore shrieked.

"We *can* return the book to the shelf," he continued. "Yes, that's a good idea. We can, quite easily. Quite easily indeed. But we must be careful."

"I shall follow your instructions to the letter."

"Come along, then," Mr. Bentwhistle said, gesturing for him to follow as he shuffled to the shelf and peered at the spot where – until a few minutes earlier – this particular book had been resting quite happily. "The operation should be simple enough, although a few necessary considerations are most certainly in order. For one thing, the book cannot merely be slid into its former position."

"It cannot?"

"Most certainly not!" Mr. Bentwhistle snapped, turning to him – before sighing as if realizing that he'd perhaps been too harsh. "My dear fellow," he went on, "I fear that I have made you worry too much. This entire situation can be resolved with just a little care and attention on our part." He hurried past, only to stop and hold up a hand as Mr. Moore began to follow. "No, remain right where you are. Do not move a muscle until I give you the command. Is that understood?"

Mr. Moore nodded keenly.

"I just need to make a few preparations," Mr. Bentwhistle continued, quietly sliding a chair over until it was almost directly behind the other man's right elbow. "Everything will surely be fine, my dear fellow, and that exceedingly valuable book shall soon be safely back on the shelf where – sadly – it seems it must linger for a while longer." He glanced over and saw the glass of wine in the other man's right hand. "I believe all is in place," he murmured, scarcely able to believe that his plan had advanced so well. "Now, if you are quite ready, I believe we are almost ready to begin."

He paused, savoring a moment of silence.

"Turn around!" he gasped suddenly.

Startled, Mr. Moore spun toward him, only to bump his right arm against the recently rearranged chair; and this action, in turn, caused his arm to jerk terribly, tipping the wine glass almost directly over and sending a great deal of its ruby red contents splashing down onto – and all over – the book he was holding in his other hand. In that moment he froze, utterly terrified by the realization of what had just transpired, and precious seconds passed as he stared at the wine that even now was soaking deeper and deeper into those aged and very valuable pages.

"The book!" Mr. Bentwhistle called out, perhaps over-egging his shock just a little. "That valuable, valuable book!"

"I -"

Unable to bring so much as another word from his lips, Mr. Moore stared at the book for a moment longer before – in a doomed attempt to improve matters – suddenly opening it up and, in the process, allowing more of the wine to dribble down toward across the page.

"Close it!" Mr. Bentwhistle shouted, rushing over and grabbing the book, slamming it shut and then setting it on the table. "Pray! Pray that it can be saved!"

"I am so sorry," Mr. Moore continued, on the verge of tears now. "I had no idea that there was a chair behind me, I am sure it wasn't there a moment earlier."

"It hardly could have moved!" Mr. Bentwhistle hissed. "We must pray that when I open it again, the pages are not too badly damaged. Although I fear that wine – especially this expensive vintage that I obtained from a dealer who regularly travels down to Italy – is a great enemy of literature. In its physical form, at least."

"Can anything be done?" Mr. Moore asked, and now his voice was trembling with fear.

"I do not know," Mr. Bentwhistle replied, adopting the tone of voice of someone mourning perhaps a beloved pet or even a young child. "Truly this is a catastrophe, and one from which there might be no recovery. Or I might be wrong, and the wine shall have left no mark at all. Pray, pray and pray again, Mr. Moore, as I open it up and see the awful truth."

They stood in silence for a few more seconds, before Horatio began to very gently open the book. As he did so, the soaked pages began to peel apart, although in places they remained resolutely stuck together and already patches of ink could be seen to have smudged beyond repair.

"Oh, it's terrible!" the revered bookseller exclaimed, performing a very convincing impression of a man genuinely horrified by what he saw. Indeed, anyone observing – and knowing the full state of the deception – might have opined that the old man had missed his calling as an actor. "Oh, it's worse than I could ever have imagined."

He seemed poised to faint, before thinking better of such an extravagance. As he finished opening the book, however, he emitted a faint whimpering sound that seemed to emerge from the very depths of his soul, and his bottom lip quivered as if he was about to burst into tears. As anyone who has tried to produce false tears will surely know, the hardest part is to make the chin quiver properly, but this old man excelled even here. He tried to wipe some of the wine away, only for more of the ink to smudge onto his fingers.

As this awful scene unfolded, meanwhile, a reverential silence has descended upon the scene – a silence such as one might find in a church or even a mortuary.

"Is it... ruined?" Mr. Moore asked finally.

"Ruined?" Mr. Bentwhistle whispered, as if he could scarcely believe what lay before his eyes. "Is that what you ask? Is it ruined?" He hesitated, before slowly turning to him. "My dear fellow, as you can surely see for yourself, it has been truly and completely destroyed."

"Oh!" Mr. Moore gasped, taking an involuntary step back.

Now the silence returned, but something was very different; now Mr. Moore very much wanted to give voice to his fears, yet he felt sure that he should wait for the expert to take the lead, that the older man was the only one in that room qualified to give voice to the disaster. Yet with each passing second, the silence seemed to twist a little more around Mr. Moore and to constrict him the way that a snake might constrict its victim, such that he felt as if he surely *must* expel air from his lungs and say something.

"Oh," he managed finally, which was merely a repeat of his last uttering.

"Oh indeed," Mr. Bentwhistle murmured mournfully, before running a hand across the book's wet pages – as if mourning the death of a favored aunt. "It is a sorry thing, to be sure, to see a priceless book in such an awful state. I almost fear – though it is too awful to speculate – that I might never fully recover."

At this, he reached up and – although no tear was evident on his cheek, at least not from where Mr. Moore was standing – he made to wipe such a tear away. Mr. Moore, in turn, assumed that this tear must simply not have been visible from where he was standing.

And the silence came back with a vengeance, filling the room with such utter quiet that even a man with no tongue would surely have felt compelled to conjure up a miracle and speak.

"How... how much did you say that book is worth, again?" Mr. Moore asked finally, although in truth he already knew the answer to that question.

"Oh, a thousand pounds," Mr. Bentwhistle explained, artfully subtracting all trace of hope from his voice. "Give or take a little either way, depending on the vagaries of the market."

He continued to stare at the book, and this time he sniffed as if trying to hold back fresh tears.

"A thousand pounds," Mr. Moore said, weighing up that terrible amount in his mind. "For a book..."

"You think it too much?"

"No, not at all! I know that books, and the knowledge they contain, are among the most valuable things in all the world!"

"That they are. That they are."

"And I -"

Turning, Mr. Moore saw the troublesome chair that – with its sudden and unexplained movement across the room – had caught him by surprise and had caused him to tip the wine glass over. He wanted to offer some profuse apology, to explain again that he had been caught entirely unaware by the chair, yet deep down he knew that mere excuses would be of no comfort now. And the more he looked at Mr. Horatio Bentwhistle, the more he perceived that the older man seemed struck by a very genuine sense of sorrow.

"I must make it good," he said softly. "I must make this whole situation good."

"I do not see how that is possible," Mr. Bentwhistle lamented, wiping the book's sodden pages once again. "Some things simply cannot be undone."

"No, but they can be... atoned for," Mr. Moore suggested, desperate to mend the other man's broken heart. "A thousand pounds, you say. Well, I certainly think that I..."

His voice trailed off to nothing and the pesky silence insisted upon making an encore.

"Yes?" Mr. Bentwhistle said after a few more seconds, half turning to him. "You were... about to say something, I think?"

He turned and nodded at a sign on the wall, which contained six terrible words:

Any damaged book must be purchased.

"You were about to say something?" he asked again. "Were you not?"

"Only that it is I, and I alone, who must make this good," Mr. Moore continued, before taking a step toward him and then stopping again. "You must forgive me, for I shall need a little time – a few days or perhaps a week – hopefully not as long as a month – but I shall make this good in the only way I know how... presuming, of course, that you will allow me."

"Allow you?"

Again Mr. Bentwhistle turned a little more, but still not quite enough to look him in the eye.

"And how exactly," he purred, "would I *allow* you?"

"I must compensate you," Mr. Moore replied. "Forgive my impunity and please do not think me a gross or common man, I do not mean to insult a great personage such as yourself, and I know that mere financial measures will never be enough to make up for the damage I have caused."

"Yes, yes," Horatio replied, attempting to hide his eagerness. "Go on."

"But it is all I have," Mr. Moore continued. "I am not a great man, nor a learned one. I do not have very much in this world, but I shall do whatever it takes to at the very least repay you the thousand pounds I now so assuredly owe. I shall pay for the damage!"

"Oh, well..."

At this, Mr. Bentwhistle finally turned and looked at him.

"I suppose -"

"If you will let me!" Mr. Moore sobbed, suddenly bursting into a quite uncharacteristic storm of tears as he dropped to his knees and clenched his hands together in prayer. "Please, Mr. Bentwhistle, I cannot repair the damage, nor can I cover the great loss I have caused you, but will you please allow me to at least repay you the financial cost of the book I have ruined?"

"Well... if you insist..."

"I do!"

Although he paused for a few seconds to give the impression that he was thinking the matter over, in truth Mr. Horatio Bentwhistle had in all truth been waiting for this exact moment; indeed, he had arrived at the culmination of his little plan and now he could almost feel the weight of a thousand pounds landing softly in his hand.

"If you insist," he said cautiously, "then it would seem that I am bound to accept. Not that any amount of money would ever cover the cost of such a volume, but I understand your need to do what you can. And my policy -"

He looked again at the sign on the wall, which still read:

Any damaged book must be purchased.

"My policy," he added, "is both fair and clear."

"Thank you!" Mr. Moore exclaimed, grabbing the other man's hand and kissing it before getting to his feet. "As I mentioned previously, it might take me a week or two before I can get the money together, but I shall be back here as soon as possible with all that I owe!"

"A week or two would be fine," Mr. Bentwhistle said, sounding almost faint now with worry. "Three might be a push, though."

"I shall be back just as soon as I can," Mr. Moore replied, hurrying to the door and pulling it open with such alacrity that the little bell swung wildly above him. "Again, you have a thousand of my apologies and I only hope that you shall not speak to too many others of my great shame here today. I have proven myself to be an oaf, I have lumbered into this fine establishment and caused such damage, but I shall pay you what I owe! Of that, you have my word!"

"Indeed," Mr. Bentwhistle said, watching as the door swung shut, then listening to the sound of Mr. Moore's footsteps hurrying away along the cobbled street.

Finally the silence returned, but this time it was silence entirely of old Mr. Bentwhistle's devising. He stood completely still in the bookshop, looking down at the wine-soaked tome in his hands, which he then set aside so that he could take a walk across the room. Reaching the mirror, he stopped and looked at his own reflection; in the old days, the sale of a book would have filled him with incomprehensible joy, yet such a time had long since passed. Now he was far more concerned with the panic and fear in the countenance of his recent visitor, and he was most focused on the idea that soon one thousand pounds would be pressed into his hand.

"After all," he said out loud, savoring every second of this momentous event, "a sale is a sale. And this is my first sale in a very long time."

He continued to peer at his own reflection as – very slowly – a broader and deeper smile began to cross his lips – a smile, indeed, that extended all the way down to his heart. He wanted to slow the moment down a little, to enjoy the sense of anticipation, but he was already starting to rumble with the first intimations of laughter, and finally this laughter burst out of him almost like a burp. He began to shake rather violently, and tears of joy rolled down his cheeks, and he had to reach out and steady himself against the nearby fireplace in order to keep from falling down. Laughter had gripped his entire body as never before, and he felt himself almost young again as he let out a series of startled guffaws.

Eventually all this laughter gave him a painful stitch in his side, yet still he could not stop. Dropping down into a nearby chair, he wiped tears from his cheek but more were already flowing. Tilting his head back, he tried to stop himself – yet the laughter actually became stronger, and he felt himself using muscles in his body that he had not used in years – or perhaps ever.

"A thousand pounds!" he called out with

glee. "A thousand pounds for a tattered old book covered in cheap wine! Has any man ever sold such a poor book for such a grand sum?"

***

II

It is at this point that we must leave Mr. Horatio Bentwhistle to his pleasures, for the course of our tale requires us to instead follow Mr. David Moore back to his home in the village of Wallophampton. There is no need for us to cover the details of his journey, save to say that it was one undertaken in a state of considerable despair – and that several people who saw him passing remarked that he looked to have the weight of the entire world upon his shoulders.

And now that we know him a little better, we can perhaps refer to him not as Mr. Moore but as David. After all, this was how he was referred to by almost all those with whom he became accustomed.

We can rejoin him, therefore, as he trudged down the muddy path that led from one end of a small stone bridge. This particular path connected the main road at the edge of Wallophampton with the mill that had stood for many years now by the side of the river, and it was this mill that David – thanks to some strokes of luck and a huge amount of hard work – had managed to purchase some years earlier. This mill came with several fields, some of which were several miles from the town. David was by no means a wealthy man, but the mill and its land afforded him a degree of comfort that he had hitherto not known in life, and he was particularly relieved that he could now provide properly for his wife of seven years and their young son.

Now, however, as he headed toward the door on the side of the mill's adjoining house, David felt as if he had let everyone down. All he could think about was the fact that he now owed one thousand pounds to a bookseller in a nearby town, and the fact that scraping together that money was going to be very difficult indeed. By the time he reached the door, in fact, he was starting to wonder whether he could find the money at all, although he quickly admonished himself. Of *course* he must find the money. He was an honorable man, and he was determined to repay poor Mr. Bentwhistle long before anyone might need to involve lawyers.

Stopping, he turned and looked over at the river, and he found himself wishing that he'd never dared to visit the bookshop at all. Why, he wondered now, had he entertained such delusions of grandeur? He was a simple man, and the day's events served only to confirm in his mind that he should stay as far away as possible from the genteel and cultured world of literature – or, indeed, any of the arts.

A moment later the front door swung open, and David found himself turning to see his wife emerging with a basket of washing for the line.

"Ah, there you are," Jane said with a pleasant smile as she walked past. "I was starting to wonder when you might return from your sojourn."

He opened his mouth to reply to her, to tell her everything, yet he was unable to quite conjure the words from his throat. Instead he watched as she set the basket down and began to hang up the washing, but sure enough after a few more seconds she glanced back at him and he immediately knew that all pretense was in vain. His wife had always been in possession of an almost preternatural ability to read his emotions.

"David?" she said cautiously, furrowing her brow. "Whatever is the matter? You're white as a sheet."

"I am?" he replied.

"What happened?" she asked, setting the shirt back in the basket and walking over to him. Reaching out, she dabbed the back of a hand against his forehead. "You're clammy. You're not coming down with something, are you?"

"If I am," he replied, "that would be a very great coincidence."

"Then something else is causing this

change?"

Exasperated, he could only nod.

"I knew it," she said with a sigh. "Don't you remember me warning you? You never should have gone to town today, the whole project was highly foolish to begin with."

She looked down at his hands.

"Did you buy a book or not?"

"I did not," he replied, before reconsidering his answer. "Not in so many words."

"And what does that mean?"

Although he wanted to bluster his way through the conversation and avoid admitting the truth, David knew that his wife's intelligence was too sharply focused to allow her to be fooled. Not that he was even *trying* to fool her, of course, but he was still completely unsure as to how he might explain everything to her and – although she was by no means a tyrannical or cruel woman – he was more than a little worried about her range of possible reactions.

"Did you go to that little bookshop you mentioned?" she asked.

"I did."

"And it was open?"

"It was."

"And you... went inside?"

"I did."

"So what is amiss?" she asked, and now she

allowed herself a wry smile, as if she was more than accustomed to dealing with her husband's trials and tribulations. "You told me that you wanted to start reading, that you hoped to improve your intellect and perhaps even build a small library. Well? Did you not find a book that you considered to be appropriate?"

"Oh, there were many," he countered. "That bookshop is a wonderful little place. I venture to say that any man could spend an entire lifetime in there and never be bored. Mr. Bentwhistle must have hundreds upon hundreds of books covering a great many subjects. Why, I am quite sure that he must be the happiest man in the entire world."

"Indeed," she said, eyeing him with a little more suspicion now. "So you went inside, and evidently you made the acquaintance of the proprietor. A Mr. Bentwhistle, I believe you said told me? And then what happened? Was he an agreeable fellow?"

"Oh, *most* agreeable," he told her. "A saint, almost."

"Did you engage him in conversation?" she asked. "Do you recall that I told him you should be honest about your intentions, so that he might offer his guidance?"

"I do remember, and I did just that."

"And was he helpful?"

"Unbelievably so. He went out of his way to

find a book that he thought I might enjoy, and he even took it from the shelf and let me handle it!"

"What generosity of spirit," Jane replied, with more than a slight twinkle of sardonic amusement in her eye. "And tell me, what did this most magnanimous of booksellers do next? Did he let you actually peruse the title that you were considering purchasing?"

At this prompting, David's remaining resilience deserted him and he realized that he could hold back no more. And so it was that, on that bright afternoon outside the mill, he relayed the entire tale to his wife in excruciating detail, telling her all about the kindly Mr. Bentwhistle and the beautiful book, and about the glass of wine that was offered and refused and still found its way into his hand regardless, and about the chair that had seemingly developed an ability to move unbidden and unaided across the room, and about the awful moment in which Mr. Bentwhistle had so kindly begun to detail the book's price, after which David had committed his most awful mistake and had inadvertently ruined the book by spilling wine all over its pages. Then there had been the sign on the wall, detailing a most understandable policy regarding such mishaps. Meanwhile Jane, having expected nothing like this tale, listened agog and tried to make sense of the events.

Finally – and blessedly – David fell silent,

wallowing now in the shame the tale had inflicted upon him.

"So you see," he added, "I am in the most terrible bind and I owe this bookseller a great sum of money. Money that we do not have, at least not readily to hand."

He waited for his wife to respond, but with each passing second he felt more and more certain that he had disappointed her. Having built up his little business for so many years, and having long assured her that eventually their lives would be more stable, he knew that in one fell swoop he had ripped everything apart and potentially left them back at the start. He wanted to leap to his feet, to clutch her arms and assure her that everything would be alright, to beg for her forgiveness – yet he knew that he would only sound desperate and that most likely she would treat his excuses with the contempt they deserved.

After a moment, still having said nothing, she merely sat down on the other side of the table.

"I have to pay the man," he said softly. "You understand that, do you not? I could never live with myself if I tried to wriggle out of the debt."

"But are you *sure* that the book is ruined?" she asked.

"I am."

"And are you sure that it is worth what he says it is worth?"

"He is a most reputable bookseller. I would not dare to question him."

She opened her mouth to ask another question, yet after a few seconds she was clearly unable to get any words out at all.

"I can pay him," David continued. "I have been thinking about it, and I believe I can draw together the necessary money. You remember Henry Kilby, do you not?"

"The man who wanted to buy the south field," she murmured.

"The very same," he pointed out. "I turned him down, but he might still be interested. If I can get him to match his original offer, I shall be able to scrape together enough money to go back to Mr. Bentwhistle and repay him for the book that I ruined."

"But that field -"

"The field is one of our best," he acknowledged, "but I only have myself to blame for this mess. Jane, you must know that I am a man of honor. I have told you what happened to the book, and there can be no doubt that I am to blame – and I insist that I must pay him every last scrap of this debt."

"Can you not reason with him?" she asked. "Would he take repayment in installments of perhaps -"

"No," he said firmly, before she could

further advance the proposition. "Please do not ask me to do the wrong thing, for I cannot."

The longer he waited for her response, the more he realized that this woman – this vital, combative woman – appeared to have been utterly crushed by the latest development. Again he felt compelled to try to comfort her, even though he knew that no words could ever soften the crushing blow of his awful mistake. All he could do, he told himself now, was put things right and then try to recover from the disaster.

"Well," he said, looking at the window and seeing that the sun was already starting to set, "it is too late to set off this evening, but tomorrow morning I must venture out at first light to visit Mr. Kilby, and I must entreat him to extend once more his most generous offer to purchase that field. He is a good man and I imagine that his interest must surely still be there."

How he dearly wished that his wife might agree, that she might leap to her feet and tell him that she understood – and that, all things considered, he was making the right choice – and indeed that the south field did not really matter a great deal in the grand scheme of things. How he begged the universe to deliver such a response, yet instead Jane merely remained in her seat and stared straight ahead before uttering four words that did not seem designed to cut to his soul... but words that cut nevertheless.

"As you see fit," she murmured softly.

"Never again shall I make such a foolish mistake," he promised her, for now promises were all that he had left to offer. "Of that, you can be sure. Never again shall I disappoint you so greatly."

His sleep that night was fitful and came only in brief, jarring starts that never lasted for long. He tossed and turned, convinced that he might yet chance upon a position in the bed that would suddenly afford him some rest, yet in truth it was not his body but his mind that kept him in the waking world. And despite occasional snatches of sleep, for the most part he heard every creak and groan and unexplained knock that disturbed the house all the way through until the time of sunrise, at which point he immediately rose from the bed and told himself that he must make haste. Indeed, he dressed himself more quickly than he had ever managed before, and he hurried out of the bedroom like a man charged with a mission of the utmost importance – and he did not look back even for one second at his wife.

After slipping his feet into his boots, he prepared the family's only horse and climbed up into the saddle, and then he commenced the fifteen mile ride to the small village of Cornstaple, where he knew he was likely to find Mr. Henry Kilby so that he could plead his case.

"Good morning, David," Mr. Yarrow said, doffing his hat in a greeting that seemed pleasant enough. "Up early, I see."

"As are you," David replied with a rehearsed smile. "Good luck to you, my good gentleman."

As he made his way past the spot where Yarrow was leaning on a fence post, David could not help but wish that he could have enjoyed such a simple pleasure. Some people, he had noted, appeared to go through life with such an easy, breezy countenance, whereas he always found something to worry about. He did not mean to be jealous, but men such as Cornelius Yarrow evidently spent much of their time mooching around and enjoying the world, and paid precious little attention to the drudgery of everyday life. All he could assume was that some men were born with such a careless demeanor, and that others – such as himself – were born with the opposite.

Such was his mood as he finally reached the home of Mr. Kilby, which overlooked the very same south field that he himself wished now to sell – and that Kilby in turn had some time previously offered to buy.

Dismounting from the horse, David was already running through all the possibilities should his intended target prove not to be at home – and already thinking of all the places he could try otherwise – when he spied the front door of the house opening and the great Kilby expelling himself into the morning sunshine.

"Moore?" the expansive – in girth, in facial hair and in everything – man boomed. "Is that you?"

"It is indeed, Mr. Kilby," David said, almost tripping on the front gate as he hurried through. "I am grateful that you remember me."

"I never forget a fellow," Kilby replied, before taking a puff from his pipe, "unless I set out to do so deliberately. A good memory is my greatest gift in this world, but tell me... what are you doing in Cornstaple at such an early hour?"

"Well, it's a difficult thing to bring up," David said, worried now that he seemed far too out of breath, "but in truth – well, Sir, Mr. Kilby, do you perhaps recall that a short while ago, six months or perhaps nine to be precise, you extended to me a very generous offer to purchase the south field that even now stands before us?"

"You mean the north field?"

"I suppose it would be the north field to you, yes," David continued, reasoning that the field lay between their respective towns. "The point is, I was very much disinclined to sell the land in question, and indeed I paid very little attention to your offer."

"I remember," the other man said starkly.

"I do hope that I was not considered rude," David replied. "That was never my intention, yet I fear now that possibly I might have seemed a little abrupt."

"That you were," Kilby admitted, "although I was perfectly able to understand. The north field is beautiful and you wish to retain it. I cannot blame you for such an attachment and, if you will recall, I did not push the matter too much. I am not one of those fellows who expend much energy trying to change a man's mind. It's about respect, you see."

"I do see," David said, "but -"

"I had visions of planting sunflowers in this field," the older man explained, raising his cane and pointing in the general direction of the field that to him lay north of his home – and to David lay south of his own. "You might think that foolish, but my Gladys does so love sunflowers, and Harriet too, and I promised them that one day I would try to plant as many as possible so that they could be seen from our window. Alas, so far that has not been possible, but again I ask you to mark that I did not try to pressure you in any way."

"Surely you did not," David told him, "but -"

"Then I tried Mr. Augustine," Kilby went on, "whose property is to the south of mine, and who is in possession of a great field. The south field, I call it, and I had designs on that too, only for him to quote a quite considerable sum that might be enough to make him consider thinking about a sale. I felt that he was out of his mind, so I broke off the negotiations and ever since Gladys and Harriet have had to content themselves with the sunflowers in the garden."

Turning, David saw that indeed a dozen or so sunflowers were standing at the garden's far end, where they seemed healthy enough but perhaps not as healthy as they would be in – for example – a field.

"One must be content with what one has," Kilby added, "and not always yearn for what one lacks."

"Indeed," David said, turning to him again, "and I wish that I had heard those words before I ever set foot in the bookshop of Mr. Horatio Bentwhistle. Alas I did not, which is why I am here. Sir, I shall not trouble you with the details of my case, for I seek neither pity nor charity. It should be sufficient for me to say that I am suddenly in need of the money I would make from selling the south field – or the north field, as it is to you – so I have belatedly arrived to inform you that I would be willing to accept your very gracious offer."

"Accept it?" Kilby asked, puzzled. "But you have already rejected it."

"And now I would like to accept."

"I have already accepted your rejection."

"I do not deny that," David said, feeling the first stirring smidgen of a headache, "yet it might be better to say that I would like to suggest that you might offer again. The answer from me would surely be very different this time."

"It would, would it?"

"I promise," David continued earnestly. "As the Lord is my witness, I swear it."

"I see," Kilby said, looking past him for a moment as if imagining the vast south field suddenly covered in as many sunflowers as any man might conjure in his lifetime. "It seems to me that this would represent not a reopening of our previous discussion, but the start of a whole new one."

"However you wish to think of it."

"And there would be no haggling? No stalling or deception?"

"None whatsoever, Mr. Kilby. Truth be told, I am rather desperate, so if you would advance your original offer one more time, I would be so very grateful and I would accept in an instant. Why, I might even have voiced my acceptance before you can finish asking."

"You might, eh? That seems to be to put you in a very disadvantageous negotiating position."

"It does indeed," David admitted, wondering now whether he might have phrased things a little better. "Does that mean that you... will no longer match the price you previously offered?"

"I would have every right to change the numbers," Kilby opined, "but I am a man of honor. And if I am honest with you, I know that neither Gladys nor Harriet can ever be satisfied by anything less than a veritable field filled with sunflowers. To that end, I am minded to advance my previous offer to you, provided you can abide by the price."

"Oh, I can," David told him, scarcely able to believe his luck. "I can indeed."

"Yet I worry that I might seem a little soft," Kilby said. "I would not want any man to believe that I am too easy to negotiate with."

"I would not think that."

"But word might get out," Kilby continued, evidently troubled a great deal by this conundrum. "Why, they would wonder why old Mr. Kilby did not extract a better concession from a man so clearly in need of the funds. What if they came to believe that I am getting weak in the head?"

"Nobody could possibly believe such a thing," David told him, "and if they did I would surely set them straight. But why do we not go inside and draw up a contract for the sale? As I might have made clear already, I am in need of a quick conclusion to this matter."

"I must improve my position in the deal," Kilby replied. "I must get something else, so that I benefit from the fact that you have returned. Just an important procedural point, you understand."

"I am not sure that I can afford to drop the price," David admitted. "Indeed – I know that I cannot."

"And I am not the type of man to take advantage when a fellow is down on his luck," Kilby said, before stopping for a moment to think. At that point he heard a whinnying sound and he spotted – for the first time – the horse upon which David had made his journey that morning to his door. "A fine horse you have there."

"He is indeed," David said. "My wife and I are very glad of him."

"A horse like that costs money," Kilby said, "and clearly he is also of sentimental importance to you."

"Both those statements are true."

"Which is why," Kilby continued, watching the horse for a moment longer before turning to him, "I think I have come to an equitable conclusion. Our shared dilemma can be resolved, my dear Mr. Moore, if you consent that as well as giving me the north field for my money, you shall also give me your horse."

"My horse?"

Shocked by the suggestion, David seemed momentarily unable to quite comprehend the idea.

"It's settled," Kilby said, holding out a hand. "I shall pay you the agreed price, but in return I shall receive not only the north field but also your horse."

"But that is my only horse," David told him, "and although I can acquire another, it would take time to train it up properly."

"I can see why that might be a concern," Kilby admitted, "but I am adamant. In order to save a little face in this deal, I shall require both your field and your horse." He hesitated for a few more seconds. "And your boots."

"My boots?"

"Just a little extra proof of my impressive business mind and my ability to negotiate," Kilby continued. "Yes, I am quite made up on the matter and my decision shall not be altered. The deal is offered and, as you well know, I am not one to beg, barter or bother. Whether you are minded to accept my offer or not, I ask only that you give me your answer swiftly."

David thought for a moment, and he had to admit that selling the south field to Mr. Kilby would allow him to almost instantly repay his debt to Mr. Bentwhistle. He could afford to take the hit of losing the south field, even if he would have to make some adjustments – and he knew that Jane would come to her senses and accept that loss, given time. Of more concern were his horse and boots, and he wondered whether Kilby might be persuaded to drop that element of the arrangement, yet he didn't want to push his luck and, besides, he still retained a little too much pride to actually beg for different terms.

Therefore, as a practical man, he reached down and began to untie his bootlaces.

"Gladys!" Kilby shouted with a greater sense of excitement than he had produced in many a year, as he looked up at one of the open windows. "Harriet! I have wonderful news!"

"Will the money be ready presently?" David asked wearily, wincing a little as he pulled off first one boot, then another from his tired feet.

"Oh, absolutely, ab-so-lutely," Kilby replied, although something about his tone suggested that he was far more interested now in the prospect of planning his great field of sunflowers. "I shall have my solicitor draw up the necessary paperwork and forward it to your solicitor, and then I'm sure we can get the bureaucracy out of the way in record time."

"I would appreciate that a great deal," David said as two women – one young and one old – hurried from the house in a state of great, excited agitation – or perhaps agitated excitement. "I don't suppose you know of anyone who might be heading in the direction of Wallophampton today, do you?"

"I can't imagine why anyone would," Kilby said, before putting his arms around the two women and leading them to the low garden wall, over which they could easily see the field in question stretching out toward the horizon. "Now, my girls," he continued, "it gives me great pleasure to inform you that my original plan to make a sunflower haven has rather surprisingly come to fruition, or at least the start of it has. Give me a year, my darlings, and there shall be nothing but sunflowers for as far as the eye can see."

"My solicitor is Mr. Dingle in Wallophampton," David said, trying to force a smile as the two girls issued a variety of joyful gasps. "Shall I tell him to expect your correspondence?"

"Indeed," Kilby replied, rather in the manner of a man answering an irritating child. "Now, my dears, I want you to try to imagine ten thousand sunflowers before you. I know, I know, it's hard to do that, but I want you to try. And I want you to imagine that I am responsible for putting them there. Does that not bring great joy to your bosoms?"

The old man was still enthusiastically discussing his plans as David, aware that his presence was no longer of strict importance, turned and headed out through the gate. He murmured something about his solicitor, and about Mr. Kilby's solicitor, and about his desirous keenness for the transaction to be completely as swiftly as possible, but soon he was back on the road and he made his way over to the horse.

"Well, old thing," he said, patting the horse's side tenderly, for he had grown exceedingly fond of this particular animal over the years, "that would seem to be that, at least so far as you and I are concerned. I'm afraid you're to start a new life here – quite as what, I don't know – but I don't think you'll be mistreated. I hoped we'd get a few more working summers out of you yet, I always enjoyed our hours on the fields, and I'd like to think that you did too. Best ensure that you're a good worker for Mr. Kilby now, though. Make me proud."

He patted the horse's flank one more time, eliciting a brief low neigh that a sentimental man might interpret as a farewell, and then he turned and began to walk away. The journey ahead of him was fifteen miles, more or less exactly, and he had not anticipated making the return on foot, and he had certainly not even considered the possibility that he might be barefoot. He could already feel the road's stones threatening to cut into the souls of his feet, so he took to the grass verge instead – and while the verge wasn't perfect, he supposed that even a slight improvement might grow to become a big one over the course of fifteen miles.

As he walked away, he could still hear Mr. Kilby grandiosely filling his companions' minds with visions of sunflowers, promising them the greatest spectacle ever seen in the county.

"I'll speak to my solicitor," David muttered wearily. "We must get the ball rolling."

The road ahead was rough and more than a

little rocky, and passed across undulating land filled with gentle dips and equally gentle inclines. The actual route was easy enough and there was no danger that David might get lost, especially since he knew this part of the world so well, and the surrounding countryside on either side was enough to gladden the heart of even the most hardened observer. Why, a painter might even stop to commit such beautiful scenery to a series of canvasses, extending the trip by several days. Truly, everything about the journey upon which David was now embarking could be reckoned as near perfect, save for the sheer length – and the fact that his bare feet were expected to carry him the whole way.

After one mile he felt pleasantly optimistic.

After two miles his feet began to feel a little sore.

After three miles he began to worry that he lacked the necessary stamina.

After four miles he was ready for a drink, although he had no means to find one.

After five miles he was passed by a coachload of gentlemen who greeted him – but who, sadly, did not offer him a lift.

After six miles he stopped for a breather, and to converse briefly with a cow at a gate.

After seven miles he found himself at the foot of a steep hill.

After eight miles he found himself at the top

of that hill, and very tired to boot.

After nine miles he began to spot more familiar buildings on the horizon.

After ten miles he felt his thirst becoming stronger still, and he briefly considered drinking from a puddle.

After eleven miles he could feel sharp cuts on the soles of his feet, but he knew that there was no point stopping to examine the damage.

After twelve miles he believed that he could hear footsteps keeping pace behind, although repeated glances over his shoulder revealed nothing and nobody – yet the footsteps returned periodically.

After thirteen miles he stopped to lean against a post for a while.

After fourteen miles he passed Mr. Yarrow again, who made several very obvious and unnecessary comments about his appearance.

And after fifteen miles he finally reached the bridge and followed the path to the mill, at which point he felt as if he was on the verge of dropping from exhaustion.

And so it was that – many hours after he'd left – David Moore stepped into his own parlor and saw his wife washing some pots, and then he looked down and saw that he'd walked bloodied footprints into the house.

"David, where have you been?" Jane

gasped, rushing over to him with an expression of alarm on her face; this expression only became stronger as she looked him up and down. "You should have been home hours ago. You're soaked in sweat and your feet are bleeding. David, were you robbed?"

"Not in the way that you mean," he replied, before reminding himself that bitterness was not a gallant quality. "Not at all. I met with Mr. Kilby and made a deal, one that cost a little more than I had expected, but the upshot is that I should have the money within a day or two, and then I shall be able to pay Mr. Bentwhistle."

"Where is the horse?"

"Sold to Mr. Kilby," he admitted, "along with my boots."

He took a step forward, but in that instant his right leg did what it had been threatening to do for at least the past six miles – and buckled completely, dropping David down with such force that he could not hold back a gasp of pain.

"Let me help you into your armchair," Jane said, taking his arms from behind and starting to haul him up. "Let's not be having any grumbling from you, David, for you simply can't stay down there on the floor. You understand that, don't you?"

"Of course I do," he murmured as she dropped him against the chair and he began to feel himself already slipping out again.

It was only thanks to his wife's efforts, as she hauled him a little higher up and then placed a chest of considerable weight against his feet, that David Moore did not in that moment slide down off the chair and perhaps end up in a feeble heap on the carpet. Instead he was held up, an agreeable outcome that at least afforded him some dignity as his wife sat on the footstool nearby and waited anxiously for him to speak. For his part, meanwhile, he felt that his throat was too parched for any words to emerge for at least ten minutes, which in fact turned out to be a remarkably accurate estimation of the time needed.

"I sold the field," he murmured finally, "and the horse and my boots too, to Mr. Kilby – and he means to grow sunflowers there."

"You have the money?"

"I shall do, in a day or two," he replied wistfully. "Then I shall return to Mr. Bentwhistle and give him what he is owed, and then I intend to never dare look at another book ever again."

"You are in no fit state to travel," she told him.

"But I must."

"Can he not wait a little while longer?"

Wearily, he shook his head.

"Then..."

She thought for a moment, trying to come up with a solution – and sure enough, after a few more seconds her chest hardened and her thoughts crystallized and she realized that there was really only one option. She knew full well that her husband would object, but she also knew that she could win him over and that eventually he would acquiesce to her request. After all, his feet were cut to ribbons and he seemed as if he might not survive another arduous journey in the near future, and Jane could think of a dozen other arguments that also served to underline the importance of her case.

"Once the money arrives," she said finally, "it shall most certainly be conveyed to this Mr. Bentwhistle fellow so that he can be paid. I agree with you wholeheartedly on that score. But since you are unlikely to recover in time, my darling... I shall deliver the money to that gentleman myself."

***

III

The weather was so bad that night, and nobody was out in the cobbled streets save for the wind and the rain themselves. As Jane Moore pushed through the maelstrom, she felt almost as if the tumult was trying to force her back, as if the natural world itself was trying to tell her that this journey was wholly unnecessary. Nevertheless, she forced herself on and on – and finally she spotted a light burning in a shop window, and she knew that she had found the place.

Several weeks had passed since her husband David had secured the sale of the southern field to Mr. Henry Kilby, weeks in which two entirely separate sets of solicitors had managed to drag their feet and slow the process almost to a standstill. David, worried that he might be seen as someone who reneged on a promise, had fussed over every stage of the sale to such an extent that the first flecks of white had begun to show in his otherwise dark hair, and his stubble in particular had begun to lighten in color. By the time the arrangement had finally been sealed and the money was delivered, David had once more been in no fit state to undertake much of a journey, while his feet had for some strange reason still not quite fully recovered from his long trek. So it was, then, that Jane's original plan to deliver the money could not be argued against, and now she found herself in that strange little town.

Stopping, she looked up at the doorway and saw a line of text embossed in the most beautiful golden gilding:

H. Bentwhistle esq., bookseller and antiquarian, established 1701

Taking a deep breath, she felt a stirring

sense of dread in her chest, but also the anticipation that had been building for weeks. More than anything, she simply wanted the whole miserable affair to be over, so after a few more seconds of rumination she reached out and rang the bell that nestled in a small alcove, and she rehearsed once again what she might say to this Mr. Bentwhistle fellow once she finally set eyes up on him.

The hour was late, perhaps a little too late, but she supposed that the bookseller would be glad of his money.

After a few more seconds she heard a rustling sound on the other side of the door, accompanied by what she believed might be the sound of footsteps, and finally a jiggling sound suggested that the lock was in the process of being operated. This took a little longer than she might have expected, but eventually the door began to creak open and Jane was just about able to make out a lined and desperately thin face peering out at her.

"Yes?" Mr. Bentwhistle – for it was he – said cautiously. "I'm not open at this late hour. You shall have to come back tomorrow."

With that, the door eased shut again.

"Mr. Bentwhistle, wait!" she called out, ringing the bell again. "Please, I implore you. My business shall be swift!"

A moment's silence was her answer, followed by the door finally opening again – but only a little, not a lot.

"Swift?" Mr. Bentwhistle said, his voice groaning like the spine of a long-unopened book finally being tested for the first time in centuries. "I think you misunderstand. Nothing about the purchase of a book can be swift. The matter must be considered in great detail, there must be a discussion concerning the purpose of the reader, and only then can a purchase be even considered. To suggest that your business here could possibly be swift... why, you make me believe that you are wholly unsuited to even set foot in this shop. I bid you good evening, and I would suggest that you might make your way home quickly so as to avoid the worst of the rain."

He pushed the door shut once more.

"Mr. Bentwhistle, I come on behalf of my husband," Jane said firmly. "Mr. David Moore of Wallophampton? He was in your shop some while ago and he left owing you a debt for a damaged book. I have come to repay that debt."

The door opened again, a little more swiftly than before, revealing Mr. Bentwhistle's beady-eyed face glaring out at her. Almost immediately, the old man's gaze fell upon the paper in his visitor's hand.

"I have here an instruction," she told him, "to pay you the sum you are owed. All is in order, my husband's solicitor is expecting you to contact him about the matter – and please, rest assured that the money is ready and there shall be no attempt made to delay your reimbursement."

"I remember your husband," he said darkly, tilting his head slightly. "I had begun to think that I might have to engage the relevant authorities in order to get what I am owed."

"You shall not have to stir in that direction," she told him, holding the note up. "It is all here."

Mr. Bentwhistle stared at the note for a moment, as if he could scarcely believe what he was seeing – which was in fact true, since he had not been sure that he would ever receive the sum. Not that he had involved any solicitors, of course, since he knew that he lacked the proof required to enforce any claim. He had merely hoped that poor Mr. Moore's sense of duty would compel him to do the right thing and hand over the money; many men over the years had fallen for Mr. Bentwhistle's little tricks, yet they had all lacked the moral fortitude to actually pay up. Finally one of his vic... visitors... had gone through with the entire business, and Mr. Bentwhistle felt a sense of great satisfaction waking and yawning in his belly and stretching its arms all the way up into his chest.

"Very good," he purred, pulled the door fully open. "It is good to see that there are least some people in this world with a sense of responsibility. Your husband damaged my very valuable book and it is only fair that I am compensated."

"My husband would never try to slip from a debt," she told him, determined to defend David's honor. "I am sure you sensed that in him when first he set foot in your shop."

As those words left her lips, she saw past Mr. Bentwhistle and spotted shelf after shelf lined with what she could only assume must be very rare books. A pair of candles burned on the table, but Jane had to note that this shop seemed like a very grand and wise place indeed, and a place in which she herself could never feel very much at home. Old Mr. Bentwhistle was evidently a wise and learned man – a man who had derived great knowledge from books over the years – and she only felt more certain than ever that she and her husband had no place in such a world. After all, they were mere farmers and millers, so how could they possibly expect to pass among the exalted company of a bookseller? She could only hope that her husband would never again entertain such delusions of grandeur.

In the far corner of the room, a warming fire burned in the hearth.

On the wall next to Mr. Bentwhistle a simple sign proclaimed a rule of the house:

Any damaged book must be purchased.

"Well," Mr. Bentwhistle said, reaching out to take the piece of paper, "I do not wish to detain you. The night is wretched and I am sure you have a journey to undertake on your way home."

His fingertips brushed against the edge of the paper and he exerted a small effort, only to find that his prize was not as yet being allowed to fully leave Jane's hand.

"If I can just take it," he added softly, putting on his broadest smile, "then I shall be happy to leave you in peace."

"Yes, indeed," she replied, yet she felt a strange reluctance to part with the note, as if – after hurrying to complete the deed for so long – something was holding her back at the last moment.

"If I can just..."

Mr. Bentwhistle adjusted his fingers a little and pulled again, once more trying to remove the note from Jane's hand.

"If you'd be so kind," he continued, trying to hide a sense of frustration, "I shall just relieve you of this weight. You are but a woman and I am sure you find it a little heavy."

Jane looked at the piece of paper and wondered why she did not yet release it, but a moment later she glanced again at the sign on the wall and then – looking at Mr. Bentwhistle – she was struck by a moment of realization.

"The book," she said calmly.

"Hmm?"

"The book," she said again, still holding the piece of paper so that he could not take it entirely. "The one that my husband damaged with the wine."

"Yes, what of it?"

"Well..."

She waited for him to understand, yet understand he did not. Instead he seemed utterly focused on the piece of paper, and he was trying to pull it from her hand in different angles – as if he perceived that this was the cause of his failure thus far to take full possession.

"You very rightly insist," she continued, "that a damaged book must be paid for."

"Indeed, indeed."

"That it must be purchased."

"Yes, yes, what of it?"

He was trying now to slide the paper from her hand from underneath, a tactic that had required him to stoop a little and reveal his rounded back.

"Do you have it?"

"Have what?" he asked, tugging on the piece of paper.

"The book."

"What book?"

"The book that my husband damaged," she reminded him, puzzled by his failure to retain much memory of the conversation. "He spilled wine all over it, did he not?"

"Oh he did, yes," Mr. Bentwhistle muttered, trying now to remove the paper from her hand by sliding it out to one side. "Lots of damage. Wine everywhere. A terrible thing, and an awful smell too. Wetted paper has a tendency to reek, especially when red wine is the culprit."

"Very regrettable," she admitted, "but... as you yourself note, a damaged book must be paid for."

"Yes," he replied, tugging a little harder now on the piece of paper, "that is the part of the transaction that I am... attempting to facilitate as we speak."

"But I do not see the book."

"Why would you see the book?"

"Because I am here to purchase it."

"It was damaged beyond repair," he insisted. "Please try to keep up. That is the very basis of our conversation."

"Yes, but I require it," she pointed out. "My husband damaged the book and must purchase it, it is a very rare book but we have scrimped and sold a valuable field – not to mention a horse and some boots – to get the money together, and now I have arrived to complete the purchase that we are bound to complete."

She hesitated, before holding out her other hand.

"Might I take the book now?"

"The book?"

"The one my husband damaged."

"The one he so carelessly spilled wine on?"

"That is the book at the center of this whole transaction."

"Why..."

Mr. Bentwhistle hesitated, still bent over as he tried to slide the note from her hand, but his expression now bore a sense of caution as candlelight danced across his features.

"Why would I still have that book?" he asked after a few more seconds had passed. "It was damaged. Destroyed, even. It was a total mess."

"I understand that," she told him, "but the arrangement is that my husband must purchase it. I have the money here, and I am ready to hand it over to you willingly. Well, if not willingly, then with a sense that this is how things must be. But the transaction goes both ways, Mr. Bentwhistle, and you must produce the book that I am purchasing."

"Produce?" he replied, as if he was still trying to process her request. "Purchasing?"

"Yes," she said with a nod, as she began to suspect that he might struggle in this regard. "You do still have the book, do you not?"

"Still have it?" he spluttered. "The book stained by wine? Why would I still have it? The nights have been cold and my hearth needs feeding. Once it had been ruined by your husband, the book was of no use to anyone so I did the only thing that any sensible man would ever do." He hesitated again, pulling just a little harder on the note. "I burned it."

"You burned the book?"

"What would anyone else do?"

"Mr. Bentwhistle," she replied, "it is that very book that I came here tonight to purchase, on account of my husband having damaged it. And now you claim that it is no longer available? Do I understand the situation correctly?"

"My dear woman," he said after a moment, "I believe that you fail to understand anything at all. Your husband ruined that book. Why, parts of the text were completely illegible once they had been stained by the wine. There was very little to be done with the thing, it certainly could not be read, and the smell meant that it was not even viable as a doorstop. So you see, I cast it into the fire so that it might at least be useful in one regard." He tugged harder on the piece of paper. "Now I am owed my money."

He began to twist the paper, still determined to slip it from her grasp, for in truth his intentions had changed over the previous few weeks. Having made a number of calculations, he had determined that the money from Mr. Moore would in fact be sufficient to allow him to retire from the business of selling books altogether. He had long known that his inventory of titles was not quite as valuable as he had long pretended, and that in truth he had been rather trapped by the shop for many years. The promise of so much money had inspired a moment of intense clarity in which he had imagined himself leaving the shop and the little town far behind, and perhaps retiring to a life of leisure in the countryside; this image had grown more and more enticing with each passing day, and he had come to realize that he could put his bookshop aside and live happily on the money he was now due.

If only he could get it out of the impertinent woman's hand.

"You are indeed owed your money," Jane told him, "but my husband in turn is owed that book."

"It was a sodden mess by the time his oafish self was finished with it," the bookseller replied, no longer able to hide a sense of frustration. "It was a reddish, stained lump of worthless paper. It was a most disgustingly fragrant and tattered thing of no value whatsoever. It was barely a book at all."

"A transaction is a transaction, nonetheless," she reminded him, and now she was starting to see that she had the man trapped – not that she had meant to trap him, yet such an opportunity had now arisen. "If you no longer have the book, in whatever state, that I came here to buy... then I cannot buy it."

"But -"

"Your own rules are very clear," she added, nodding toward the sign on the wall. "A damaged book must be purchased. Are you telling me now that the book no longer exists?"

"It no longer existed to be purchased from the moment your slovenly husband spilled his glass of wine all over it!" the old man snapped furiously. "Do you not understand? He ruined it!"

"It is still his to take," she informed him, and now she began to pull a little harder on the note in her hand, trying to get it away from Mr. Bentwhistle's grasp. "Sir, perhaps I am not the one lacking in understanding here. If two parties agree to a transaction and then one party destroys the very item that is to be exchanged... well, then, I fear that the whole thing arrangement has come to naught."

"Are you serious?" he spluttered. "You cannot be. That book was worthless once it left your husband's hand, except as a piece of kindling!"

"Worthless?" she replied. "I think not. I think it was worth a thousand pounds, according to your estimate."

"But that was before it was ruined!"

"You were still asking a thousand pounds for it, even in such a state," she pointed out. "An agreement is an agreement."

"I -"

Suddenly stopping completely, as if the very mechanism of his mind had been stilled, Mr.

Bentwhistle stared back at her with an expression of utmost bemusement. In his mind's eye, he was seeing the life he had begun to imagine for himself, the life in which that thousand pound payment would allow him to escape to a whole new existence far out in the countryside – a life, indeed, that he believed might grant him the respect he had always wanted. A thousand pounds might seem like a small sum for a man determined to achieve such freedom, yet Mr. Bentwhistle's finances were arranged in such a complicated manner that even this amount of money was enough to get the gears turning and facilitate his relief. It is to be remembered, too, that desperation plays a part in this story... for Mr. Bentwhistle was by this stage in his life so very desperate, and as such his thoughts were colored and tinged by something approaching madness.

Not that the author feels qualified to diagnose madness, necessarily; but certainly something in that direction is proposed, especially in an attempt to explain what happened next.

"Fine," he said, letting go of the note and taking a step back, then turning to indicate all the books on the shelves in the room. "I confess that the exact specimen your husband damaged is gone, but I have many other titles from which you might choose. He is not here, but I am sure he would trust your judgment. Be my guest, choose any of these books here and you can take it with you in lieu of the title now gone."

"That is hardly the point," she told him. "My husband was very keen on that particular title. I am really not sure that any other book would be the same."

"Look at this one!" he said, hurrying to the nearest shelf and pulling out the first book he found, then taking a moment to read the title from the spine. "An account, I see, of the habits of ordinary nesting birds along the Medway. Would your husband not benefit a great deal from such knowledge?"

"He has never suggested himself to be so inclined."

"Or this one!" he continued, tossing the first book onto the table before grabbing another from one of the shelves. "Look! How much does your husband know about the history of forts in and around the Chatham dockyards? I bet he knows nothing, or at least next to nothing. Think how much more knowledgeable he could be on the subject if you take this book to him!"

"It is not the book he -"

"What about this?" he said, taking yet another tome from the shelf. "When first I saw your husband in my shop, I instantly marked him out as a man particularly ignorant of -"

He took a moment to check the title of this

latest book.

"The habits of successful haberdashers," he continued, before stopping for a few seconds to ponder that title. "Yes, I'm sure he has a gaping lack of knowledge on that matter. And to think! This ignorance can be so easily fixed!"

"Yet it is not the book that he -"

"Snails," he muttered, pulling out yet another book. "See here, this book is all about snails! How much does your husband know about snails?"

"I venture to say very little, but it is not the -"

"And what of buttercups?" he went on, and now he was taking books from the shelves with such speed that he seemed almost to be juggling them as he set them on the table. "Can a man really be called a man if he does not know the anatomy of the different types of buttercup?"

"Mr. Bentwhistle -"

"Which book do you want?" he snapped angrily – and breathlessly too. "You must buy a book from me!"

"I must buy that one particular book," she replied, "that you have already admitted is now no more than ash. It is you, I must point out, who has removed the possibility of completing the transaction."

She looked down at the piece of paper in her

hand.

"I believe I must go home with this," she continued. "and -"

"I need that money!" he shouted, staring at her with wild, rounded eyes that seemed almost to be on the verge of springing from their sockets – indeed, the madness that would eventually confine him to a lunatic asylum perhaps began in that very instant. "Do you think I want to spend the rest of my days in this place, surrounded by books that nobody in their right mind would ever want to purchase? Of course not! Most of them are barely worth the paper upon which they are printed! So how about this..."

He took a moment to try to get his breath back as he worked on the plan that even now was starting to form in his mind.

"How about this?" he continued. "Take all of them. Take every last title in my shop, in exchange for that money. I implore you, you can build your own little library and become more knowledgeable than you ever dreamed. You can impress all your neighbors as you expound upon the subject of -"

He looked at one of the books.

"Brass doorknobs," he muttered, seemingly a little taken aback for a moment before quickly recovering his enthusiasm – or, some might venture to say, his desperation. "I'm sure there is a great deal to be said on the subject of brass doorknobs. Why, I have never given such things much thought before, but now I reckon that one could trace the entire history of our great nation through a vigorous study of the doorknobs that line every respectable street in every town and city. How could one not be fascinated by such a prospect?"

"You do indeed make a good point," she told him, "but... the book I came to purchase is a very specific one, and it is one that was damaged by wine. If that transaction cannot be fulfilled, then -"

"Of course it can be fulfilled," he said, hurrying to the table in the far corner and picking up his decanter, then removing the stopper and heading to the middle of the room again. "Just tell me which one you want, and it shall be yours! I can even repeat the damage that was caused, if that is what matters!"

He began to pour the wine over the books, soaking their pages just as David Moore had soaked the pages of the earlier book.

"Tell me when to stop," he stammered. "Say when!"

"I rather think that I should leave now," Jane told him, "and -"

"Or one on the shelves!" he shouted, rushing across the room and splattering the decanter's contents all over the volumes he found there. "Look, they're all soaked now! You can have your pick!"

Finishing the decanter, he rushed back to the small table and examined his other bottles, quickly picking up two – one containing red wine and the other filled with a rather strong brandy. He opened both bottles, and then he poured these too over the books on his shelves, as if he meant to saturate every single title in his possession.

"I don't care which one you take," he continued, "but just pick one! Look, soon they'll all be stained! You have free choice! Or take them all!"

"This has gone a little farther than I intended," Jane mused, genuinely shocked by the gentleman's behavior as she took a step back out into the rain – and slipped the piece of paper away in the process. "Mr. Bentwhistle, I must bid you farewell. I fear that I have rather ignited something in your bosom that should better have been left undisturbed, and for that I am profoundly sorry. I can only hope that, once I have departed, you are able to regain your senses... and that you can undo any damage to these books."

"These ones are covered in brandy," he stammered, pouring another bottle over the books on the large table. "That makes them more valuable, does it not? Just take your pick!"

He hurried around the table and took more books from the shelves, setting them down and soaking these too with brandy.

"You must choose!" he shouted. "You cannot walk away with that money! You have no idea how much I need it! No idea at all!"

He turned and stumbled, bumping against the table and knocking it over, sending some of the books spilling into the hearth. It is at this point that he probably regretted purchasing his brandy from a certain retailer in Faversham known for a particularly high alcohol content, for contrary to most expectations this particular liquid immediately caused a veritable fireball to issue forth from the hearth, briefly filling the room with enough force to start fires on all the shelves.

"My word," Jane gasped, "I am sorry. I am so dreadfully sorry."

Too horrified to witness whatever Mr. Bentwhistle might do next, she turned and hurried away through the rain, determined to find her way home to Wallophampton and – if possible – to pretend to herself and to others that she had never visited the bookshop at all on that dark night. As soon as she reached the end of the street, she stopped and looked back through the darkness, only to see that the darkness was now punctured by flames roaring from the property in which she had just been standing. Her first thought was for poor Mr. Bentwhistle, and the reader must be assured that she would have gone back to help him – had she not in that instant spotted him stumbling unlit from the front door and dropping to his knees in the street, where he proceeded to issue a series of wails and moans.

People were emerging from other houses now as the fire continued to rage, and Jane chose in that moment to turn once more and hurry away. She had intended only to pay the bookseller what he was owed, and then she had chanced upon a loophole that she had hoped might render the entire transaction null and void. She had certainly intended to cause no mare harm than that, and the idea that the entire bookshop might go up in flames would have been beyond her wildest imagination even a few minutes before she made her escape.

Continually glancing over her shoulder as she departed, she could hear the townsfolk organizing to put the fire out, plainly concerned that the flames might spread to other buildings. She told herself that there was no real need to worry in that regard, that they would surely extinguish the fire before it posed a wider threat, although she had seen enough to be sure that the bookshop itself would most likely never recover. Part of her felt a little sorry for Mr. Bentwhistle, at least until she recalled the way that he had tried to cheat her out of the money owed for a book he had already destroyed. Her heart began to harden with respect to that gentleman, even as she hurried away into the night and heard his wailing cries somehow rising up into the night sky.

Later that night, once she returned home, Jane regaled her husband with the whole tale, including the various twists and turns. Once he understood that the money was safe, and that old Bentwhistle had ended up half mad on the street outside his burning shop, David began to laugh; indeed Jane joined him in this, such that soon they were both in hysterics as they repeatedly mocked the stupid and feeble bookseller. They made fun of his name – Horatio! Bentwhistle! - and his appearance, and his mannerisms, and his clothing and his little shop and every aspect of the man that entered their minds.

Oh – how they laughed well into the next day and beyond.

Back outside the bookshop, men from neighboring houses had indeed worked quickly to douse the flames during the night, and they had enjoyed great success in doing so. Mr. Horatio Bentwhistle, meanwhile, had remained on his knees in the street – and seemingly out of his mind as he struggled to contemplate the very real fact that all his books were now burning and he had lost everything. Looking down, he saw a solitary page that had blown out from the shop. He picked the page up and saw that it was stained by wine, but in his mind's eye he was instead seeing the note that Jane had been holding – the same note that would have changed his life completely had only he been able to persuade it to leave that feminine hand. A few seconds later he blinked and found himself peering at a page from one of his few fiction volumes, and this happened to be the final page since he saw two words at the bottom:

THE END.

He stared at those words for a moment as he listened to the sound of his entire shop burning, and slowly he began to formulate a plan – and this plan grew like a cancer through his mind. That wretched Jane Moore woman had humiliated him, and he was starting to wonder whether she had done so on purpose, in which case – ruined and poor now – he told himself that he might yet exact his revenge. He knew of a priest who traveled the nation seeking out witches, and he knew that this particular priest was most desperate to capture young married women who might possess such powers. And since Jane Moore clearly possessed some kind of wicked ability to influence the minds of others – a power she had utilized to trick him into burning his own shop – he reasoned that he had a solemn duty to report her actions to the famed Mr. Hopgood.

Even in a moment that should have delivered clarity, he believed that he had been undone by a witch's curse. He had no idea that he shared the same supposed curse as so many men and women in this world – the curse of his own foolishness.

"You shall pay for this," he whispered through gritted teeth, imagining Jane Moore hurrying back to her husband. "For humiliating me... for manipulating me and making me act like a fool... you are a witch, and you shall pay with your life. Mr. Hopgood will see to that."

THE END.

AMY CROSS

Also by Amy Cross

1689
(The Haunting of Hadlow House book 1)

All Richard Hadlow wants is a happy family and a peaceful home. Having built the perfect house deep in the Kent countryside, now all he needs is a wife. He's about to discover, however, that even the most perfectly-laid plans can go horribly and tragically wrong.

The year is 1689 and England is in the grip of turmoil. A pretender is trying to take the throne, but Richard has no interest in the affairs of his country. He only cares about finding the perfect wife and giving her a perfect life. But someone – or something – at his newly-built house has other ideas. Is Richard's new life about to be destroyed forever?

Hadlow House is brand new, but already there are strange whispers in the corridors and unexplained noises at night. Has Richard been unlucky, is his new wife simply imagining things, or is a dark secret from the past about to rise up and deliver Richard's worst nightmare?
Who wins when the past and the present collide?

AMY CROSS

Also by Amy Cross

The Haunting of Nelson Street
(The Ghosts of Crowford book 1)

Crowford, a sleepy coastal town in the south of England, might seem like an oasis of calm and tranquility. Beneath the surface, however, dark secrets are waiting to claim fresh victims, and ghostly figures plot revenge.

Having finally decided to leave the hustle of London, Daisy and Richard Johnson buy two houses on Nelson Street, a picturesque street in the center of Crowford. One house is perfect and ready to move into, while the other is a fire-ravaged wreck that needs a lot of work. They figure they have plenty of time to work on the damaged house while Daisy recovers from a traumatic event.

Soon, they discover that the two houses share a common link to the past. Something awful once happened on Nelson Street, something that shook the town to its core.

AMY CROSS

Also by Amy Cross

The Revenge of the Mercy Belle
(The Ghosts of Crowford book 2)

The year is 1950, and a great tragedy has struck the town of Crowford. Three local men have been killed in a storm, after their fishing boat the Mercy Belle sank. A mysterious fourth man, however, was rescue. Nobody knows who he is, or what he was doing on the Mercy Belle... and the man has lost his memory.

Five years later, messages from the dead warn of impending doom for Crowford. The ghosts of the Mercy Belle's crew demand revenge, and the whole town is being punished. The fourth man still has no memory of his previous existence, but he's married now and living under the named Edward Smith. As Crowford's suffering continues, the locals begin to turn against him.

What really happened on the night the Mercy Belle sank? Did the fourth man cause the tragedy? And will Crowford survive if this man is not sent to meet his fate?

AMY CROSS

Also by Amy Cross

The Devil, the Witch and the Whore
(The Deal book 1)

"Leave the forest alone. Whatever's out there, just let it be. Don't make it angry."

When a horrific discovery is made at the edge of town, Sheriff James Kopperud realizes the answers he seeks might be waiting beyond in the vast forest. But everybody in the town of Deal knows that there's something out there in the forest, something that should never be disturbed. A deal was made long ago, a deal that was supposed to keep the town safe. And if he insists on investigating the murder of a local girl, James is going to have to break that deal and head out into the wilderness.

Meanwhile, James has no idea that his estranged daughter Ramsey has returned to town. Ramsey is running from something, and she thinks she can find safety in the vast tunnel system that runs beneath the forest. Before long, however, Ramsey finds herself coming face to face with creatures that hide in the shadows. One of these creatures is known as the devil, and another is known as the witch. They're both waiting for the whore to arrive, but for very different reasons. And soon Ramsey is offered a terrible deal, one that could save or destroy the entire town, and maybe even the world.

AMY CROSS

Also by Amy Cross

If You Didn't Like Me Then, You Probably Won't Like Me Now

One year ago, Sheryl and her friends did something bad. Really bad. They ritually humiliated local girl Rachel Ritter, before posting the video online for all to see. After that night, Rachel left town and was never seen again. Until now.

Late one night, Sheryl and her friends realize that Rachel's back. At first they think there's on reason to be concerned, but a series of strange events soon convince them that they need to be worried. On the outside, Rachel acts as if all is forgiven, but she's hiding a shocking secret that soon starts to have deadly consequences.

By the time they understand the full horror of Rachel's plans, Sheryl and her friends might be too late to save themselves. Is Rachel really out for revenge? What does she have in store for her tormentors? And just how far is she willing to go? Would she, for example, do something that nobody in all of human history has ever managed to achieve?

If You Didn't Like Me Then, You Probably Won't Like Me Now is a horror novel about the surprising nature of revenge, about the power of hatred, and about the future of humanity.

Also by Amy Cross

The Soul Auction

"I saw a woman on the beach. I watched her face a demon."

Thirty years after her mother's death, Alice Ashcroft is drawn back to the coastal English town of Curridge. Somebody in Curridge has been reviewing Alice's novels online, and in those reviews there have been tantalizing hints at a hidden truth. A truth that seems to be linked to her dead mother.

"Thirty years ago, there was a soul auction."

Once she reaches Curridge, Alice finds strange things happening all around her. Something attacks her car. A figure watches her on the beach at night. And when she tries to find the person who has been reviewing her books, she makes a horrific discovery.

What really happened to Alice's mother thirty years ago? Who was she talking to, just moments before dropping dead on the beach? What caused a huge rockfall that nearly tore a nearby cliff-face in half? And what sinister presence is lurking in the grounds of the local church?

AMY CROSS

Also by Amy Cross

American Coven

He kidnapped three women and held them in his basement. He thought they couldn't fight back. He was wrong...

Snatched from the street near her home, Holly Carter is taken to a rural house and thrown down into a stone basement. She meets two other women who have also been kidnapped, and soon Holly learns about the horrific rituals that take place in the house. Eventually, she's called upstairs to take her place in the ice bath.

As her nightmare continues, however, Holly learns about a mysterious power that exists in the basement, and which the three women might be able to harness. When they finally manage to get through the metal door, however, the women have no idea that their fight for freedom is going to stretch out for more than a decade, or that it will culminate in a final, devastating demonstration of their new-found powers.

AMY CROSS

Also by Amy Cross

The Ash House

Why would anyone ever return to a haunted house?

For Diane Mercer the answer is simple. She's dying of cancer, and she wants to know once and for all whether ghosts are real.

Heading home with her young son, Diane is determined to find out whether the stories are real. After all, everyone else claimed to see and hear strange things in the house over the years. Everyone except Diane had some kind of experience in the house, or in the little ash house in the yard.

As Diane explores the house where she grew up, however, her son is exploring the yard and the forest. And while his mother might be struggling to come to terms with her own impending death, Daniel Mercer is puzzled by fleeting appearances of a strange little girl who seems drawn to the ash house, and by strange, rasping coughs that he keeps hearing at night.

The Ash House is a horror novel about a woman who desperately wants to know what will happen to her when she dies, and about a boy who uncovers the shocking truth about a young girl's murder.

AMY CROSS

Also by Amy Cross

Haunted

Twenty years ago, the ghost of a dead little girl drove Sheriff Michael Blaine to his death.

Now, that same ghost is coming for his daughter.

Returning to the small town where she grew up, Alex Roberts is determined to live a normal, quiet life. For the residents of Railham, however, she's an unwelcome reminder of the town's darkest hour.

Twenty years ago, nine-year-old Mo Garvey was found brutally murdered in a nearby forest. Everyone thinks that Alex's father was responsible, but if the killer was brought to justice, why is the ghost of Mo Garvey still after revenge?

And how far will the real killer go to protect his secret, when Alex starts getting closer to the truth?

Haunted is a horror novel about a woman who has to face her past, about a town that would rather forget, and about a little girl who refuses to let death stand in her way.

AMY CROSS

Also by Amy Cross

The Curse of Wetherley House

"If you walk through that door, Evil Mary will get you."

When she agrees to visit a supposedly haunted house with an old friend, Rosie assumes she'll encounter nothing more scary than a few creaks and bumps in the night. Even the legend of Evil Mary doesn't put her off. After all, she knows ghosts aren't real. But when Mary makes her first appearance, Rosie realizes she might already be trapped.

For more than a century, Wetherley House has been cursed. A horrific encounter on a remote road in the late 1800's has already caused a chain of misery and pain for all those who live at the house. Wetherley House was abandoned long ago, after a terrible discovery in the basement, something has remained undetected within its room. And even the local children know that Evil Mary waits in the house for anyone foolish enough to walk through the front door.

Before long, Rosie realizes that her entire life has been defined by the spirit of a woman who died in agony. Can she become the first person to escape Evil Mary, or will she fall victim to the same fate as the house's other occupants?

AMY CROSS

BOOKS BY AMY CROSS

1. Dark Season: The Complete First Series (2011)
2. Werewolves of Soho (Lupine Howl book 1) (2012)
3. Werewolves of the Other London (Lupine Howl book 2) (2012)
4. Ghosts: The Complete Series (2012)
5. Dark Season: The Complete Second Series (2012)
6. The Children of Black Annis (Lupine Howl book 3) (2012)
7. Destiny of the Last Wolf (Lupine Howl book 4) (2012)
8. Asylum (The Asylum Trilogy book 1) (2012)
9. Dark Season: The Complete Third Series (2013)
10. Devil's Briar (2013)
11. Broken Blue (The Broken Trilogy book 1) (2013)
12. The Night Girl (2013)
13. Days 1 to 4 (Mass Extinction Event book 1) (2013)
14. Days 5 to 8 (Mass Extinction Event book 2) (2013)
15. The Library (The Library Chronicles book 1) (2013)
16. American Coven (2013)
17. Werewolves of Sangreth (Lupine Howl book 5) (2013)
18. Broken White (The Broken Trilogy book 2) (2013)
19. Grave Girl (Grave Girl book 1) (2013)
20. Other People's Bodies (2013)
21. The Shades (2013)
22. The Vampire's Grave and Other Stories (2013)
23. Darper Danver: The Complete First Series (2013)
24. The Hollow Church (2013)
25. The Dead and the Dying (2013)
26. Days 9 to 16 (Mass Extinction Event book 3) (2013)
27. The Girl Who Never Came Back (2013)
28. Ward Z (The Ward Z Series book 1) (2013)
29. Journey to the Library (The Library Chronicles book 2) (2014)
30. The Vampires of Tor Cliff Asylum (2014)
31. The Family Man (2014)
32. The Devil's Blade (2014)
33. The Immortal Wolf (Lupine Howl book 6) (2014)
34. The Dying Streets (Detective Laura Foster book 1) (2014)
35. The Stars My Home (2014)
36. The Ghost in the Rain and Other Stories (2014)
37. Ghosts of the River Thames (The Robinson Chronicles book 1) (2014)
38. The Wolves of Cur'eath (2014)
39. Days 46 to 53 (Mass Extinction Event book 4) (2014)
40. The Man Who Saw the Face of the World (2014)
41. The Art of Dying (Detective Laura Foster book 2) (2014)
42. Raven Revivals (Grave Girl book 2) (2014)

43. Arrival on Thaxos (Dead Souls book 1) (2014)
44. Birthright (Dead Souls book 2) (2014)
45. A Man of Ghosts (Dead Souls book 3) (2014)
46. The Haunting of Hardstone Jail (2014)
47. A Very Respectable Woman (2015)
48. Better the Devil (2015)
49. The Haunting of Marshall Heights (2015)
50. Terror at Camp Everbee (The Ward Z Series book 2) (2015)
51. Guided by Evil (Dead Souls book 4) (2015)
52. Child of a Bloodied Hand (Dead Souls book 5) (2015)
53. Promises of the Dead (Dead Souls book 6) (2015)
54. Days 54 to 61 (Mass Extinction Event book 5) (2015)
55. Angels in the Machine (The Robinson Chronicles book 2) (2015)
56. The Curse of Ah-Qal's Tomb (2015)
57. Broken Red (The Broken Trilogy book 3) (2015)
58. The Farm (2015)
59. Fallen Heroes (Detective Laura Foster book 3) (2015)
60. The Haunting of Emily Stone (2015)
61. Cursed Across Time (Dead Souls book 7) (2015)
62. Destiny of the Dead (Dead Souls book 8) (2015)
63. The Death of Jennifer Kazakos (Dead Souls book 9) (2015)
64. Alice Isn't Well (Death Herself book 1) (2015)
65. Annie's Room (2015)
66. The House on Everley Street (Death Herself book 2) (2015)
67. Meds (The Asylum Trilogy book 2) (2015)
68. Take Me to Church (2015)
69. Ascension (Demon's Grail book 1) (2015)
70. The Priest Hole (Nykolas Freeman book 1) (2015)
71. Eli's Town (2015)
72. The Horror of Raven's Briar Orphanage (Dead Souls book 10) (2015)
73. The Witch of Thaxos (Dead Souls book 11) (2015)
74. The Rise of Ashalla (Dead Souls book 12) (2015)
75. Evolution (Demon's Grail book 2) (2015)
76. The Island (The Island book 1) (2015)
77. The Lighthouse (2015)
78. The Cabin (The Cabin Trilogy book 1) (2015)
79. At the Edge of the Forest (2015)
80. The Devil's Hand (2015)
81. The 13th Demon (Demon's Grail book 3) (2016)
82. After the Cabin (The Cabin Trilogy book 2) (2016)
83. The Border: The Complete Series (2016)
84. The Dead Ones (Death Herself book 3) (2016)
85. A House in London (2016)
86. Persona (The Island book 2) (2016)

87. Battlefield (Nykolas Freeman book 2) (2016)
88. Perfect Little Monsters and Other Stories (2016)
89. The Ghost of Shapley Hall (2016)
90. The Blood House (2016)
91. The Death of Addie Gray (2016)
92. The Girl With Crooked Fangs (2016)
93. Last Wrong Turn (2016)
94. The Body at Auercliff (2016)
95. The Printer From Hell (2016)
96. The Dog (2016)
97. The Nurse (2016)
98. The Haunting of Blackwych Grange (2016)
99. Twisted Little Things and Other Stories (2016)
100. The Horror of Devil's Root Lake (2016)
101. The Disappearance of Katie Wren (2016)
102. B&B (2016)
103. The Bride of Ashbyrn House (2016)
104. The Devil, the Witch and the Whore (The Deal Trilogy book 1) (2016)
105. The Ghosts of Lakeforth Hotel (2016)
106. The Ghost of Longthorn Manor and Other Stories (2016)
107. Laura (2017)
108. The Murder at Skellin Cottage (Jo Mason book 1) (2017)
109. The Curse of Wetherley House (2017)
110. The Ghosts of Hexley Airport (2017)
111. The Return of Rachel Stone (Jo Mason book 2) (2017)
112. Haunted (2017)
113. The Vampire of Downing Street and Other Stories (2017)
114. The Ash House (2017)
115. The Ghost of Molly Holt (2017)
116. The Camera Man (2017)
117. The Soul Auction (2017)
118. The Abyss (The Island book 3) (2017)
119. Broken Window (The House of Jack the Ripper book 1) (2017)
120. In Darkness Dwell (The House of Jack the Ripper book 2) (2017)
121. Cradle to Grave (The House of Jack the Ripper book 3) (2017)
122. The Lady Screams (The House of Jack the Ripper book 4) (2017)
123. A Beast Well Tamed (The House of Jack the Ripper book 5) (2017)
124. Doctor Charles Grazier (The House of Jack the Ripper book 6) (2017)
125. The Raven Watcher (The House of Jack the Ripper book 7) (2017)
126. The Final Act (The House of Jack the Ripper book 8) (2017)
127. Stephen (2017)
128. The Spider (2017)
129. The Mermaid's Revenge (2017)
130. The Girl Who Threw Rocks at the Devil (2018)

AMY CROSS

131. Friend From the Internet (2018)
132. Beautiful Familiar (2018)
133. One Night at a Soul Auction (2018)
134. 16 Frames of the Devil's Face (2018)
135. The Haunting of Caldgrave House (2018)
136. Like Stones on a Crow's Back (The Deal Trilogy book 2) (2018)
137. Room 9 and Other Stories (2018)
138. The Gravest Girl of All (Grave Girl book 3) (2018)
139. Return to Thaxos (Dead Souls book 13) (2018)
140. The Madness of Annie Radford (The Asylum Trilogy book 3) (2018)
141. The Haunting of Briarwych Church (Briarwych book 1) (2018)
142. I Just Want You To Be Happy (2018)
143. Day 100 (Mass Extinction Event book 6) (2018)
144. The Horror of Briarwych Church (Briarwych book 2) (2018)
145. The Ghost of Briarwych Church (Briarwych book 3) (2018)
146. Lights Out (2019)
147. Apocalypse (The Ward Z Series book 3) (2019)
148. Days 101 to 108 (Mass Extinction Event book 7) (2019)
149. The Haunting of Daniel Bayliss (2019)
150. The Purchase (2019)
151. Harper's Hotel Ghost Girl (Death Herself book 4) (2019)
152. The Haunting of Aldburn House (2019)
153. Days 109 to 116 (Mass Extinction Event book 8) (2019)
154. Bad News (2019)
155. The Wedding of Rachel Blaine (2019)
156. Dark Little Wonders and Other Stories (2019)
157. The Music Man (2019)
158. The Vampire Falls (Three Nights of the Vampire book 1) (2019)
159. The Other Ann (2019)
160. The Butcher's Husband and Other Stories (2019)
161. The Haunting of Lannister Hall (2019)
162. The Vampire Burns (Three Nights of the Vampire book 2) (2019)
163. Days 195 to 202 (Mass Extinction Event book 9) (2019)
164. Escape From Hotel Necro (2019)
165. The Vampire Rises (Three Nights of the Vampire book 3) (2019)
166. Ten Chimes to Midnight: A Collection of Ghost Stories (2019)
167. The Strangler's Daughter (2019)
168. The Beast on the Tracks (2019)
169. The Haunting of the King's Head (2019)
170. I Married a Serial Killer (2019)
171. Your Inhuman Heart (2020)
172. Days 203 to 210 (Mass Extinction Event book 10) (2020)
173. The Ghosts of David Brook (2020)
174. Days 349 to 356 (Mass Extinction Event book 11) (2020)

175. The Horror at Criven Farm (2020)
176. Mary (2020)
177. The Middlewych Experiment (Chaos Gear Annie book 1) (2020)
178. Days 357 to 364 (Mass Extinction Event book 12) (2020)
179. Day 365: The Final Day (Mass Extinction Event book 13) (2020)
180. The Haunting of Hathaway House (2020)
181. Don't Let the Devil Know Your Name (2020)
182. The Legend of Rinth (2020)
183. The Ghost of Old Coal House (2020)
184. The Root (2020)
185. I'm Not a Zombie (2020)
186. The Ghost of Annie Close (2020)
187. The Disappearance of Lonnie James (2020)
188. The Curse of the Langfords (2020)
189. The Haunting of Nelson Street (The Ghosts of Crowford 1) (2020)
190. Strange Little Horrors and Other Stories (2020)
191. The House Where She Died (2020)
192. The Revenge of the Mercy Belle (The Ghosts of Crowford 2) (2020)
193. The Ghost of Crowford School (The Ghosts of Crowford book 3) (2020)
194. The Haunting of Hardlocke House (2020)
195. The Cemetery Ghost (2020)
196. You Should Have Seen Her (2020)
197. The Portrait of Sister Elsa (The Ghosts of Crowford book 4) (2021)
198. The House on Fisher Street (2021)
199. The Haunting of the Crowford Hoy (The Ghosts of Crowford 5) (2021)
200. Trill (2021)
201. The Horror of the Crowford Empire (The Ghosts of Crowford 6) (2021)
202. Out There (The Ted Armitage Trilogy book 1) (2021)
203. The Nightmare of Crowford Hospital (The Ghosts of Crowford 7) (2021)
204. Twist Valley (The Ted Armitage Trilogy book 2) (2021)
205. The Great Beyond (The Ted Armitage Trilogy book 3) (2021)
206. The Haunting of Edward House (2021)
207. The Curse of the Crowford Grand (The Ghosts of Crowford 8) (2021)
208. How to Make a Ghost (2021)
209. The Ghosts of Crossley Manor (The Ghosts of Crowford 9) (2021)
210. The Haunting of Matthew Thorne (2021)
211. The Siege of Crowford Castle (The Ghosts of Crowford 10) (2021)
212. Daisy: The Complete Series (2021)
213. Bait (Bait book 1) (2021)
214. Origin (Bait book 2) (2021)
215. Heretic (Bait book 3) (2021)
216. Anna's Sister (2021)
217. The Haunting of Quist House (The Rose Files 1) (2021)
218. The Haunting of Crowford Station (The Ghosts of Crowford 11) (2022)

AMY CROSS

219. The Curse of Rosie Stone (2022)
220. The First Order (The Chronicles of Sister June book 1) (2022)
221. The Second Veil (The Chronicles of Sister June book 2) (2022)
222. The Graves of Crowford Rise (The Ghosts of Crowford 12) (2022)
223. Dead Man: The Resurrection of Morton Kane (2022)
224. The Third Beast (The Chronicles of Sister June book 3) (2022)
225. The Legend of the Crossley Stag (The Ghosts of Crowford 13) (2022)
226. One Star (2022)
227. The Ghost in Room 119 (2022)
228. The Fourth Shadow (The Chronicles of Sister June book 4) (2022)
229. The Soldier Without a Past (Dead Souls book 14) (2022)
230. The Ghosts of Marsh House (2022)
231. Wax: The Complete Series (2022)
232. The Phantom of Crowford Theatre (The Ghosts of Crowford 14) (2022)
233. The Haunting of Hurst House (Mercy Willow book 1) (2022)
234. Blood Rains Down From the Sky (The Deal Trilogy book 3) (2022)
235. The Spirit on Sidle Street (Mercy Willow book 2) (2022)
236. The Ghost of Gower Grange (Mercy Willow book 3) (2022)
237. The Curse of Clute Cottage (Mercy Willow book 4) (2022)
238. The Haunting of Anna Jenkins (Mercy Willow book 5) (2023)
239. The Death of Mercy Willow (Mercy Willow book 6) (2023)
240. Angel (2023)
241. The Eyes of Maddy Park (2023)
242. If You Didn't Like Me Then, You Probably Won't Like Me Now (2023)
243. The Terror of Torfork Tower (Mercy Willow 7) (2023)
244. The Phantom of Payne Priory (Mercy Willow 8) (2023)
245. The Devil on Davis Drive (Mercy Willow 9) (2023)
246. The Haunting of the Ghost of Tom Bell (Mercy Willow 10) (2023)
247. The Other Ghost of Gower Grange (Mercy Willow 11) (2023)
248. The Haunting of Olive Atkins (Mercy Willow 12) (2023)
249. The End of Marcy Willow (Mercy Willow 13) (2023)
250. The Last Haunted House on Mars and Other Stories (2023)
251. 1689 (The Haunting of Hadlow House 1) (2023)
252. 1722 (The Haunting of Hadlow House 2) (2023)
253. 1775 (The Haunting of Hadlow House 3) (2023)
254. The Terror of Crowford Carnival (The Ghosts of Crowford 15) (2023)
255. 1800 (The Haunting of Hadlow House 4) (2023)
256. 1837 (The Haunting of Hadlow House 5) (2023)
257. 1885 (The Haunting of Hadlow House 6) (2023)
258. 1901 (The Haunting of Hadlow House 7) (2023)
259. 1918 (The Haunting of Hadlow House 8) (2023)
260. The Secret of Adam Grey (The Ghosts of Crowford 16) (2023)
261. 1926 (The Haunting of Hadlow House 9) (2023)
262. 1939 (The Haunting of Hadlow House 10) (2023)

263. The Fifth Tomb (The Chronicles of Sister June 5) (2023)
264. 1966 (The Haunting of Hadlow House 11) (2023)
265. 1999 (The Haunting of Hadlow House 12) (2023)
266. The Hauntings of Mia Rush (2023)
267. 2024 (The Haunting of Hadlow House 13) (2024)
268. The Sixth Window (The Chronicles of Sister June 6) (2024)
269. Little Miss Dead (The Horrors of Sobolton 1) (2024)
270. Swan Territory (The Horrors of Sobolton 2) (2024)
271. Dead Widow Road (The Horrors of Sobolton 3) (2024)
272. The Haunting of Stryke Brothers (The Ghosts of Crowford 17) (2024)
273. In a Lonely Grave (The Horrors of Sobolton 4) (2024)
274. Electrification (The Horrors of Sobolton 5) (2024)
275. Man on the Moon (The Horrors of Sobolton 6) (2024)
276. The Haunting of Styre House (The Smythe Trilogy book 1) (2024)
277. The Curse of Bloodacre Farm (The Smythe Trilogy book 2) (2024)
278. The Horror of Styre House (The Smythe Trilogy book 3) (2024)
279. Cry of the Wolf (The Horrors of Sobolton book 7) (2024)
280. A Cuckoo in Winter (2024)
281. The Ghost of Harry Prym (2024)
282. In Human Bonds (The Horrors of Sobolton book 8) (2024)
283. Here & Now (The Duchess of Zombie Street book 1) (2024)
284. Blood & Bone (The Duchess of Zombie Street book 2) (2024)
285. Dust & Rain (The Duchess of Zombie Street book 3) (2024)
286. Hope & Hail (The Duchess of Zombie Street book 4) (2024)
287. Blood of the Lost (The Horrors of Sobolton book 9) (2024)
288. Rust & Burn (The Duchess of Zombie Street book 5) (2024)
289. Red-Eyed Nellie (The Horrors of Sobolton book 10) (2024)
290. Echo of the Dead (The Horrors of Sobolton book 11) (2024)

AMY CROSS

For more information, visit:

www.amycross.com

AMY CROSS

Printed in Great Britain
by Amazon